My Dear

PRUDENCE

SEVEN VIRTUES RANCH ROMANCE BOOK 6

BECKY DOUGHTY

BraveHearts

Press

My Dear Prudence: A Seven Virtues Ranch Romance Book 6
Copyright © 2020 by Rebecca Doughty

Published by BraveHearts Press

Book Cover by BraveHearts Press Designs

ISBN: 978-1953347329

PRUDENCE

This little light of mine; I'm going to let it shine.

ONE

"It's beautiful, isn't it?" Prudence whispered, leaning her head on her father's shoulder. Her hand rested in the crook of his elbow as they stood in the foyer of the little church, peering through the open doors into the sanctuary. The room was hushed, anticipation heavy in the air. A champagne-hued satin runner covered the dated burgundy carpet of the aisle, and the pews were cordoned off with draped ribbon, each wooden bench festooned with bouquets of dried flowers, sprays of autumn leaves and curling willow branches. At the front of the church, up on the dais, a stunning arched trellis made of woven birch saplings stood ready, decorated with similar gold, red, and brown foliage. On either side of it, matching waterfall candelabras were lit, the flames aglow in their elegant crystal globes.

"It makes my chest ache to look at it," Daddy murmured, more to himself than to her, she thought. Then he patted the back of her hand and turned to smile down at her.

Prudence's heart, too, felt enormous and tight in her chest. It overflowed with love for the family and friends gathered together for this momentous occasion, to celebrate the beginning of a life-long journey for her sisters, Courage and Justice, and for the men to whom they were, at that very moment, preparing to pledge themselves. How right that the twins should share this most precious day, and how noble that Joe Lynxwilder and Brandon Stillwater were only too happy to stand together before practically all of Plumwood Hollow in order to make their brides happy.

Even God seemed to be granting special favors today. There was a definite nip of pending winter in the air outside, but the sun was shining crisp and warm in a cerulean sky. The trees had burst into riotous color over the last two weeks, and the rain that typically fell sporadically all month long had taken an unexpected sabbatical a few days earlier. The local weather forecaster—and Daddy, who was usually more accurate than any old weather channel—wasn't calling for more precipitation for at least another three days.

"You've done a beautiful job, sweetheart," Jed said, leaning over to plant an affectionate kiss on Prudence's temple. "Your mother would be so proud. As am I."

"It wasn't only me," she corrected. "I just helped. Trilby and Alexia, they're the wedding planners."

Jed turned toward her and cupped her upper arms in his big, gnarled hands. "Pixie Cut, look at me." He'd started calling her that the day she discovered the pair of scissors in the bathroom cabinet and chopped off the majority of her near-black curls. Her five older sisters had produced a variety of responses, all negative—Faith had actually cried—but her mother had smiled and hugged Prudence to her rounded belly; Mama had been well into her pregnancy with Abby at the time. Then with those same scissors, and with patient, gentle hands, she'd cleaned up the mess her daughter had made.

A pixie cut, Mama had said. *It suits you perfectly, my little fairy child.*

She'd been Pixie Cut to Daddy from that day on.

And Prudence had pretty much kept her hair the same style since. It was her clearest memory of her mother, and every time she cut it, a task she'd grown much better at over the years, she imagined her mother's sweet smile of approval, of acceptance.

"What?" She looked up into her father's face. His expression was equal parts stern and adoring as he studied her.

"You have worked hard to make this day special for your sisters, just as you worked hard to make Faith's wedding day special, and Hope's wedding day special, and even Charity's anniversary party last month special. I know how much of yourself you pour into these events, and I want you to *know* that I know. I look around and see your love for your sisters everywhere in this sanctuary." He pulled her into a sturdy hug, holding her a little longer than he usually did. She heard him swallow hard before he added, "I see you, Pixie Cut."

"Stop, Daddy," Prudence whispered against his bony shoulder. Age had whittled away at the thick layers of working-man muscles Jed had once sported, but he would always be a giant of a man to her. She sniffed his neck, breathing in the old-fashioned scent of his shaving soap, and willed herself to keep it together. "You'll make me cry and ruin my makeup."

He set her away from him, gave her shoulders one last squeeze, then bent forward and kissed her on the forehead. "You don't need any makeup."

Prudence rolled her eyes at him, but she knew he only said it to tease her. Back in her early high school years, they'd had it out about her creativity with hair products and cosmetics, and he'd come to terms with her blue and pink streaks, her false eyelashes, green nail polish and purple lipstick, accepting that it was just her way of expressing herself. By the time she graduated, she'd toned things down considerably, and although he still insisted that he preferred his girls 'without all that goop' on their faces, it was never really an issue with him. In fact, he got a kick out of the elaborate makeup and costumes Prudence donned when she did photo shoots for her Pixie Cut Botanicals website. She'd disappear into the woods for hours with her camera, a tripod, and an assortment of flowery, fluttery outfits, all made up to look like something straight out of a Tolkien book. She'd return after the sun had set with a whole new series of otherworldly images featuring her as part human, part forest creature.

"I love you, Daddy," Prudence said, reaching up to pat his cheek, appreciating the smoothness of his freshly shaved jaw under her palm. "You look quite debonair today, you know."

Jed stepped back, smoothed his jacket front and squared his shoulders. "You think?" he asked, arching one brow, an expression the eldest Goodacre sister, Faith, had down pat. It always made Prudence laugh when she saw it on either of them.

"Mama would fall head over heels for you all over again," she assured him. Then in a softer voice, she added, "I so wish she were here today."

"Well, now, I do believe she is, daughter of mine." Jed gestured out the large foyer windows to the glorious day outside. "Who do you think petitioned God for the weather this week?"

"Of course," Prudence agreed, but she didn't miss the telltale glisten in her father's eyes. She knew full well that he would prefer his sweet Caroline to be standing right there with them, too.

With all his daughters getting married and moving on, Prudence couldn't imagine how Daddy must be feeling, the house he built for his wife and girls emptying out around him. It had to be a little like saying goodbye to Mama all over again, but in bittersweet increments, one piece of his heart at a time. Was it any wonder he'd made the decision last year to buy the property across Carpenter Road where he planned to build something new for himself?

All his daughters except for her, that is. Abby wasn't getting married any time soon, at least not that anyone was aware of, but she was definitely moving on. She'd unofficially migrated to Nashville the week after graduating from high school when some big country music hotshot had scooped her up after seeing her play at The Smokehouse last year.

Prudence, however, had no plans to marry or move on from Seven Virtues Ranch and Plumwood Hollow. Then again, she really had no plans at all. All she knew was that she wanted to stay right where she was, plant her gardens, make her body products in what Daddy called her Mad Hatter's Workshop, and only leave the ranch to go to work at Trilby's Flowers and Books. Part time. Except when she was helping Trilby and her wedding planner, Alexia, put together events like this one.

Now that Courage and Justice were moving forward with their trick riding school at Seven Virtues, however, would there still be a place for Prudence in the home where she'd grown up? The only home she'd ever known?

Was she destined to become the old maid of the family, living off the good graces of her sisters?

Courage was moving in with Joe and his delightful mother, Sarah, but Justice and Brandon would make the ranch house their home. Like that wasn't going to be awkward, especially once Abby headed back to

Nashville in a few days. Just her and Daddy and the two newlyweds in the bedroom across from Prudence. And once Daddy moved out? Ugh.

Maybe she should talk to her father about her moving to the new place with him. Her heart wilted at the thought.

She didn't want to move. She might be floundering, unsure of what she wanted out of life—.

No, she knew what she wanted, but what she wanted, she couldn't have.

So until she could figure out where she belonged, she needed to stay in the safety and security of the ranch.

"Aunt Pru? Where are you?" Her niece's voice echoed down the corridor that led to the Sunday School classrooms the wedding parties had commandeered as dressing rooms. Faith's daughter, Jasmine, came darting around the corner, dragging along with her Yvette, her best friend turned cousin by marriage, thanks to Hope winning the great big heart of the great big town butcher and Yvette's father, Levi Valiente. The cousins were still young enough to relish the role of flower girls, and they looked lovely in matching garnet dresses, black patent leather Mary Janes, and twig and berry crowns—handmade by Prudence—in their hair. Their faces sparkled with a combination of sheer giddiness and a touch of glittery makeup, and they each touted delicate wicker baskets nearly overflowing with colorful autumn leaves they'd be scattering in the path of the brides and Grandpa Jed in less than an hour.

"We're here, you beautiful girlies," Prudence said, greeting the two with a wide smile. They looked like something right out of a bridal magazine, Jasmine with her sun-burnished chestnut curls, golden skin, and moss-green eyes, and Yvette, her exotic mocha coloring and straight blue-black hair swept away from her face, eyes the color of brown velvet set off by sooty lashes and slashing brows.

"Grandpa! You're here, too. Good." Jasmine gave him a quick squeeze around his waist then leaned back to look up at him. "Mommy wants to know if you've seen Abby. She still isn't here."

Jed hugged her back, then stretched out a hand to Yvette, who still waited to be invited into the affectionate relationship he offered her; Hope and Levi's marriage made Jed Yvette's grandfather, too. He didn't push her, though; he just kept making a point to include her, to involve her, in the hopes that one day, she'd feel just as comfortable with him as Jasmine did. "I haven't seen her yet," he told them.

Jasmine turned to Prudence. "And we've been waiting for you so we can take pictures of all of us dressing and doing each other's hair and makeup and all that girlie stuff."

Jed chuckled and tugged on one of Jasmine's curls. "Why don't you three head back to the girlie stuff room and I'll see if I can hunt down Abby. She should have been here by now."

Abby had arrived in town late the night before, and she had begged off going to the church with the rest of them first thing in the morning. She'd promised to get ready at home, and be there at least an hour before the wedding, in plenty of time for pictures. Unable to attend in person, she'd video chatted with them during the rehearsal the evening before, and assured Prudence she knew exactly what was expected of her.

"Thank you, Daddy," Prudence said, stepping forward to join the girls. "I hope you don't have to go home and drag her out of bed. She called half an hour ago and said she was almost ready, but you know how she can be."

Jed waved her and the girls off. "I'll deal with Abby. You scoot."

TWO

When the wedding invitation first arrived, Collin was surprised by the unsettling wave of what felt like jealousy that surged through him. Jealousy toward his buddy, Joe Lynxwilder... but not because he coveted his friend's soon-to-be bride, Courage Goodacre. Actually, how that had all come about was still a bit of a puzzler to him. How on earth had the quiet farmer Joe won the heart of one of the fancy pants trick riding twins, The Twisted Sisters? Surely, that was a love story worth hearing.

No, the surge of jealousy, swift and unprecedented, was because he had once entertained illicit thoughts of having one of Jedediah Goodacre's lovely young daughters for himself. The second to last one, specifically.

Prudence, with her elfin features, those luminous eyes that seemed to see right into people's souls, her skin so pale it was almost translucent. That dark hair all choppy and messy, like she hadn't even thought to run a comb through it. Knowing her—and he liked to think he had, at least at one time—he wasn't sure if she even owned a comb. Or a brush. Or whatever women used to fix their hair these days.

Well, he knew she owned a pair of scissors. She'd once told him she cut her hair herself.

Did she still dress in the chaotic mismatched outfits she'd once preferred? Tops pieced together from scraps of fabric and other people's castoffs, skirts with jagged hemlines that looked like something out of Picasso's wardrobe. Boots in various colors and styles, or strappy gladiator sandals that looked like an insurmountable chore to lace up.

And the flowers. She always had a sprig of something colorful tucked into her hair, in a pocket, or a small bouquet clutched in her hand.

He stared at the double wedding invitation from Joe and Courage and Brandon and Justice. Now that was no surprise. Brandon Stillwater had practically imprinted on Justice Goodacre when they were kids. Collin had heard that story more than once during his time in Plumwood Hollow.

No, his eyes weren't focused on the letters of the invitation, or the words they formed.

A wedding. He imagined, just for a moment, standing before his friends and family, watching Prudence and her father walking toward him, her crystalline gaze locked with his, her bow-shaped lips curved in a smile of anticipation, her snowdrop skin tinted pink with happiness...

Then he replayed the last moments he'd spent with her, the things he'd said—the things he'd left unsaid. Her enormous eyes glistening with shame before she lowered her chin, her mouth a thin line of repressed pain.

No, he'd done nothing to ever deserve a celebration like the one to which he'd been invited, and he'd be the first to acknowledge as much.

But it didn't change the fact that he still longed for it with every fiber of his being, a longing that hadn't lessened in the five years that had passed since he'd last set eyes on Prudence Goodacre.

THE INVITATION WAS STILL there, splayed out accusingly on his kitchen counter when he came home from work the next day.

Of course it was. Like it was going to get up and throw itself into the trash? Collin walked right by it, and recklessly tossed his messenger bag on the couch, momentarily forgetting that his laptop was inside. He tensed as the thing flopped precariously close to the edge of the cushions, then released a huff of relief when it didn't crash to the floor. He schlepped down the short hall to his bedroom, tugging roughly on his tie as he went.

He liked his job, the kids in his class, his fellow middle school teachers. He didn't care much for Vice Principal Trooper, he admitted; the students not so affectionately called her "Storm Trooper" because of her affinity for lurking in the hallways hoping to catch someone doing something worth making a stink about. The woman was notorious for lurking similarly in the teacher's lounge, hoping to catch snippets of conversation worth filing away to use against her staff when she felt the occasion called for it.

Collin liked his neighborhood, too. There was the family of four who lived in the condo on his right, and the three single women who rented the place on his other side, Jessica, Belinda, and Tracy. He especially liked the three women.

Not that he had any romantic inclinations toward any of them.

Not that he hadn't given it the old college try, either. But after a few pleasant, but inconsequential dates with Jessica, Collin had made the decision to enjoy the company of the women as neighbors. Having lived next to them long enough to have witnessed the comings and goings of significant others in their lives, he was quite content with remaining friends. He made for a good plus-one if any of them needed arm candy at a date—they were quite adept at dressing him up—and at least one of them was usually available if he needed a companion for an outing, an extra chaperone or a driver for a school event, or someone to share a bowl of popcorn and a beer in front of the television. In fact, Belinda had one of those instant pressure cooker pot things that she used at least two or three times a week. The meals she put together with it were amazing, and she had no concept of portion size, which was rather fortuitous for him. Inevitably, there was always an enormous amount of food left over when she used the pot, which meant Collin ate well. He'd never had chicken breast so tender or pulled pork so delicious.

The thought of some of Belinda's pulled pork—followed by the last piece of the homemade cinnamon cake Tracy had brought over last night—had his mouth watering as he slipped into an old comfortable pair of jeans and a t-shirt. He was starving. He'd ended up with lunch hour detention duty and had forgotten to bring a lunch. Hank, a quiet sixth grader who'd made it a habit to forget his homework, had offered him a piece of the Kit-Kat bar he'd pulled from his hoodie pocket. Collin had turned down the slightly deformed piece of candy—it had borne little resemblance to the mouth-watering break time snack in the television commercials. But by the end of the last period of the day, he'd berated himself about that missed opportunity more than once.

He grabbed up his cell phone from the bed and thumbed in "Got any leftovers?" to the group text with Jess, Belinda, and Tracy.

It was Tracy who responded. "J&B went out. Making chicken enchiladas for Beau here. Want me to send him over with some? Still hot."

A moment later, she clarified, "Beau's still hot, I meant. But so are the enchiladas."

He grinned at her text. Before he could reply, the three dots popped up to indicate she was adding something else.

"Fine. You're still hot, too. At least, that's what Beau says."

All joking aside, she hadn't invited him to join them, but he wasn't surprised. Tracy and Beau had been spending a lot of one-on-one time together lately. He didn't mind eating alone, and really, he might not be the best of company, not with the siren call from Plumwood Hollow in the form of that stupid wedding invitation driving him a little mad.

"Thanks. You're a lifesaver. Tell Beau I'm not on the market right now, but he can bring me a plate of enchiladas anyway."

Back in the kitchen, he put on the kettle to boil water for his French press. It made strong, muddy coffee that he shouldn't drink at night, but it was still early, and he had a folder full of papers to grade.

Less than ten minutes later, Beau and Tracy both showed up on his doorstep, the whole casserole dish in hand. "We didn't want you eating alone," Tracy said in response to the question on his face before slipping around him and into his kitchen. "Can we come in?" she asked over her shoulder as she set the enchiladas on the stove top. She didn't wait for an answer but let out a twinkly giggle. "Besides, Beau was afraid to come alone. He thought I might have given you the wrong idea about him."

The man was the last person to be afraid of anyone or anything. The size of a Mac truck, Beau towered over them both, his shoulders practically filling the door frame as he entered behind Tracy. "Hey, man," he said, bumping a fist into Collin's shoulder by way of greeting, hard enough to knock him backward a step or two. He carried a large, still sizzling cast iron skillet of onions, peppers, and asparagus in the other hand as though the pan weighed no more than a couple of ounces.

Collin gestured grandly with one arm. "*Mi casa es su casa.* Come on in." He glanced at Tracy just in time to notice her gaze homing in on the invitation he'd left on the counter.

"What is this?" she asked, plucking it up before Collin could get halfway across the room. "A wedding invitation! I love weddings," she gushed. "Oh my goodness! And it's a double wedding, Collin. How cool is that?"

Collin closed his eyes briefly, then nodded. "Very cool," he agreed, keeping his voice as nonchalant as possible. "The brides are twins."

Tracy clutched the cream-colored missive to her chest. "Really?" Her voice rose in escalating giddiness. "Twins having a twin wedding? I might just die from the cuteness of it all." She turned to Beau. "Doesn't it just make you want to die, Beau?"

Beau, a man who knew which side his bread was buttered on, said nothing, but slipped an arm around Tracy's waist and tugged her close so she could lay her head against his shoulder, probably on the off chance she might swoon.

"Who are these twin sisters?" Tracy gushed. "Do we know them?"

Unsure of who the collective "we" included, Collin spoke over his shoulder as he crossed to the kitchen to pull plates and glasses from a cabinet. "You might. Have you heard of The Twisted Sisters? The trick riding twins?"

"Oh my stars, yes!" Tracy gasped, thrusting the invitation out in front of her to gawk at it again. "I love them. I heard something terrible happened to them this year, though. I thought one of them died, but they're just getting married? That's not so bad." Collin snorted quietly, wondering if she realized what she'd just said. He, too, could think of worse things than getting married. Like being over thirty and single. Collin wanted a wife. He loved the kids he worked with, but he wanted children of his own. He wanted to be a family man in a bad way.

She lifted wide eyes to his. "Collin, how did *you* get an invitation to their wedding? Wait. Do you actually know them? I mean, you know The Twisted Sisters personally and you never told us?"

It was all he could do not to roll his eyes, but he didn't want to hurt Tracy's feelings. He liked her genuine enthusiasm for life, even if being around her sometimes felt like trying to eat a meal made up solely of cotton candy. "A little, but it's Joe Lynxwilder I'm friends. One of the grooms."

"You're going, right?" she said, cocking her head to one side and narrowing her eyes at him. "Collin," she added, a warning note in her voice.

Had he made a strange face, or had he said anything that implied in any way that he wasn't sure? Was he that transparent?

"Collin!" Tracy said, lifting a finger and pointing at him. "You're going. Don't you dare even considering not going. If not for you, then you have to go for us, because you're going to send a boatload of pictures and we're going to go vicariously through you." She suddenly gasped again and snatched up the RSVP card from the counter. "Sweet potato chips, Coll! This says you and a guest! A guest!" Every word she spoke was followed by an exclamation mark. "Who are you going to take with you?" She darted a look at Beau, bit her lip, then turned back to Collin. "You should ask Jess or Bell to go. I know either one of them would *totally* be your plus one."

Collin was pretty sure her offering up her roommates to him instead of herself was one of the hardest things Tracy had done in a long time. Her desire to go to The Twisted Sisters' double wedding was a palpable thing. Beau must be something really special to her. He handed Beau the stack of plates and held out his hand to Tracy for the invitation. She gave it to him reluctantly, going so far as to plant a tiny kiss on the corner of it before laying it on his palm and patting it gently.

"I haven't decided yet," he simply said, then tucked the invitation and the response card back into the parchment paper envelope it had come in, and then slipped it under the tray that held his wallet, pocket change, and keys at the other end of the counter. He held up a hand when she protested. "But I'll be sure to keep you girls in mind if I do go, okay?"

Oh, how she wanted to push him, he could see, but with Beau there, she was holding back her enthusiasm. Collin ducked his head and grinned as he filled three glasses with ice cubes. "I've got water, unsweetened iced tea, beer, or coffee."

The conversation was pleasant enough as they dug into Tracy's delicious enchiladas, but things wound down pretty quickly once they'd eaten their fill. It was evident that Beau hadn't planned on having Collin around as a third wheel, and more than once, Collin was pretty sure a whole different conversation was going on under the table between his guests. Tracy had run her toes up the side of his foot to his ankle, then twitched violently in her seat before taking a big chug of her tea to hide her face. Beau wore work boots, while Collin had on his comfy loafers, and it had taken her only a moment to realize her mistake. Collin didn't acknowledge the faux pas for Tracy's sake, but as soon as he could do so politely, he thanked them for the fine meal, told them he had a bottomless stack of papers to grade, and assured them he'd make quick work of the cleanup. "It's the least I can do."

They didn't argue, but right before she stepped out onto his front stoop, Tracy turned back to Collin with a finger pointed at his face. "You're going to that wedding, Collin Stewart, you hear? And you're taking one of—one of my roomies."

It didn't take a genius to know she'd almost said "one of us."

Collin just nodded agreeably, but he made no promises one way or the other. He was glad when Beau put a large hand on his neighbor's back and ushered her out into the night.

Back inside, he made quick work of the dishes, fixed himself another small cup of coffee—one he really shouldn't drink, but he had that last piece of cinnamon cake to eat. And he didn't even feel bad about not offering to share it with Tracy and Beau. Knowing Tracy, she probably had some rich dessert waiting for the two of them back at her place, one they hadn't offered to share with him, either.

Nearly three hours later, he stood and stretched, pleased by how well his fifth-grade students had done on their first big research papers of the semester. He showered, pulled on a pair of flannel pajama bottoms and an old comfortable t-shirt, made sure he had a clean, pressed shirt, and trousers for the next day, and crawled into bed with Michael Crichton's *Timeline*, a book he'd read back in high school. One of the students had mentioned it in her research paper and Collin had been pleased to find his old copy still on his bookshelf.

By midnight, Collin was lamenting the coffee he'd enjoyed earlier that evening. He was exhausted, but sleep kept eluding him. It wasn't the coffee keeping him awake, though; he kept dozing off, only to be awakened by the quandary of the upcoming wedding in Plumwood Hollow.

Finally, he threw back his covers, shoved his feet into a pair of what the girls next door called his "old man house shoes" and shrugged into a thick, hooded sweatshirt. Before he could talk himself out of it, he stomped through the kitchen, shoved the RSVP response into the accompanying stamped envelope, and sealed it. He'd left the plus one line empty—he'd be going alone. Mainly because he wanted to be able to duck out of there without a fuss if he needed to. That would not be possible if he had any one of the trio next door on his arm.

The air was damp and chilly as he strode down the sidewalk toward the bank of mailboxes centrally located in the middle of the block. The cursed envelope felt heavy and hot in his hand, like it might spontaneously combust if he wasn't careful with it. He just wanted to be rid of the stupid thing; he was sure sleep would come now, having made up his mind to go.

Collin was surprised to find that he wasn't the only one taking a midnight stroll to the mailboxes. A elderly man, one he hadn't seen before, stood in front of the unit, a little dog on a leash sniffing around the bushes close by. As he approached, the man glanced at him and smiled in greeting, then turned his gaze back on the bank of boxes, as if he were waiting for something.

Collin hesitated, not wanting to interrupt the old guy's ponderings. He stooped to greet the little dog with an ear scratch and a hushed "Hello, pup." Then he straightened and turned to study the mailboxes, too. The two of them, Collin and the elderly gentleman, both in flannel pajama pants, old man house shoes, and rumpled bed heads, standing side by side in the middle of the quiet night... It felt a bit like standing beside a future version of himself. His heightened fatigue made it all feel a little surreal.

"What are you waiting for, young squire?"

Caught off guard by the question, Collin wasn't exactly sure how to respond. He just lifted the small envelope and waved it briefly instead of speaking, and the old man nodded slowly.

"Better drop it in before you lose your nerve." Then, without waiting for a response, the guy turned and started off in the opposite direction, the dog trotting agreeably along behind him, leaving Collin standing there feeling rather unsettled by the encounter.

Brow furrowed, he shook his head in consternation, pulled open the outgoing mail flap, and shoved the card into the box with a little more vehemence than was necessary.

Weariness dragged at his ankles as he made the short trek back to his apartment. He was asleep within minutes of resting his head on his pillow.

THREE

IN THE LARGEST OF the Sunday School classrooms, the twins were breathtaking in wedding gowns as different as night and day. Courage's was simple and old-fashioned with a wide boat-neck that showed off her collar bones. The hem of the full A-line skirt hovered just above the ground as she moved. Her sleeves were long and fitted, coming to a delicate point at the back of her hands and trimmed with tiny seed pearls. Justice's gown wasn't much more elaborate, but the style she'd chosen was perfect for her more petite frame. Topped with a square neckline over a fitted bodice decorated with delicate hand-stitched lacework, and from the slightly dropped waist, a skirt made up of yards and yards of the sheerest silk organza fluttered and swirled with every step she took. While around Courage's neck was a choker made up of three strands of seed pearls, Justice wore a vibrant necklace of beadwork handcrafted years ago by Brandon's mother, a bridal set she'd made for herself before he was born. She'd never worn it—she'd never married—and she'd given it to her son to save for his future bride.

Their headdresses, however, were nearly identical twig and berry crowns with delicate chiffon veils falling down their backs. Each of the bridesmaids had similar pieces, sans the veils, of course, and all made by Prudence.

Prudence paused in the doorway, her hand at her throat, swallowing back a fresh wave of love that threatened to turn to tears. "You all look so… enchanting," she gushed.

Jasmine headed straight for the corner of the room where Ollie, her baby brother, gurgled contentedly in a playpen. Yvette followed in her wake, her eyes wide with wonder at all the feminine accoutrements everywhere. Raised primarily by her father and her elderly grandmother, fancy dresses, hair dressing equipment, and overflowing makeup kits were things she'd only experienced vicariously through Jasmine in the past. Now that she'd officially become a member of the Goodacre family of seven sisters and their offspring, that had all changed, but she still sometimes wore that expression of awe and wonder when all the womenfolk were gathered in one place. Especially when the menfolk were absent.

It only took a glance for Prudence to recognize the tight lines around Justice's mouth. She met Faith's eyes in the mirror and saw the quiet concern there, too. "What's wrong?" she asked, pulling the door closed behind her.

"Where is Abby?" Justice demanded, shooting a narrowed glance at a clock on the wall. "She was supposed to be here ten minutes ago."

"Daddy's gone to look for her. She's coming—she texted me about half an hour ago to say she was heading out shortly." When Justice's expression didn't change, Prudence added, "She'll be here. She won't let us down. Now what can I do to help?" She stepped confidently into the room, then drifted from one sister to another, tucking and tweaking and touching up, depending on each one's needs. Even though Faith was the eldest and the most mother bear of the lot, it was Prudence who brought an air of calm and serenity into the fold with her.

The photographer, a young woman named Teresa Meadows, was one Trilby and her staff had worked with before, and Prudence had chosen her specifically, liking the images she captured through her camera lens. Teresa moved quietly among them, taking both candid and posed shots that would document these final moments of preparation for the wedding soon to take place.

A knock sounded at the door.

"I'll get it," Prudence declared, raising a hand to quiet the young girls who were doing their best to remain calm. She opened the door to find her father standing there, an inscrutable expression on his face. She stepped out into the hall in case he'd brought bad news. "What is it?"

"It's Abby." He spoke low, his gaze darting into the room past Prudence's shoulder. "She locked her keys in the car at the gas station, but she's on her way now. Said she'd be here in less than ten minutes."

"Oh, Abby." Prudence grinned and rolled her eyes. "Well, I'm glad she's okay. Thanks, Dad."

"And folks are starting to arrive."

Prudence nodded. It was way early, but she wasn't surprised. This wasn't just any old wedding. Plumwood Hollow's only twins were marrying two of the community's most eligible bachelors today, and the whole town would likely show up to witness it. Arriving an hour early would assure they'd get the best seats in the church, if nothing else. "I think I'll keep that bit to myself for now," she murmured, ducking her head to be sure no one heard inside the room. "Send Abby in as soon as she gets here."

"Yes, ma'am," Jed said, giving her a little salute before turning on his heel.

Eight minutes later, Abby charged into the room, almost clocking the photographer when she threw open the door. Teresa was crouched low, taking a photo of the tips of Courage's turquoise cowboy boots peeking out from under the hem of her gown. "Oops! Sorry!" Abby gasped, halting dramatically, her arms akimbo.

They all turned to gawk at her, and Justice let out a sound that, coming from anyone else, might have been a sob.

Abby's gorgeous auburn hair was windblown and wild, the full skirt of her champagne dress scrunched messily in one hand, and she was barefoot, the straps of her gold sling-backs hooked on one finger. "What?" she said, looking around at everyone's shocked expressions. "I'm here, aren't I?"

Justice turned her back on her and Courage moved to stand at the window, Teresa right on her heels since the afternoon light cast a lovely glow into the room. Hope and Charity, who had been talking quietly to each other about Charity's new pregnancy, cast sympathetic looks at their youngest Goodacre sister, then went back to their conversation.

"What happened?" Faith demanded impatiently. She pointed at a chair in front of a mirror propped on a student's desk. "Get over here so we can get you put in order."

"I'm sorry," Abby said, then angled a quick, toothy grimace at Prudence. But a glint of mischief in her eyes that belied her words. "I locked my keys in my car—"

"We know," Faith said, cutting her off, but her tone was gentler now. "Dad told us. Now hush and fix your makeup. I'll work on your hair."

Prudence knelt down in front of Abby to smooth the skirt of her dress, but it was wrinkled badly. "I'll have to steam this," she said, glancing up at her little sister. "Do you trust me to do it while you're wearing it? We can drape a towel over your legs under your skirt as an extra precaution."

"Sure," Abby said almost unintelligibly, holding her mouth in an awkward position as she touched up her eye makeup.

Prudence got right to work on the dress, frowning at the smudge of what looked like grease on the back of the skirt. She didn't point it out, not wanting to give the twins anything else to worry about, but when she was finished, she sat back on her haunches and eyed Abby. "There. That's as good as we're going to get." She glanced up in time to watch Faith settle Abby's crown on her head. Prudence nodded in approval. "Nice work, Faith."

"You're lucky," Faith told Abby, bracing her hands on the younger woman's shoulders and eying her reflection in the mirror. "You have the most gorgeous hair, and there isn't much you can do to it to make it not look amazing." She gave her a quick squeeze, then stepped back as Abby leaned forward to slip her feet into her shoes.

"I'm almost afraid to ask," Justice said from the window where she now stood next to Courage, their arms linked, heads tipped toward each other as Teresa continued to take pictures. "But did you get a ride over in a feed truck or something? How did you end up in such a mess?"

Abby made a sheepish face at her reflection in the mirror before getting to her feet. "I really am sorry, guys. I stopped at Lock 'n' Stock for a Honeybun and bag of nuts, but only because I still had plenty of time. I skipped breakfast to get here early, but on my way over, my stomach was growling something fierce, and I didn't think that would go over well in the middle of the Wedding March." She'd developed a bit of a Tennessee twang in the time she'd been away. Prudence thought it a vast improvement to the bored monotone Abby had spoken with for most of her early teen years. It struck her that the little girl had done more than become a woman; she'd become her own person while out from under the shadow of all her older sisters.

Abby paused in her explanation to let Teresa position her between the twins, then gave the camera her "performance face," the smile she wore when she took the stage with her guitar.

"Relax," Prudence murmured gently from behind Teresa. "Try to look casual. Sisterly."

Abby turned toward Justice and took both her hands, the stage look disappearing immediately. Genuine love shone from her eyes as she spoke. "I love you, Justice. You're beautiful and you look absolutely gorgeous today. Brandon is one lucky man, and I hope he knows it. Actually, no." She shook her head, then hugged Justice gently. In a quieter voice, she said, "I know he knows it. Which makes you a lucky woman."

She turned to Courage. "And I love you, Courage. You're beautiful and you look absolutely gorgeous today. Joe—" Her voice caught momentarily, so she hugged Courage quickly. "Joe is one lucky man, and I know he knows it. Which makes you a lucky woman, too."

Teresa's camera never stopped working.

Turning back to the room, Abby continued her story, her expression much softer, her rich songstress voice rising and falling with the telling of it. "Well, I locked my keys in the car—and before you ask me why on earth I locked my car to run into the food mart, just remember that I've been in Nashville for the last nine months. I now lock everything, okay? So anyway, I was trying to hurry, and as I got me and this big old dress out of the car, I just automatically hit the lock button on the car door and closed it behind me, with the key still in the ignition." Like the pro she was becoming since moving to Music City, she let Teresa pose her as she talked, smiling on command. "So I ran inside and asked Harv if he had a Slim Jim. The old fart tried handing me one of those nasty beef sticks he keeps in a jar on the counter." She grimaced and shuddered melodramatically for emphasis. "When I told him I needed the tool, not a beef stick, he claimed he didn't have one." She shook her head in disbelief. "I still think he was lying."

"We need to wrap this up," Faith interrupted, swirling her finger in a circle at Abby. But the smile tugging at her lips softened her words.

Teresa used the break in the story to gather them all into some group shots, then Abby picked up where she'd left off.

"So, yeah. Anyway, I went back out to the parking lot, because, surely, someone else had one, or maybe a coat hanger, or something, you know? But there was only one other guy out there." She chuckled and shrugged. "On a motorcycle. The only vehicle in the world that wouldn't have any use for a Slim Jim, right?" She didn't wait for a response but wagged her finger between the twins. "No one was there because everyone is coming here today to watch you two tie the knot."

"You hitched a ride on some stranger's motorcycle?" Faith gaped at her, no longer smiling.

"No, of course not!" Abby shot back. "On a motorcycle, yes, but not with a stranger. It was—"

"Girls?" Jed's voice sounded through the closed door right before he knocked. After a chorus of 'come ins', he poked his head inside the room, then straightened in the doorway and closed his mouth, apparently at a loss for words at the sight before him. His eyes grew misty, then he cleared his throat. "Well," he said when his voice started working again. "I am a man undone." He nodded slowly, his gaze roving adoringly over each one of them, then he cleared his throat again and squared his shoulders. "That Alexia woman sent me to get you. They're ready for us to line up."

A hush fell over the room, breaths held, eyes wide. Then suddenly, everyone moved at once. Jasmine and Yvette squealed with excitement and began jumping up and down until Justice shot them a narrow-eyed look. Faith scooped up Ollie and hurried out into the hallway to find her friend, Beth, who'd readily agreed to watch the chronically happy baby during the ceremony. The rest of them followed her out into the hallway, Teresa trailing behind with her camera raised.

In the foyer, Cord Overman, Levi Valiente, and Frank Flanners, all three looking quite dashing in their sports jackets, stood waiting to escort their wives up the aisle. When "Ode to Joy" began, Alexia gestured for the wedding party to move forward.

Cord and Faith led the way, a few moments later, Hope and Levi followed after them, then Charity and Frank, his military stance almost completely masking the slight limp he had due to the prosthetic leg he wore. He'd worked tirelessly to get this far after his amputation last year. Charity beamed beside him, her baby bump obscured by the cut of the dress she wore.

Prudence made sure Jed and the twins were in position, then whispered encouragement to Jasmine and Yvette before stepping into place beside Abby. They stood shoulder to shoulder in the foyer and waited for their cue to head up the aisle together. She and Abby were the ring bearers, each holding a bird's nest found in the woods at the ranch, in which the rings were tucked.

"Oh, look!" Abby whispered, tipping her head slightly toward a man sitting in the last pew on the right side of the sanctuary. "There he is. My white knight to the rescue."

At that moment, the piano stopped, then started up again, the first resounding bass notes of "The Bridal March" filling the sanctuary. The guests all rose to their feet and turned in accord toward the foyer, all eyes on them.

Including the stormy eyes of the man Abby had pointed out.

Prudence froze, her heart coming to a standstill in her chest.

Collin.

His gaze locked with hers, and for what seemed like an eternity, time simply stopped.

"Come on, Pru," Abby murmured urgently, nudging her side with an elbow. "We're up."

A tremor passed through Prudence and the spell was broken. She jerked her gaze toward the front of the sanctuary where Joe and Brandon stood waiting for their brides, where Reverend Treadwell beamed down upon the good people of Plumwood Hollow, where Trudy Huckster pounded out the triumphant chords of the traditional wedding song.

"We're up," Prudence echoed, then they started down the aisle.

FOUR

Abby Goodacre had changed dramatically since Collin had last seen the girl. She'd been a gangly young teenager then, all elbows and knees, with a smile that was almost too big for her face. If he recalled correctly, her hair had been long and a little frizzy, a faded strawberry blonde, and the only reason he even remembered her at all was because of the remarkable sound that flowed out of her when she started singing. Even back then, the girl had a voice that could melt the coldest of hearts. Now, she was a young woman, filled out in all the right places, long burnished mahogany curls artfully framing her face, brown doe eyes highlighted by expertly applied makeup that made the nineteen-year-old look twenty-five to anyone who didn't know her. An up-and-coming country singer in the middle of recording her first album under the guidance of none other than Remington Sounder, a country superstar who had a penchant for discovering up-and-coming music artists and making them famous. Apparently, Abby's maple syrup voice was one thing that hadn't changed.

Even so, Collin recognized her almost immediately. It was that smile, warm and wide, that stopped him in his tracks. It hadn't changed, either. And the fancy dress she wore. It didn't take a genius to figure out that she was on her way to some big shindig, and in a town the size of Plumwood Hollow, it was likely the same shindig he was still trying to talk himself into attending. He'd come all this way, and he still hadn't quite made up his mind whether to actually make an appearance at the double wedding or not.

"Harv, I need a Slim Jim," she called out as she pushed through the door of the Lock 'n' Stock and hurried to the counter, cutting in front of Collin who stepped back to avoid being run over. "Sorry," she said to him over her shoulder, then turned back to Harv. "Do you have one I can borrow?"

Collin chuckled quietly when the old codger behind the counter furrowed his bushy brows in confusion at her, then plucked one of the foot-long beef sticks from a jar he kept next to the cash register and held it up. "Well, now, borrow? No. But I got one you can buy."

"Ew. Gross. Not one of those," Abby retorted, stepping back as if Old Harv wielded a weapon at her. "The tool. You know, to unlock my door. I locked my keys in my car."

But Harv was shaking his head before she finished her explanation. "Sorry, missy. I loaned out my last one to some young whippersnappers a few months ago and they took off with it. I hain't replaced it and I hain't goin' to. Them things don't work so good on all these newfangled cars, anyway."

"Yeah, well, they work fine on my ancient jalopy," Abby shot back, a hint of panic at the edge of her voice. "What am I going to do? I'm supposed to be at the church already. You know everyone is probably freaking out by now." She glared at Harv, a ferocious scowl on her face, and planted her hands on her slim hips. "If I die at the hands of my sisters today, and any or all of them go to jail for murder, it's going to be your fault. I expected more from you, you know."

Collin stood in the aisle with his bottled water and bag of unhealthy, overpriced trail mix in hand, and watched the drama play out. For a moment, he actually thought Abby might be serious, but then Old Harv shook his head and rolled his eyes.

"I don't envy any man who ends up with one of you Goodacre girls. You got yourself a young man yet? He know what he's signin' up for?" Harv asked.

"Ha!" Abby shot back. "As far as I can tell, all my sisters seem to be keeping their men pretty happy these days. How many weddings have there been in the last few years?"

Old Harv shook his head. "Poor old Jed. Yer daddy won't have two nickels to rub together by the time he gets you married off."

"Well, lucky for him, I'm not getting married any time soon. I'm too busy singing about love to get caught up in it."

Collin was no longer smiling. Did he understand their conversation correctly? Was Abby the only Goodacre girl still unmarried? Did that mean his Prudence—no, not *his*, he'd seen to that. Did that mean Prudence was already—? He couldn't bring himself to finish the thought.

"And I don't know why I'm standing here shooting the breeze with you. I need to get to the church." She started back toward the door. "Maybe someone out at the pumps has one."

"Ain't nobody out there," Harv told her, shaking his head again. "It's been fair quiet since just after the noon hour, what with everyone heading to the wedding."

"Seriously?" Abby wailed. She crossed back to the counter, shooting Collin another apologetic look over her shoulder before turning back to the old man at the register. "Can I use your phone? I have to call Triple A, then. Mike will have to come over here and unlock it for me."

"You gonna make Mike leave the wedding to bail you out?" Harv asked, his brows raised in censure.

Abby pressed the heel of her hand to her forehead. "Gah! Of course not." Then she held out her hand, palm up. "Give me your truck keys. I promise I'll bring it back as soon as the wedding is over."

Once again, Harv shook his head. "My truck is over at Charley's getting a new head gasket."

"I'll take you," Collin said, stepping forward. He hadn't realized he was going to offer until the words were halfway out his mouth. Heck, he hadn't realized he was even going to the wedding for certain until the exact same moment. "You probably don't remember me, but I used to teach over at Plumwood High. Collin Stewart." He set the water bottle down on the counter and thrust his hand out for her to shake. "You're Abby," he added, as if him knowing her didn't sound creepy at all.

Her eyes narrowed suspiciously as she looked him up and down. Finally, she said, "You do look familiar. How, exactly, do you know me?"

She still hadn't taken his hand, and now Collin wasn't sure whether to withdraw it or hold out a little longer. "I'm a friend of Joe's. I knew—I know your sisters. I had a few of them in my classes."

Abby suddenly reached out and shook his hand in a quick, firm grasp. "Do you have a Slim Jim—the tool, I mean?" she clarified, rolling her eyes at Old Harv.

"Sorry." Collin shook his head and made a show of patting his pockets. "Not on me today."

"He wouldn't need one now, would he?" Harv chortled. "Fella here is on that fancy motorcycle parked out front."

Abby's eyes grew wide with surprise and, if he weren't mistaken, a smidge of excitement. "That's your bike? Nice."

"It is. Thanks." His Honda Shadow wasn't anything remarkable, but as far as bikes went, it was reliable, comfortable, and had the beefy appeal of a cruiser without the extra weight or hefty price tag. Collin wasn't a big guy, anyway, and he liked the wide, low lines of the machine that made long rides easy. He'd bought the thing for a steal from a fellow teacher who needed the cash to pay for a kitchen remodel, and although the purchase had been on a bit of whim, it hadn't taken Collin long to realize he really enjoyed the freedom and solidarity of taking the bike out on the road.

Abby nodded slowly, sizing him up once again, then flashed him that wide smile that showed a whole lot of straight, white teeth. Stepping back, she dropped into a coquettish curtsy, then straightened and said, "I accept your offer of a ride, kind sir. I'll even pay for your goodies as a way of thanking you." Turning to Old Harv, she grimaced. "Except I locked my purse in the car, too, so you'll have to put it on my tab."

Harv crossed his arms over his chest and stepped back from the register. "Tabs went out of style long before you were old enough to sign your name on one, young missy."

"No need," Collin said as he pulled out his wallet, quickly counting out a few dollar bills to cover his purchase. "I've got this."

Abby leaned forward over the counter and made a ridiculous wide-eyed damsel-in-distress face at Old Harv. "Please make sure no one breaks into my car and steals my stuff," she simpered. "I'll fill my gas tank all the way to the top when I come back for my car after the wedding, I promise. And I'll make Daddy top his off, too. Deal?"

"Get on outta here, girlie. Nothin's gonna happen to your stuff." Harv handed Collin his change, then made a shooing gesture at them.

Once outside, Collin handed her his helmet and insisted she wear it; there was no way he'd let her get on the back of his bike without it.

"Thank you," Abby practically gushed as she made quick work of buckling the helmet and tightening the chin strap so that it sat snug on her head. Then she hitched up her skirts and threw her leg over the bike behind him. As she settled into position, Collin got the impression that she was quite comfortable on a motorcycle.

"You ride a lot?" he asked.

After a brief pause, she said. "Nah. I used to ride with a friend, though. Good times." Then she wrapped her arms around his waist. "Ready when you are."

The moment Collin put his feet on the ground in front of the old white church, Abby was already unbuckling the helmet and dismounting. "You're a lifesaver, Collin," she said, handing him the helmet. Then she threw her arms around his neck and kissed his cheek. "You're here for the wedding, right?"

"I am, yes," he said with a nod.

"Good. I'll catch you later, okay? I gotta run."

"Go." He shot her a grin, then watched as she held her skirts high and hurried up the steps to the double doors of the sanctuary. How she managed to move that quickly in the strappy heels she wore boggled his mind, but she disappeared inside the building without a mishap.

Collin found an empty parking spot halfway down the first row in the lot, then took his time heading back to the church. The wedding didn't start for another hour, but he had his water bottle and the trail mix he'd tucked inside his jacket. Circling the side of the building, he made for one of the benches at the edge of the small play area. It was a beautiful day; he'd wait outside until folks started showing up for the ceremony. He wasn't ready to run into anyone else he knew just yet.

By the time he worked up the courage to head inside, the sanctuary was nearly full. He slipped into the first empty spot he came to, a single seat in the last row, where he hoped he'd go unnoticed by the wedding party from their positions up front on the dais.

It hadn't occurred to him that he'd be one of the first people seen by the wedding party as they entered the chapel, not until it was too late to find another seat.

When Abby and Prudence stepped through the double doors and into his line of sight, time stuttered to a standstill.

Abby Goodacre may have changed in the years since Collin left Plumwood Hollow, but the same couldn't be said for Prudence. He drank in the sight of her; the same choppy black hair and pale, creamy skin, the slight, delicate lines of her body, the way she seemed to almost float as she moved....

And those eyes.

Look away, man. While you still can, look away.

FIVE

WHAT WAS HE DOING here? Who invited him? She hadn't seen his name on the mailing list; surely, she'd remember if she had. And if she'd come across it, she'd have made sure his invitation got lost in the mail. Well, maybe she wouldn't have actually done anything about it, but at least she'd have had warning. She'd have been prepared.

It was all Prudence could do to focus on the pastor's words as he led Courage and Justice and their grooms through the age-old ceremony that would bind them together until death parted them. At most weddings, Prudence would be enraptured by the romance and dabbing at the tears that inevitably fell, but today, her whole body felt frozen in place. She was afraid to even turn her head lest her eyes find Collin's of their own accord. Instead, she kept them fixed on the faces of Joe Lynxwilder and Brandon Stillwater, her soon-to-be brothers-in-law.

Talk about two very happy men.

Was Collin here alone? She hadn't noticed anyone with him... then again, she hadn't noticed anyone else at all once their eyes met. He could've arrived with a whole bevy of babes, and she wouldn't have noticed. Dare she take a quick peek?

Wait. No, he'd been on a motorcycle. He'd given Abby a ride to the church, so he had to be here alone.

A motorcycle? Prudence couldn't picture it. Her gentle, soft spoken, loafer-wearing Mr. Stewart rode a motorcycle? She tried to conjure up an image of him in biker boots and black leather. *Hmmm. Not bad.* Mess up his hair a little, give him a two-day scruff, slap on a pair of aviators? *Not bad at all.* Her cheeks grew warm at the visual and she forced her attention back to Reverend Treadwell's words. *Focus, Pru.*

"A good marriage must be nurtured, tended, protected, and defended. Never be satisfied with bringing fifty percent into the union. Instead, each of you bring one hundred percent, and do so one hundred percent of the time. Never let a day go by without saying I love you, in words and in actions. Look into each other's eyes and say 'I love you' every day. No matter how hard the day or night has been, no matter how good or bad your circumstances, take the time each day to stop and look each other in the eyes, to really see the person whom you are standing here today promising to love and cherish and treasure above all others." He paused and wiggled his brows at the couples in front of him. "And remember, you are never too old to hold hands and kiss."

Soft chuckles echoed around the room, but the pastor's words sent Prudence's mind reeling backward in time. Maybe you were never too old to hold hands and kiss, but she knew from her own personal experience how it felt to be too young.

Oh, Collin. Why are you here?

Had he ridden all the way from Cincinnati for the wedding? Or was he just passing through and heard about the much talked about event and decided to sit in for the fun of it?

Was he hoping—or dreading—to see her?

The unending stream of questions parading through her head made it all but impossible to pay attention to what Pastor Treadwell was saying. It was something about the special bond between twins and how it would be Joe and Brandon's responsibility to care for that aspect of their wives' relationship, too. Prudence wanted to hear it, wanted to take it all in. She bit down on her bottom lip hard, forcing her attention back to the ceremony. She didn't want to miss this wonderful moment for anything. Not even for Collin Stewart.

Beside her, Abby ducked her head and whispered, "You alright?"

Prudence nodded once, darting her youngest sister a quick, reassuring smile. Then she squared her shoulders and turned her attention back to the two couples preparing to say their vows to each other.

When the pastor declared Joe and Courage man and wife, then Justice and Brandon, Prudence cheered with the rest of the family and friends gathered in the old church. And when Prudence and Abby followed the wedding party down the aisle and out the back doors of the sanctuary, Prudence kept her eyes averted from the last pew of guests.

It didn't matter. Her heart knew he was there, and when she passed by him, she felt his gaze on her.

Would he come to the reception? Would he *dare* after what he did the last time he'd been out at Seven Virtues Ranch?

Thank goodness they were scheduled to do wedding party pictures immediately after the ceremony while the guests made their way out to the ranch for the reception. Prudence would have time to compose herself before she had to face Collin in the receiving line.

PRUDENCE, FAITH, HOPE, AND Charity headed for the ranch as soon as their part in the photo shoot was over. Charity's catering crew had everything well in hand, as expected, and Prudence felt a keen sense of accomplishment and pride at how picturesque everything looked as they pulled into the reserved-for-family parking section just past the big barn. The enormous tent canopy on the lawn was festooned with fall foliage and draped with shimmering champagne-colored tulle and twinkle lights that would be switched on when the sun started going down. On round tables draped in gold and burgundy tablecloths, each centerpiece was unique, globed candles set into various treasures gathered from the woods: a section of a fallen tree branch, a chunk of moss-covered bark, bundled twigs of dried berries, a grouping of colorful stones, assorted birds' nests.

One of the DJs from The Smokehouse, Hank Mosely, had the music rolling at just the right volume—loud enough for folks to appreciate the songs, but not so loud they couldn't converse. Prudence stopped in front of his set up and flashed him a grateful smile.

"It sounds great, Hank," she told him. "Can I get you anything? A drink? Something to eat?"

Hank winked at her and leaned forward over his equipment. "How about a dance later on?"

Prudence waggled a finger at him, laughing at his forwardness. "Not until after I get my money's worth out of you, sir." Hank loved the ladies, but he was a sworn bachelor. And why not, Prudence mused, when half the single female population in Plumwood Hollow and the surrounding counties were giving up the milk for free to him. As Pastor Treadwell had said, marriage required work, commitment, and effort, and Hank was little more than a kid out to have fun packaged in a very attractive thirty-something-year-old body. He was harmless enough, though, Prudence thought; at least he knew that no meant no. And he was a great dancer, too, she had to give him that. Tall and broad in the shoulders, he held a woman in his arms in a way that made it easy to let him lead. Was it any wonder the ladies liked him as much as he liked them? Even Prudence, who wasn't especially drawn to big brawny men, couldn't help feeling a little giddy after a spin on the dance floor with Hank Mosely.

"I'll take that as a yes, then, Ms. Goodacre." He looked past her shoulder and thrust his chin in the direction of the milling folks. "It's a great party already, and the guests of honor haven't even arrived yet."

"Thank you," she said, feeling her cheeks warm with pleasure at his compliment. "And yes. That's a yes." She mimed writing something on the palm of her other hand with a flourish. "Your name is on my dance card, Hank. Catch you later." She turned and threaded her way through the tables, greeting folks who were already seated, double and triple checking to make sure everything was as it should be.

"Everything is so beautiful, dear." Trudy Huckster laid a plump brown hand on Prudence's arm. "Your mama's surely beaming from ear to ear up there in Heaven today. I know she's happy right where she's at, but I'm certain the Good Lord is allowing her front row seats to today's events. Why, you Goodacre girls have turned this place into a wedding wonderland today. No one would ever believe this was a working ranch every other day of the week." The roly-poly woman plucked a pale yellow pillow mint out of a candy dish on the table and popped it in her mouth. "I hear this is mostly your doing, too," she said around the mint tucked into her cheek. "You know, Miss Prudence, you could make a good living holding weddings like this out here." The church secretary tapped her silver-streaked temple. "I know your daddy is getting out of the ranching side of things altogether once that house of his is built across the way. Something has to come of this beautiful piece of property, right? What are you girls planning to do with it?"

It wasn't the first time someone had said as much to Prudence. The last two events she'd helped put together had garnered much praise. But this was the first time she'd commandeered the whole thing, and the first one they'd held at Seven Virtues Ranch. And although she wasn't quite ready to say it out loud, she was seriously considering going into the wedding planning business for herself. She enjoyed working with Trilby and Alexia, and she didn't want to take any work from them, but she couldn't deny the exuberant flutter in her stomach every time she thought about it.

That said, with Courage and Justice's plans for their trick riding school already underway, Prudence couldn't quite see how her ideas fit into the grand scheme of things.

"Of course, there's the twins' trick riding school," Trudy said, as though reading Prudence's mind. "It's all the youngsters can talk about these days. That, and the rodeo plans coming together for next year at Whispering Hills." She made a clucking sound and wiggled her shoulders excitedly. "Imagine that," she said, her eyes lit up. "Our own official rodeo right here in little old Plumwood Hollow. All those cowboys gathered in our neck of the woods? Mm-mm!"

"Mrs. Huckster!" Prudence gasped with exaggerated shock.

"Oh, don't give me that look," the ebullient woman shot back, reaching up to pinch Prudence's cheek. "I may be old, but I'm not dead, and there isn't anything wrong with these eyes the Good Lord gave me."

Prudence gave the woman a quick hug. "I do love you, Mrs. Huckster."

"Speaking of handsome cowboys, where is that daddy of yours?"

"He'll be here soon. They're still finishing up pictures at the church."

"How's he doing, what with giving up two of his girls in one day?"

"Just fine," Prudence assured the woman. She leaned in close and lowered her voice. "I have a feeling he's congratulating himself a little extra today. Not only did he get a massive family discount on all of this, but he got a two-for-one deal on everything but the dresses. He even got the catering at cost," she exclaimed in a conspiratorial whisper.

Trudy chuckled appreciatively. "Good for him. I can only imagine retirement will come a little easier, knowing all you girls are set right."

Except for me. Prudence smiled brightly around the thought and focused on her father's plans instead of what was to become of her. "Daddy's place is coming along nicely. Have you been over there yet? But between you and me," she added, "I'm not so sure he's going to be able to give up ranching altogether—he's already talking about taking a couple of his favorite heifers with him to do some breeding."

"Well, of course, dear Prudence. Everyone knows ranchers never retire." Trudy paused for comedic effect, and Prudence had no doubt there was a punchline coming. Sure enough. "They just get deranged." Trudy let out a low, full-bellied laugh at her own joke, and Prudence joined in.

Trudy and her zany sayings; she was famous for them all over the hollow, and she took great pride and joy in putting up a new one each week on the church's marquee. Although it held details of the wedding celebration today, last week, the sign outside the old-fashioned white clapboard church had touted an oldie, but goodie: *Faith is a journey, not a guilt trip.*

Prudence made her excuses, then moved off before she could get roped into further talk of the future of Seven Virtues Ranch. Now was not the time. Today was all about her sisters and their new husbands. Her intention was to flit from table to table, from station to station, from moment to moment, making sure the whole event went off without a hitch. Now that the ceremony was over, she could breathe a little easier; receptions were always a little less regimented. And once the dancing started, well, she'd give it a few songs, then she'd kick off her shoes and join in on the fun.

That is, unless she encountered Collin Stewart. Then she'd hide in the barn or in her workshop, or even in the chicken coop if the hens would stay quiet. She glanced around at the folks mingling on the lawn, but she didn't see the man anywhere. Maybe he'd only stayed for the ceremony, and he'd driven off into the sunset on his motorcycle by now.

Then again, there were still vehicles coming down the long driveway off of Carpenter Road, still cars being valet-parked by a couple of the younger ranch hands from Whispering Hills in the cleared pasture beyond the ranch house.

Would he even approach her if he came? Would he try to speak to her? What if she saw him first? Did she have to acknowledge him? Could she somehow avoid him altogether? Find excuses to be anywhere he wasn't throughout the reception?

"Stop it," she muttered to herself, then stepped aside to let a young couple pass with their little plates of appetizers. She exchanged smiles with them—she'd gone to school with the girl, but they'd never been more than acquaintances. Then again, there were very few people Prudence could really call friends. Sure, she knew a lot of folks, and she had a knack for reading people, a gift that made putting together events like this one come easy to her.

A gift that could also be a little off-putting, if she wasn't careful how and where she wielded it. Folks didn't always appreciate her discerning intuition, something she'd learned the hard way. Outside of her father and sisters, she could only count on one hand those who were comfortable getting beyond her quirky exterior.

Which was okay with Prudence. Most of the time.

Sometimes, though, like on days such as today, when love hung in the air like the sweet fragrance of jasmine at twilight, Prudence longed for more. Even as she found great joy in the culmination of all her hard work in creating, as Trudy said, this wedding wonderland for her sisters, she also felt the ache of that hollow place inside of her. She already knew she'd end the night alone out under the moonlight. Once the newlyweds had been sent off in style, after all the guests were gone, when the candles had burned out and the twinkle lights were unplugged, she'd make her way to the gnarled old apple tree that stood sentinel over her garden. There, seated on the little bench with her feet tucked up under her, she'd pray for her sisters' happiness and for her father's contentment in the new stage of life they were each entering. And there, she'd be free to let the tears of loneliness fall unchecked, without anyone around to ask her what was wrong.

But that was later. Right now, it was time to celebrate. Prudence squared her shoulders, lifted her chin, and forced her mouth into a wide, welcoming smile for the next group of people who crossed her path.

By the time the rest of the wedding party finally showed up, Charity's crew had the food hot and ready to serve. Hank put on a huge production of introducing the newlyweds as the strains of Manfred Man's "Do Wah Diddy Diddy" played out over the loudspeakers. Folks clapped and cheered in congratulations while the two couples and their entourages danced their way to their places at the wedding party tables. Prudence motioned for Hank to let folks know it was time to eat, then Joe's Uncle Sheldon, who'd flown in from Ohio for the occasion, said the blessing over the whole event. Hank directed the brides and their grooms to the buffet table, and the rest of the guests began falling in line behind them.

For the next hour, Prudence flitted rather frantically, until her father put an arm around her shoulders and thrust a plate of food into her hands. "Take a load off, Pixie Cut," he murmured close to her ear before planting a quick kiss on her temple. "No one is going without today, not on my watch, and that includes you."

Prudence leaned into him for just a moment, then straightened quickly when she noticed a woman comforting her daughter who'd just spilled a cup of juice at a nearby table. "I will, I promise. I just need to—."

"No, you don't," he interrupted, steering her toward her reserved spot at the wedding party table. It was the only place setting that remained undisturbed. "You've been bouncing around like a cat in a room full of rocking chairs. Just hold still a minute and get some food in your belly, you hear?"

"Yes, Daddy," she murmured, setting the plate of food on the table and dropping into the chair he held out for her. "Oh, wow," she said, the words coming out as more of a groan as she kicked her shoes off under the table and stretched out her toes. "My poor feet. I still don't understand why I couldn't wear boots today," she half-grumbled.

"I still don't understand why you girls insist on wearing those torture contraptions you call shoes, either," her father agreed. Then he ruffled her hair. "Eat. And don't get up until that plate is empty." He started to pull out the seat next to her to join her, but then paused when he noticed Justice cutting through the crowd toward them.

"Hey, Dad! There's someone I want you to meet," the younger twin said, her face radiant in the late afternoon sunlight. "Mind if I steal him?" she asked Prudence.

"Go," Prudence insisted. At her father's stern look, she added, "I'm eating, see?" She scooped up a fork full of creamy mashed potatoes drenched in brown gravy and brought it to her mouth. They were, as expected, absolutely delicious.

Jed allowed Justice to drag him off, offering a nod at Brandon who joined them, and Prudence relaxed back in her seat.

She wasn't exactly hungry, even though she'd eaten very little that day, but it felt good to sit still a minute, as her father had instructed. And it made it easier to take it all in when she wasn't darting around from place to place. As her gaze swept over the party, her heart warmed again at the sight before her. It seemed that the whole town—and then some—had shown up to celebrate the double wedding of Plumwood Hollow's only set of twins. Most of the folks she recognized, but there were a few faces who were new to her. Charlotte Rawlings for one, a woman who'd arrived with Joe's mother, Sarah. Prudence had heard all about her and her part in bringing Brandon and Justice back together after their terrible breakup, but she'd yet to officially meet the woman. She'd have to make that a priority... as soon as she could convince her feet to shove themselves back into her shoes.

Justice, with Daddy and Brandon in tow, made a beeline toward Charlotte and Sarah. Prudence's eyes widened and she quickly covered her smile with a hand, tickled by the sight of her father standing a little taller, his shoulders a little straighter, his chin a little higher, as Justice introduced him to the fiber artist-turned-sheep rancher from Colorado. Charlotte stood a good three or four inches taller than Daddy in her wedge sandals, and with her long silver hair and billowing turquoise skirt, even from afar, she looked a right formidable woman. Nothing at all like Prudence's petite, demure mother, Caroline. Jed's reaction to the woman sent a prickle of anticipation—or was it apprehension?—up the back of Prudence's neck.

Nor did she miss the back-and-forth glance that Sarah, Joe's lovely mother, sent between Jed and Charlotte, followed by a slightly furrowed brow. Prudence's momentary giddiness vanished at the sight, and not for the first time, she wondered if Sarah harbored secret hopes of spending evenings with Jed in matching rocking chairs on his future front porch. Prudence adored the kind, gregarious widow, and of all the women who'd set their sights on Jedediah Goodacre over the years since his Caroline's passing, Sarah seemed the most well-suited match for Daddy... *if* Daddy was looking for a match. Oh, he'd dated off and on over the years, letting his daughters know who he was with and when he'd be home, showing the girls the same courtesy he demanded of them. But nothing had ever stuck, and since the terrible tractor accident that had nearly taken his leg, leaving him with a significant limp and recurring debilitating back pain, Jed had seemed to grow content with slipping into retirement on his own. It certainly helped that, save Abby, all his daughters and his growing brood of grandchildren remained in the hollow close at hand.

Watching the two attractive single women sizing up her father—and each other—not to mention the way Daddy appeared to puff up under their perusal, Prudence couldn't help wondering if all that contentment was about to get upended.

"Yo, Pru!"

Startled out of her musings, she jumped, and the glass of water she held sloshed down the front of her, leaving a large wet splotch darkening the pale gold of her bodice. She gasped in shock at the chilled liquid against her skin and turned to gawk at Abby, who'd come up behind her.

"Oh, geez! I'm so sorry!" Abby declared, then snatched up one of the large linen napkins from the table and started dabbing at the front of Prudence's dress. "I didn't mean to startle you."

"Cut it out," Prudence said, batting her sister's hands away. She stood, plucking the sodden fabric away from her chest.

Abby brought the napkin up to hide her expression, but it was no use. It was obvious by the way her eyes crinkled at the corners that she was doing everything she could to hold back a laugh... and not succeeding very well. "Oh dear. I'm—I'm—"

Then they were both laughing. "You dork," Prudence admonished as she tried in vain to mop up the worst of the spill. "It's no use," she said. "I'll have to go change."

"Yeah, you'd better. You can see right through the wet patches." Abby wiggled her eyebrows before busting up again.

Prudence gasped and snatched the napkin from Abby, clutching it to her chest. "You can? Seriously?"

"You're wearing your butterfly bra, aren't you?" Abby asked, then before Prudence could respond, she took her elbow and steered her away from the party and toward the ranch house. "Go change, but hurry back. You need to meet my knight in shining armor."

"Your kni—knight?" She tried not to stammer but failed miserably. She let out a slighty hysterical giggle and fluttered the napkin a little, hoping to distract Abby enough that she wouldn't notice her sudden breathlessness.

"It's Mr. Stewart. Collin Stewart. You remember him, don't you? You probably had him in high school. Anyway, he's friends with Joe. And he's cute in a kind of professorial way." Abby grinned mischievously. "Way too old for me, but you might think—"

Prudence cut her off. "I have to go change." She took a step toward the house, but Abby grabbed her arm and stopped her.

"But you're coming back, right? You're not going to go hide inside?"

"No, of course, not. I have a wedding party to see to." Prudence swept an arm toward the

"Good. He's really nice, Pru. He wasn't going to come out to the ranch, but he stuck around after the ceremony to congratulate Joe and Courage while we were taking pictures. I convinced him that he had to join the party, and we wouldn't take no for an answer. I wanted to make sure he got a chance to meet the whole fam."

Somehow, Prudence's feet kept moving, but her heart ground to a stuttering stop. He was here.

After five years, Collin Stewart had returned to Seven Virtues Ranch.

SIX

Collin leaned casually against the low rock wall that bordered the sprawling lawn, having stepped away from the fray for a moment. He carefully sipped from the steaming mug of coffee he'd just served himself from one of the carafes on the drink table, then nodded in satisfaction at the robust flavor.

He'd spent the first hour of the reception catching up with Joe and Brandon and several of the other guys he'd known back when he'd called Plumwood Hollow home. He'd greeted Joe's mom, Sarah, and her artist friend, Charlotte Rawlings, had spoken with Levi Valiente, the town butcher who was now Hope Goodacre's husband—from what he'd learned, a second marriages for both—and he'd met Cord Overman, the lucky man who'd wooed—a second time—and wed the eldest Goodacre sister, Faith. He hadn't yet gotten around to speaking with the family patriarch; for a man who had a long-standing reputation for not stringing more than two sentences together in one sitting, Jed Goodacre had been hard to get close to, surrounded as he was with well-wishers.

But try as he might, he couldn't figure out how to bring Prudence up in conversation with anyone without sounding sketchy. He just wanted to know if she had someone in her life *before* he ran into her. And run into her, he would, come hell or high water. It was why he'd come, after all, and he wasn't leaving Plumwood Hollow until he'd had his say. But he wanted to be prepared if, after all this time, he had to face her again with some guy at her side.

He'd seen the way the DJ—Hank? Was that his name?—watched her as she moved among the guests, but he wasn't the only one. Walt Trager couldn't keep his gaze from landing on her throughout the afternoon, and then there was Terrell Jackson, the man who ran the Quarter Horse stables next door at Whispering Hills Ranch. Terrell had a way with the ladies that didn't sit well with Collin. Not because he behaved badly, but because it seemed to come so naturally to the man. In fact, Terrell seemed to have it all—he was a good-looking guy who knew how to wear a Stetson, and he moved with a sense of confidence that made Collin uncomfortably aware of his own slighter stature. It didn't help that Terrell made Prudence smile easily—and often—every time they crossed paths.

"You're acting like a fool," Collin muttered under his breath before taking another sip of the strong brew. He'd seen Abby startle Prudence, witnessed the spilled glass of water and the comedic attempts to clean up that followed, then watched Abby shoo her sister away from the party toward the ranch house, presumably to change. He'd seen it all... because, like Hank, Walt, Terrell, and probably a good half a dozen other men spending the relaxing afternoon in the Goodacre's back yard, he couldn't keep his eyes off the lovely, enigmatic Prudence, either. And what was he doing now? Sitting off by himself nursing a cup of coffee while he watched and waited with bated breath for her return to the party. "Pitiful," he growled, then he straightened up and headed back toward the tent just as Hank cranked up the volume on the music.

"Hope you all enjoyed that phenomenal food, folks!" the DJ practically bellowed into the microphone. "Because now it's time to make some room on the dance floor and work off some of those calories. To kick things off, we have our newlyweds' first dance." People were already scooting chairs and tables to the outer edges of the tent, clearing the space for dancing. "Ladies and gentleman, let's give it up for Mr. And Mrs. Joe and Courage Lynxwilder and Mr. And Mrs. Brandon and Justice Stillwater..." His voice faded out as the music swelled, the bluesy acoustic guitar of Greta Van Fleet's "You're the One" spilling from the speaker system. Brandon and Justice were alone on the dance floor for most of the first verse, but then Joe and Courage joined them, to the accompaniment of cat calls and wolf whistles. Joe's smug grin and the pretty blush on Courage's cheeks before she buried her face against her new husband's chest indicated the couple had quite possibly been rounded up from some dark corner where they'd been doing a little celebrating of their own.

By the time the song ended, folks were rallying to storm the dance floor, and Hank was ready with a party favorite from Train.

Collin took his cup of coffee and headed over to where Jed now sat with Frank Flanner, Charity's husband. He'd gotten to know Frank a little before the man had headed overseas to serve in the military. He'd been shocked to learn about the loss of Frank's leg, but Collin was not surprised by his dogged pursuit of a whole life and the subsequent journey toward recovery he'd made over the last couple of years. Frank had always been driven, just like his father before him, but Collin got the sense that much of Frank's healing was due to the woman who loved him.

"Hey there," Jed said, his voice raised to be heard over the music as Collin approached the table. "Pull up a chair, young man."

They exchanged a few words before it became evident that conversation this close to the festivities wasn't going to be feasible. In silent agreement, the three of them settled back into their chairs to watch the chaos on the dance floor that typically followed most weddings. A few songs in, Collin was surprised to find that he was rather content to just sit and watch.

Until he saw Prudence in the middle of the dance floor in the arms of the horse whisperer, Terrell Jackson. Her face was lifted to his, her eyes bright under the twinkle lights that glowed overhead, then she laughed as he leaned in close to murmur in her ear. A surge of something liquid and dark bubbled up inside Collin, and he clenched his fists in his lap to keep from lurching to his feet and cutting in on the couple.

Evidently, Terrell wasn't just a horse whisperer. He was a woman whisperer, too, because he certainly did a lot of whispering in Prudence's ear over the next three—count them, *three!*—songs. Terrell handed her off to someone who cut in on them, then Collin lost sight of her when Prudence left the floor with yet another man to mingle with folks gathered around the drink table. He sighed deeply and leaned back in his chair.

"Someone out there you keen on dancing with, son?" Jed's gruff voice rose above the throb of the music, and Collin looked over at him, a little taken aback by the straightforward question.

He took his time answering, doing his best to present a cool front. "Actually, sir, I'm feeling like one of the old codgers sitting here watching all that energy out there. Makes me tired just looking."

"Who you calling old?" Jed released a scoffing laugh that was echoed by Frank.

"And I don't see anything wrong with your legs," the Frank said, leaning forward to rap a knuckle against the front of his prosthetic leg.

"That's not—I didn't mean—." Great. Now he'd offended both of them. Maybe it was time to call it a night. He hadn't even planned on being here, anyway, and the peaceful solitude of his comfy hotel room awaited him.

Jed clapped a hand on his shoulder. "I'm just giving you a hard time," he said with a slow grin. "Caught you eying my daughter and wanted to let you know, that's all. But since I owe you for getting my Abby to the wedding this afternoon, I'll let you off the hook."

Collin wanted to slide off the chair and under the table, then slither out the back of the tent on his belly so he could disappear into the gathering darkness. He caught Frank's eye across the table, and he wasn't sure whether the smile on the man's face was one of pity, ridicule, or warning. He cleared his throat and said the first thing—the only thing—that came to mind. "Um, thank you, sir."

Frank released a guffaw, then planted both hands on the table. "Well, I don't know about you two," he said, rising. He gestured at Charity, who was making her way toward them between the tables. "But I see the most beautiful woman in the world coming my way, and I intend to dance with her. Even I can pull off a little two-stepping, and I only have one good leg." He gave Collin what appeared to be a challenging look and turned smartly in place to watch his wife draw near. Charity shot an adoring smile at her husband.

She stepped into Frank's arms, rose up on tiptoe to kiss him on the mouth, then peered over his shoulder at Jed. "Hey, Daddy. You gonna dance tonight? Should I send Pru over to get you off your backside?" Then, slipping an arm around Frank's waist, she turned to face Collin. "Well, hello, Mr. Stewart. I'm so glad you could come out to the ranch tonight. You enjoying yourself?"

"I am," he said politely. Did she call him that out of habit because he'd once been a teacher at Plumwood Hollow High? Or was it a subtle line in the sand, a warning that he no longer belonged on the inside. Should he insist she call him by his first name? After all, she was only a few years younger than he was. Feeling completely out of his element, he opted to play it safe, and simply said, "The food was delicious. I hear we have you to thank for it."

Charity beamed. "It's what I do; cook good food."

"The best," Jed confirmed. "And don't you dare send anyone over to dance with me, darlin' girl. I've been on my feet too long already."

Charity broke away from Frank and circled the table to give her father a quick kiss on top of his head. "Love you." Then pointing at her husband, she said, "What are you waiting for, stud? I'm only going to be fit to dance in public for another few months, you know. Time's a-tickin' away on us."

Jed watched the couple swirl away, a pleased grin on his face, before turning back to Collin. "Don't feel obligated to sit here and keep an old man company, son. Go on out there."

He was about to argue when he saw Sarah's friend, Charlotte, heading their way. She wore a wide, friendly smile, but it was obvious she was coming to join them because of Jed, not him. Collin rose when she approached, held a chair for her, then made his excuses.

"Enjoy yourself, Mr. Stewart." Jed said, his chin lifted in farewell. Then he made the universal "I'm watching you" gesture, pointing two fingers first at his own eyes, then toward Collin.

"Good to know," Collin replied with a nervous chuckle, before turning toward the dance floor. Was that a warning? Did Jed know anything about the last time Collin had been at Seven Virtues Ranch?

For the next several minutes, he meandered from one group of people to the next, exchanging greetings and platitudes, but not really engaging with anyone. He'd never felt like more of an outsider in his life. This town, these people, they were once *his* town and people. But he'd cut and run, hadn't he? He'd left them—and left them kinda high and dry and without much of an explanation, either. Could he blame them for not readily opening up the inner fold to him again?

Prudence seemed to have vanished altogether, and he'd just made up his mind to call it a night for real, when Hank's voice boomed out over the sound system. "Well, well, well, folks! Looks like it's time to say goodbye—and good luck!— to our favorite newlyweds! At each table are little baskets of bird seed and bubble blowers. Grab yours and let's give them a sendoff they won't forget!"

And with that, Collin was swept up in the melee of people swarming out of the tent and onto the lawn toward a stretch limousine, its doors flung open, parked at the head of the driveway.

SEVEN

Prudence pushed to the front of the group crowding around the limo, dragging Hank with her. "Tell them to split up so there's a path down the middle!" she hollered at him above the clapping, cheering throng. Everything seemed especially loud to her, and she thought she could actually feel her pulse thrumming at her temples. The big, outside lights glared overhead, and even though it wasn't quite completely dark, they seemed overly bright to her. She blinked and squeezed Hank's hand. "Help me get them split up," she said. "No one is listening to me."

Hank let go of her hand, let out a piercing whistle, and raised both his arms over his head to get everyone's attention. Then he faced his palms straight out in front of him like a traffic controller. "Make way, folks!" he commanded. "Be like the Red Sea, people! Make way, make way!"

Prudence moved back, stumbling a little when she backed into Jasmine, but her niece just took her hand and grinned up at her. "Isn't this awesome, Aunt Pru?"

Prudence hugged the girl, then turned to peer up the cleared path toward the back porch of the house just as the two couples made their way down the steps toward the limo. Before they'd even made it into the gauntlet, guests were already throwing birdseed and flower petals, and thousands of bubbles drifted up into the twilit sky overhead. Prudence tipped her head back, watching one bubble flit higher and higher, drifting up to dance with the first star of the night twinkling overhead.

Star light, star bright, she murmured to herself. But instead of wishing for happiness for her sisters, she found her thoughts were on Collin. *I wish I may, I wish I might.* She hadn't seen him in quite some time; had he left the party without even speaking to her? *Have the wish I wish tonight.* And what, exactly, *did* she wish for tonight? To see him? To talk to him? To dance with him?

To dance with him.

To be held in his arms.

To press her cheek to his shoulder and sway with him.

The very thought of it—the very dream of it—made her whole body grow warm.

The bubble popped.

She lowered her gaze... and there he was. Directly across the driveway from her.

Staring right at her.

Those dark hazel eyes outlined in sooty lashes, eyes she could see clearly now. No more Clark Kent glasses—although, she'd loved those, too. His hair, the soft Afro he'd once worn a little long on top with a distinct side part, was now cropped close to his perfectly shaped skull, making his cheekbones more pronounced, his nose a prominent arrow that pointed to his wide mouth. Full lips and straight white teeth, always ready with an encouraging smile for a student who needed one. Even without the glasses, without the wiry curls he'd once struggled to control, without the cardigans with elbow patches he used to wear, she saw that he still had that iconic professorial look. A little otherworldly. A little distracted.

Except he didn't seem distracted at all right now. That smile, his eyes, they were turned not on the brides and grooms sweeping down the lawn, but on her.

She raised a hand to her throat above the sweetheart neckline of the dress she'd changed into. She could feel the heat of her own skin against her fluttering fingertips. Was that her pulse beating so erratically?

She had to get out of there. Had to get away. She needed to disappear, preferably without making a scene.

Behind her, the crowd pressed in, surging forward. Try as she might, she couldn't back up, couldn't escape.

And suddenly, Courage and Justice were in front of her, both of them stopping to hug her and thank her one last time before their husbands swept them off to the waiting car. A moment later, the twins popped up through the open sunroof, arms around each other's waists, waving and calling out their goodbyes, barely able to be heard above the cheers and shouted congratulations.

Prudence stood perfectly still as the hubbub continued around her. Tiny lights pinged at the edges of her vision, and for a moment, she thought the sky was suddenly filled with stars. But when she looked up, she only saw bubbles... and then they, too, blinked out of sight, and everything faded, ever so slowly into quiet blackness.

She felt herself falling, but there was nothing she could do about it.

She felt hands reaching for her, but she couldn't grab on.

She heard someone—a child?—calling her name, but try as she might, she couldn't force out a response.

EIGHT

Collin was halfway through the throng of people when he saw her sway. He lunged forward and reached for her as her legs seemed to simply give out beneath her. There were too many people around for her to fall unhindered, and directly behind her, a young girl, maybe eleven or twelve, had her slender arms wrapped tightly around Prudence's waist, doing her best to hold her up.

"Aunt Pru!" the child cried out, her voice frantic. "Somebody help!"

Collin wasn't a big guy, nor did he make a habit of spending time in the gym, even though a membership to the local YMCA was one of the perks of his teaching job. But whether it was pure adrenaline or the fact that Prudence was petite and fine-boned, he managed to scoop her up in his arms without making a fool of himself. Granted, it wasn't easy, not at all like the way they made it look in the movies. It was tough trying to maneuver a limp noodle, even one as diminutive as Prudence Goodacre, but he managed to lift her high against his chest without dropping her.

He started to push through people who were now crowding around with concern. Should he ask if there was a doctor among them? Or was that also only something they did in Hollywood?

"Move out of the way, you guys!" the young girl called out as she moved along beside him, her high voice bordering on hysterical.

Then Hank the Tank was there, his arms out like he was going to take her from him. For a moment, Collin had the insane notion that they were going to start fighting over who got to carry her. He turned a steely look up at the guy who stood a good six inches taller than him. "I got her," he said, his voice firm, and, thankfully, not winded at all. Then he stepped around the DJ, his precious bundle held even tighter.

Hank gave him a nod, then began to clear the way for him. "Get back, folks," his voice boomed above the noise of the concerned crowd.

Prudence made a sound but didn't seem aware of what was going on. Her breath fluttered warm against his neck, making his pulse race.

"Bring her in the house." Faith appeared out of nowhere and rested her hand on Collin's shoulder. To his relief, she didn't seem too concerned about her younger sister's unconscious state. "I'll bet she hasn't eaten a thing all day." Her other arm was draped comfortingly around the shoulders of the girl who'd been so heroic. "She'll be fine, honey," Faith said to her in a soothing tone.

Collin made it up the porch steps without embarrassing himself by tripping or stalling, then paused to catch his breath while Faith held open the back door for him. The last time he'd been inside the Goodacre's sprawling ranch house, he'd gone in that same way, except without Prudence in his arms. The long table still sat in the same spot in the middle of the large farm kitchen, all twelve chairs scooted in around it. The table itself was covered with all the accoutrements of party preparation—extra serving platters and bulk jars of condiments, half-used packages of plastic cups and utensils and more.

"Wha—" Prudence's half-whisper got his attention, and he glanced down to find her staring up at him, her eyes widening in shock. Her whole body tensed, and for a moment, Collin thought he might stumble, or worse, loose his grip on her.

"It's okay," he quickly assured her. "I got you." Okay. So he did sound a little winded. But he wasn't sure if that was from the effort he was expending, or from the close proximity of the woman—*the* woman—he held in his arms.

"I—I can walk," she stammered, but her arm went around his neck and she held on tightly, as though suddenly realizing just how precarious her predicament was. "You can put me down."

"He'll do no such thing, you ninny," Faith said, glancing back at them over her shoulder. "Let me guess. You didn't eat any of that food I sent Daddy with, did you?"

Collin could practically hear the woman's eyes roll.

"I—I—" Prudence began.

"Take her in there and lay her on the sofa." Faith directed him through to the living room. "I'll get a cool washcloth." She turned to the young girl. "Honey, will you please go get your aunt something to eat and a glass of water? A handful of a almonds and maybe a few of those peanut butter cookies. She needs a little protein and sugar."

Collin moved through the arched opening and made a beeline toward the larger of two sofas. They were all alone in the quiet room, and now that Prudence was awake and aware of all that was happening, Collin found himself getting more flustered with each passing moment. He grunted slightly as he bumped his knee against the corner of the coffee table, and Prudence squeezed her eyes shut. "I won't drop you," he assured her when her arm tightened around his neck.

"Okay," she whispered, her reply shaky.

Collin commanded himself to be more manly, and nudging the coffee table out of the way with his foot, he maneuvered around it. But when he bent to set her down, he leaned forward too far, nearly toppling over on her. He caught himself just in time by bracing his hands against the armrest on either side of her head, his face was only inches from hers.

Inches from her pale blue eyes.

Inches from that pretty, pink mouth.

Those eyes went wide, and her mouth opened in a tiny sound... and time seemed to hold its breath right along with him.

Don't look at her mouth. Don't look at her mouth.

Prudence blinked once, then twice, and Collin straightened and pushed away from her so fast, he stumbled over the coffee table again.

At the exact moment that Faith walked back into the room.

A curious look crossed her face. "Everything all right in here?" she asked, cocking her head in question.

Collin couldn't look at her lest she see the turmoil roiling around inside of him, so he busied himself straightening the coffee table. "Just a little shaken," he said, then grimaced at his choice of words. Hopefully, Faith would think he was referring to Prudence, not him. From the corner of his eye, he saw Prudence smoothing her skirt over her legs. He secretly patted himself on the back for making sure he'd kept her modest while carrying her, but he was grateful the dress she'd changed into after she'd spilled water on the other one had such a long full skirt, or his task might not have been quite so heroic.

"Thank you, Coll—Mr. Stewart." Prudence's voice came out breathy and ragged, but she still wouldn't meet his eyes.

"Are you okay?" he asked, and he didn't sound much more stable than she did. He stepped back, feeling suddenly useless. What did one do with their arms after setting down a rescued damsel in distress? His seemed to just hang there like lifeless noodles, reminding him of a scene in one of the Harry Potter movies when a spell had gone comically wrong, and the bones in one of Harry's arms had to be regrown. If he shook his, would they wobble around like a water balloon? And why was that suddenly the funniest thing in the world to him? He clenched his jaw to keep back the laugh that threatened to launch itself out of his throat.

What was wrong with him? He was making quite the impression on the whole Goodacre gang tonight.

Faith laid a wet washcloth over Prudence's forehead, then dropped into one of the armchairs nearby and sighed dramatically. "Yes, thank you," she murmured, resting her head on the chair back and closing her eyes. "Both of you."

Collin looked over at her. Both of them?

"Why me?" Prudence asked, echoing his thoughts.

Faith opened one eye to peer at her sister. "Because I needed a break," she said with a grin. "I handed the baby off to Dad a few minutes ago, and I was going to sneak away to put my feet up in here for a few minutes. But then I got roped back into the send-off party. Which was fine." She snorted affectionately. "Except that I saw Cord making a beeline for me with a crying Ollie in his arms, that helpless dad look on his face."

Collin's eyebrows furrowed in confusion.

"Don't judge me, Mr. Stewart," she declared, pointing a finger at him, both eyes open now. "Not until you've walked a mile in my shoes."

"I'm not judging," Collin assured her, raising his hands in surrender. Apparently, the bones in his arms were present and accounted for.

"Good." She closed her eyes again.

"And I'm Collin," he blurted out. "Call me Collin, please. My students call me Mr. Stewart."

"Sorry," Faith replied, not bothering to open her eyes. "Old habit."

There followed a brief, but awkward silence, and Collin dropped his gaze to the floor, completely out of his element. If only Faith would find a reason to step out of the room again so he could speak to Prudence alone.

"Hold tight, Pru," Faith suddenly commanded, her eyes still closed.

It was like Faith had a sixth sense or something. Was it a mother thing? Because sure enough, Prudence was pushing up to sit, sliding her legs toward the edge of the couch cushions. She dropped back down with a huff at Faith's firm command.

"Jasmine will be back any second now with something to eat. Neither of us are moving until she gets here."

What about me? Collin wanted to ask. He looked back and forth between the two women, but with Faith's eyes closed and Prudence homing in on anything and everything but him, he was at a loss. "Well, I guess I'll take my leave, then. Unless you need anything else," he amended when Faith raised her head to look at him. He was at such a loss; she seemed to be taking all of this in stride, almost as if Prudence fainting was no big deal. He didn't want to question her judgment, but her casual response, or lack thereof, to the whole situation disturbed him. Where were all the concerned guests who'd crowded around them only moments before? Where was Jed? Surely, he'd seen the whole incident. And if not, someone must have told him about it by now.

"We're good," Faith assured him. "Go. Enjoy the party."

He paused for just a moment more, and Prudence finally lifted her gaze, but only for the few moments it took to express her gratitude.

"Thank you," she said, a little more firmly this time. "And I'm sorry for... for all of this."

Collin opened his mouth to reply, to assure her she'd done nothing wrong, but Faith spoke first.

"And if you see my husband wandering around with a crabby baby, don't tell him where I am." She sighed wearily.

With those words, he was dismissed.

As he passed back through the kitchen, Collin paused at the table to brush his fingers over the curved back of the chair where Prudence sat the last time he'd been there. His eyes rested on the next seat over where he'd been, close enough for their elbows and knees to bump throughout the meal they'd shared. He stood there, awash in the memory of how those fleeting touches had made his pulse race. The way the memory made his pulse race even now.

High-pitched giggles brought him out of his reverie, and he jerked his hand back just as the kitchen door was flung open by the preteen girl from earlier. She'd brought a friend with her. "Mom?" she called out. "I'm back. And Vetty came, too." She smiled at him as she rushed past.

Mom? So that was Faith's daughter? Was it possible she'd grown so much in the years Collin had been away? Which meant her little friend must be Levi Valiente's daughter. He'd heard from both Levi and Hope that the two girls were inseparable.

Suddenly feeling older than his thirty years, Collin slowly made his way down the porch steps and out toward the party tent.

So much of Plumwood Hollow felt the same, unaffected by the passage of time. He'd driven through the small downtown, past the familiar shop fronts: the hardware store at the corner of Main and First, Nesbit's Grocery, the book and coffee shop, the ancient post office; it was all there. Even Old Harv at the Lock 'n' Stock gas and convenience store where he'd rescued Abby. Harv had greeted Collin as though he'd just been in the day before. And the old guys in the plastic lawn chairs under the awning of the hardware store. They'd smiled and waved at him as he drove past, a telltale wistful look on at least one of their faces.

But then he'd stumble across something—usually some*one*—and it would catch him by surprise at how nothing ever really stayed the same. The last time he'd seen the girl—Jasmine, that's what Faith had called her. He remembered now. The last time he'd seen Jasmine, she hadn't even started school yet. She'd been a goofy little five-year-old, doted on by the whole Goodacre gang.

And with that realization came the memory of the scandal that had swirled around Faith all those years ago. Collin was still working on his teaching degree when she'd been a pregnant teen, but even three years later after he'd taken his first teaching job at Plumwood High, her sordid story came up now and again because her younger sisters all attended Plumwood High after her.

Collin stopped short at the edge of the crowd as his rambling thoughts suddenly took shape, pieces of a puzzle falling into place. Those whispered stories about Faith included tales of her entanglement with Frank's cousin, Cord, who came out to visit Whispering Hills Ranch every summer. Cordell Overman, who now owned the ranch. Who was now married to Faith. According to the rumors, Faith and Cord had been pretty serious back in their high school days, and then he'd left her high and dry—and pregnant—to chase after his superstar football dreams.

Jasmine, he realized, was the spitting image of her father. There was no denying the blood ties there. By the look of things, those rumors, the gossip, it had all been true.

And yet, somehow, they'd managed to find their way back to each other, and apparently, things had worked out.

A frisson of hope skittered up his spine, but he shook it off. He would not allow himself to entertain any such thoughts until he'd had the chance to talk to Prudence. He owed her that much.

The party across the lawn had kicked up a notch in his short absence, and he was reticent to return, especially since the person he was there to see was inside the house under her sister's guard. "Time to call it a night, young squire," he muttered to himself. He'd been calling himself that since the old man at the mailboxes had dubbed him as such. For some reason, it resonated with him. "Give it another shot in the morning." Surely,

Prudence would be at church with her family. The Goodacre's took up a whole pew, and that was before any of them were married or had children. And without fail, every Sunday, Jed and his tail of pretty ducklings took their places in the fifth row from the front.

Tomorrow, Collin would be there to greet them all, except for the newlyweds, of course.

NINE

"How are you feeling, Aunt Pru?" Jasmine plunked down beside her on the couch and took her hand, holding it between hers. Yvette, who was rarely far from Jasmine's side, dropped to the floor and leaned her head against Prudence's shoulder.

"I'm fine, girlies," she assured them. "Your mom is right, Jazzy-girl. I went too long without eating, I guess."

"You guess?" Faith asked dryly, but her smile was kind. "Pru, when will you learn? You have the metabolism of a hummingbird. You can't just go without sustenance for hours at a time. Especially on an all-day event like today."

"I know, I know," she groaned, flopping back against the armrest again, and draping the damp washcloth over her eyes. "I was going to eat when Daddy brought me that plate of food, I really was."

"Well, why didn't you?" Jasmine asked, her slashing brows so like her father's furrowing in question.

Prudence took a deep breath and blew it out, then removed the washcloth and pushed up to sit on the edge of the couch. The girls shifted to accommodate her. "I was just getting ready to when Abby came up behind me and scared me." At Faith's stern expression, she quickly explained. "Not on purpose. She was just trying to get my attention. But I was in the middle of taking a sip of water and when I jumped, it spilled down the front of me, and do you know how see-through that chiffon fabric is when it's wet?"

"I wondered why you'd changed," Faith interjected with a chuckle.

"So yeah. I went inside and changed, and by the time I came back out, Justice was looking for me and asking about getting on with the bouquet and garter toss stuff." She rolled her eyes and grinned at Faith. "I have no idea why, but the twins seemed in an awful big hurry to get the festivities rolling so they could hit the road with their new husbands."

"Selfish, demanding divas," Faith said with exaggerated scorn.

"They just wanted to go somewhere they could kiss with their tongues," Jasmine said, her eyes wide with false innocence.

"Jasmine!" Faith blurted out, straightening abruptly in her seat.

"What? We saw them doing it already," the girl said, then nudged Yvette. "Didn't we?"

"Yep," Yvette agreed, although she kept her eyes lowered to her lap where she toyed with the decorative stitching along the hem of her skirt. Prudence could still see the silly smirk on her averted face, though. "At least, we saw Mr. Joe and Aunt Courage."

"They were totally tongue kissing," Jasmine said. "Can we call him Uncle Joe now?"

Faith had a hand over her mouth, but her eyes were tearing up with the effort to keep from laughing out loud. "Yes," she managed to eke out. "You may now call him Uncle Joe. And Uncle Brandon."

"What?" Jasmine looked aghast at her mother. "Why? Just cuz he married Aunt Justice?"

"That's exactly why, darling girl. He is now your uncle by marriage. Which is a good thing, after all, with all that tongue kissing going on," Faith added with a snort.

"Mom, gross," Jasmine said before making a grossed-out face.

"I'm gross? You're the one who brought it up," Faith countered. "But anyway," she went on, not letting Jasmine interrupt again. "You get to call Yvette your cousin now, don't you? Because your aunt married her daddy, who is now Uncle Levi to you. Get it?"

Jasmine let out a long-suffering sigh. "Yes," she said, drawing the word out. She straightened and turned her attention back to Prudence, who was also trying to quell her giggles. Poor Joe. He had a big learning curve, marrying into their family of seven sisters and their husbands and offspring. Nothing was sacred among the Goodacre sisters, and quiet, solid, Oak Tree Joe, as Courage sometimes called him, having been raised an only child by two quiet, solid parents, would need to watch his back a little more carefully if he wanted to get away with necking in the shadows.

"Are you sure you're okay?" Jasmine asked, turning to Prudence again.

"Thanks to you," Prudence said, stroking the girl's cheek with the back of her fingers. "Not only did you keep me from falling on my backside, but you two also brought me the perfect cure." She pointed at the half-eaten roast beef sandwich Charity had put together and given the girls for her. "Did the twins get off okay? They didn't notice me go down, did they?" She wouldn't want them to have worried.

Faith shook her head. "Nope. I doubt they noticed anyone or anything as they took off, all wrapped up in their bubble of love." She gave Prudence a scrutinizing look. "Thank goodness for the dashing Mr. Stewart and how he swept you off your feet like that." One of her eyebrows arched, and Prudence felt her cheeks grow warm.

"It was a very gallant thing he did," she agreed, like it was no big deal.

"I thought it was very romantic, Aunt Pru. Didn't you?" Jasmine asked. "Yvette does, too."

"Yep," echoed her cousin. "Picking you up and carrying you off to safety. Like that Jane Austen movie where Mr. Willoughby carried Marianne—"

"No, not Mr. Willoughby, Vetty!" Jasmine interrupted emphatically. "We like Colonel Brandon, remember? I mean, Mr. Willoughby carried her, too, but he's not the real hero."

Yvette paused a moment, then nodded. "Yeah, I think Mr. Willoughby was just showing off." The two girls, almost the same age and in the same grade, had been best friends for years, but since joining the family by marriage, Yvette's schooling in chick flicks, rom coms, and tear-jerkers that came with the family of seven sisters had been amped up. The thirteen-year-olds were currently saturating themselves in the timeless pleasure of Jane Austen's brilliant mind.

"Thinking he was all hot and stuff." Jasmine gave an exaggerated eye roll.

Faith said nothing, but her lips quirked up at the corners as she listened.

"But that guy who carried you, Aunt Pru? He's like Colonel Brandon. I mean, even though he's kinda old, he's still pretty yummy." She paused to study Prudence thoughtfully. "You know, maybe he'll marry you." She said it in a manner that suggested there might still be hope for Prudence after all. Prudence didn't know whether to laugh or cry.

"Girls," Faith said, still trying to hold back her smile. "Run along and tell Grandpa that Aunt Pru is doing fine. And bring us some cake, will you? I already had a piece, but I'm a nursing mom, so I need at least twice as much as everyone else."

"Where is Ollie?" Prudence asked as the girls hustled from the room. It was well after eight o'clock and they didn't look like they were running out of steam any time soon.

"Last I knew, Cord had him. Dad must have handed him off when he started getting fussy." She chortled softly. "I'm so glad you pulled that little stunt, Pru. This is the most relaxed I've been in about six months."

"It's the least I could do," Prudence said with a bright smile, but Faith's eyes stayed locked on her as the silence between them stretched out.

Prudence recognized the ploy for what it was. A mom trick, the "A long enough silence will force a confession out" method Faith had used on all of them as far back as Prudence could remember. But it was a trick of the trade she'd come by honestly. Their mother had been sick off and on long before those last few months when her weakened state had left her bedridden and unable to do much on her own, and Faith, being the eldest sister at twelve, almost thirteen, had taken it upon herself to step into the adult-sized shoes no preteen should have to fill. Their mother had been a pro at using silence to garner answers, and in taking over the matriarchal role in the family, Faith had mastered the talent over the years.

But Prudence didn't feel like talking about Collin. There was nothing to tell, anyway. So what if he'd picked her up and carried her off to safety like the girls said. If he hadn't been there, some other guy would have done the same thing. Hank, or Walt. Even one of her brothers-in-law.

She picked up her glass of water and downed the rest of it. "Well, I should probably get back out there. Thanks for looking out for me, Faithy." She wasn't exactly anxious to go out and face everyone after making such a scene, but she had no desire to stay inside and be interrogated by her big sister, either. That was something else Faith was good at... the ability to somehow just *know* when something wasn't quite as it should be. Besides, she couldn't hide inside the rest of the night. She was the official wedding planner, after all. And even though the newlyweds were off on their honeymoon adventure, there was still a whole lot of partying going on out there, and she still had lots of work to do before she could call it a night.

"Eat the rest of your sandwich first," Faith said.

"I'm fine, really."

"Eat. I'm bigger than you are, and I can make you stay until that sandwich is gone." She shrugged, then added, "Or you can just eat it like a normal person. Which is probably your better option. You know, so you don't faint again." Although her tone was dry and sarcastic, the look in her eyes was one of concern, and if Prudence read her right, curiosity.

Prudence picked it up and took another bite. It really was delicious. Charity had spread a thin layer of horseradish aioli between the slices of roast beef and provolone cheese, and the roll was soft and yeasty.

"It really was nice to see Mr. Stewart again, wasn't it?" Faith asked directly.

Well. There it was.

"Not like that, it wasn't," Prudence deflected. "Poor guy. Welcome back to the Hollow, Mr. Stewart." She lifted the back of her hand to her brow. "Would you mind catching me while I swoon?"

"Exactly," Faith said, her gaze unwavering. "You did, indeed, swoon over him."

"No, I didn't swoon over *him*. I got dehydra—"

"Dehydrated. Light-headed. Low blood sugar. Yes, you said." Faith was sitting forward in her chair now. "Sorry, girlie. But that was the closest thing to a legitimate swoon if I ever saw one. And I did see it, Pru. The whole thing. The way you locked eyes with each other. How you tried to run away from—"

"That is not what happened. I got dizzy watching the bubbles," Prudence interjected, cutting her off. She felt her cheeks warm at how silly her excuse sounded, but it was true.

Faith let the words hang between them for another moment or two, then she shrugged one shoulder. "Not that I blame you. He is rather swoon worthy in all that geeky professorial appeal. And didn't he used to wear glasses?"

Prudence opened her mouth to defend herself, but she was saved by the sound of the back screen door slamming closed behind someone coming through the kitchen.

A moment later, Abby sashayed into the room carrying a tray with several pieces of cake on it. "How's it going?" she asked in a sing-song voice, handing out the plates of cake to each of them, keeping one for herself. "I swear that was the most romantic thing I've ever seen in real life, Pru, and that's saying something, considering today we had us a ridiculously romantic double wedding."

"Right?" Faith concurred.

"And my goodness, girl. When did Mr. Stewart get so hot?" Abby kicked her shoes off and stretched her bare feet out in front of her. She pointed her fork at Prudence. "I mean, if he wasn't so old, I'd put dibs on him. Remember, I saw him first." She turned to Faith and explained, "He's the one who brought me to the church this afternoon, did I tell you? At first, I didn't recognize him—thought I might have to fight him off with my handy dandy tire iron, you know? I mean, he used to have super old-school side part and those doofy glasses. And didn't he wear Mr. Rogers cardigans?" She polished off the last bite of her piece of cake, set her empty plate on the table in front of her, then slouched lazily back in her chair. "Such a dork. I mean, he was cute with that whole geeky professor thing he had going, but wowzer! Who would've ever guessed he could look like he does now?"

"That whole geeky professor thing," Faith echoed softly, like she was conjuring up memories from the past. And even though Prudence remained laser focused on the delicious piece of wedding cake she was savoring, she could practically feel Faith's eyes boring into her.

Abby continued, unperturbed by the interruption. "But then he laid those big brown eyes on me, and, well..." She lifted both hands in the air in surrender, leaving the statement hanging.

"Well?" Faith prodded.

"Well, I think I would've considered going just about anywhere with him had it not been for the wedding," Abby admitted dreamily.

"His eyes aren't brown," Prudence stated. "They're hazel. Or amber." *Like fine whiskey....* She glanced up to fine Faith staring at her, both brows raised in question. "What?" Prudence asked, trying to sound nonchalant. "The guy was all up in my face not more than ten minutes ago, okay?" She forced a little belligerence into her voice, too. "Talk about no respect for personal space."

"Something you should be grateful for, considering that otherwise, you'd still be sprawled on the lawn out there, your skirt up over your head," Faith pointed out.

"Really? Because he's the only guy out there who'd be able to haul my skinny butt up here to the house?" Now the belligerence was genuine. "And I never hit the ground, thanks to your heroic daughter, *not* Mr. Stewart. Nor was my skirt ever up over my head," she added.

"Hey, I'm certainly grateful for his lack of personal space issues," Abby interjected. "He didn't seem to have any qualms about me throwing a leg over the back of his bike, even in this dress, mind you." She flapped her skirt a few times. "I mean, I was like, all snuggled up close and personal, hanging on his back like a little monkey. I'm just glad I wore underwear today."

"Abby!" Faith's eyes went wide with alarm and Prudence nearly choked on the bite of cake in her mouth.

"Just kidding, you guys!" Abby chortled gleefully at the responses she'd goaded out of them. "Not only am I wearing underwear, but I'm also wearing my workout shorts." She hitched up one side of her skirt to show them. "Keeps my thighs from chafing," she explained, then added, "I'm a no-thigh-gap girl and proud of it."

"Preach!" Faith declared, raising a supporting fork in the air.

"Anyway, at least he recognized me, even after all these years." She touched her face coquettishly, turning this way and that. "But then, who could forget a face like this, right?"

Faith rolled her eyes at their beautiful nineteen-year-old sister. "I'm so glad you don't suffer from the sin of vanity," she teased.

Abby chuckled good-naturedly, but then frowned and changed the subject. "Ugh. I totally forgot. My car is still at Lock 'n' Stock. Old Harv said he'd be sure it stayed safe, but I'll need Daddy to take me over there soon and get it. My phone and purse are locked inside, too."

"Why don't you ask Cord to take you?" Faith suggested. "Dad has got to be exhausted after today."

"That's all right. I'll catch a ride with someone heading out shortly. Some of the folks with kiddos are starting to round up their offspring to go home." She grinned impishly. "Or maybe I'll ask that hottie horse whisperer Terrell Jackson if he'll be my knight in shining armor and drive me over there. He's got that sweet old Chevy pickup out there, and I'd do just about anything to get to ride in it."

"Please don't let him hear you say that," Faith admonished. "He might just take you up on it."

Abby snorted and waved off Faith's warning. "T.J.? Ha. He may know how to work magic with the horses, but us girls?" She shook her head. "As Daddy says, he's all hat and no cattle."

"Don't be too sure about that, Abs," Faith entreated again, a worried crease forming between her brows. "Just be careful, okay?"

"I'm always careful," she shot back, her smile bright. "Trust me, Faithy."

But something in the way Abby said those words had the fine hairs on the back of Prudence's neck standing up.

They chatted for a few more moments, then Prudence excused herself to the bathroom so she could freshen up. She hoped if she stayed in there long enough, her sisters would be gone when she came out. In fact, maybe if she stayed in there long enough, everyone outside on the lawn—including Collin—would be gone, too.

No such luck on either count. When she re-emerged, she could hear the boisterous ruckus from outside through the back screen door, and Faith was still sitting in that same chair.

Her eldest sister eyed her seriously. Her voice had lost all trace of levity. "No more funny fainting business, okay? It's been a while since you let it go so far—when was the last time you actually fainted like that? Years, hasn't it been?"

"At least," Prudence agreed vaguely, although she remembered the last time as clear as day. They'd all been pretty frightened for her in the few years following high school, had worried that their mother's weakened constitution might have somehow been passed down. But Dr. Piper had finally narrowed it down to the simple fact that Prudence was starving herself. It wasn't one of the typical eating disorders that plagued teenage girls. No, Prudence was suffering from a failure to thrive, and it had happened without her even being aware of it. Granted, she hadn't been aware of a lot of things back then. "I'm feeling much better now, I promise."

Faith didn't say a word, but she pointed two fingers back and forth between her eyes and Prudence's like some threatening mobster, a gesture their father used all the time. It made Prudence smile.

She crossed the room and planted a kiss on the top of Faith's head. "Thanks for always taking care of me," she murmured, then headed out of the room.

She could hear Ollie's warbling cry before she made it through the kitchen, and she stepped out onto the back porch in time to hold the door open for the cranky baby carried by his similarly cranky father. She shot Cord a commiserating smile when she heard Faith holler, "You found me. I'm in here, boys."

Cord, however, paused and turned back to Prudence. "You doing all right?" His brow stayed furrowed, and he tipped his head away from the baby crying against his shoulder, but his eyes gave her a quick, brotherly once-over. "Jasmine said you fainted."

"I'm fine," she said with a slow nod. "Just forgot to eat today." She'd be saying the same thing a hundred more times before the night was over. "Your wife took good care of me, as usual."

"She's good at that, isn't she," Cord shot her an affectionate grin that quickly changed to a grimace when Ollie got hold of a clump of chest hair poking out of Cord's open collar. "Let go," he grumbled as he used his thumb to pry the baby's fist open. Then to Prudence, almost as an aside, he said, "My wife and the dashing Mr. Stewart, from what I hear. Jas and Yvette are talking marriage, you know. After the success of today, they're in wedding planning mode. Just a heads up."

Prudence's cheeks blazed and she covered her eyes with the hand that wasn't holding the screen door open. "Great. Just great. Poor Collin."

"Collin, is it?" Now Cord was teasing her, too. "Already on intimate first name ba—Ouch!" Ollie tugged on the chest hair again, then stopped whimpering at his father's yelp. The baby lifted his big teary eyes while Cord loosened his grip once more, and then let out a delighted baby chortle before reaching for the same spot again.

"No, Ollie," Cord reprimanded, but anyone could see the relief in his eyes now that his son had stopped crying.

"Serves you right," Prudence said. "Good boy, Ollie. Pull harder next time. Rip it out at the roots," she commanded in a silly, baby talk voice. Then she let the screen door close just as Faith called out again from the living room.

"Where are you guys? I'm not getting out of this chair for at least another thirty minutes, so you'll have to come to me. But better make it quick; my milk just let down."

"Coming!" Cord called back, grabbing Ollie's wrist before the baby could latch on again. Peering through the screen at Prudence, he said, "In case you're wondering, the dashing Mr. Stewart left the premises about ten minutes ago. But he promised to look for us in church tomorrow." And with those parting words, he turned away to find his wife.

"Well, it looks like I'm going to be super busy with cleanup all day tomorrow," Prudence muttered under her breath as she made her way down the steps and started back toward the party. She shot a brief glance heavenward. "You'll understand, won't you, God?" But God wasn't really going to be the problem. Convincing Daddy that she had to stay home from church would be a far bigger hurdle to clear.

"Of course, I *did* faint from exhaustion just now," she mused calculatingly. "And I am definitely still feeling wobbly." She slowed and did her best to look a little less fine than she had a moment ago. Maybe that hurdle wasn't going to be such a tall order after all.

TEN

He made a quick circuit of the party until he found Jed, congratulated him on the fine festivities and thanked him for his hospitality, then made his way to where he'd parked his bike.

Back at his hotel, he kicked off his boots and tossed his jacket over the back of a chair in one corner of the room. Dropping to sit at the edge of the bed, he scrubbed his face with both hands. His eyes felt a little gritty from the long hours spent on the road yesterday, followed by a fitful night's rest, and then the events of this day, and he was suddenly terribly tired. The cushy king-sized bed was calling, but he needed to get his contacts out before his eyes dried up and fell out of his head.

Half an hour later, Collin lay sprawled on his back, his fingers laced behind his head as he stared up at the ceiling. A narrow beam of moonlight pried its way through the crack in the drapes and shone directly on his face. He closed his eyes.

Then he opened them again.

It didn't matter. Either way, he still pictured Prudence up close and personal, still felt the weight of her in his arms, still felt the rush of her breath against his neck when she gasped, fearful he might drop her. Over and over, he heard that little sound—a coo? A squeak?—she'd made when he all but fell on top of her.

Again and again he saw her crumple just out of his reach, her eyes rolling back in her head, her body going limp.

He saw her dancing in the arms of Hank. Terrel. Walt. Talking, smiling, giggling. Not frightened, wounded, or confused at all when she looked at any of them. No, those emotions she reserved for him.

And she had every reason to.

No, tonight as he'd watched her mingle with the people of Plumwood Hollow, he'd seen a lovely, content woman who belonged right where she was... in a place he no longer called home.

Maybe he should just check out in the morning and go back to Cincinnati. Heck, since sleep seemed to be eluding him no matter how tired he was, maybe he should just get on the road tonight. He could be back in his own bed in his own Kennedy Heights neighborhood by dawn. He had nowhere to be for another two days, and he could just hole up in his apartment, all alone, and feel sorry for himself. And hopefully, the girls next door wouldn't figure out that he was back; he certainly wouldn't be in any mood to regale them about wedding stories.

"You are such a pitiful schmuck," he groaned, then grabbed the pillow from behind his head and held it over his face.

No. He came here for a reason—two, if he counted the wedding—and he'd be hanged if he wasn't going to see it through. Prudence was no longer one of his students. She was no longer a seventeen-year-old siren on the verge of ruining his reputation, his career, his life.

Collin had come to see her, to explain why he'd done what he'd done. Why he'd treated her so coldly. Why he'd run like a scared little boy.

He'd come to apologize, to beg her forgiveness. He'd come, he admitted there in the cool dark room, to see if maybe, just maybe, there might still be some flicker of what once was.

Because if there was, he intended to fan it back into flames.

In spite of all the years that had passed between them, seeing her today had confirmed something he already knew to be true.

There were, indeed, some things that never changed, and his feelings for her were on that list.

Tomorrow, he'd get up, grab breakfast at Serendipity, then head over to church where he'd pull her aside and do his best to convince her to meet him somewhere to talk. It didn't have to be tomorrow. Or even the next day. But he wasn't leaving the hollow until he'd given it is best shot.

ELEVEN

The party was still going strong even with the couples of the hour gone, but it was to be expected. Mid-October often came with a respite for farmers and ranchers alike, and folks were ready to gather and celebrate a good year and a good harvest, or to commiserate over a rough year and a bad harvest. Or just to enjoy each other's company in their fancy duds. And there was nothing more convivial than a Midwest wedding, no matter what time of year. The fact that the weather was cooperating, and the moon was out in all its glory, shining down on the swarm of humanity milling about on the Goodacre lawn only added measure to the success of the event.

Her father waited for her at the edge of the canopy. When she drew close, he tipped her chin up and looked her in the eyes. "How you doin' Pixie Cut?"

She assured him she was just fine. "Faith was in there mother-henning me to death," she added for extra measure.

"Well, I'm glad Mr. Stewart was there to catch you, too." He crooked his finger under her chin and lifted her face to the light. He said nothing, but she saw the concern in his eyes as he studied her.

"I'm fine, Daddy. Really." She went up on tiptoe to kiss his cheek. "I feel much better." But she felt his watchful eye on her while she made her rounds, offering her apologies for the disruption and a simple explanation to anyone who asked. And of course, most of the guests did. Because they cared about her, she knew.

"I just forgot to eat, silly me," Prudence assured one concerned party after another. "But Charity put together a plate for me, Faith watched me eat every bite, and as you can see, I'm fully recovered. I just feel terrible for causing such a scene."

That last line always got gracious smiles and hand pats, people wanting to comfort her and console her. They said pretty much the same thing all around. "You're just so focused on everyone else, that you forget to look after yourself."

Prudence wasn't fishing for compliments, not at all. She just knew that folks around these parts had long memories, and most of them had seen her mother faint a time or two, and it hadn't ended well for Caroline Goodacre. Prudence saw the concern in people's eyes, knew they wondered if she might fall victim to the same fate as her mother, and she also knew that the only way to quell that worry—a worry that would quickly turn to gossip, then to rumor, then to "fact"—was to nip it in the bud now. Which was why she'd garnered the courage to come back outside and face the teeming mass in the first place.

What she hadn't counted on was that Collin had, indeed, as Cord had told her, called it a night before she'd returned to the party. Apparently, he hadn't even cared to stick around long enough to find out if she was all right. Nope. He'd cut and run. Without saying goodbye.

But wasn't that his *modus operandi*, after all?

Sheesh. Would she never learn?

Prudence must have given Daddy enough evidence of her well-being to satisfy him for the night, because when she circled back around to the table where she'd left him, he was engaged in a lively conversation with the pastor and his wife. Always the gentleman, her father rose and offered her his chair when she approached. "I'm good, Daddy," she told him before turning to smile at the Treadwells. "You two enjoying the party?"

"Of course," the reverend said with a warm smile. "We were just commiserating on the fact that our energy stores get depleted a lot quicker these days. I think we are just about ready to call it a night."

"Hear, hear," Jed said from beside her. He hadn't taken his seat again. He did look pretty wrung out, but then, the man had just given away two of his beloved daughters. He had the right to feel a little drained. Besides, she knew her father liked nothing better than to end his days sitting quietly in the living room with whichever of his girls was underfoot, either reading or watching television until he drifted off in his easy chair. Eventually, he'd give up trying to convince everyone that he was just resting his eyes, and he'd take himself off to bed.

The Treadwells also rose, obviously preparing to call it a night. "It was all so lovely, Prudence, dear," said Mrs. Treadwell, hitching the strap of her purse over her shoulder. Her kind eyes shone bright with affection. "Just lovely."

"Thank you," Prudence replied, returning the woman's hug. "I'm so glad you enjoyed yourselves."

She and her father watched as the pastor and his wife wended through the tables on their way to where the cars were parked. They snagged their disappointed daughters, both still in high school, on their way.

"You've put on a good party, Pixie Cut," he told her with great affection. "Your mama would have been proud." It wasn't a direct answer to her question, but there was no higher compliment, coming from Jed.

She slipped her arms around his waist and rested her head on his bony shoulder. "I didn't get to dance with you tonight."

"That's all right," he said with a chuckle that rumbled in his chest beneath her ear. "I think I've had all the dancing this old man can handle for the day. For the year, for that matter," he added.

Prudence leaned back to look up at him. "Your Father-Daughter dances do you in? You *are* getting old, Daddy," she teased.

"Hey now. I took a spin or two out there, I'll have you know."

She stepped back and cocked her head at him. "You did? When was that? And how come I missed it?"

"I did. I danced with Ms. Sarah while you were making eyes at that young horse fella from next door."

Prudence snorted. "I wasn't making eyes at anyone, Daddy. Besides, Terrell Jackson isn't my type."

"Well, he was certainly making eyes at you." Jed ruffled her hair, then snatched back his hand like he'd been burned.

Prudence frowned up at him. "What?" She reached up to touch her hair, wondering if maybe he'd been poked by a twig from the garland crown she'd worn earlier. "Is there something wrong with my hair?"

"No, no," he assured her, holding his hand up, palm out toward her. "I just sometimes forget my little girls are all grown up. I shouldn't be patting you on the head like that. You're a young woman now, child." He let out a short guffaw at his contradictory endearment, then amended, "You're a grown woman, *not* a child."

"Daddy," Prudence said, grabbing his hand with both of hers and placing it on her head. "Every time you ruffle my hair you tell me you love me. It's like a blessing to me." She shifted his hand, so his work-roughened palm now cupped her cheek, and she pressed into it. "If you stop doing it, I'm going to think you don't love me anymore."

Jed drew her in for another quick, tight hug. "I'll always love you, Pixie Cut. Always." Then taking her by the shoulders, he set her away from him and peered down into her eyes, his expression growing serious. "That Mr. Jackson wasn't the only one keeping tabs on you tonight, you know. I got the feeling there are a few young men here who wouldn't mind spending more time with you."

Prudence rolled her eyes. "Are you trying to get me married off or something? You tired of me?"

"Never." He gave her a gentle shake and repeated, "Never."

"Good. Because for now, at least, you're stuck with me." *And please, please, please don't leave me alone in that big old house with the newlywed love birds,* she wanted to add, but she kept her words to herself and just beamed up at him.

"Like a bug on fly paper," he said with a laugh.

"Ew. Which one am I? The fly or the sticky paper?"

"Well, if those young fellas swarming you are any indication, I'd say you're probably the sticky paper," he teased with a wink.

"Daddy!" she exclaimed, then turned and slipped her arm into the crook of his and turned him toward the house. "I think it's time for you to go to bed. You're getting a little out of control. Too much mulled apple cider, I think."

"Jedediah?" The rich voice from behind them could have been a man or a woman's, and they both spun around to see who was beckoning. It was Charlotte, the woman who'd come from Colorado, the fiber artist who raised her own sheep for the wool with which she created her gorgeous designs.

"Miss Rawlings," Jed said, reaching up to touch the rim of his absent cowboy hat. A good number of the men at the reception had on their Sunday hats, but Jed had taken his off hours ago. He still had a full head of hair, a beautiful sweep of frosty white that gave him a rather debonair flair when he got all dressed up. In a surprisingly formal tone, he said, "I hope you're having a fine evening."

Prudence glanced from her father to the woman and back again. What was going on here? She'd seen something earlier, too, hadn't she? And now, Daddy looked like he might actually be... could it be? Was he blushing? Sure enough, two spots of color appeared on his cheeks, bright enough to be seen in the lights under the tent canopy.

"Why, thank you. Yes, indeed, I am." She turned to Prudence, reaching out a turquoise and silver ringed hand to graze her fingertips over Prudence's shoulder. "I'm Charlotte Rawlings. I don't think we've officially met," she said in her molasses voice. "Your sisters wouldn't stop talking about the way you brought magic to their special day."

"Nice to meet you, Miss Rawlings," Prudence said, beaming up at the tall, handsome woman. "We're so glad you could be here to celebrate with us."

Her father nodded in agreement beside her, but he said nothing.

"Are you sticking around the hollow for a bit? Justice mentioned you might be considering moving out this way."

When Charlotte smiled, her whole face changed. Her features weren't exactly masculine, but they were bold and sturdy, almost austere, framed by all that steely silver hair. When she smiled, though, laugh lines shot rays of sunshine from the corners of her eyes, her lips opened wide over large teeth, and something about the way she cocked her head gave her a rather sultry appeal. An appeal that seemed to be having a surprising effect on her father. Prudence felt him stiffen beside her.

"Yes, to both, my dear. I'll be staying with Sarah Lynxwilder." She chuckled. "I just can't get over that fantastic name, so I say it whenever I can drum up the opportunity."

"It is pretty great, isn't it?" Prudence agreed.

"Anyway, I plan to take a few days and do a little scouting in the area, including Indiana and Tennessee, too, but we'll see where the good Lord leads."

Jed cleared his throat. "This is God's country, there's no question about it," he said. "We don't raise sheep on Seven Virtues Ranch, but I know folks who do just fine with the animals in these parts. Plenty of green pastures and still waters to be had, that's for certain."

Prudence pressed her lips together to hide her delight. Although he was never standoffish or unfriendly, her father was rarely so loquacious, especially with newcomers. Or women.

"Well, that's good to know, Jedediah Goodacre," Charlotte said, the rasp in her earthy voice giving weight to each syllable, almost like she was tasting his name, testing how it sounded coming out of her mouth.

Prudence turned wide eyes on her father, fascinated by the myriad of emotions warring on her father's face as the woman spoke. Emotions he seemed determined—in vain—to mask. She ducked her head, not wanting him to see her amusement

After an awkward beat of silence, Charlotte said, "So Prudence, Justice told me about your botanical interests, your flowers and herbs, and what you do with them. I'm not much of a gardener, I'll be the first to admit. I can grow a few rows of tomatoes, corn, and beans, of course, but the only flowers I seem to get along with are those that grow wild along the hedge rows and in the pastures where the good Lord does the tending. That said, I'm all about doing things nature's way. I'd love a tour of your garden and workshop, maybe check out some of your products for myself."

Hmm. Was the woman really interested in Pixie Cut products? Or was she just looking for a good excuse to come back to the ranch and see Daddy? "I'd be happy to show you around. You know, Charity is serving up brunch here after church tomorrow for anyone willing to come back over and help with putting this place back to order." Prudence flinched when her father's fingers closed over hers a little tighter than necessary. He said nothing, though, and his carefully blank expression gave nothing away. Did he not want the woman to join them? She hesitated, giving him the opportunity to speak up if he wanted to, then continued. "I think Sarah plans on being here, so of course, you're welcome to join us."

Charlotte turned her all too knowing gaze on Jed. "Well, I wouldn't want to intrude on family."

When Daddy still didn't speak, Prudence elbowed him gently in the ribs.

He grunted softly, then said, "It's an invitation, Miss Rawlings. Not an intrusion."

"Daddy!" Prudence peered up at him, her eyes grown wide. He sounded nothing like the warm, friendly man he'd been a moment before. It was like a switch had been flipped. She turned back to Charlotte and said, "You're more than welcome to join us for both, of course. I'm sorry I didn't officially extend the invitation to you earlier. Please say you'll come. I'll show you around the place tomorrow in the daylight."

Charlotte studied her father for a moment longer, then nodded. "Maybe I will."

Before Prudence could respond, Jed lifted his chin a notch. "Then it seems we'll be seeing you here tomorrow, Miss Rawlings."

Aghast at what could only be called a polite dismissal, Prudence's mouth fell open.

But before she could speak, Charlotte reached out and laid a hand on Daddy's forearm just for a moment. "Charlotte. Please. Calling me Miss Rawlings only emphasizes my single status, and it's the one area of my life I'm seriously reconsidering these days."

Well, well, well. If Ms. Charlotte wasn't just putting it out there....

Jed stepped back like her touch had scorched his skin, causing Prudence to stumble into him. To her delight, the flush that had colored his cheeks earlier deepened noticeably, suffusing the rest of his face and neck now. He opened his mouth to speak, but nothing came out.

Charlotte didn't seem in the least bit offended or surprised by his reaction. Instead, she smiled warmly at him, and in her molasses voice, said, "Thank you, Jedediah. I'm looking forward to joining your family."

Jed made a quiet strangling sound that likely only Prudence heard, but it was enough to tell her that he was reading as much, if not more, into Charlotte's declaration with its potential double-entendre. Joining their family? Was the woman really so brash?

Charlotte winked—she actually winked!—at Daddy. "And thank you for the wonderful dance, Jedediah. You certainly know how to hold a woman, and you're surprisingly light on your feet."

The strangling sound he made this time wasn't quite so quiet, but Charlotte was already moving away. Her shoulders shook just the tiniest bit, and Prudence was certain she was chuckling under her breath, presumably having elicited the exact reaction she'd wanted out of Jed.

Prudence turned to look up at her father. "Oh my gosh, Daddy! What was that all about? She was hitting on you! And you didn't tell me you danced with her. When did you dance with her?"

"Hush, child," Daddy said, attempting to draw his arm from Prudence's grip.

She held on tighter. "Oh, no you don't. I'm not letting you get away that easily. What is going on between you two?"

"Between who two?" Abby appeared and twirled around them in time to the thumping song playing over the loudspeakers. "Hey, Pru. You should have seen Daddy tonight. He was on fire out there on the dance floor!"

"What?" The word came out almost a shriek. "Where was I?"

"You were passed out on the sofa inside," Abby said. "Come on, Daddy. Come dance with me again."

"Wait, wait, wait," Prudence said, not loosening her hold on her father's arm. "I have dibs." She pointed at their linked arms. "See? If he's going to dance with anyone right now, it's me."

"But I'm his favorite!" Abby performed a ridiculous shimmy in front of them. "Right, Daddy?"

"Stop it, girls," Jed admonished gruffly, but one side of his mouth was twitching, belying his furrowed brow. "You're all my favorites, Abby."

"But he's dancing with me," Prudence insisted, then in a tone that matched Abby's, she added, "Right, Daddy?"

"I don't know if I have it in me. I'm an old man, girls, and I'm about done in."

"Fine," Abby cajoled. "Then how about a two-fer? Dance with both of us, then we'll let you call it a night." She linked her arm in Jed's other one, and the two girls escorted him through their guests to the middle of the party. Hank, ever the attentive DJ, smoothly transitioned from the boisterous number that had been playing to Nathan Turnbull's "Daddy's Girl."

As soon as the instrumental introduction started, Hope pulled out of Levi's arms and joined them. By the end of the first verse, Faith and Charity both appeared, and as the guests realized what was happening, they cleared the dance floor to make room for Jed and his daughters. Justice and Courage's absence was evident, but when Jasmine dragged Yvette out to the floor with her, everyone agreed that, in their matching flower girl dresses, they were the perfect stand-ins for the twins.

By the time the last of the guests had said their goodbyes, leaving behind only immediate family, Prudence was exhausted. The October moon had sashayed itself across the night sky and now hung low over the pasture, looking rather fatigued as well.

Prudence's garden still pulled at her, in spite of her weariness, like a lover who'd waited patiently on the sidelines. She stepped through the whimsical gate she and Daddy had built together, wooden chair backs pieced together inside a frame of gnarled walnut branches.

Tonight, especially, the garden hung heavy with nostalgia. It wasn't as lush and vibrant as it had been a few weeks ago, but fall had its own share of flowering plants, mostly wild, and Prudence welcomed them in her space, too. Spikes of goldenrod along the back fence line, large yellow and purple blossoms polka-dotting chrysanthemum bushes, a grouping of Blue Mist caryopteris with its silvery green foliage, and of course, the ancient lavender bushes just inside the garden gate that flowered without fail right up to the first real freeze. Most of her coneflowers had cooperated with a second burst of color after their midsummer deadheading, and a few other late bloomers were still putting out, too. But things were definitely winding down now that the autumn harvest was upon them. The season was on the brink of change, and over the next few months, Prudence would pull up bulbs and wrap them carefully in brown paper, trim roses and other perennials back and cover them in burlap for the winter, and she and Daddy would bring in a trailer full of leaf mulch and straw to create a thick winter blanket for the ground.

But right now, the apples on the old tree weighted the gnarled branches like ornaments on an overloaded Christmas tree, and the sweet fragrance of the fruit wafted tantalizingly in the air as Prudence meandered among the beds toward the bench beneath it.

Seeing Mr. Stewart—Collin—again today, and dancing to music that had shaped so much of her high school world, had brought back wave upon wave of memories that she could no longer keep at bay. As she sank down onto the bench, she murmured his name as they washed over her.

TWELVE

Five years earlier...

Prudence started her senior year at Plumwood High with as much excitement and anticipation as most teenagers did. She'd turn eighteen a few months before graduation. She'd saved up enough money working her part time job at Trilby's to buy a sturdy used pickup, and if she managed things right, she'd be able to afford the down payment for the herbal academy she had long dreamed of attending in Colorado.

She also had a boyfriend, a nice guy named Bruce Cutter. They liked each other well enough, enjoyed spending time together, and Bruce was a really good kisser who didn't often push for more from her. He liked holding her hand in public, and he told her she was pretty all the time. But she wasn't so naive to believe that they were in love with each other. She figured that once they'd graduated and headed off to their respective colleges, they'd end things amicably and remain friends.

But it was nice having someone to belong to, someone to sit with, to stand next to in the middle of a crowd. It gave her the sense of being on the inside without her having to exert too much effort. And she was happy to be his arm candy. Bruce never called her as much to her face, but she wasn't fooled; she knew he was as glad to have a girlfriend as she was to be one. What she wasn't so sure about was whether or not it was specifically her he wanted.

It wasn't until the junior-senior winter social dance in early December that she learned the truth. They'd gone all out with their formal wear. Bruce had rented a midnight blue velvet suit that was ridiculously flamboyant, which, of course, made him that much cooler to his peers.

Under it, he wore an ice blue shirt that matched Prudence's sequined strapless party dress with its full skirt that poofed out over white tulle crinoline. The winter social was notoriously a couple's dance, a night out away from school to celebrate the end of the first half of the year with the one you loved. Although Bruce was doing and saying all the right things, she could tell something was off between them. He seemed distracted. It wasn't their flamboyant outfits—in fact, they'd been his idea. The theme of the social was Starlight Madness, and Bruce never shied away from pulling out all the stops with activities like this. He knew how to have a good time, and he was the kind of person to make sure everyone around him was having a good time, too.

Which was why his preoccupation felt so odd to Prudence. Although she knew they weren't super serious, they'd come to the dance together, and she was a little wounded by his inattentiveness. She'd always believed they were good enough friends that if either of them wanted out of the relationship, they'd be up front and open about it. Surely that wasn't it, was it? She put on a brave face and her usual bright smile and tried not let the hurt she felt show.

She was in a bathroom stall just getting ready to flush the toilet when a group of girls burst in, startling her. "Oh. My. Gosh, you guys!" It was Holly Larsen, a girl Prudence had always considered a friend. Her words came out in short, choppy sentences. "You guys. You won't believe it." Then she squealed like a little girl with a secret she wasn't supposed to tell. "Oh my gosh," she gushed again. "Okay, so you have to promise not to tell anyone. No one. I mean it, okay? At least, not yet. Not until I tell you it's okay."

A sense of foreboding washed over Prudence like a cold shower. She should leave now. She should flush the toilet, so they knew she was there, exit the stall with her smile back on her face, and leave the room. Now.

But she didn't. For whatever reason, she just didn't. Instead, she lowered the toilet seat and sat down on it. Her skirt was short, but she carefully tucked it into her lap so nothing would show beneath the door, then she drew her knees up and wrapped her arms around them, so nothing showed beneath the stall door. They'd have to really try hard to see her.

"You guys, it's Bruce!" Holly's exclamation echoed around the room like a freight train bearing down on Prudence.

Bruce. Bruce. Bruce. Bruce.

Holly squealed again, not so quietly this time, unable to contain her excitement a moment longer. "He finally kissed me!" Then she let out a long, dreamy sigh as the other girls with her—were there two? Three others?—pushed her for details. "Oh, you guys. He's such a good kisser. His lips." Each word was drawn out and breathless. "He had one hand on the back of my neck like he didn't want to stop." She breathed out, and the others cooed dreamily along with her.

"Where was his other hand?" Donna. She *would* ask that question. The girl seemed to have her mind in the gutter all the time and had no qualms about it. "Did he discover that fancy new thong you wore for him tonight?"

"Donna!" Holly practically shrieked, but then giggled. "Not yet. But there's still time," she added in a singsong lilt. "The night is young."

"What are you going to do about Prudence, though?" And that was Rachel, Holly's sidekick. Of course, she was there, too.

Donna snorted. "Prudence the Prude, you mean?

Holly's voice grew bolder, a little snippy. "Bruce says she never lets him do anything more than kissing; can you believe it? I mean, we're not fifteen anymore."

"Seriously," Donna agreed in a bored drawl. "Or in my case, twelve," she added.

"Oh, my gosh, Donna!" Rachel gasped. "You did it when you were twelve?"

"It was no big deal." But the edge in her voice told Prudence that maybe it had been a big deal after all. That maybe her experience as a twelve-year-old had made her into the hardened, crass girl she was now.

"How can you say that?" Rachel asked, her shocked question almost a whisper.

"Hey, you guys. Let's not get off track," Holly cut in. "Rachel, if Donna says it was no big deal for her, then it was no big deal, okay?"

"Yeah. Stop judging me, Bambi."

"Don't call me Bambi."

"Guys!" Holly raised her voice. "We're talking about me and Bruce, remember? Focus, focus."

"Sorry," Rachel said meekly.

"If it weren't for Prudence, Bruce would have asked me to the social. But he was too nice to break up with her right before the dance since they already had their outfits."

Donna scoffed. "Wait a minute. He was too nice to break up with her before the dance, but he didn't have a problem sticking his tongue down your throat in the hallway just now?"

"Don't be disgusting," Holly reprimanded in a bit of a whine. "He didn't stick his tongue down my throat. And we couldn't help it, okay? We saw each other out in the hallway by the drinking fountain and it was like some kind of crazy fireworks went off between us, you know? And the next thing I knew, he'd pulled me around the corner and was kissing me."

"So you preserved your dignity, demanded his respect, and told him he could kiss you all he wanted after he broke up with his girlfriend, right?"

For a moment, Prudence wondered whose side Donna was on, but the girl's next words made it clear that she wasn't Prudence's friend.

"That's the only way to get what you want from a guy, you know. Offer him the goods, give him a taste of what he's missing, but then hold out until he's begging for it. That's when he'll do just about anything for you."

"Well, I don't know about that," Holly responded. The girls seemed to be hovering around the sink and mirrors. Were none of them in there to use the toilet? Prudence prayed they were indeed only touching up their makeup and checking their hair and clothes in the vanity mirrors over the sinks. "I don't think I should have to bribe a guy to get what I want from him. That doesn't seem like much of a relationship."

"But stealing kisses while he's dating someone else is?" Donna shot back.

"You know what?" Holly snapped. "You're kind of acting like a jerk, Donna. Are you jealous or something?"

"Of Bruce? You're kidding, right?"

"You guys," Rachel cut in, her baby doll voice pleading. "Don't fight, please. Let's just be happy for Holly, okay? We're happy for you, Hols. We really are, right, Donna?"

"We really are, Hols," Donna echoed drolly.

After a brief hesitation, Holly said, "Fine. You two ready?" And with that, they exited the room.

So many emotions roiled around inside of her, that Prudence wasn't sure which one to focus on. Betrayal, yes. If Bruce had wanted to be with Holly, he should have told her. Sure, she would have been hurt and even a little embarrassed to break up right before the dance so he could go with someone else, but better that than this.

Anger at the girl she'd thought was a friend. Hurt at the betrayal. Embarrassed that she hadn't seen it coming.

Both disgust and sadness over the words that came out of Donna's mouth. Words that masked some deep wounds, Prudence thought. No teenager, twelve or seventeen, should be that cynical about guys and sex and love. There was tragedy there, she was certain, and it saturated Donna's behavior like black ink in water.

What emotion she finally landed on was sorrow. This was supposed to be a happy night. A fun night. A night to celebrate being young and on the brink of something new and exciting. For most of the students at the winter social, they were halfway through their last year of high school, and after one more semester at Plumwood High, they'd be launched into that transition period between childhood and adulthood.

Now, for Prudence at least, the night had been sullied. Not destroyed, she realized. Bruce apparently didn't have the power to do that to her. It was just emptied out of its effervescence. Like a can of soda that had lost all its fizz and was no longer worth drinking.

Which only confirmed what she already knew in her heart; that he wasn't the guy for her. However, he clearly wasn't the gentleman she'd thought he was either, and that made her sad for both of them.

Prudence knew she'd need to head back out to the decorated auditorium soon or Bruce would—presumably—miss her. But she wasn't sure if she could just go out there and pretend like everything was peachy.

She went to the sink, wet a paper towel with cold water, and pressed it to her flushed cheeks and chest. "Stupid dress," she muttered, suddenly hating how much of her pale flesh it exposed above the sweetheart neckline. She needed to get out of the bathroom just in case the trio circled around again.

She paused, a thought crossing her mind. Maybe if she waited long enough, Bruce would come looking for her. Hadn't Holly just said she'd encountered him by the drinking fountain in the hall? "I'll never drink from that one again," she muttered under her breath. If he was still out there, she could tell him what she'd overheard without having to set foot back in the auditorium. She'd assure him he was free to go after Holly to his heart's desire, but to take her home first.

Yes, she decided, that's what she would do. Taking a deep breath, she set her shoulders and headed out into the corridor. It was quiet except for the muffled sounds of the music pulsing through the auditorium doors. And it was empty. No Bruce. She wondered if he even realized she was still gone.

With a sigh, as unobtrusively as possible, Prudence slipped back into the party and wended her way through different groups of students and chaperones, looking for her date. When she spotted him, she felt the last hint of wind go out of her sails. Bruce and Holly were out on the dance floor together, looking like the couple they apparently wanted to be. Anyone could see it. *Everyone* could see it, the way they smiled at each other, the way her fingers rested like a caress against his neck....

No, it was pretty clear that Bruce Cutter wasn't wondering where Prudence Goodacre had disappeared to.

She couldn't believe she hadn't seen it before. She didn't usually miss things like that.

Flustered, and now horribly embarrassed, she made a quick detour toward the refreshments table. She needed fresh air, but they weren't allowed to leave the building without permission from one of the chaperones. She wasn't about to humiliate herself even more by admitting as much to a teacher. A cold drink would have to suffice. Then maybe she'd need to use the bathroom again.

With her head down so no one would notice the flush on her cheeks, Prudence moved forward, then crashed into something... no, some*one*, halting her in her tracks so suddenly that she almost toppled backwards. Hands gripped her bare shoulders and kept her from going over.

"Whoa. You alright?"

Prudence gaped up at Mr. Stewart. The hot English Lit teacher. Of course. Because she wasn't mortified enough already. "I'm so sorry," she murmured, stepping back as he lowered his hands to his sides. "I wasn't watching where I was going." She must have looked more distressed than she hoped, because he frowned and bent forward a little to look her in the eye.

"Are you sure you're okay, Ms. Goodacre?" The concern on his face embarrassed her; the fact that he could tell she was upset made her feel more vulnerable than ever. She couldn't tell him that she'd just become a victim of the most cliche of all bad high school cliches—the girl in the bathroom stall overhearing the mean girls gossiping. And she'd sat there and let it happen.

"I'm fine, really. I—I just needed a drink," she stammered, suddenly desperate to get away from him. "Sorry I ran into you." She tried to skirt around him, but he fell into step beside her.

"Did something happen? You came with Bruce Cutter, didn't you?" From the corner of her eye, she saw him glance over his shoulder at the dance floor, then back at her.

"Um... yes, I did." How did he know that? Granted, the school wasn't huge, and it was only juniors and seniors there that night, but were all the chaperones that well-informed? Then again, she and Bruce had been dating since shortly after school started, so it wasn't like it was a secret or anything. But still, it felt kind of strange to have Mr. Stewart ask her about her love life.

"I don't want to pry, so let me just say this. Plumwood High is a safe place. If you need to talk, we have teachers available to speak to. A female teacher, of course."

"I'm fine, Mr. Stewart," Prudence insisted again, wishing he'd just leave her alone before she made a fool of herself. She felt the tingle of tears behind her eyes and blinked quickly, willing them away.

But to no avail. When the first tear fell, Mr. Stewart reached out like he was going to touch her, then withdrew his hand as if he'd thought better of it. "How can I help you?" he asked instead.

"I—I just need somewhere—somewhere to hide for a few minutes," she managed to get out, then lifted her eyes to his, wordlessly pleading with him to understand, to not keep pushing for answers.

"Here." He pulled his keys from his pocket, separated one out, and handed the set to her. "This is the key to my classroom. You're welcome to go sit in there."

The surprise must have registered on her face, because Mr. Stewart grinned at her. "It's okay. Take your time and come back when you're ready. No one will bother you."

With a murmured, "Thank you," Prudence took the keys from him and fled the auditorium.

The moment the doors closed behind her, the muted silence of the halls surrounded her, and she felt her shoulders relax. She made her way quickly to Mr. Stewart's classroom, not wanting to get stopped by any students or teachers alike. She didn't think students were allowed to wander the halls or loiter in the classrooms during events like this one, even with a teacher's permission, nor did she want to get Mr. Stewart in trouble. His kindness was unexpected and greatly appreciated.

Prudence made it into the dark classroom without any trouble, then leaned against the closed door where she took several deep calming breaths. The darkness soothed her nerves even more, and she closed her eyes, breathing in the smells that would forever mean high school to her senses. It was an odd combination of chalk dust and dry erase markers, textbook pages that had absorbed the residue from too many teenagers' hands, and a strange chemical plastic smell that could be attributed to any number of things in the classroom: the world maps on the walls, the laminate bookshelves, the uncomfortable student chairs.

There was a hint of something else in the air, too. Something that made Prudence think of flickering sunlight and walks in the woods. Daffodil yellow and moss green. She couldn't quite place it.

Finally, feeling a little better, and now that her eyes were adjusting to the darkness, Prudence opted to leave the lights off. She moved carefully to Mr. Stewart's desk and dropped into his chair. She didn't feel like trying to cram her flouncy skirt under one of the student desks, and his chair with its wheels and the cushions seemed like a much more comfortable seat for her to regain her composure in. She closed her eyes and let her head rest on the back of the seat, her arms on the arm rests. The fingers of one hand toyed with the drawer pull in front of her.

She gave it an experimental tug, then sat up straight when it opened without any resistance. Surprised—she just assumed the teachers all locked their desk drawers—she went to close it again, but she caught a whiff of what she could only describe as completely and utterly Mr. Stewart. Not Axe Body Spray or one of the other overpowering cheap colognes the high school boys drenched themselves in. No, this was that something else she'd caught scent of when she'd first walked in. Mr. Stewart.

She inched the drawer open a little more and peered inside. From the rectangle of light coming in through the window of the classroom door, she could make out a tray with compartments that held a collection of pens, paper clips, rubber bands, and other classroom paraphernalia. Beside it was a stack of what looked like notepads or file cards. Then she saw it. There, tucked toward the back of the drawer, was a small bag that looked like a travel kit. She stared at it, warring with herself. Dare she pull it out? All she wanted to do was smell it. Surely there was no harm in that. Was there?

But she suddenly wanted to do more than that. She wanted to unzip it, root around inside the tweed pouch to see what secrets it held about Mr. Stewart. That little bag offered a glimpse into a private part of their teacher's life that no one else in his class had access to.

No one would know. She'd put everything back exactly the way she'd found it.

Almost of their own volition, her fingers stretched toward the bag. "Don't do it," she whispered into the stillness around her. *Just a quick look,* said another voice inside her head.

Prudence leaned forward and sniffed, then closed her eyes as that smell of spring filled her senses. It was definitely coming from the back of that drawer. From that bag.

She held her breath, grasped the zipper pull with her thumb and forefinger, then eased the bag out slowly, carefully. She set it on his desk and stared at it, hardly believing she'd already gone this far. A tag hung from the zipper pull, and Prudence tipped it toward the light. Collin F. Stewart, it read.

Collin F. Stewart.

Might as well open it, the voice in her head that sounded like a dreamy version of herself said.

What did the F stand for, she wondered? Frank? Fred? Floyd? Did anyone else in her class know that Mr. Stewart's middle name started with an F?

Open it.

"Why not?" she muttered, then tugged open the zipper and peered inside the kit.

A small electric razor, one of those rechargeable ones Brandon took on the road with him when he and the twins did the rodeo circuit. A travel-size bottle of aftershave, a wide-toothed comb, and was that a small pump bottle of what looked like some kind of hair product. She pulled it out and turned the label toward the light. Argan oil. It smelled a little like olive oil, but with a slight hint of citrus to it.

There was also a packet of tissues inside, the kind Faith kept in her purse at all times, just like the one Mama used to keep in hers.

Before she could talk herself out of it, she gingerly pulled out one of the tissues, popped the top off the bottle of aftershave, and dabbed a tiny drop of it on the tissue, then brought it to her nose.

Mr. Stewart.

Mr. Collin F. Stewart.

She quickly recapped the fragrance before it completely permeated the air and tucked it back into the kit, suddenly afraid she'd be caught—wouldn't it be the most humiliating thing ever to be found sniffing his shaving kit? That just sounded so wrong, so... well, *perverse*. Prudence's pulse ratcheted up, and before panic could set in, she carefully slid the kit back in place at the back of the drawer, then closed it as noiselessly as she could. She tucked the perfumed tissue into her little clutch purse, then lifted the beaded bag to her nose. The scent was barely discernible. Good.

She sat in the darkness, not moving, just breathing. And thinking about Mr. Stewart.

Collin Stewart. The perfect name for an English teacher. "Collin," she said under her breath. Collin F. Stewart. Even his name sounded old school and poetic, like he'd just stepped out of a Jane Austen novel. She said it again, this time with a British accent. "Collin F. Stewart." Not that Mr. Stewart was British—he often talked about his blonde-haired, green-eyed mother of Germanic descent and his African American Cincinnati-born father who'd met and married in graduate school—but with a name like that, he certainly could be.

And he taught all the literature classes, including British Lit, didn't he?

"Collin," she murmured, liking the sound of it rolling off her tongue. What would he do if she called him Collin the next time she saw him? Would he be surprised? Offended?

"Of course, I'd never do that," she said aloud, but even to her own ears, it sounded like she was trying to convince herself. "At least not until after I graduate," she admitted to the empty room.

After I graduate. She mulled over that thought for a few moments. By then, she'd be an adult. She wouldn't be in his classes anymore. She wouldn't be his student. *After I graduate, we'll be peers.* She wouldn't have to call him Mr. Stewart anymore.

The more she thought about it, the more she *wanted* to think about it. She could picture it now. Maybe they'd run into each other at Serendipity's at lunch. "Hey, Collin," she'd say. "How is your day going?" And she wouldn't just ask for propriety's sake. She'd really want to know.

"Well, hello, Miss Goodacre," he'd reply, and with a warm smile, of course, because Mr. Stewart—*Collin*—always smiled warmly.

"Call me Prudence," she'd say with a smile of her own. "All my friends do."

He'd nod in acknowledgment. "It's been a long morning, Prudence, but then, you know those high schoolers. They can keep a guy on his toes."

She'd laugh sympathetically. "They sure can," she'd agree.

Or they'd bump into each other in the produce aisle at the grocery store. No, not the produce aisle. Whatever produce they didn't grow themselves, the Goodacres usually got organically and locally grown from Joe Lynxwilder's organic farm. The frozen foods aisle? Sure. They'd cross paths in front of the ice cream freezer. They'd reach for the door handle at the same time, because they'd inevitably have the same taste in ice cream. "Oh, hi, Collin!" she'd say. "Let me grab my Peanut Butter Moose Tracks, then it's all yours."

"Grab one for me, too, will you?" he'd ask her. "It's my favorite."

"Really? Mine, too. Oh no," she'd say with a slight frown. "There's only one carton left."

Collin would flash that grin at her again. "Hm. So how good are you at sharing?"

She'd roll her eyes. "I am one of seven sisters, remember? Sharing is my middle name."

"Then how about dinner at my place tonight?" he'd ask, taking the ice cream from her and putting it in his basket. "I'll pay for this, and we'll have it for dessert."

Prudence straightened in Mr. Stewart's seat and put her hands to her face. Her cheeks felt flushed under her palms. Was she actually imagining that her teacher would invite her to dinner? That he'd ask her out? Or in? What did you call it when you stayed in for a date?

A date! "Of course not," she said in as firm a tone as she could muster.

Who was she kidding? Hadn't most of the girls in Mr. Stewart's classes suffered from at least a minor crush on the handsome teacher?

"But I won't be just one of the girls in his class after I graduate," she reminded herself, lifting her little black clutch to her nose and breathing in that delicious smell again.

The longer she lingered in his classroom, the longer her thoughts lingered on her teacher. And the more she thought about him, the more she realized that Mr. Stewart—Collin—was exactly the kind of man she'd like to date. He was calm, kind, and sensitive. Look how he'd handled her situation tonight. He had a gentle spirit about him, and his amber eyes behind those black rimmed glasses were thinker's eyes. His cardigans were kinda goofy; she'd heard other students, mostly the guys, call him Mr. Rogers behind his back. Prudence, however, thought they made him seem more approachable than if he wore a sports coat like the history teacher, or the polo shirts Vice Principal Truman favored. There was something sweet about a man who wore cardigans, that was all there was to it.

Yes, she could imagine herself with someone like Mr. Stewart one day. Not someone *like* Mr. Stewart. With Mr. Stewart, himself.

She didn't want to marry a football player or a cowboy or any of those guys who were into all that macho stuff. She wanted a thinker, maybe even a dreamer. Someone romantic who would see her heart and soul, who wasn't ready to set her aside the moment something better—or someone with lower standards—came along.

By the time Prudence made it back to the auditorium, she was in much better spirits. And her sights were set on much loftier targets. She returned Mr. Stewart his keys and thanked him sweetly for being so kind. "It was exactly what I needed to get my head on straight," she assured him.

Then she hunted down Bruce, who, a little frantic over her prolonged absence, asked her where on earth she'd been.

"It doesn't matter where I've been," was her evasive response. "But I think it might be over between us, don't you agree? I feel like maybe we should start seeing other people." She darted a look around the room, caught Mr. Stewart's eye and gave him a reassuring nod, then returned her attention to Bruce. "It's been a fun night, but I think I'm ready to go home. You stay, though. I can call home and get a ride from one of my sisters." And she said it all with a friendly—and only slightly condescending—smile on her face.

Bruce, who wasn't really such a bad guy after all, insisted on taking her home himself. Then he thanked her for being so great about breaking up with him, admitted that yes, he agreed they should see other people, and yes, he was going to head back to the dance if she was absolutely sure she was all right with it.

Prudence floated through the remaining weeks of the first semester on a little cloud that smelled like yellow daffodils, green moss, and Argan oil. She never went anywhere without the tissue; she kept it in a plastic sandwich bag to preserve the scent for as long as possible. She'd tuck it into her pocket, or her bra, or the inner compartment of her backpack or purse. Every time she passed a fragrance counter, she'd sniff all the samples in hopes of finding that particular one, but to no avail. The last day of class before school got out for the holidays, Prudence set a small, gift-wrapped box on Mr. Stewart's desk as she left his class. "Merry Christmas, Mr. Stewart," she said, then caught herself swaying back and forth a little and stilled. She wore one of her favorite skirts that swished hypnotically around her calves when she moved, but she didn't want him to think she was being flirtatious or coy. She didn't want to try any feminine wiles on him at all. No, she wanted him to see her for the adult she—almost—was, not some starry-eyed teenage student.

Over Christmas break, she was the first one ready for church on Sundays, knowing she'd get to see her teacher at the morning service. On New Year's Eve, her family all headed to the town green to usher in the new year with the rest of Plumwood Hollow who gathered as a community to celebrate together. She made a point to be close enough to Mr. Stewart that he would see she wasn't kissing anyone on the stroke of midnight, and so that she could be one of the first to wish him a Happy New Year.

By the time she returned to school in January, Prudence was head over heels in love. Her heart raced every time she entered Mr. Stewart's classroom and saw him waiting there, one hip propped on the edge of his desk as he greeted each student by name. She practically floated whenever he acknowledged her in the halls. But she could tell no one. She wouldn't be eighteen for another two months, and even then, she'd still be in Mr. Stewart's class for a few more months. She wouldn't put him in any kind of an awkward position. She had to bide her time, be patient, and love him from afar. He was worth the wait.

Prudence went over and above in Mr. Stewart's class the rest of the semester. Her grades were exceptional, the highest of any student he'd had before, he told her. She poured over her essays and research papers, making each one of the assignments love letters to literature. Her final paper on her career choice—to become an herbalist, to study herbal medicine, lore, and history—was some of her best work; she even submitted it along with her application packet to the School of Clinical Herbalism she planned to attend the following year.

After she turned eighteen, she became more intentional about getting his attention. She didn't do anything drastic, like dress differently or act like she was suddenly someone else now that she was an adult. No, it was little things, like offering thoughtful responses to his questions so that he'd engage with her more often. Gathering up her things slowly at the end of class so that by the time she stood from her seat, he was saying goodbye to the last of the other students, and she'd have his full attention. She wanted to be the last face he saw at the end of his teaching day, the last student he spoke to, the last girl he smiled at.

Her patience and determination paid off. She felt the subtle shift in the air between them over the following months, and by the end of April, she was certain his eyes lit up the same way hers did when their paths crossed. She knew he watched her as she left his classroom. She noticed the way he straightened his shoulders and toyed with the cuffs of his sleeves whenever they spoke, something he didn't do when he discussed Charlotte Bronte or Thomas Hardy with any of the other girls. And more than once, she'd lift her gaze during a silent reading to find his eyes on her. They'd smile at each other, then both look away, but there was no denying that there was something there between them just waiting to be unwrapped.

She already knew what it was, and she was beginning to believe that Collin Stewart knew what it was, too.

She could hardly wait until after graduation; it was all going exactly the way Prudence had hoped it would.

Until that fateful Sunday in late May when Mr. Stewart accepted their invitation to join them for supper. That terrible day when Prudence, unable to hide her love for him a moment longer, offered him her heart, only to have him crush it beneath his feet as he practically ran from her, leaving her standing in her garden with nothing but his cardigan sweater draped around her shoulders.

She claimed a headache the following Monday and stayed home from school, then again on Tuesday. On Wednesday, she forced herself to go back to class, only to find a substitute at Mr. Stewart's desk. When she asked one of the other students, Jill Archer, where he was, she told Prudence that Mr. Stewart had taken a leave of absence, and he was planning to be gone the rest of the school year.

"Will he be back for graduation?" she asked, appalled at the possibility—no, the probability—that she, not an ailing mother, was the reason for his absence.

"I don't know," Jill said, then squeezed Prudence's hand and grinned. "But who cares, right? We're almost done, Pru. We'll be outta here in less than two weeks! I can hardly believe it!"

He wasn't there for graduation, although Vice Principal Truman read aloud a letter Mr. Stewart wrote to the graduating students.

He didn't come back that summer, so he wasn't there to witness Prudence grow wan and miserable, eaten up inside by guilt and shame.

He didn't return that fall when school started up again, so he wasn't aware that she'd withdrawn from the herbal academy, unable to leave home because of the crippling anxiety she'd developed.

Nor did he return after the holiday break, so he wasn't around to know how lost Prudence seemed to those who cared about her, and how uncertain she became about every decision set before her.

When the high school replaced him permanently with a new English teacher, when his little house sold early that spring, he wasn't there to see the last flicker of hope fade from Prudence's eyes.

THIRTEEN

PRESENT DAY...

Collin awoke with a start, and for a moment, had to wrack his brain to remember where he was.

No, no, no! To remember where he'd been; that's what he wanted. *Please, oh, please.* He closed his eyes, willing himself back into the dream that lingered on the edge of his consciousness. He saw her, as if through a frosted windowpane; Prudence, swaying back and forth in that fluttery dress she'd changed into last night, her eyes bold and challenging and so... well, so *unlike* her. Her finger crooked his way in a beckoning gesture. "Come to me," she'd whispered, or at least he thought she had, but her lips never moved. "Do you—will you..."

Had she finished the sentence? In frustration, he thumped his pillow with his fist. Try as he might to hang on to the dream, it slipped away. He simply couldn't remember.

But like it had been yesterday, he could remember the last time she'd stood before him, asking for something he couldn't give. Back then, her eyes hadn't flashed with suggestion the way they did in his dream. And she certainly hadn't moved her lips in that hypnotic rhythm that brought him awake with his pulse pounding and the blood thick in his veins.

But the words she'd whispered, they were the same, and were forever seared into the flesh of his heart. Those unfinished questions haunted his waking hours almost as much as they did his dreams.

FIVE YEARS EARLIER…

The school year was winding down and graduation for Plumwood Hollow's seniors was a month away. So was the end of Collin's fourth year of teaching high school English Literature at Plumwood High, a job he profoundly enjoyed.

It was a triumphant and bittersweet time for the community; young people flying the nest usually led to most of them never coming home again for anything more than holidays, weddings, and funerals. It seemed to be a tradition in the hollow for families of graduating students to thank their teachers by feeding them. Collin had broken bread around more than a dozen dinner tables over the last few months, and as much as he enjoyed the variety of home-cooked fare—usually delicious, sometimes less than—there was one invitation he was determined to dodge.

For the last several weeks, Collin had produced one excuse after another to turn down the Sunday dinner invitation from Faith Goodacre. He'd even taken to arriving at church at the very last minute and sitting at the back so he could escape quickly if he got desperate. But she'd cornered him in the vestibule right before church began, almost as if she'd been lying in wait for him, and she wore an expression that made it clear she wasn't going to let him decline her again.

"So you *are* joining us for Sunday dinner, right, Mr. Stewart?" She said it like he'd already committed to it.

Granted, last Sunday he'd mumbled something along the lines of "…maybe next week." But that was only to buy him time to come up with a valid reason to say no.

"I'm sorry, Faith," he responded, making a valiant attempt to sound remorseful. "I already have plans after church. With the Thompsons," he added for good measure. There were no *official* plans, but he did have a standing invitation to join Garrett and Sherry Thompson whenever he felt the need for good food and company. Garrett taught high school history and shared an adjoining classroom with Collin, and the two of them got along well enough. Of course, Sherry's single sister inevitably showed up for the meal, but Annie was kind and thoughtful, and he genuinely enjoyed her company.

"Well, that will work out perfectly," Faith assured him. "We're heading to Bowling Green to watch the twins perform at a fundraiser, so we're doing our Sunday dinner for supper, instead."

Before he could protest, the opening worship song started up, and Faith shooed her young daughter up the middle aisle ahead of her, leaving Collin standing there with his mouth opening and closing wordlessly.

"Lucky dog," someone muttered beside him. It was Doyle Wayne, his eyes following Faith's movements, the look on his face not exactly appropriate for church. "What's she see in you?" he asked, as though the very idea was unfathomable.

"Put your eyes back in your head, man," Collin muttered just loud enough for Doyle to hear. "A little respect, okay?" Faith saw nothing in him, at least not anything romantic. Everyone in Plumwood Hollow knew Faith Goodacre was officially off the market. Her life revolved around her daughter, her father, her sisters, and their ranch. No, Collin was pretty sure the invitation to join the Goodacre Sunday Dinner tradition was borne out of small-town hospitality. Between Prudence and the twins, he'd had three of the sisters in his classes already. Abby would start high school next year and would eventually end up under his tutelage, too. In fact, two years ago at the end of the twins' senior year, he'd enjoyed a delicious pot roast and the best apple pie he'd ever tasted around the Goodacre dinner table.

Doyle just shrugged and headed up the aisle to find a seat while Collin slipped into the last pew, hoping he'd start feeling sick to his stomach or get a debilitating headache halfway through the service and he could bail early. It wasn't likely; in spite of his slightly unkempt, scholarly appearance, Collin had the constitution of a work horse, and he'd awakened that morning feeling hale and hearty as usual.

Needless to say, he was twitchy, on edge the whole service, and had a difficult time focusing on Pastor Treadwell's message. As soon as the last note of the last song died out, Collin was on his feet and hurrying toward the exit... only to bump into Faith in the vestibule again. He hadn't even noticed her slip out of the service early with her daughter,

Jasmine, but there they were, once again standing in his path. Well, at least Faith was. The child was talking animatedly to herself underneath a linen-draped table that held an assortment of church literature and spare Bibles. Apparently, she, too, was having trouble sitting still, but being five years old, he supposed she had a better excuse than he did.

"Oh good," Faith said with a bright smile. "I'm glad I caught you. I forgot to give you a time. We plan to eat at six; will that work? Joe and his mom will be there, too. You know him, right?"

He nodded. He did know Joe. Quite well, in fact. They'd met in college, and it was Joe who'd told Collin about the Plumwood High teaching position that brought him to the hollow. During his summers, Collin worked for Joe Lynxwilder at his organic farm. They'd discovered similar interests in literature during their college years, but it was during those hot and humid dog days of summer working side by side with Joe on the farm that Collin unearthed a fascination with plant lore, particularly in literature. He didn't have the green thumb Joe did, that was for sure, but along with becoming familiar with growing things, he also gained a deep sense of understanding of the importance of traditional and organic farming practices in the modern world.

Faith rambled on, not giving him an opportunity to speak. "Brandon Stillwater—you know him. You had him and the twins in your classes their last two years of high school, right? Anyway, he'll be there, of course, because where there is Justice, there is Brandon. Hope is back from school for the summer, and Charity's bringing her fiancé, Thad." Without waiting for his response, she added, "So you don't have to be afraid of being alone at the table with Daddy and all of us girls. You'll have plenty of male companionship."

When she finally stopped talking, he opened his mouth to defend his manhood—he wasn't afraid of a bunch of women and one old man—but she shook her finger at him. "And if you say no again, I'm going to tell Daddy that you're purposely avoiding us."

Fine. So he was afraid. A little. She was joking, of course. He could tell by the twinkle in her eyes. But she didn't know how spot on her words were.

He wasn't avoiding all of the Goodacres, though. Just one of them.

Just Prudence.

Collin racked his brain for anything, *anything*, that might get him out of it, but he drew a great big empty blank. He closed his mouth, his teeth clacking together in frustration.

Faith nodded is that was all the answer she needed. "Good. We'll see you this evening at six sharp. And don't be late. If you are, Daddy will make you say the blessing."

Now, here he was, seated painfully close to his favorite—no, his *least* favorite—English Literature student, Prudence Goodacre, their arms and elbows brushing, their knees periodically bumping under the table. He could hardly think straight with her so close, the sunshine fragrance of her wafting around him with every move she made, the sound of her voice almost a tangible thing, like delicate fingers feathering over the surface of his skin. At one point, they both reached for the same serving dish and his long fingers momentarily covered hers. She pulled her hand away so quickly, that he almost dropped the bowl of mashed potatoes.

"Sorry," she murmured, the hitch in her voice making his pulse do a little hitch of its own. "Please go ahead." She gestured at the bowl, not meeting his eyes.

"That's all right. Why don't I hold it for you while you dish up?" But when he looked at her plate, she already had a surprisingly large pile of potatoes there. His brow furrowed; she wanted more?

"No, no. I was just going to—" She broke off, her cheeks going bright red. "I was going to offer you some."

"Oh. Right. Yes." *Quite the conversationalist, Stewart.* "Thanks."

Fortunately, at that exact moment, Jasmine accidentally knocked over her glass of water. There wasn't much in it, so the spill was quickly sopped up with a few napkins, but the timing of it couldn't have been more fortuitous.

By the time dessert was served, he felt like a tightly coiled spring, afraid with every point of contact that the trigger would snap and this thing he'd kept under lock and key would fly free and wreak all sorts of havoc on this family who'd been nothing but good and kind to him. And if he let that happen, no amount of damage control would be able to set things right; none that he could see.

"Prudence, tell Mr. Stewart what you're doing after graduation," Faith said, then handed Collin a slice of apple pie with an enormous scoop of ice cream already beginning to melt and puddle on the hot crumb crust.

He turned to look at Prudence, but she was staring at Faith across the table from them, her eyes open wide with what could only be dismay.

"Tell him," Faith cajoled, apparently oblivious—or purposely ignoring—her little sister's desperate expression. "He'll appreciate it if he's anything like you say he is."

Prudence let out a tiny "Eep!" and ducked her head.

"Could you, um, pass me the water," Collin said, hurrying to distract everyone from Prudence's embarrassment.

"It's right in front of you," the fourteen-year-old Abby said, waving her fork at it. She studied him owlishly from across the table.

"Oh, right." Better he look the fool than have Prudence suffering.

"And your glass is already full," the young teenager added, still gesturing with her fork.

Next to Faith, Justice lifted one brow and peered suspiciously at him. "You okay, Mr. Stewart?" she asked.

"Collin," he said after clearing his throat. It wasn't the first time he'd asked them to call him by his given name. "Please. I'm Mr. Stewart at school. Principal Val's rule. Collin among friends."

"Sure. You okay, *Collin*?" Justice asked, a bit of a sardonic emphasis on his name. "You seem... I don't know... flustered? You and Pru, both."

This time, the noise Prudence made sounded more like a sob, and Faith elbowed Justice. "Really? Why?"

Justice just shrugged. "Just asking," she said, then turned to say something to Brandon, whose attention never strayed far from her.

"Good pie, Charity," Jed said, his gruff voice cutting through the tension in the room. To Collin, he added, "You'll never have a better apple pie than one made by my daughter."

Collin nodded politely at Charity, who sat at the far end of the table from him. She sat very close to her boyfriend, Thad, whose arm was draped loosely around the back of her chair. Collin lifted his first bite to his mouth and chewed quickly. It was delicious, but still piping hot, and it was all he could do not to snatch up his glass of water to cool off his tongue. Somehow, he managed to get a few more words out. "Your father's right. This might be the best apple pie I've ever had."

"Nailed it, sis," sing-songed Abby, waving her fork at Charity now.

There followed a short lull in conversation as everyone around the table indulged in their desserts, then finally, Charity spoke. "What's the name of that herbal school you're going to attend, Pru? I don't know why I can't seem to remember it."

"That's because your brain is addled by love," Abby teased, then giggled when Thad drew Charity close and kissed her temple. "Gross. Not at the table, please. You'll make me lose my appetite." Turning to Collin, she said, "She wants to be an herbalist, Mr. Stewart. Isn't that cool?"

"Hey, chicky," Faith said elbowing Abby. "She can speak for herself."

All eyes turned to Prudence. A pretty blush stained her cheeks, and she took a quick, fortifying drink of water. "Yeah, I love all things homeopathic. I totally believe in the adage, *Let food be your medicine*, you know? But if food is going to be our medicine, we have to know what to eat and how to eat it." When she spoke, her voice was a little tremulous, but her chin was up and he sensed a determination in her spurred on by her obvious passion for the subject. "So I'm planning to go to an herbalist school next year."

"You're already so good at it, Pru," Charity complimented, smiling down the length of the table at her. "Mama would be so proud of you."

"We're all proud of you, child," Jed concurred with a nod.

Prudence straightened in her seat beside Collin, almost as if she'd been waiting for her father's stamp of approval before continuing. "I've been accepted into this herbal medicine program in Colorado. I have to be there in person for the first twelve to fifteen months, but then once I get the hands-on stuff out of the way, I can do a lot of the rest of the coursework online. So my plan is to find a place to rent out there this summer in time for me to start school in the fall. Then hopefully, I'll be back here in another year to help out with the ranch and gardening."

Faith lifted her glass to Prudence. "She just sent off her down-payment earlier this week."

"Non-refundable!" Prudence exclaimed on a breathy note. "Yikes!"

Joe's mom, Sarah, spoke up. "It's wonderful that you already know what you want to do with your life, Prudence. I was the same way. I knew I always wanted to help people who'd were sick or injured, but I never had any inclination to be a doctor. No, I wanted to be on the healing end of it, the part that came after the initial trauma and the hospital stay. As soon as I learned what role a Physical Therapist played, I knew it was the perfect job for me. I still love it."

Collin's head moved side to side, feeling a bit like he was watching a volleyball game, the conversation bouncing back and forth from one end of the table to the other. Sure, every once in a while, someone—usually Justice or Abby, sometimes young Jasmine—would pull a surprise move and lob the ball out of bounds with an inappropriate comment, throwing the rest of them off for a moment or two. But all in all, it was quite a thing to behold, the comfortable ebb and flow of discussion as it circled around the occupants seated together over their meal.

Prudence shrugged, the motion causing her shoulder to bump his, and Collin did his best not to flinch. It wasn't her fault he was so jumpy.

No, not just jumpy.

Hypersensitive. Hyper-aware. Hyper... hyper wound up.

Actually, it *was* her fault. He wouldn't be like this if she wasn't sitting so close to him. In fact, why was she practically cuddled up against his side? Did she not have enough room? Why couldn't she cuddle up to Joe? He didn't seem unduly fazed by her, and not once had the farmer said anything that made Justice's eyebrow crook.

But the idea of Prudence cuddling up to Joe struck a sour note in his gut. Not because there was anything wrong with it—Joe was a good guy, if a little old for Prudence, but he was a farmer who loved planting things, and an organic one at that, which made him a good match for someone like Prudence.

In fact, the more he thought about it, the more it bothered him. He sent Joe a sideways glance.

Uh, no. It was a glare. A short one, but a glare, nonetheless.

Wait. Was Prudence leaning into Collin because she had a thing for Joe? Was she avoiding touching the guy because of the things he stirred in her? Was that why she was so flustered; not because of Collin at all, but because of Joe? He was solid as a rock. Quiet and patient, a farmer down to his very bones. He cared for people the way he cared for plants, patient and focused, gentle, but firm at the same time. And should a storm threaten, Joe was out there fighting rain, wind, snow, sleet, and more to protect his precious crops. Why on earth *wouldn't* Prudence want a man like Joe?

Who was he kidding? Collin couldn't compete with that specimen of a man on Prudence's other side.

Stop, he reprimanded himself. *There is no competing with anyone or for anyone here!* The voice in his head was practically shouting, all but drowning out the conversation around him. *There is one blaring reason you're not even in the running, remember, Mr. Stewart?*

By the time he tuned back into the conversation, he was just in time to hear Prudence respond to something Brandon asked her.

"Yeah. I'll be gone for just over a year if I leave right after graduation. I kinda need to go early to make sure I have a place to live. They don't have dorms or any kind of housing on campus, but they did say that students often come to their summer meet-and-greets to find roomies they can share rentals with. They have a group gathering the end of next month I plan to attend. We'll see from there."

"So you'll be leaving next month?" Collin hadn't meant to ask the question out loud, but he'd been caught by surprise. He already knew about her plans to attend school in Colorado; she'd written her last research paper on it. But he hadn't realized she'd be leaving so soon. Or that she'd be gone for so long. The thought of it caused a dull ache in his sternum and he took a deep breath in an effort to relieve the pressure.

"Yes," Prudence confirmed, glancing briefly at him before dropping her eyes to her plate again.

"And you'll be gone for a whole year?" *Really, Stewart?* Isn't that what she'd just said? Why was he parroting her?

"Um, yes," she murmured quietly.

Well, at least he wouldn't have to worry about Farmer Joe getting first dibs on her.

Yeah, well, what about all of the Rastafarian nature guru wannabes who'll be attending this flower power hippie school in Colorado?

Good grief. Where had that voice come from?

"Right. Good. Good for you," he said. He didn't have to be looking at her to see her shoulders slump. He tried one more time. "I'm sure you'll love Colorado. I hear it's beautiful country."

"Yeah," Prudence said, sounding almost a little angry. "I'm sure I will."

What had he said wrong? Maybe he should just call it a day. He plucked his napkin off his lap, wiped his mouth, and laid the square of fabric on the table beside his plate. To Jed, he said, "Sir, I think I'm going to have to pass on that second helping of pie." He smiled at Charity down the way. "It really is delicious, but after every other delicious dish on the table, I don't know if I can squeeze in another bite of anything."

"You'll take a piece with you when you go, then," Jed said, patting his stomach and nodding in apparent understanding. "So tell us. How did you get into teaching, son? And how did you end up in our little holler?"

So much for making his escape.

In as few words as possible, Collin explained that his father was a college literature professor and his mother a magazine editor. "I grew up reading everything I could get my hands on. The good, the bad, and everything in between. Like several of you have said around this table today, I knew early on what I loved, and as soon as I figured out how to make a living doing what I loved, I never really thought of doing anything else."

"Stewart and I met in college," Joe added when Collin paused to let Charity refill his coffee cup. "We were pretty much the only two nerds hanging out in the library on game days."

Collin took a sip of the hot brew, grimaced as it scalded a bit going down, his tongue still a little tender from the first bite of pie. But he nodded, hoping no one would notice his eyes tearing up a little behind his glasses. He set the cup away from him so he'd have to think a second before picking it up again, then cleared his throat, hoping his voice would work. "Yep. Which is how I ended up here. Joe told me all about his hometown, his farm, his parents—he bragged on your cooking all the time, Mrs. Lynxwilder," he added, smiling over at the woman.

"*My* cooking?" Sarah asked, pressing a hand to her chest. "I'm a terrible cook, boys, and you know it."

"That's how bad I missed home, Ma," Joe said with a chuckle. "I even missed your cooking."

"I'm only allowed to bring chocolate chip cookies to any potluck," Sarah declared, smiling good-naturedly at Joe's teasing. "And only because the recipe is written on the back of the bag. Even I can't screw that up."

Appreciative laughs erupted around the table at the woman's self-deprecating words.

"So I lied," Joe teased. "But Stewart here believed me long enough to come check out our little town when they had an opening for an English teacher at Plumwood High."

"Took the job they offered, and here I am."

"Well, we're right glad you're here," Jed said with a solemn nod. "My daughters tell me you're a fine teacher, Mr. Stewart. Which is good to know, what with Abby taking one of your classes next year."

And just like that, he'd just been reminded of his place by the one man at the table whose opinion of him mattered the most.

A long, excruciating hour later, the evening was pronounced over by Jed. The whole group had moved into the living room to let their food settle, but it wasn't long before Joe and his mother made their excuses, then Justice and Brandon disappeared out into the night. Shortly after, Faith took the flagging Jasmine off to bed, and Collin was making a concerted attempt to disengage from a stomach turning conversation with Hope about how to treat a sheep with a prolapsed uterus. Something Collin fervently prayed that he'd never be called on to do. Never ever. How Hope kept her legs under her—and the contents of her stomach down—while working for the local veterinarian was nothing short of a miracle.

"Hope," Faith interrupted, coming back into the room without Jasmine. "Collin will never want to set foot in our home again if you don't stop sharing your disgusting animal doctor tales with him."

As if snapped out of a trance, Hope's eyes grew wide as they bounced from Collin to Faith and back to him again. "Oh my gosh. I'm so sorry." She covered her face with her hands, and Collin bit back a grimace as he imagined just where those hands had been.

"It's fine," he said, swallowing hard against the bile that was trying to make its way up the back of his throat. "I'm fine."

Faith laughed out loud, and Jed chuckled softly from his recliner, surprising Collin; he'd thought the man was sleeping.

"Why don't you take your teacher outside for a breath of fresh air," Faith said to Prudence. "He's looking a little green around the gills."

"I'm so sorry," Hope said again, her long blonde ponytail bobbing emphatically as she nodded at Prudence. "I never know when to stop talking about guts and growths—"

Collin fervently wished he hadn't eaten so much.

"Right now would be a good time to stop, sister," Faith cut in, crossing the room to open the front door. "Please. For all of our sakes!" She wiggled her fingers at Collin. "Come on. Fresh air awaits. Out you go. If you're going to puke, do it in the bushes, not in our living room."

He lurched to his feet. "Right," he managed to get out. It sounded like someone had a grip around his throat.

"Go with him, Pru," Faith ordered again, giving her young sister the eye. "He's all yours."

"Well, now, I don't know about that," Collin heard Jed say right before Faith closed the door behind them. And then it was blessedly quiet, except for the singing of the frogs down by the lake and the spring breeze that whispered through the trees nearby.

FOURTEEN

"Sorry, Mr. Stewart," Prudence apologized from behind him. Her voice carried in the hushed night. "Between horses, cows, and a house full of females, things can get pretty graphic around here."

Collin nodded slowly, finally getting himself together enough to meet her eyes. At least he wasn't going to throw up at her feet. "Your poor father," he acknowledged, then wished he could suck the words back in.

But to his surprise, Prudence laughed out loud. "I know, right? That man deserves a sainthood, that's all I can say. Raising all of us without a mother? Who would do that on purpose?"

"My respect for him has grown exponentially this evening, I have to admit. He just seems to take it all in stride."

"He does. He's had to learn to do so over the years just to survive." She stepped up beside him at the top of the front porch steps. They stood a good foot or more apart, looking up at the stars flung out into the night sky. "It's beautiful, isn't it?" Prudence murmured so softly, he thought maybe she'd not meant to speak aloud.

"It is." From beyond the house, he heard the nicker of a horse.

"Have you met Cyrano?" The question caught him by surprise.

"Who?" he asked, turning toward Prudence.

"My Andalusian. My horse." She shrugged. "Actually, I'm pretty sure I'm his human. That was him just now. I swear he can hear my voice a mile away."

"An Andalusian? Aren't they those huge black horses with the long tales and manes?" He couldn't picture the petite Prudence with the giant of horse he pictured in his head.

"Yep. They're not all black, of course, but Cyrano is. Except for his rump. It kind of fades to gray with spots. He's got a freckled butt," she added with a giggle. "It's very rare."

"Well, how can I say no now? I must see this mythical beast."

"Come along, then," she said, darting down the steps in front of him, the hem of her short sun dress flipping provocatively as she moved. "He's shy at first, but that's because he had a rough start," she said over her shoulder.

Collin hurried down the steps after her, his eyes following her appreciatively. For a moment, he wished he could stay behind her just to watch the way her slender hips moved under her skirt when she walked, but he quickly stopped that train of thought from careening off the tracks. He caught up quickly. *Think about the giant horse,* he ordered. "What kind of a rough start? Have you had him since he was a baby? A colt? A foal? What's the right word—sorry, not a horse person here."

"They're foals for the first year. A male foal is a colt and a female is a filly." She didn't laugh at his ignorance, which wasn't a surprise. He'd never known Prudence to mock or make fun of anyone. "They're called yearlings their second year of life, then two-year-olds during their third year of life, which is typically when you can start riding them because they're mostly done growing. They reach adulthood at four years old, and then around their late teens or early twenties, they become geriatric. In the wild, they go downhill pretty quickly from there, but a well-cared-for horse can live into his or her thirties these days."

"Wow, thirty years." He was parroting her again, but she didn't seem to notice. "Can you still ride a geriatric horse?"

"It all depends on the animal. Cyrano is most likely getting close to twenty, but that's only a guess. Without papers or any other kind of a record, we can only estimate his age within three or four years. I do ride him now and then, but not hard, and I don't weigh a whole lot." She shrugged one shoulder in that shy way of hers. "Bigger breeds like Andalusians typically have shorter life spans than other horses, and the quality of their care can certainly influence how long a horse lives, too." A tinge of sadness inflected her words, but he liked hearing her talk. It was obvious she really loved that horse of hers.

He remained silent, hoping she'd keep filling the space between them with her sweet voice.

"Cyrano is a rescue. I found him a few years ago tied to a tree way back in the woods between our place and Whispering Hills next door. He was all alone, but I could tell someone else had been there recently," she explained as they circled the house and headed for the largest of the three barns. "Someone had made a fire ring and the grass around it was flattened like people or animals had been sleeping there for a while."

"Someone abandoned him?"

"When I found him, the fire was cold, so we kind of assume that was the case. He was in bad shape. Just skin and bones, a shadow of a horse, really. It broke my heart to know that someone had treated him so badly. It wasn't just that they'd abandoned him; it was obvious he'd been abused, too. He had marks on his neck and hind quarters, and one of his ears was badly torn. It's healed nicely, you'll see, but he's still got a chunk missing."

They'd reached the big double doors and Prudence went to lift the latch, but Collin stepped forward. "I got it," he said, then pulled the door open to let her pass through ahead of him. It was all he could do not to let his eyes wander over her again.

A horse whinnied loudly from the dark barn, but a moment later, Prudence hit a switch, and the place lit up. Several animals thrust their heads out into the main passage to see who was disturbing their slumber, but Collin knew immediately which horse was Cyrano. The beast's head was enormous, it's arched Roman nose giving it an ancient, almost austere appearance. "Ah," he said with a chuckle, tapping his own prominent nose. "Cyrano de Bergerac. On account of the nose."

"Shh," Prudence said, darting a quick look at him. Her eyes twinkled impishly. "You'll hurt his feelings."

As if in agreement, the horse pawed fitfully at the iron bars of the gate that kept him in his enclosure.

"I'm coming, you big oaf," Prudence said, her words lilting and gentle. "Hush now. You're waking up the whole neighborhood." Halfway there, she stopped and popped the top off of a metal trash bin, stuck her hand in, and pulled out a small fistful of what he assumed were oats. "I'm coming," she said again, then turned to Collin. "Grain treats. Want to feed him some?" she asked, holding the lid above the open bin.

"That's okay. I'll watch. He's... um, kinda big."

Prudence arched her brows at him, but again, she didn't laugh. "Yes, he is. His size can be intimidating, believe me. He was a little scary even back when he was nothing but skin and bones." She replaced the lid and pushed down hard on it to make sure it was locked tight in place. "But he's just a big softy. Come on. I'll show you."

Collin stood back as she approached the horse, her handful of grain held behind her back. She cooed and murmured to the beast, blew softly against his nose, then let the animal bump at her head and neck with his huge nose in greeting. He made a loud whuffling sound, then nudged her shoulder on the same side where she held the treats. Prudence laughed, let the horse push her around a little, then finally batted his head away and held up her cupped hands. Collin didn't miss the way she kept her fingers flat and away from those gigantic chomping teeth.

"You're such a sweet lost boy, aren't you?" Prudence gushed, stroking the horse's nose as he made quick work of the treats she offered him.

"Did you ever find out where he came from?" Collin asked, venturing forward a few steps. "Who left him in the woods?"

Prudence shook her head. "No, not really. A family of squatters was discovered a couple ranches over about a week later, but they swore they had no knowledge of this guy and they didn't seem to have any paraphernalia that would indicate they'd cared for a horse. It was a family, too. Young kids and all. Sheriff Dougal thought they might have come from one of the cannabis farms that got raided the year before, but there wasn't any evidence of that, either. And they seemed appreciative of the help that was offered."

Collin wasn't sure if she believed what she was telling him or not. A furrow had formed between her delicately arched brows, and she'd gone back to stroking the horse with slow, sweeping passes over his neck in a way that probably soothed them both.

"They moved on after they spent a few nights in the local shelter." She spoke in only a murmur now, more to the horse than to him. "I guess the husband—or boyfriend or guy or whatever he was—got a hold of his parents, and they took a bus to some small town in eastern Tennessee where he was originally from."

Collin nodded slowly, fascinated by the story. His literary side wanted to explore the human nature of it all, what brought people to a place in their lives, in their minds, where squatting became less of a choice and more of a necessity. Especially with young children. And a horse? He moved a little closer, then stopped when he caught a whiff of the perfume Prudence wore. He breathed in through his mouth, instead. "At least Cyrano here gets his happy ending."

Prudence looked over her shoulder at him, and for moment, she seemed surprised to find him so near. But then she smiled. "Unlike Roxanne, I like big noses and shy heroes." Then she stiffened, almost like she'd just realized what she'd said. She moved to stand a few feet away from him. "Um, so you can pet him if you want. He won't bite."

Trying not to read anything into what she'd said—she'd been talking about her horse, right?—Collin reached up a tentative hand to stroke the horse's nose. Cyrano tossed his head, startling him, and he stumbled backward a step or two, his hand still raised.

"It's okay," she assured him, not looking at him. "He's just messing with you. Come closer so he can get a good whiff of you."

Taking a firm grip on his nerves, Collin moved forward again and held his hand toward the horse, palm up. To his astonishment, Prudence wrapped her fingers around his wrist and brought it even closer, just under Cyrano's nose.

"Keep your hand flat. His hairy lips will tickle, but he won't bite."

Sure enough, the horse lowered his head until his nose all but rested in Collin's hand, then it blew softly against his palm. Collin grinned at how the dry, prickly muzzle felt on his skin.

But when Prudence drew Collin closer to Cyrano, she inevitably drew him closer to Prudence, too, and it wasn't long before he was having a hard time focusing on the horse. His gaze drifted sideways to the lines of her profile, the pert ski jump nose, the shapely lips that always looked like they were on the verge of puckering up. Her lashes, long and as sooty as her hair... and the way she smelled. Like something green and edible. Moss and wild blackberries. Like being in the woods after a spring shower. He breathed in quietly, deeply, inhaling that fragrance as if he could draw it in and take it with him when he left.

Prudence must have sensed the change in him. She released his wrist and stepped away again, tucking her hands behind her back, leaving him feeling suddenly bereft of her touch, her proximity.

What was he doing? He was supposed to be resisting her, not smelling her. He cleared his throat and nudged his glasses up a little higher on his long nose. *She likes big noses.*

"Um, so do you want to see my garden?" She sounded so young.

She *was* so young, he reminded himself. He should go. He should leave right now. And never come back. At least not until next year when she came home from school. "I'd like that," he said instead.

"Oh." She sounded surprised at his answer. "Okay. It's not quite at it's prime yet, and with it dark out, you might not be able to really tell, but things are starting to bloom. Um, well, follow me, then." She turned and headed back down the corridor toward the big doors, apparently having forgotten to say goodbye to her horse.

"Nice meeting you, Cyrano," Collin murmured quietly to the beast, then did as Prudence instructed and followed her. Only the horses were witness to him giving in to the temptation of letting his eyes wander. But just for a moment.

"Wait up," he called after her. "I'll get the door."

Outside again, he made sure he was at a safe distance from her, then took in a deep cleansing breath. It was growing chilly, even though it had been in the low eighties that afternoon, and he glanced over at Prudence, wondering if she was getting cold. Her sun dress had only short fluttery sleeves, and the skirt barely reached the middle of her thighs. At least she wore a pair of army style boots, he noted, so her feet were probably warm. Should he offer her his sweater? It was pretty lightweight, but maybe if he wrapped it around her quickly, it would retain some of his body heat long enough for her to feel it.

The thought of wrapping her up took him places he shouldn't go.

She was off, and once again, he hurried to keep pace with her. She reminded him of a dragonfly or a hummingbird, the way she flitted from place to place, never landing anywhere for too long, whimsical, but always on guard, too.

They reached the garden gate and he marveled at the design. "Daddy and I built it," she told him when he commented on it. "We had this old table and chair set that used to sit on our back porch. My parents brought it with them from Texas back when we first moved here. The table got too wobbly to use and the leg on one of the chairs broke while my dad was sitting on it. Fortunately, he wasn't doing anything stupid like leaning back on two legs or anything, so nothing bad happened, but we knew that meant the rest of them probably weren't fit to keep using. But because it was my mom's, we were hesitant to get rid of it. So we pulled all the backs off the chairs because the scrolled woodwork is so pretty, right?"

Prudence talked freely, he noted, when she spoke about things—animals, people, places—she loved. But rarely about herself. And yet, he found he was learning quite a bit about the young woman.

She ran her fingers over the detailed ridges and patterns of a tooled spindle. "Then we pieced them together inside this cool frame my dad made, and now we have this awesome gate. It's like having my mom hanging out with us in the garden whenever we're working out here."

"Does your dad come out here often?"

"That's his section over there." Prudence pointed to the other side of a row of espaliered fruit trees that divided the garden into two sections. "He grows most of the vegetables we eat, and I grow mostly edible and medicinal herbs and flowers." She touched the petals of a rose that glowed pale pink in the starlight. "And the ornamental flowers, too. I love flowers of all kinds."

Collin nodded. She reminded him of a flower. Or a flower fairy, maybe.

A dragonfly. A hummingbird. A flower fairy. *Listen to yourself, man. You sound like you're going soft in the head.*

"Oh! And you have to check out my favorite spot." She reached out like she was going to take his hand, but right before she touched him, she paused, her fingers curling in on themselves. "Um, over here."

He maneuvered down the narrow path between rows of some kind of flowering bush that gave off a heady scent. It reminded him of laundry day back when he was a kid and his mom hung their sheets out on the line to dry. A step ahead of him, she subconsciously reached out to skim her fingertips along the tops of them. He did the same.

"That's lavender," she said over her shoulder when she saw him bring his fingers to his nose to sniff. "Isn't it nice?"

"Reminds me of my childhood," he said.

Prudence giggled, the twinkly sound swirling around him in the near dark. "Reminds me of little old church ladies. People seem to love it or hate it; no in between."

"Do you love it or hate it?" He watched her as she, too, paused to bring her fingertips to her nose.

"Lavender is a marvelous plant with a myriad of uses, so yes, I love it, even though the scent is a little overwhelming to me. This one isn't my favorite, though. I have another row of them over there." She pointed across the way. "It's got a much sweeter, almost vanilla note to it. I had to order it from a specialty seed company."

He just nodded, glancing around the garden and marveling at the evidence of her love for growing things.

They reached the end of the row and she cut across a few more to the back corner of the large, fenced off plot where a squat tree loomed low and wide, like a mother hen spreading her wings over her babies. Even in the dark, he could see that it was lush and leafy, but the trunk and branches were gnarled and twisted, as though it had stood watch over the garden patch for a thousand years.

"This is Henrietta," Prudence said proudly. "She's our grandmother apple tree. She came with my parents from Texas, too. They planted her closer to the house at first, but in this different climate, the tree actually spread out wider instead of growing taller, so we eventually moved her out here to our garden patch where she thrives."

Collin peered up into the branches of the old girl and surprised himself when he greeted the tree out loud. "Nice to meet you, Henrietta. Or should I call you Grandmother Apple?"

Beside him, Prudence giggled again, the sound childish enough to remind him that he was walking on dangerous ground.

And hallowed ground, the way she talked about it. The spirit of her beloved mother imbued this place, and he couldn't let himself forget that.

"Come. There's a bench over here. You can see all the way out past the lake when you're sitting there, at least in the daylight." She paused, then without looking at him, she added, "It's perfect for star gazing, too." She skirted the thick trunk of the tree.

Like a lamb being led to slaughter, he followed the sound of her siren voice. She brushed debris from the bench, then sat down, patting the empty spot beside her.

They sat in silence for several moments. She was right. Across the near pasture, the surface of the small lake, ruffled by the gentle spring night breeze, reflected the starlight in a twinkling display. Beyond it, things faded to black, but he could make out the ragged cutout of the treetops that marked the horizon line where land met deep velvet sky.

She shivered. It was just a slight movement, but he saw it. Without hesitation, he peeled off his cardigan and draped it around her shoulders. "It's not much, but I have long sleeves," he said, tugging on his cuffs.

"Thank you," she whispered, drawing the lapels around her. He thought he saw her bend her head forward like she was smelling it, and worried for a moment if it needed to be washed. Mortified at the thought, he averted his face and grimaced. "I like your cologne," she said, no longer whispering. "It smells really nice."

His relief was a palpable thing and he let out a long exhale as quietly as he could. "Thank you," he managed to say, reminding himself over and over again that it was just a compliment and nothing more.

"I come out here a lot." Her words were soft, sounding almost like a confession. "There are a few places around here where I feel like I'm closest to my mom. This is one of them."

It was obvious that she—and presumably the rest of her sisters, too—missed their mother terribly, had suffered greatly over her loss, and he was simply at a loss of anything to say that didn't sound trite or platitudinous.

"She's buried out in those woods," she continued when he didn't speak. She pointed toward the thick section of trees off to the west of them. "There's a clearing," she added. "We all visit it often, but I'm the one who takes care of it."

"She's a lucky woman," Collin said, picturing a place among the trees and wildflowers, a peaceful tribute to a woman adored by her family.

"You could come out there with me some day." The offer sounded sincere, but she was probably being polite. "It wasn't always a grave. She stumbled upon the clearing one morning on a walk, and for several weeks, she headed out there alone and turned it into this little magical hideaway. Then she surprised us all with a picnic out there. We still spend Mother's Day and her birthday out there. Or whenever any of us wants to spend time alone with her." She braced her hands on the bench on either side of her and leaned forward a little, giving him a clear shot of her elfish profile in the moonlight. She smiled and ducked her head. "I know she's not out there or here in this garden. It's just that these are the places where her memories are the brightest. The strongest."

"I think I understand," Collin said, as reverently as he could. He'd never lost someone close to him, and although he didn't fully comprehend all of it, he'd seen others deal with grief in much less healthy ways. "She sounds like a remarkable lady."

"She was," Prudence concurred, then turned to look at him. In the darkness, he couldn't quite make out her eyes at first, but the longer she looked at him, the clearer they became. "I hope I'm like her, Mr. Stewart. I mean, everyone says I look like her, but I don't really care about that. I want to *be* like her."

"Collin," he insisted, then blinked slowly, wishing he hadn't. "I think you're more like her than you know."

Prudence shook her head, but she didn't avert her face. "No." It came out more of a sigh than a word. "My mom, she wasn't afraid of anything. Not even death. I'm afraid of everything."

"That's not true," he countered. "You're going away to Colorado next month. You're following your dream. That might be the bravest thing anyone could ever do."

Prudence rose and took a few steps away. "Yeah, but I'm only doing it because I know home is going to be here waiting for me if it doesn't work out. And I'm not brave. I'm terrified. I don't want to go, Mr. Stew—Collin. I want to stay here where I'm safe, protected. I'm happy here. I love Seven Virtues Ranch and Plumwood Hollow. My Dad, this land, all of this—this is my home. I'd be happy if I could just stay here forever."

After a few moments, she shifted her stance so her back was no longer to him. Her expression gave away how unsettled the topic made her.

"Then why are you going?" The question came out with a little more edge than he'd intended, but before he could rephrase it, she turned to face him. Backlit against the starlit sky, she was only a silhouette, but he didn't miss how her spine stiffened and her shoulders straightened. He half expected her to plant her hands on her hips, but instead, she crossed her arms in front of her.

"I'm going because I want—I want—well, I do want to go, but more than that, I want to make my mom proud. I know she would have wanted this for me, too."

Collin stood slowly so as not to intimidate her. He kept his posture loose and tucked his thumbs in his front pockets, his gaze fixed, not on her, but on the glittering lake. "Is that reason enough to go? Because you think she'd want you to?"

"Of course it is. My mom is the reason we do a lot of things around Seven Virtues."

Collin frowned. "I don't mean to sound obtuse, but why do you think she'd be proud of you for going if it's not what you really want to do?"

"It *is* what I really want to do, Mr. Stew—"

"Collin," he interrupted, this time without regret. Their conversation had taken a pretty serious turn into something deeply personal, and now was not the time for formalities. "You can call me Collin. We're not in class right now."

"Fine. *Collin.*" But the bitterness got a little thicker. "It *is* something I want to do, *Collin*, and I'm also doing it because she'd be proud of me for going, *Collin*." Every time she said his name, it reeked of something he didn't quite grasp. "I'm not brave, okay, *Collin?* I'm scared to go, and I'm scared to stay. And after our conversation tonight at dinner, I've decided I'm more scared to stay. *Collin.*"

He turned to face her now, his own dander rising at her persistent verbal attack. "Hey. What's going on? Did I say something to upset you? To offend you? Why are you so angry with me?" He kept his thumbs in his pocket, but every muscle in his body had coiled up again. His pulse raced in response to her anger and his scalp tingled as if in warning of something to come.

"I'm not angry with you," she shot back. He could see her eyes now, glistening in the starlight. Were those tears making them shine like that? *No, no. Please no tears.*

"You could have fooled me." Now he sounded a bit like an argumentative kid. He dropped his chin to his chest for a moment and gathered his thoughts. "Sorry," he said, looking at her again. "Please help me understand, Prudence. It feels like you're lashing out at me, that's all. I just want to know why." He tipped his head to the side a little and forced his shoulders to stay relaxed. "Help me understand."

"Don't use your teacher psychobabble on me, Mr. Stewart."

Sarcasm now. He waited, holding his tongue, something he'd learned to do when trying to figure out what was going on in his students' minds. More psychobabble, he supposed, but without the babble.

"Are you glad I'm going away next year?" Her question shot out of the darkness at him, taking him by surprise. Not only because of the bitterness in her voice, but also because of the sudden change of subject.

"Um, yes?" It came out a question. "Yes," he said more definitively this time. "I'm happy for you. I want you to pursue your dreams, to do what makes you happy." He lifted one shoulder in a half-shrug. "It's what I want for all of you," he added, suddenly remembering he was her teacher and she, his student.

"All of us?" Prudence sounded confused.

"All of my students. All of you," he expounded.

"Right. All of us." She started to turn away from him, but Collin reached out and took her shoulders, forcing her to stop and face him.

Forcing everything to stop.

The rustling of leaves overhead stilled.

The frog song in the distance became muted.

Even her breathing stopped.

So did his.

The only thing that didn't stop was his heart. It surged forward, pounding out a frantic rhythm between his ears, drowning out all sound, all time. All sense.

Prudence Goodacre stood before him, her face lifted to his beneath the scattered-diamond sky, her eyes wide and full of questions. Full of... hope?

"Collin?" This time, his name came out of her like a tentative caress. It made his knees go weak.

"I want you—you to be happy, Prudence." Somehow, he got the words out past the lump in his throat, and then it was as if the flood gates had burst open. "If you want to go to Colorado, if it will make you happy to do that, then that's what I want. If you want to stay here at Seven Virtues, if that's what makes you happy, then stay here. If you want to ride a motorcycle from here to Alaska and back because that's the one thing that will make you happy, then that's what I want you to do." *Where on earth had that come from?* He was practically shaking her now, his fingers gripping her shoulders hard, and he wasn't finished. "What is it you want, Prudence? Tell me. Be brave like your mother. Tell me what will make you happy. Because if it makes you happy, then that's what I want for you."

He felt her draw in her breath, hold it... and release it with the words, "Okay. Then... it's you. I—I want you."

This time, his heart stopped, too. Just for a moment, but stop, it did.

His silence must have given her hope because she took a tiny shuffle step forward and lifted her hands to press her palms against his chest. Could she feel it? The absence of the pounding of his heart? The jagged-edged hole her words had blown through him?

"I want you, Collin," she said again, every word like whip lashes on his tingling flesh. "Do you—will you—?"

Yes. I do. I will. Yes. Every cell in his body cried out for her. Every part of him leaned toward her as though she had some magnetic force drawing him in. His gaze roved over her face, from her brimming eyes to her pale cheeks, to the curve of her jaw.

To her lips, soft, slightly parted in anticipation, in invitation, so ready to be kissed. So ready for *his* kiss.

"No!" he gasped, then thrust her away from him, pulling back his hands and locking his fingers together behind his head to keep from reaching for her again.

She stumbled slightly, but quickly righted herself.

"Oh, God, I'm sorry, Prudence. No. No," he said again, this time with more vehemence. "I'm sorry. I—I have to go. Are you—are you okay?" Had he hurt her when he set her back like that?

"Don't go," she pleaded. "Oh, please, Mr. Stewart. Collin. I'm sorry." She stood before him, wringing her hands, clearly afraid to come any closer. "I shouldn't have—"

He cut her off with a firm shake of his head. "I shouldn't have come out here with you. I knew it, that it could only lead to... to.... This is my fault, not yours." The words kept gurgling out of him, like blood seeping from a femoral wound. "I'm the one who—I should have known better. I should have behaved better. I'm better than this." The last words were uttered in an angry growl, and in the light of the moon, her face seemed to blanch paler, if that were even possible.

"Collin." She breathed his name, her hands reaching for him.

"Don't!" He stepped back, his fingers still locked behind his head. "Don't touch me." It came out raw and rough. "You can't touch me." *Or I won't be responsible for what happens next.*

"I'm so sorry," she whimpered, barely above a whisper. There were tears now. They tracked slowly down her smooth cheeks, and it took every ounce of willpower not to pull her hard against him and wrap himself around her. To protect her from monsters like him.

"I can walk you back—" he started to say. But he couldn't. He simply couldn't. Just being in close proximity to her had him on fire for her. Jed would take one look at him and know the thoughts he harbored toward the girl. *The girl! She's a girl, Stewart, you sicko.* Surely, Jed would smell the desire—the lust—oozing from his pores. And he'd see the pain, the humiliation on Prudence's face. He'd know.

And Jedediah Goodacre most certainly had a gun. Guns, plural.

Someone would end up dead tonight, and on a property this size, it might take years before the authorities discovered the body.

But that wasn't why he couldn't do it.

"I can't," he said, softly this time. He unlaced his fingers and took a deep breath, fortifying his will before he reached out to cup her face in one hand. For a brief moment, he let his thumb brush the curve of her bottom lip. "I'm sorry."

With that, he turned around, back ramrod straight, head forward, no looking to the left or right, and headed back to the house. At the last minute, he veered toward his car in the driveway. He hadn't left anything inside, and he was too hot right now to worry about the sweater he'd draped around Prudence's shoulders. She could keep it, for all he cared.

Or throw it away.

"Or burn it, more likely," he ground out through the emotions that clogged the back of his throat. He flung himself into the driver's seat of his car and slammed the door hard. By the time he made it back to town and was pulling into the driveway of his little row house, his mind was made up. There was no going back; not after tonight.

FIFTEEN

PRESENT DAY...

Sunday morning dawned bright and cheery, but Prudence rolled onto her side in bed and lay still, listening to the sound of the house stirring to life. Daddy woke with the roosters, and she was certain he'd already have a pot of coffee brewed and waiting for Abby and her to dose up on their caffeine. She held her breath and listened for Abby's off-key humming that would indicate she was up and listening to music in the bathroom across the hall. Even though the girl sang like an angel, put sound-blocking headphones on her, and she couldn't carry a tune in a bucket.

"La-la-la-la-la... I love you," Abby crooned, most of the words drowned out by the sound of the bathroom vent fan. Good. That meant Abby would be going to church with Daddy, and Prudence wouldn't feel so badly about begging off. She wouldn't let him go alone, but she was dreading facing Collin so soon.

She'd waived everyone's concerns off last night, then danced into the wee hours to prove that nothing was wrong with her. Collin had left before she emerged from the sanctuary of her home, but surely, if he'd stayed in town last night, he'd be in church, wouldn't he? And if so, then just out of politeness, he'd surely seek her out to see how she was doing after her fainting spell last night.

Besides, she'd made sure there would be plenty left to do this morning before everyone gathered again for the after-church family brunch. The party rental company would come dissemble the tent, but she still had to unwind all the twinkle lights and take down the sheers she'd hung to mask each support pole. The linens were all heaped on top of the tables ready to be carted off, too, but she needed to locate the large laundry bags they'd given her to put them in after the event. Someone had tossed a pair of high-heeled, strappy sandals up in the branches of the old redbud tree at the top of the driveway, and she'd need to pull out the extension ladder to get to them. There was no way she trusted those ancient branches to hold up under anyone's weight. She still had no idea whose shoes they were, but eventually, someone would come by to get them.

Then there were the hundred and one other things that had to happen at the end of an event like this. The kitchen was still in utter chaos, although, Charity had made a point to clear off the counter where the coffeemaker was so they could have breakfast without too much fuss. The bathrooms in the house were in shambles, even Daddy's, and she needed to give them all a quick wipe down before everyone convened back here again. Those out in the barns would have to wait for another day to get cleaned.

The back porch had taken quite a bit of abuse from the catering crew, and the whole thing could use a good hose down before she set it up again with their assortment of patio furniture. They'd take advantage of the extended stretch of good weather and have brunch outside.

One of the best things about living in such a close-knit community was that everyone pitched in. Prudence had been forced to practically run helpful folks off the property the night before. The only reason the kitchen and back porch weren't spotless was because Daddy had gone to bed. Otherwise, the happy group who hadn't wanted the night to end would have charged the back door and set everything to right just so they could hang out together a little longer.

She finally pushed up out of bed, slid her arms into a beautiful kimono robe she'd bought in a vintage secondhand store in Owensboro, and padded through the house barefoot to find her father. She wouldn't leave it to the last minute to tell him her decision not to attend church that morning, nor would she make Abby bear the tidings for her.

He was sitting on the top step of the back porch with Jack, Faith's dog, who'd made his regular morning sojourn from next door to spend a few minutes with his second favorite human. Jed was muttering something to the border collie and Jack had one ear pricked, his expressive eyes staring up at the old man adoringly as he listened.

Prudence poured herself a cup of coffee and pushed out through the screen door. "Hey, Daddy," she said and dropped down to sit on his other side. "Hey, Jack," she added, peering around her father to meet the dog's eyes. His tail thumped against the wooden porch planks a few times, but his devotion, especially at this time of the morning, was all for Jed.

"Mornin' Pixie Cut," Jed replied, darting a sideways glance at her. He didn't seem surprised to see her still in her pajamas.

"I just wanted to let you know I'm staying home this morning. I have a lot to do before people show up here for brunch, and I just couldn't get it all done before I crashed."

After a few moments of mulling that over, he said, "You know folks will come ready to help out. That's what the brunch is all about, right?"

He was right. No one expected her to do it all herself, and knowing her sisters, they'd all have something to say if she tried. "I know, Daddy. I'm just still a little wiggy after last night, okay?" She didn't want to pull the fainting card, but she'd been prepared to, anyway. "I'd really like to spend a little time alone this morning, if that's okay with you. I think I need it."

"Are you asking my permission, my blessing, or are you telling me?"

Prudence hesitated, but then set her cup down on the step and stretched out her legs in front of her. She smiled down at the bright green toenail polish she wore. "You know, Daddy? I guess I'm telling you. But I'd still like your blessing, if not your permission."

Jed bumped her shoulder with his. "You got it, darlin'." Then he pushed slowly to his feet, gripping the handrail for support. Prudence frowned as she watched him, but she didn't dare put out a steadying hand to help him. He wouldn't want that. He'd once yelled at Faith; "If I want help getting my sorry old ass up out of my chair, I'll ask for it!" Faith had lifted her chin and shouted back about how she should have left that same sorry old ass under the tractor where she'd found him after the accident that nearly took his life. Then Daddy had yelled at her for using crass language.

Faith had followed that up with something even crasser, after which both of them had stormed out of the room in opposite directions. Faith, of course, had moved much quicker than Jed, and by the time he made it halfway down the hall toward his bedroom, he'd been at it long enough to know he needed to be the one to apologize. It had surely taken both physical and mental willpower for him to turn around and make for the bedroom door Faith had slammed behind her, but by then, she'd been ready to patch things up, too.

Even so, the girls knew to let their father do as much on his own as possible in order to maintain his dignity for as long as he could. So even though it was obvious to Prudence that he was dealing with some significant pain this morning, she didn't say a word. Nor did she let him catch her watching him. Nor did she let him catch her with anything but a neutral, relaxed expression on her face when he turned back to her.

"If I were you, child, I'd leave a few messy spots for your sisters to clean up. She might have moved over to the big house next door, but Charity still thinks she's got squatter's rights to that kitchen in there."

"I know, Daddy." When he offered her his hand, she took it, but only squeezed it and brought it close to plant a kiss on the back of his knuckles before letting go. "I think I'll stay out here and enjoy the quiet a little longer, okay?"

"Be my guest," Jed said, then headed back inside. Jack watched after him until the door closed behind him, then flopped back down on the porch next to Prudence. She reached over and scratched his head between his ears and the dog let out a long-suffering sigh.

SIXTEEN

To his surprise, Prudence wasn't in church the next morning. She wasn't sitting with the rest of her family in the service, all of them looking a little wrung out, but happy and content with the success of the wedding day, enjoying the handshakes and back pats and hearty congratulations that were handed out all around. Pastor Treadwell even congratulated the family and the congregation from the pulpit on how beautiful a thing it was to see the whole church family come together to celebrate and support and send off the couples the way the good Lord would want them to.

Maybe the whole fainting thing had affected Prudence more than everyone let on. Maybe she was feeling sickly today. Did he dare call on her at the ranch? Should he ask her family after her?

Sarah Lynxwilder had phoned him before church and invited him to join them at The Smokehouse that evening. "We're all getting together again to celebrate; we're going to milk this party for all it's worth!" She'd chortled gleefully into the phone, and Collin thought he heard someone hoot something in the background, probably that tall Colorado sheepherder woman. Charlotte? Was that her name? He thought she was staying with Sarah while she was in town.

He liked Joe's mother a lot, with her sparkling eyes and bubbly personality. His own mother was equally wonderful, but in a quiet, settled way, and when he'd met Sarah Lynxwilder, he'd marveled at how different people could be and still be happy in their own skin. Now it sounded like she'd discovered a like-minded soul in her new friend, and it made Collin smile.

"Little Abby will be singing tonight, too, just so you know," she added, as if he needed convincing.

"Well, in that case, sure, I'll come. I haven't heard that girl sing in far too long." Of course he'd go. But not because Abby was singing. If the Goodacre tribe was gathering at The Smokehouse, then Collin would be in attendance.

When church let out, he greeted folks he'd missed seeing at the wedding and reception the day before. He made a point to thank Jed again for his hospitality and asked Abby how Prudence was feeling. He thought he sounded perfectly polite, but the twinkle in Abby's eyes when she responded made him wonder.

"Oh, she's fine. Don't you worry. You coming to the Smokehouse tonight? We'll all be there, you know. Even Prudence."

"Joe's mom invited me, yes," he said, trying to keep his tone casual and unaffected. "I hear you'll be performing some of your own music tonight, too."

"You heard correctly, gallant rescuer of fainting fair maidens," she said with a slow nod. "I'll be sure and pull out some of my ballads so you can ask a certain pretty girl to dance."

Collin tried not to roll his eyes. The girl was incorrigible. Was he really that transparent? "Looking forward to hearing them," he said. "I'll see you all later, then." And with that, he headed out of the building and into the midday sunshine where he ran into Garret and Sherry Thompson. They invited him to join them for lunch at their favorite little Italian food place, Pepito's, and he readily agreed, happy to spend the next hour or so catching up with his friends and the comings and goings of the town he found he still felt such an affinity toward.

After lunch, he got on his bike and drove around Plumwood Hollow, visiting his old stomping grounds. His first stop was the the high school, of course, where he got off his bike and walked around the main building, peering in windows and glass doors, taking it all in, awash in memories of those hallowed halls.

After leaving the school, he cruised slowly through the town square where the high school marching band led the Founders Day Parade. He saluted the coal miner sculpture in the center of the fountain in front of the town hall, a monument to the men on whose backs Plumwood Hollow and the surrounding communities had been built. With the controversial methods now being used to ferret the coal from the mountains, men brave enough to risk their lives going into those deep, dark mines weren't in such high demand anymore, but coal mining, both past and future, continued to take a toll on the people of the area. Collin remembered the day the statue had been erected and the celebratory potluck held by everyone in town bringing their casserole dishes and homemade pies to share with their neighbors. The folks of Plumwood Hollow were a proud, tightly knit community who knew how to do life together.

He drove by Trilby's Flowers and Books where Prudence had worked her senior year. If he wasn't mistaken, she still worked with Trilby, if not in the store, then at least as an event planner. He'd seen the older women and Prudence with their heads bent over a folder at the back of the sanctuary right after the wedding. He'd also heard Trilby tell several people that she'd had little to do with the planning of the event, that Prudence had commandeered the day almost completely on her own.

Next door to the flower and book shop was the post office where Mitch Krautzman, Trilby's husband, worked. On the other side of the street opposite Trilby's, was Suzi's Sweet Treats, a new place to him, but one that seemed to compliment Trilby's well. There was Nesbit's Grocery Store on the corner—did Russ Timmons still work the checkout line there? Legend had it the man had worked the same station for more than a hundred years, never aging, never taking a day off.

Braxton's Hardware and Feed brought back a swarm of memories; he'd spent many an afternoon in the expansive store the semester he'd been asked to cover for the shop teacher who was out on maternity leave. Upon her return, he'd handed over the keys to the classroom with its table saws, hydraulic car lifts, and rolling toolboxes with great relief. He'd never been more relieved to see a woman in his life than on the day Sookie Langer came back to work.

Until Prudence, of course. Except relief wasn't the right word for the way he felt when he saw her.

So many of the businesses were closed for Sunday; it was a little like stepping back in time. Kennedy Heights offered a mixed urban and suburban feel that made it unique from so much of the rest of Cincinnati, but businesses—there were lots of coffee shops, bars, and restaurants, especially—were all open long before noon on Sundays.

Thankfully, Serendipity's was open, and he stopped in to grab one of their famous cinnamon rolls to take back to his hotel room. He wasn't really hungry now, and he'd hold off and have dinner at The Smokehouse, but he'd been craving one of the decadent pastries all day, and since the little diner wasn't open on Monday's, he decided to get it now and have it for breakfast in the morning.

Cass Whitehouse was at the counter, another familiar face that made the sense of loss inside him throb. Another good friend he'd left behind when he walked away from Plumwood Hollow.

Her face lit up at the sight of him, and she came out from behind the register to greet him, throwing her arms around him in a warm, welcoming hug. She smelled of sugar and vanilla, and something herbal. Basil, maybe? It was rather pleasant and made him salivate just the tiniest bit. Maybe he was hungry after all. At least his appetite would be good for The Smokehouse's famous ribs.

When she released him, she stepped back and patted his cheek with her palm. "It's so good to see you, Collin. You here for the wedding?" She leaned back against the counter, with one elbow propped on the glass top. Her buxom curves were well-suited for the tight t-shirt she wore under her hunter green bib style apron. Cass was the kind of woman who should be married, who flourished when she was taking care of someone, of everyone. Cass was committed to the people in her life the way so many of the folks in the hollow were, and when she made you her friend, you were her friend for life, come hell or high water. She didn't turn her back on anyone in need, and she made sure no one to her knowledge went without.

"I am," he said, then frowned. "Where were you last night? I didn't see you at the reception." She'd been at the church, sitting near the back. She'd waved at him when he slipped into the pew a few rows behind her and he'd felt instantly more at ease, knowing that someone he knew was happy to see him.

"Oh, you know," she said, waving a hand flippantly in the air between them. "Someone had to man the shop."

"Serendipity's stayed open?"

"We did," she insisted, straightening up and heading back around the end of the counter. "Didn't have any customers," she admitted with a rueful chuckle. "But I was fine manning my post." She blinked rapidly, and only then did he notice the telltale glisten in her eyes.

Ah. Joe Lynxwilder. Of course. He nodded slowly. "Right. Sorry. I understand."

"I think I'll always carry a torch for that man, Collin. I'm a sucker for the strong silent type and there aren't that many of them around these parts. At least not any who don't eventually start throwing punches and getting loud, you know?"

Cass had ended a relationship with a man who'd started out strong and silent, but who'd ended up drunk and disorderly a few too many times before he finally got put behind bars for practically beating her to a pulp several years ago. Joe had been one of the volunteers on Brandon Stillwater's First Responder crews that night. They'd received a call from a neighbor that it sounded like someone was getting killed over in Cass's little house. Joe had arrived moments before the rest of the crew, but he hadn't waited for assistance. Through the kitchen window, he'd taken one look at Jimbo with his fist raised above Cass who was huddled in a corner, her arms up in front of her face. Joe had kicked through the back door, surprising the big man enough to get a jump on him, and with the adrenaline coursing through him at breakneck speed, it hadn't taken much for him to get the drunken fool face down on the floor, one arm twisted behind his back, his hand crooked high between his shoulder blades. Cass had watched it all through swollen, bloodshot eyes, her quiet sobs fueling Joe's barely contained fury.

"I'm okay," she kept saying, over and over, even though it was obvious she wasn't. But she'd fallen hard for Joe that night, her hero, her champion. She'd pursued him quietly, but relentlessly, for almost a year afterward, finally realizing he wasn't interested in more than friendship when she bluntly asked him if he'd go out on a date with her. In his gentle way, he'd told her that he wasn't the kind of man to lead a woman on, and that she deserved someone who could love her the way a woman should be loved. She'd never quite gotten over him.

Well, Collin couldn't really blame her, could he? If it had been Prudence's wedding day, he wouldn't have been able to attend, either.

"I'm heading over to The Smokehouse tonight to hear Abby sing. I heard there's going to be a gathering of the Goodacres and extended family there, and since it will be sans the newlyweds, I figured I could handle myself." She eyed him up and down, then said, "You clean up well, Collin. Want to be my platonic escort? Or I'll be yours, if you prefer. That way, I don't have to show up as a hungry single."

He hesitated for just a moment, but she noticed.

"It's okay, big guy. I'm fine being single. Folks around here already know I'm looking for a man of my own; it's not like I'd be fooling anyone, right?"

Collin shook his head to stop her. "No, stop. It's just that I'm on my bike this weekend and I only have one helmet, that's all." It wasn't quite why he'd hesitated, but it was the truth, nonetheless. "Want to pick me up? I'm at the Holiday off Booker Road. Or would you rather I drive over to your place, and we can go from there? I'd be honored to escort you, Cass, and don't you believe otherwise."

"You sure?" She grinned up at him, but he could see the uncertainty in her eyes. It bothered him because it reminded him of the way Prudence looked at him last night. Men who put that look in a woman's eyes had a lot to account for, and he hated that he was one of them.

"Absolutely. Just tell me where and when."

"Come to my place at seven," she said, a new light in her eyes. "I close up here at six. That'll give me time to get all gussied up before you get there." She pulled one of the cinnamon rolls from the pastry case and deftly nestled it into a takeout box. "Here. On the house."

"How did you know?" he asked, taking the box from her.

"I never forget my customer's favorites, Mr. Stewart. Remember?"

So, he had a date. But not really a date. He had an escort.

Well, that sounded even worse.

He was going to The Smokehouse with a friend, that's what it was.

But would Prudence see it that way? Collin had a sinking feeling in his gut that things might not go quite the way he'd hoped they would, not if he planned to show up with the lovely Cass on his arm. Especially if she still got all gussied up the way he remembered. She had a penchant for animal prints and plunging necklines, a little too much makeup, and a whole lot of hair spray.

"Well, Lord," he muttered as he threw his leg over his bike out front of Serendipity's. "You're not going to make this easy, are you?"

The good Lord had nothing to say to that.

He headed back to his hotel room for a nap, worn out by his trip down memory lane coupled with the restless sleep from the night before. He was more determined than ever to speak with Prudence, to set things right, and he wanted to be fresh and well rested when he next saw her.

Especially now that he had Cass Whitehouse to consider.

SEVENTEEN

Just before eleven, the gang started trickling in. Daddy and Abby arrived first, followed by Hope and Levi, Yvette, and Nana, Levi's mother. With her father's permission, Yvette headed out to the swing in the big tree that perched up on the high point of the property. From there, she could see Jasmine and her family approaching, whether they opted to come through the narrow strip of woods that bordered the two ranch properties, or up the long driveway from Carpenter Road.

Just as Jed had said they would, when Faith and Charity made their appearances, they both turned admonishing frowns on Prudence. "You were supposed to wait for us to help you this morning," Charity chastised, sweeping an arm around the almost spotless kitchen. "I would have taken care of all of this, you know that, right?"

"Well, now you don't have to. I freed you up to focus on cooking," Prudence said, doing her best not to sound defensive.

"She's got a point there," Abby said on her way through the kitchen to the back porch. "Love you, Pru, but your cooking? Not so much." She dodged the damp rag Prudence threw at her. "Hey, I'm going to round up Jasmine and Yvette. We'll go tend to the boys." The twins had left the care of their horses, Flash and Fire, to Abby while she was home, and Jasmine had promised to take over once Abby headed back to Nashville. "Unless there's something else you need us to do," she added, turning around to face the three older girls as she kept taking backward steps toward the door.

"Go," Faith told her. "Prudence did everything else around here already."

"Not everything," Prudence countered. "The bathrooms still need to be cleaned and the tables and chairs out there need to be folded up and made ready for the rental company to pick up this afternoon."

"Looks like Cord and Levi are already on that," said Charity, peering out the kitchen window in the direction of the big tent. "Where's Frank? Did he head out there, too?"

"I'm here." Frank entered from the living room with Ollie perched on his shoulders. "I'm on Ollie duty," he said reaching up to tickle the baby in the ribs. Ollie chortled gleefully and smacked the top of Frank's head with his fat little hands. "Ouch, you little hooligan," Frank said before swinging the little guy down. "Lets go outside and join the menfolk, shall we?" He came up behind Charity and leaned in to kiss her neck, then holding Ollie out like an airplane, he flew the child out the door and into the sunshine.

"When are you two going to have one of those?" Faith directed the question at Hope, who shook her head slowly.

"I'm not sure," she said. "We talk about it now and then, but I'm still trying to make this hospital run in the red, so I'm doing most of the after-hour calls. Which means my schedule can be pretty unpredictable." She paused, then poked her head around the arched doorway that led into the living room before turning back to her sisters. "Daddy and Nana are both dozing in the easy chairs in there, but I don't want to say this too loudly. She's fooled me before when I thought she was asleep." She drew closer and said in a hushed voice, "She keeps saying I need to have a baby before my eggs die, can you believe it? I'm hardly dead egg age yet, you guys."

"Dead egg age?" Faith repeated, snorted appreciatively. "Hardly."

"Anyway, whenever I tell her I don't have time to raise a baby right now, she just tells me all I have to do is get pregnant and she'll do the rest."

"What?" Charity covered her mouth, clearly aghast, but she was smiling behind her hand. "What on earth does she mean by that?" She stroked her barely-there baby bump with her other hand in what looked like a sympathetic protective gesture.

"What do you think it means?" Hope shot back. "She wants me to get pregnant, pop out a baby boy—and it must be a boy, by the way—and leave him with her to raise." Hope was now giggling, too, and Faith stood with her arms crossed over her stomach, trying in vain to hold back her own mirth.

"Stop. My bladder still hasn't fully recovered from pushing out melon-headed Ollie," she gasped.

"But what if you don't produce a boy?" Prudence ventured to ask.

Hope snorted. "She didn't say, and I didn't ask, but I assume Levi will have to just keep knocking me up until I get it right."

"I could think of worse ways to spend your time," Charity teased, her eyes sparkling.

"Hello." Prudence waved her hands in the air in surrender. "Not married here, so no dirty married jokes."

"Sorry, Pru." Charity giggled, then to Hope, she said, "Does she seriously think you'd just hand over your baby for her to raise?"

Hope nodded vehemently. "Oh, believe me. She does. She says she did a fine job with Jasmine, and with Levi before her." Hope leaned in even closer, lifting her hand to the side of her face as if that would help prevent her words from being overheard by the old woman in the next room. "I just can't imagine having a baby with Nana still living with us. Is that awful of me? I mean, she still smokes like a chimney, even though she does only do it outside. But secondhand smoke and all that? And she's getting old, you know? She spends more time sitting than anything else."

"That would be a deal breaker for me right there. The only time I sit is when Ollie is under someone else's supervision. Even then, I'm constantly jumping up, thinking I've forgotten him somewhere."

"And what if she were to drop him or her? You guys, I feel like a terrible person even admitting these things out loud, but I just don't see how it could work."

"What does Levi have to say about it?" Charity asked, finally lowering her hand. A small frown line formed between her brows as the conversation started to take on a more serious bent.

"He'd love another baby," Hope readily admitted. "A boy or a girl, don't worry," she added with a rueful smile. "He's not picky. But he agrees that Nana does pose a bit of a wrench in the works. I think we're both kind of tiptoeing around things. Which means I guess he's okay with waiting for now, right? No decision is really a decision, isn't it?"

Faith crossed the room and put an arm around Hope's shoulder. "Honestly, it sounds like the timing just isn't yet right for you guys, and that's okay. You're not even close to dead egg age yet, so ignore Nana. You'll know when you're ready."

"Or God will decide when you're ready, whether you think you are or not," Charity interjected, patting her baby bump again. She and Frank had been surprised by her pregnancy, but they'd quickly adjusted to the change in their plans, and now, no one could possibly accuse them of not looking forward to the arrival of their baby boy. Frank Flanner the Fourth, he'd be, and Frank couldn't be more thrilled by the prospect.

"Oh, please don't say that," Hope wailed. "I'm so not good with surprises."

Prudence lowered into one of the chairs at the table and sat quietly on the sidelines, enjoying the camaraderie of her three oldest sisters. She was definitely the outlier in the room, but she was used to it. It was one of the reasons she was able to read people so well, she decided. All her life she'd been on the outside looking in, studying life as an observer. Faith, Hope and Charity were all in relatively similar stages in life. The twins had each other and needed no one else until they finally agreed to let their husbands join them. When her parents told her they were having another baby, Prudence, even as a tiny girl, had been certain the new baby would be hers. But then Mama had died, and Faith had taken Abby for herself, leaving Prudence untethered and alone once more.

Now, she accepted it as her role in life. There were even times she almost reveled in it. Being a wallflower wasn't always a bad thing; it gave her a sense of freedom to come and go as she pleased, to not feel obligated to anyone or anything unless she chose to be.

Sure, she felt a heightened responsibility to look after Daddy, but that was because of proximity more than anything else. Other than her part time hours at Trilby's, Prudence worked from home, which made her the daughter most available to him these days. It was common knowledge that she was also, of all the sisters, the most like Mama, and for that reason, although Daddy would never acknowledge it, she was the daughter he most easily gravitated toward.

But Daddy had surprised her—surprised them all—last year when he bought the property across Carpenter Road and started building his own small ranch house where he planned to retire, leaving Seven Virtues Ranch to his daughters, who pretty much ran the place themselves, anyway. If she was being honest with herself, it more than surprised her. With Abby off pursuing her career in music, and the rest of the sisters settling into marriages and careers of their own, Prudence had harbored the notion that it was just going to be the two of them against the world, planting their gardens, tending a few head of cattle, and spending the evenings on the back porch together talking about the beauty around them. Instead, he was abandoning her, and it hurt.

No, he was freeing her from one more obligation. That was how she needed to look at it. He'd said as much when he told them all about his purchase. "You girls shouldn't have to feel obligated to tend to your old man. At least not yet. I'll still be here, right across the way, but not *in* your way." His new home was almost ready for him to move into, and once he was settled, Seven Virtues Ranch would officially be under the care of the seven Goodacre sisters. Faith would still run her herd of Dexters on Goodacre property, and the twins planned to open up their trick riding school in the spring, so the ranch would be sustainable for the time being. It would be there for Abby to come home to, and with Brandon and Justice living in the ranch house, the property would be in good hands.

No one had asked about Prudence's gardens and workshop, her business. The general assumption was that she'd just continue to stay on, doing her thing, whatever her thing was. And when she'd offered to contribute to the expense of running the property, they'd made it clear—gently, kindly, and completely unaware of how patronizingly—that her job was simply to keep the vegetable garden producing and the chickens happy.

Prudence hated chickens. Oh, she liked the fresh eggs and the chicken manure for her gardens, but the birds, not so much. She'd been attacked by a rooster when she was a child, and she'd never quite gotten over the lingering sense of panic whenever she had to go gather eggs.

Besides that, she actually wanted to contribute to making Seven Virtues Ranch successful. Her botanical product line had taken off over the last few years, and she was making far more money than she knew what to do with. She'd finally opened a savings account that had a slightly higher interest rate than her checking account, but she felt guilty every time she saw the growing balance.

Maybe if she actually knew what she wanted to do with her life, they'd take her more seriously. And that was the million-dollar question, wasn't it? Gardening with Daddy and sitting on the back porch watching the sunset sounded lovely in her head, but it wasn't the kind of thing you said out loud, especially to people you were trying to convince to believe in you.

There was also her beloved Cyrano. Although she tried not to think about it, Prudence knew that he was not long for this world. She'd be grateful to get another two or three years with him before he crossed the rainbow bridge. But once he was gone, there'd be no one left to keep her here.

The thought terrified her.

With her older sisters' attention on meal prep and conversations about married life, no one noticed when Prudence slipped out of the room to check on Daddy and Levi's mother. Sure enough, they were both sound asleep as Hope had said, so she headed out the front door, pulling it closed quietly behind her. Maybe she'd go visit Mama's grave in the woods until it was time for brunch. Charity had said it would be about an hour. Stopping by the gardening shed, she grabbed a shovel, the long-handled loppers, and a pair of sharp snips, then she headed off toward the trees.

Within minutes, Prudence stepped through the circle of fall-festooned redbuds, green ashes, maples, and sweetgum and into the little clearing where Caroline's body had been laid to rest. For the next thirty minutes, she worked her way around the circle, trimming and cutting back, clearing some of the debris from the stone cairn they'd built in Mama's memory. When she was finished, she smiled up at the interlacing branches overhead, the tricolored leaves waving down at her, feeling much better about herself and the day ahead.

She was also secretly looking forward to watching how things were going to unfold between Daddy and Charlotte Rawlings. "I think you'd like her, Mama," she murmured, her face still lifted to the sky. "I sure do. She's not like you and me at all, and I think maybe that's exactly why I like her."

With a little skip in her step, Prudence gathered up her tools and headed back to the house.

Her good mood wasn't even shaken by the news that Sarah and Charlotte wouldn't be joining them until that night at The Smokehouse. "Sarah told us at church that she was exhausted and needed a bowl of soup and a good long nap if she was going to be able to enjoy going out tonight," Faith explained to everyone. "That woman cracks me up."

"What about Charlotte?" Prudence asked, passing a bowl of bright yellow scrambled eggs down the table. "Why didn't she come?"

"She decided to borrow Sarah's car and go check out some properties in the area. Said she'll definitely be joining us tonight, though."

Prudence turned to see what Daddy's reaction was to that, but he kept his eyes focused on his food and didn't say a word.

EIGHTEEN

Cass was on her front stoop waiting for Collin when he pulled up on his bike. She waved at the numbered carport parking nearby.

"I'll pull my truck out of my spot and you can park your bike there. Less likely to have any issues with it."

He wasn't sure he liked the sound of that. Issues? Like someone stealing it? A jealous boyfriend? He nodded and waited for her to pull out. By the time he had parked, Cass was already in the passenger seat of her little pickup. She'd left the driver's side door open for him to get behind the wheel.

"You look nice," they said in unison, then laughed companionably.

Cass eyed him speculatively. "Who you going to see tonight?"

"I'm—I'm sorry?"

"You're not fooling me, Mr. Stewart," she scoffed, her eyes twinkling with good humor. "I'm sure Joe invited you to his wedding, but you could have been back home in your own little circle of friends by now if you'd only come to see him. Is there someone else here in the hollow you're looking to reconnect with? Someone you left behind?"

Geez. Maybe he really *was* that transparent. Everyone seemed to be able to see right through him these days. Even the old man at the mailbox back home, come to think of it.

"That's all right. You don't have to tell me." Cass gave his arm a conciliatory pat. "I'll figure it out soon enough, won't I?"

Collin waited until he'd pulled out of the apartment complex parking lot. "What would you do if I asked you not to try to figure anything out?"

"Oh." She drew the word out long and low. "So there *is* someone." Cass clapped her hands together gleefully.

"Cass, please," Collin groaned, but he couldn't bite back a grin.

"Need to make someone jealous? Or should I do a little matchmaking for you?" She was clapping again. "Oh, let me arrange a meet-cute, will you? I'll trip you so you *accidentally* spill your drink down the front of her. That always works in the movies. Or how about—?"

"Stop!" Collin was laughing now, but he wasn't about to let Cass stick her nose in things tonight. Not anymore than she would be just by being there with him. It was all too fragile a situation. Tonight, all he wanted was the chance to ask to speak to Prudence alone, so he could tell her why he'd done what he'd done, why he'd walked away all those years ago. He didn't need anyone interfering, even with the best of intentions. "I'd tell you there's no one, but I know you won't believe me."

"I won't." She nodded so vehemently, the high topknot she wore her hair in threatened to come loose. At least she no longer went for the hair-the-size-of-Texas look she used to sport. Her makeup was a little more subdued, too, but she apparently still like small, leopard print tops and push-up bras.

"I just can't decide whether I should tell you who it is or not. If I don't tell you, you'll be giving the stink eye to every woman in the joint—"

"And every man," she interjected, her brow crooked in question.

"No. I'm not—she's a woman."

"Oh, I can't tell you how excited I am right now," she cackled, playfully punching him in the shoulder. "For me, not for you. I mean, for you, too, if you can figure out how to get the girl, of course. But for me because, well, romance is just... so... well, it's romance. And we all need a little romance in our lives, you know? Even if it's vicariously. You don't mind if I live through you, do you?"

"You're kinda crazy, Cass."

"Not just kinda," she shot back. She held her nails to her mouth and breathed on them, then rubbed them against her shoulder. "I am certifiably mad." Then she punched him again. "So? Who is it?"

"Ouch. Stop hitting me." He massaged his shoulder with his other hand. "I'm a fragile nerd, remember? And I still haven't decided if telling you is the best thing, either."

"You might as well," she said. "I'll only drive you crazy until I figure it out." She turned in her seat, so she was facing him a little more. "And you're no nerd, Collin Stewart. You're every high school girl's fantasy hot teacher."

Exceedingly grateful that twilight had settled in, Collin felt the heat of something—shame? Guilt? Lust?—creep up the back of his neck and prickle his scalp. Why did his feelings for Prudence still seem so illicit to him? "I'm just afraid you'll drive me crazy if you know, too. You'll poke and prod me for details I'm not ready to give anyone, or you'll just jump to conclusions and run with them."

"I can see your point," she agreed, nodding sagely. She crossed her arms and pondered a moment, then said, "Is this someone you're serious about? I mean, serious enough to come back to the hollow for? To move back here for? Permanently?"

His immediate answer was *Yes*, but he wasn't quite ready to admit it out loud. It was his pride, he knew, that prevented him from declaring it from the rooftops, because if he really examined his heart, he'd do just about anything if Prudence would have him. Move back to Plumwood Hollow? Yes. Become a hippie herbalist guru? If that's what she wanted him to do, then yes. Take a cross-country motorcycle road trip to Alaska with her? Yes, and again, yes.

"Listen, Collin." Cass had grown suddenly serious. "It's been a long time since we've spent time together, but I get the feeling there's a lot hanging in the balance for you tonight."

When she didn't go on, he nodded. "There is."

"Then I promise you, I won't do anything that might mess things up for you, okay? You don't have to tell me anything if you don't want to, but sometimes it's good to have someone in your court, someone who knows what you're fighting for, someone to cheer you on. If you need a someone like that, I can be her. I do know how to keep my mouth shut when it's important, okay?"

A lump rose in his throat, and he reached over and briefly squeezed Cass's hand where it rested on the console between them. "Thank you." He didn't say anything else until they'd pulled into the parking lot at The Smokehouse. He turned off the ignition, but he continued to gaze out the windshield at the front entrance of the bar and grill.

"Collin?" Cass prodded. "You okay with this? Want me to go ahead of you so she won't think we came—" She broke off and waved a finger back and forth between them. "Together? Or, God forbid, that you and I are an item?"

Something in her voice made him angry all over again. Not at her, though. At guys like Jimbo. At Joe, for that matter. At all the men who hurt women like her, even unintentionally.

At men… yep. At men like himself.

He needed to start setting things right immediately. And not just with Prudence.

He shook his head, swallowed hard, then turned to face her. "I would never, not in a million years, be embarrassed to be seen with you, Cassidy Whitehouse."

Her eyes teared up instantly, glistening under the bright glow of the streetlight overhead. "You know," she murmured, her voice choked up. "I think that might be the nicest thing anyone has said to me in a very long time."

"Then you need to get yourself some different friends," he said, taking her hand and squeezing her fingers in his. "You are lovely. You are kind. You are generous. You are perfect, just the way you are. That's the kind of thing you should be hearing from the people in your life. Every day."

"Well, now, I think *that's* the nicest thing anyone has said to me in—well, since the last nicest thing you said to me two seconds ago." She laughed shakily, then leaned in and hugged him hard. "Are you sure I can't just keep you to myself? I'd take good care of you, you know."

Collin grinned at her when she pulled back. "How about you take good care of my secret instead?"

Cass's eyes went wide, and she did that quick, quiet clapping thing again. She nodded and pressed her lips together, then mimed drawing a zipper across her mouth.

"It's kind of..." He couldn't think of the right word to describe the situation, at least not one single word. "Well, I broke this person's heart, but I had to. I had no choice; it was for her own good."

Cass frowned and cocked her head at him. "Really? You dumped her for her own good? You're going to pull that card?"

"Really. I'm not pulling any card, either. It's the truth. I had no choice but to walk away, and I assure you, it nearly killed me to do so. From what I can tell, she didn't fare much better. I want to try to make amends, Cass."

"Amends? That's all?" Her brow furrowed as she narrowed her eyes at him. "A simple apology would be enough to make amends. A letter. A card. A bouquet of flowers if you're going all out."

"Nope. Not for this person."

"Because you're not back here to just make amends, are you?"

"Not anymore," he admitted out loud for the first time. "I think I'd convinced myself that was all I needed to do, you know, look her in the eye and tell her why, that I'm sorry, and we'd all have closure and I could get on with my life. But the moment I saw her, I knew—I knew—" He broke off, the things he knew filling him so fully that he could hardly catch his breath.

"You knew what?" Cass whispered into the still cab.

"I can't walk away again, Cass. Not without knowing for sure that there's no hope for a second chance between us."

"Who is she?" Cass was still whispering, and her hands were now pressed to her bosom, crossed over her heart.

He hesitated, but then, before he could lose his resolve, he acknowledged the woman he loved for the first time to someone other than his own reflection. "Prudence Goodacre."

To his surprise, Cass gasped, then laughed, then punched him in the shoulder again, this time really hard. "I think I *hate* the Goodacre girls. They get all the good ones."

"Oww," Collin growled, rotating his shoulder painfully. "That's going to leave a mark."

"Dang straight," she muttered, crossing her arms like a pouting child. "Sorry. Not sorry."

"Maybe I shouldn't have told you," he snipped back at her, but the relief that washed over him the moment he'd made his admission nearly wiped out the pain in his shoulder.

"Oh, please. I'm allowed to throw a hissy fit, okay? I haven't indulged in one for ages."

Collin couldn't help but laugh. "Fine. But just don't hit me again. You, of all people, should know not to hit." And there he went, cramming his foot into his mouth and shoving it down his throat again. "Ah crap," he muttered. "I'm sorry. I shouldn't have said that."

"Actually, no, you're right," Cass quipped, surprising him. "I'm the one who's sorry. You're absolutely right. Hitting is hitting, no matter what, and I would be really ticked off if the roles were reversed." She sounded like she'd just had an epiphany.

"It's fine," he assured her. "No big deal. I'm just a wimp."

"It is a big deal, Collin. And I'm glad you said something." She waved away anything else he might say. "So tell me. Why did you think you had to break dear Prudence's heart? That girl is an angel. A fairy wood-elf magical being angel. And she deserves someone like you." She pointed at his chest. "You deserve someone like her. I can totally see you two making it work."

"Think back, Cass." He didn't know if he could bring himself to say the words out loud. He took a steadying breath, then waved a hand in a circular motion gesturing at his face. "A single black male teacher only a few years older than my teenage students—"

"God. Bless. America!" Cass gasped and brought her hands to her cheeks as understanding donned. "She was still in high school when all this went down? In your class?"

He nodded. "Yep. She was my student."

"You naughty boy, Collin. Or should I say Mr. Stewart. Every high school girl's fantasy hot teacher. What did I tell you?" She was cackling now like a mad hen. "Oh my gosh, Collin! Although, honestly, I doubt you being black would have made things any worse."

Collin shook his head. "Not true, Cass, and you know it. The color of my skin isn't something folks ignore."

Cass frowned, but didn't disagree. Maybe it didn't matter to her, but she was a local girl, and she knew well that old prejudices ran deep in some circles. "Still," she finally said. "Why couldn't you wait until she graduated?"

"I wanted to," he said, not sure how much—or how little—he could get away with telling her. "But things, um, happened too fast, and—"

"Whoa. Things *happened*? Tell me, Collin," she demanded, reaching out to grab his chin, turning his face so he had to look at her. "Are you telling me that you two—you and that delightful little Goodacre girl—hooked up when she was still in high school? In your class? That's so wrong, Collin."

"No!" He jerked back like she'd struck him again. "Get your mind out of the gutter, Cass. Nothing happened, at least not like that. It just wasn't the right timing, okay?"

Cass shook her head slowly, absorbing what little he'd told her. Then she let out an explosive sound and with her hands, made a gesture that mimed fireworks over her head. "Mind blown, dude. Seriously."

"Okay, okay. I get it." Collin was suddenly regretting having shared his deep, dark secret with her now. "Pick your jaw up off the seat."

"I don't get it. If nothing happened..." She shook her head, her eyes distant, like she was going back through old memories. "You left town so sudden like; I remember now. Something *had* to have happened between you two," she insisted softly.

"It wasn't like that. I mean, yes, I found myself..." He stumbled over his words, stuttering and backtracking as he tried to explain. "I kind of—I mean, I did fall—I was drawn to her."

"Drawn to her? What are you? Some regency romance hero?" Cass was teasing, but not really mocking him.

"Drawn to her, yes. And she to me." He ignored the regency romance hero quip. "But it wasn't some sordid, perverse, creepy thing, okay?" And yet, even now, it still felt like it was. "It happened slowly, without me even realizing until it was there. Here." He thumped his chest with his fist. "Until I realized I was in love with her."

"Oh, Collin. What did you do? Did she have the hots—" She broke off at his scowl and rephrased her question. "Did she care for you?" Cass's hands were pressed to her chest again. "Wait. She must have. You said you broke her heart. Oh, Collin."

"Yes. Yes, to all of it."

"Did you, um, *act* on any of it?" The question was asked quietly, her words chosen carefully, he could tell.

"I acted, all right. I acted on it by resisting temptation and humiliating her." He let out a rueful snort. "I basically ran from her, leaving her standing in her garden holding onto my sweater." He scrubbed at his face with one hand, then added, "Holding my heart."

Cass sat quietly for several moments, then finally, she said, "And now you've come back for it. Your heart, not the sweater."

He nodded.

"If I know anything about women, and I'd like to think I do, then I would bet she still has your sweater, if you want that back, too."

Collin chuckled wryly. "Actually, I don't want my heart back. I want *her* heart. And she can keep my sweater, too."

"Then go get it. Go get her," she reiterated. "Come on. I'm in your court, Mr. Hottie McStewart."

"Cass," he said, his voice dark with warning.

"I promise to be on my best behavior," she said, holding her hand up. "Because I want at least one of us in this decrepit old truck to get their happily ever after, okay?"

He shook his head. "Let's shoot for both of us getting that."

"Sounds like a plan. You ready, you big stud?"

Collin rolled his eyes, then pushed open his door, suddenly feeling claustrophobic inside the close confines of the vehicle. He circled the hood of the truck and opened Cass's door, then waited patiently while she did a last-minute check of her lipstick in the visor mirror.

"How do I look?" Cass asked, straightening her shirt and smoothing down the legs of her tight jeans. She planted her hands on her hips and struck a pose.

"Beautiful," Collin assured her, and he meant it. Everyone had their own version of outer beauty, and hers may not be in line with his personal taste, but that didn't mean she wasn't beautiful. "Inside and out. Just the way you are."

Cass patted his cheek tenderly. "You know, if she turns you down, I'm not too proud to accept her castoffs. You remember that, okay?"

"I'll keep that in mind," he said. Then with a hand on her back, he ushered her toward the front door of The Smokehouse.

Inside, the music pulsed hard and loud, and the place was packed, especially for a Sunday night. But then, word had gotten out that Abby Goodacre was back in town and would be live on stage for one night only. Folks from all over were crowding the tables and booths, there to see their darling hometown up-and-coming country superstar. The girl about whom they could say, "I knew her when..."

Collin took Cass's hand, but let her lead the way through the crowd on a hunt for some place to sit. They paused often to greet folks one or both of them knew, and all the while, he kept his eyes peeled for any of the Goodacre clan. But the room seemed devoid of them. He spoke loudly near Cass's ear. "I don't see her here. Any of them," he added.

"They're probably in the family room," she shouted back. "It's new since you were last here. For bigger parties. Come on. I'll show you."

"Wait! Hold up," he said, trying to tug her backwards. He wasn't ready for this. Not yet.

"Don't be a coward, Collin Stewart. This is your moment. Seize it." She tugged harder, and he stumbled along after her.

"Howdy, folks!" A familiar voice boomed over the sound system. Hank the DJ from the wedding. Hank... a man who'd spent a great deal of time flirting with Prudence. Dancing with her. Teasing her. Making her laugh.

Competition.

He fought the sudden urge to throw in the towel, to admit that this was going to require too much work, and without any promise of succeeding.

He probably didn't have what it took, anyway, especially compared to Hank the Music Man. Or Terrell Jackson the Horse Whisperer. Or Taylor Baucom, the Brick Layer. Or...

"Shut up," he snarled to himself.

"What was that?" Cass asked over her shoulder.

"Nothing," Collin answered with a quick shake of his head. "Lead on," he simply said, putting his head down to push through the crowds with gritty determination. Then he plowed into her when she stopped directly in front of him.

"There they are," she declared, gesturing grandly beyond a wide arched doorway that led into a room sectioned off from the rest of the open floor plan. It was only slightly quieter in the large party room, but not because of the music or Hank's booming voice. There were a lot of people seated around the two long tables, and everyone seemed to be talking at once. Cass waved at Faith who'd looked up when they appeared n the doorway.

Collin, however, had eyes only for Prudence, and the moment his gaze landed on her, it was like she felt it. Her head lifted sharply, and she swiveled in her seat away from the conversation she'd been having with Faith and Hope's daughters, and she stared wide-eyed at him. Then her eyes darted to Cass, down to their clasped hands, and back to Collin, narrowing just the tiniest bit.

Well, dang it.

Oblivious, Cass dragged him into the room behind her. "Hello to the largest family in the whole Lanner County. I see you got the best tables in the house." They were off to the side of the main room, but they had a direct shot of the stage, and they were close enough to see and be seen by whoever stood behind the microphone. A young man named Bucky was their server, and he couldn't stop ogling Abby between refilling water glasses and taking orders. Cass directed her dazzling smile at the man at the head of the table. Unlike all the ladies, Mr. Goodacre's mouth was set in a grim line. "Why, Mr. Goodacre, you're outnumbered tonight, aren't you? Where are all the menfolk?"

She was right, Collin realized. Other than Baby Ollie and the silent, salivating Bucky, Jed was the only representative of the male species in the room. Five of the seven Goodacre sisters were present and accounted for, Faith's daughter and Hope's stepdaughter were there, and seated side by side a few chairs down from Jed, were Sarah Lynxwilder and Charlotte Rawlings. The eldest sisters' husbands, Cord, Levi, and Frank were glaringly absent. And Collin hadn't even noticed, so focused was he on Prudence.

"There was an incident at the ranch." Faith waved at the air in front of her as though the explanation was hardly worth giving. "A randy bull got loose. He manages to do so at least once about this time of year." The single arched eyebrow was the only indication that she was bothered by the incident. "They'll be here as soon as they round him up. They've only got a skeleton crew on site tonight with it being the weekend, and Cord wasn't about to let old Binks try to corral the stupid bull on his own."

Collin looked at her in surprise. "Binks is still around?" The foreman at Whispering Hills had been ancient for as long as he could remember.

"That old geezer won't retire," Faith scoffed. "He insists he'll know when it's his time to go, and he plans to just wander off into the woods and lie down somewhere."

"Like a dog," Jasmine said in a hushed, reverent tone.

"Jasmine!" Faith balled up a napkin and flicked it across the table at her daughter.

"What?" The girl flicked the napkin back at Faith, and Ollie let out a delighted squeal at the game.

"You could join us and boost the odds. Do poor old Jedediah a kindness," Charlotte Rawlings said with a teasing glance in Jed's direction. The man caught the look, and his brows drew together as he scowled back at her.

"Please do," Faith said, waving them inside. "We've got lots of empty chairs, and it's crowded as sin out there."

Cass lifted questioning eyes at Collin, but she didn't wait for his response. "We'd love to, right, Collin?"

He nodded against his will. This wasn't happening quite the way he'd planned.

"Here. Take my seat," Abby said, pushing to her feet from where she sat on Prudence's other side. "I'm up in a few minutes and you can see the stage better from this side of the table." She flashed Collin a wide-eyed grin, all artificial innocence, if he read her correctly. She patted the table in front of her. "Best seat in the house right here, Mr. Stewart." Then she skirted her chair and actually held it out for him, waiting for him to come around the table and sit.

There was nothing for him to do but capitulate or make a scene, and he had no desire to make a scene right now. It didn't help that Cass practically shoved him in that direction, almost forgetting to release his hand first, so that he stumbled awkwardly right in front of Jed.

The Goodacre patriarch greeted him with a nod. He didn't smile, and he said nothing.

Once again, Collin resisted the urge to turn tail and run. Instead, he made it around the end of the table without further mishap and sat gingerly in the chair Abby still held for him. "Thank you," he said, barely glancing up at her. The knowing look on her face made him want to accidentally scoot his chair back and set one of the legs on her booted foot. It was a vicious thought and he felt terrible as soon as it arose in his mind. But as she hurried out of the room, Collin could feel the lingering sentiment squat like a nasty little toad in his gut. He didn't need any help right now. Not from Cass, not from Abby. He needed to take back the reins and do this the right way. His way.

Beside him, Prudence glanced at him quickly, and said, "Mr. Stewart," then turned back to continue her conversation with the two girls on her other side.

Dismissed. Why had he let Cass drag him in here?

He shot her a disparaging look as she took a seat on the other side of the table next to Sarah Lynxwilder. Sarah greeted her, introduced her to Charlotte Rawlings, then flashed one of her warm smiles at Collin.

"It's so good to see you again, Collin. I hardly got a chance to visit with you last night, so I'm thrilled that you've joined us here. You've met Charlotte, right?"

"We've met," Charlotte confirmed, but she stretched her long arm across the table anyway and offered him her hand to shake.

"Nice to see you again, Ms. Rawlings." When he released her hand, he bumped Prudence's water glass with his elbow and had to scramble to catch it before it toppled. "Sorry," he said to no one in particular, since Prudence continued to pay him no attention.

The surly "hrrumph" from the end of the table had him glancing up to see Jed watching the whole exchange with a scowl on his face. "Some people shouldn't be allowed out in public."

Shocked by the harsh words, Collin opened his mouth to apologize again, but Jed had turned his scowl in the direction of Charlotte.

"Stop looking at us like we're a bunch of ill-behaved children, Jed," the woman said, flipping her silver hair over her shoulder and tossing the man a saucy smile. Was she *flirting* with him?

"If the shoe fits," Jed shot back, still frowning, but Collin thought he saw one side of the man's mouth quirk up for just an instant.

"That's what the prince said to Cinderella, and look where it got them," Charlotte replied, her slow drawl overly sweet. "Happily ever after, that's where."

She *was* flirting with him. And if Collin was reading things right, Jed wasn't completely immune to it. Or completely unreceptive. He may not be handling it with much aplomb, but his indignant frown felt oddly disingenuous.

"Be mindful of the company you keep, son." Now the old man's attention was back on Collin. Great.

"Why, Jedediah Goodacre," Charlotte interjected. "Aren't you the pot calling the kettle black? You're the only one at this table apparently not having a good time."

Lord, have mercy, Collin did not want to see any more of this, and he certainly didn't need to get caught in the crossfire between Mr. Goodacre and Ms. Rawlings, whatever was going on. He had his own battle to wage, although he hoped he and Prudence would be ending things with a peace treaty. He had no desire to lob hand grenades at each other the way the older combatants were.

He turned to say something to Joe's mother, but the words died on his tongue. What he saw in her eyes looked suspiciously sad, like surrender, as she, too, watched Jed and Charlotte exchange one-liners. Oh, no. Not the lovely Mrs. Lynxwilder, too. Why were so many women in the hollow walking around with unrequited love and wounded hearts?

"Oof." Someone kicked him under the table. He grimaced in pain and reached down to rub his shin. He looked up to catch Cass staring open-mouthed back and forth between Charlotte and Jed before making a goofy face at Collin. So he wasn't the only one who'd noticed the unsettling interplay.

"You all right?" Prudence's soft question beside him caused him to snap to attention. He straightened in his chair, his throbbing shin forgotten.

"Um, yeah. Just bumped my leg under the table." But by the time he got the words out, Prudence's attention was on Cass, the expression on her face mirroring some of the surliness on her father's.

"How are things at Serendipity's?" Prudence asked politely. Collin could hear no trace of anything untoward in her question, but with all the mixed messages and convoluted emotions swirling around the room, he felt a little like he was sitting in the eye of a storm. One wrong move, one wrong word, heck, one wrong thought could send him tumbling end over end.

"This weekend was a little slow, of course, with the wedding, but otherwise, it's going like gangbusters," Cass said, her smile bright.

Maybe a little too bright, Collin thought. Was Cass putting on her Rom-Com-Meet-Cute-Matchmaker hat?

"Everything was so beautiful yesterday, Prudence," Cass continued. "Even the weather cooperated, didn't it?"

"Thank you," came Prudence's carefully modulated reply. "I didn't see you at the reception."

"No," Cass confirmed, her smile slipping just a bit. "Someone had to man the counter, and everyone wanted to be there for the big event. I chose to go to the ceremony and let the rest of my team attend the reception."

"That was really great of you," Sarah interjected kindly, resting a hand on Cass's arm. Cass's old obsession with Joe was no secret, so it stood to reason that Sarah would know about it, too. Collin thought his friend's mother was one of the most gracious women he'd ever met, even more so now as he watched her maintain her dignity while her new friend appeared to be getting quite a kick out of flirting with Jedediah Goodacre. Apparently, Sarah's eye had been on him, too, but she now appeared to be stepping back to let whatever was going on between Jed and Charlotte play out.

Then again, maybe the woman knew what she was doing. Charlotte wasn't from around here; she'd come in from Colorado just for the wedding, hadn't she? Once she was gone, Sarah would have Jed all to herself again.

Collin mentally shook his head. It was like one big soap opera and he couldn't keep up.

"So have you found anything in this area to your liking?" Prudence directed the question at the silver-haired woman across the table, drawing Collin's attention back to her. What did she mean by that? Was Charlotte considering moving to the hollow? And had Prudence read his thoughts?

Charlotte's eyes lit up. "You'll never believe it, but I met a man named Dan Lanyard out in Benton County this afternoon, and he raises sheep. They're nothing like the specialty breed I raise, but they're sheep, nonetheless." She laced her heavily ringed fingers together on the table in front of her and leaned forward a little, excitement radiating off of her. "He assured me that they thrive out here."

"Well, that's good to know," Prudence said, her expression pleasant as she nodded at Charlotte. But Collin wondered what was going on in her head as he watched her fingers tracing patterns into the condensation on the water glass he'd almost knocked over. The way she couldn't seem to stop fidgeting made him think she might be as nervous as he was.

"It certainly set my mind at ease. I've seen two properties on the market around here that I could probably manage, although they'd both require a significant amount of work to accommodate my flock and my wool production operation. But the sale of my place in Colorado would bring in plenty to take care of what I'd need. It would just be timing the transition right for all of us. I've never moved the whole flock at once, and certainly never this far. Lord willing, I'll figure it out, though. The more time I spend out here, the more reasons I'm finding to make me want to stay." She nudged Sarah's shoulder with her own. "I've lived out in the middle of nowhere for so long, I've almost forgotten how nice it is to have friends." She shot a teasing grin at Jed. "Even cranky ones."

Jed shook his head and muttered something under his breath, then homed in on the stage where Abby was getting set up. The crowd was still buzzing with activity beyond the private room, but the noise had diminished greatly, the air electric with anticipation.

Abby hadn't just changed physically, Collin soon discovered. She'd grown into her voice, and her voice, in turn, had matured and blossomed into something that legends were made of. Not that Collin was an expert in music, but from the first drawn out note that poured out of her mouth, the room of people were transfixed. Enthralled. She held everyone, including him, in the web of emotions she cast over them with her songs.

Beside him, he could hear Prudence sniffling softly, likely as overwhelmed by her sister's talent as he was. He heard her sharp intake of breath when she accidentally—or was it intentionally? Dare he hope?—brushed her arm against his as she reached for one of the paper napkins from a dispenser in the middle of the table. She didn't pull away when he slid the old-fashioned metal contraption close, causing their shoulders to bump. Nor did she do more than flinch ever so slightly when he shifted in his seat and his knee nudged hers under the table.

Collin mustered every ounce of courage he could manage and leaned toward her. In a quiet voice, one he hoped no one else at the table would pay attention to, he said, "You look... lovely, Prudence." Was that word too poetic, too cheesy, too English professor? It was true, though. She was ethereal, not fragile. Reserved, not shy. Careful, but not afraid...

At least, he didn't remember her as being afraid.

Prudence made a soft derisive sound behind the napkin. "Even with a red nose and tears?"

"Tears for the right reason are always lovely," he murmured.

NINETEEN

What was she supposed to say to that? Did he have any idea the oceans of tears she'd shed because of him? Any clue how much pain—not loveliness—each tear represented?

Prudence couldn't bear it. She couldn't bear the closeness of him, right there beside her, breathing the same air as she was. She could feel warmth radiating off of him; the whole left side of her body felt combustible. When their arms brushed, she half-expected sparks to crackle between them. And his smell. Oh, mercy, she could confirm that the olfactory senses did, indeed, have long memories. It wasn't a typical men's barbershop cologne he wore; there weren't any woodsy undertones or hints of Middle Eastern spice markets. Whatever he used reminded her of sunny days in the herb garden, where everything was green and earthy, making a person want to touch, bend closer, draw in the aroma of goodness and life.

Now she was being dramatic. He just smelled good. He smelled like Collin Stewart. He may have gotten a new look with his close-cropped hair and contact lenses. He may have traded in his cardigans with their elbow patches for a black leather jacket, his loafers for boots, and his economy Toyota for a roadster, but he still smelled exactly the same as he had the last time that she sat this close to him.

"Are you feeling better after last night?" he asked, leaning in so he didn't have to speak louder. It was all she could do not to pull away.

"I'm much better. Thank you for asking," she said, praying her voice wouldn't give out on her. "Yesterday was a long day, and I didn't get to bed until pretty late. So I played hooky this morning since I had the house to myself, and I rested."

"I'm glad to hear that. I missed you in church this morning."

So he'd noticed. Had he looked for her? Had he come here tonight looking for her, too? Then why did he arrive with Cass Whitehouse?

Cass. The woman was perfect in all the ways Prudence wasn't. Confident, secure in her feminine bounty, a successful business owner, and Plumwood Hollow's favorite baker to boot. Most importantly, she was Collin's age. Oh, and she was single and looking for a husband; something she wasn't reticent to admit. And not in a sleazy way, either. She simply had no qualms about letting folks know that she was on the lookout for a good man who would love and respect her for who she was, a man whom *she* could love and respect for who he was. Nor should she be ashamed, either. Cass Whitehouse was good people. She was kind and warm to everyone who crossed her path, she was a good friend to those in her circle, and she was generous and loving and loyal to a fault. So much so that the few times she'd been in any kind of serious relationship, it had been with men who took advantage of her goodness. She'd make someone a fantastic wife, Prudence had no doubt, if only she could figure out how to find a man who would make a fantastic husband.

Cass needed someone like Collin Stewart.

No. Prudence clenched her jaw to keep from heading down that mental rabbit trail. *Thank goodness he doesn't live here anymore.*

The thought was bittersweet. Thank goodness he didn't live in the hollow so she wouldn't have to see him courting Cass. Thank goodness he didn't live in the hollow so she wouldn't have to face her own heartbreak, her shame, her humiliation every stinking day. Thank goodness...

"Your sister sounds amazing." Collin leaned close again, their shoulders bumping. "Cass said she's been in Nashville for the last year working on an album. That's fantastic."

"She is." Prudence nodded and reached for her water glass. She took a slow sip. "Some big music guy came through town last year and heard her sing here at The Smokehouse. He's kinda taken her under his wings. Justice, our family lawyer," she said, forming air quotes around the words, "still doesn't quite trust him." She chuckled, then gestured at the stage. "But as you can see, she's come a long way since leaving home."

"She sounds like she'll go a lot farther, too," he agreed. "I remember being blown away by her back when she was just a kid, so I'm glad to see she's pursuing her dreams. You Goodacre women are all pretty amazing. Gifted in your ways, and not afraid to go after what you want. Your father must be proud."

Prudence nodded slowly, considering his words. *Except for me.* Surely, he wasn't mocking her, was he? But then, how could he possibly know what her life had been like in the five years since she'd graduated from high school? Since he'd walked out of her life and away from Plumwood Hollow? "Yes," she said, forcing her voice to remain steady. "Dad is proud of all of his girls." Hopefully, he'd take the subtle hint and not try to engage her in any more conversation. She wanted to hear Abby sing, but more than that, she *didn't* want to hear Collin speak. Especially when he leaned close to do so. She needed to get away from him before she did something to betray the way his mere presence in the room made her feel.

"Hey, Pru!" Tanner Baucom sauntered into the room. "Your sister's playing our song. Wanna dance?" He lifted his arms as if he held an invisible partner and did a quick shimmy, thrusting his hips forward in a way that made Prudence's father frown and Faith laugh.

Pru closed her eyes. Which would be the lesser of two evils? Dance with the gregarious Tanner to Abby singing Shania Twain's "I Feel Like a Woman," or remain sitting there beside a man who made her insides quiver with each mundane word he spoke? She pushed to her feet.

"Excuse me," she murmured to Collin, then fixed her smile on Tanner. "Are you leading, or am I?" she teased as she let him draw her out to the floor where several folks were already singing along with Abby.

This was supposed to be a night of celebrating, after all. They were here to have fun, not to sit and wallow in what once was, what could have been, and what would never be. Things were already a little off kilter because of whatever was going on between Charlotte and Daddy. She'd never seen him behave so bristly toward a woman before, and as much as Charlotte fascinated Prudence, she could tell the woman made Daddy uncomfortable. No, more than uncomfortable. Charlotte unsettled him. And Jedediah Goodacre was, if nothing else, settled, steady, unshakable.

Or so Prudence had thought.

And now, with Collin back in the hollow, even if only for the weekend, everything seemed to be on shaky ground. So, she was going to dance with Tanner Baucom. She was going to let the man sweep her out onto the dance floor, spin her around the room, leave her breathless, her heart pounding from the exertion, and hopefully, in so doing, take her mind off the man who'd caused her heart to almost stop beating altogether.

Even as she moved, light and loose in Tanner's arms, her mind kept scrambling back to Collin Stewart. As Tanner spun her past the room where her family held court, her eyes locked with Collin's. The look on his face as he watched her—intense, heated, brooding—made her knees go a little weak. She misstepped slightly, and Tanner pulled her up against him to keep her from stumbling.

"You all right, Miss Pru?" he asked, grinning down at her from under the brim of his hat. "Am I wearing you out already?"

"Whew!" She laughed and shook her head. No. Collin Stewart wasn't going to steal this evening from her. She straightened her shoulders and leaned back to look up to meet Tanner's smile. Fanning her face with the hand she'd rested on his shoulder, she said, "You're a hard man to keep up with, Mr. Baucom."

"I'd slow down for you any day, darlin'. You just say the word." He pressed her closer, his splayed fingers on her back sliding a bit lower.

"Now, that is a lie if I ever heard one," she countered, reaching around to nudge his hand back up again. "It would take a very special woman to bring you to heel, my friend, and if I can't keep up with you for one song, I'm certainly not the lady to lasso your heart."

"Aw, come on now," Tanner teased, two-stepping with ease around the other dancing couples. "You haven't even given me a fair shake."

It was the same conversation they'd had—or a variation of it—since they'd shared one date a couple years back. It had been obvious to her that theirs would never be a romantic relationship, but Tanner had refused to believe it without her giving him a fair shake. "One date," he'd insisted. "If I can't change your mind in one date, then I'll stop asking." Less than an hour in, Tanner had tossed his napkin on the table, and with a capitulating grin, said, "Change of plans. Let's go have some fun, instead." They'd ended up at Ladies Night at The Smokehouse, and the women cheered when Tanner danced to Shania's warrior cry right along with the best of them.

"I'll give you a fair shake," she said with a laugh, and reached up to cup his chin and shook his head back and forth. "That's a no, darlin'." She used the same endearment he had a moment before. "Besides, I couldn't stay friends with you if you broke my heart, and I don't have enough of them to risk losing even one. Especially one as good looking as you are, Tanner Baucom."

He rolled his eyes. "Now, I can't even be offended by that rejection," he said, then spun her around with one hand lifted above her head and dipped her into a back bend as Shania sang out her final, "Man, I feel like a woman."

"Let me buy you a drink," Tanner said when Abby switched gears on stage and transitioned into an old Patsy Cline crowd pleaser. "This song always makes me wanna cry, and I hate cryin' or drinkin' alone."

"Sure," she said agreeably. Prudence wasn't ready to go sit quietly beside Collin again, pining for what could never be hers. This was her life, the life she'd chosen. Maybe by default, but she knew as well as the next gal that not choosing anything is still making a choice. She had more than enough to be content with—her family all close by or at least within visiting range, her father in good health, a roof over her head, at least for now, and her garden and the things that came out of it. Even if nothing ever came of her ideas for Seven Virtues Ranch, she loved planning events with Trilby and making her botanical body care products, and she'd be satisfied with that if that's how the chips fell.

They ponied up to the bar, and while Tanner ordered them a couple of drinks from Badger the bartender—so called because of the nearly white streaks at his temples in his otherwise black hair—Prudence greeted those around her.

Tanner helped her up onto the only empty stool, then stood close behind her with one arm resting on the bar on her other side. He wasn't quite touching her, but Prudence found his protective posture endearing. A warning, she thought, to other guys that she was under his watch.

The conversation around her was pleasant and comfortable, although the volume of the music made anything more intimate impossible, but Prudence found she was enjoying herself more than she'd thought she would. When Hank approached and asked her to dance, she didn't hesitate to take his proffered hand. She slid off the stool and made her way out to the dance floor with him.

Hank was taller and more solidly built than Tanner, and while Tanner moved with agility and enough energy for both of them, Hank had about him a quality that made her want to lean into him, to rest her head on his shoulder and let him lead. It was nice to be held by someone so much larger than she was. It reminded her of when she was little and she and her sisters used to take turns dancing with Daddy. That was before his accident, though. He didn't do much dancing these days, which was why it had been such a surprise—albeit a pleasant one—to hear that he'd done more than his perfunctory dance duties at the wedding reception last night.

But Prudence wasn't the kind of girl to lead a man on, and although she liked Hank well enough, she kept her boundaries firmly in place. She moved gracefully in his arms—he made it easy for her—and she thanked him again for his part in making the party out at the ranch such a memorable one. Hank responded by spinning her out, then tugging her back into him... but not before she'd caught sight of Daddy on the dance floor with the willowy and lithe Charlotte Rawlings in his arms, their eyes locked in what appeared to be either a fearsome battle of wills, or a magnetic pull neither of them were strong enough to break.

For a moment, Prudence wanted to squeal with glee, but right on the heels of that emotion came a wave of trepidation, one so strong it made her stumble a bit. Prudence's heart felt bruised by what she'd just seen, a deep ache for the way things used to be.

Things were changing too quickly. Why couldn't time slow down? What was wrong with the way things were?

"You alright?" Hank asked close to her ear so she could hear him.

"I'm fine," she assured him, then closed her eyes and rested her forehead against his chest. She didn't want to see anymore. Too much, too fast. She stayed that way until Abby crooned out the last line of the song.

Hank suddenly stopped moving, making her lift her head in surprise to find Collin beside them.

"May I cut in, Hank?" Collin asked, but he was watching her.

"Sure," the big man said, obviously not nearly as affected by Collin's sudden appearance as Prudence was. "Thanks for the spin, Miss Pru," he said, and then he was off, leaving her standing alone in the middle of the dance floor with the last man in the room she wanted to see.

Collin smiled tentatively at her. He held out a hand to her, palm up, leaving her with no choice but to agree or embarrass them both. She placed her hand in his, hoping he couldn't feel the slight tremor that coursed through her. He didn't pull her to him, but instead, he moved into her. As Abby began to play one of her own numbers, a song that whispered of cutting ties, second chances, and finding heaven, Collin slid his arm around her waist.

She forced herself to take a steadying breath, but inside her chest, it felt like she'd just drawn in the whole ocean, and that surely, she would drown.

As he pulled her closer, Prudence locked eyes with Faith over his shoulder. Her sister wore an expression that, for once, Prudence couldn't read. Then Faith nodded slowly before turning her attention to her husband and the other menfolk who'd just arrived from rounding up the runaway bull.

"Prudence." Collin said her name, but that was all. She lifted her gaze to meet his, letting the plaintive notes of Abby's voice soothe her spirit and quiet her mind.

Like a scene out of a Jane Austen movie, the rest of the room seemed to fade into the background. All around them, couples swirled and swept by in a blur, while the two of them moved slowly, out of time, out of place, lost in a memory of what might have been.

TWENTY

COLLIN COULD HARDLY BELIEVE he was actually holding Prudence Goodacre in the circle of his arms. She felt so fragile there, but like glass; stiff and unyielding, yet likely to shatter into a million pieces if he lost his grip on her. He dipped his head to speak close to her ear. "You're making me nervous," he said, only half-joking. "I'll relax if you will. I'm harmless, I can assure you."

Something in her eyes told him she knew better, and he stumbled.

"Sorry," he muttered. This was not going well. He closed his mouth and focused on the rhythm of the song, hoping the sweet melody would calm both their nerves. Finally, he tried again. "Prudence, I'd like to see you while I'm here."

She stared just past his shoulder as they moved around the dance floor. "You're seeing me now."

"No, not like this." So she wasn't going to make this easy. Fine. He deserved that. "Can I come out to the ranch to see you? Maybe sometime tomorrow? Or can we have lunch or dinner somewhere quiet where we can talk?" He couldn't get much blunter than that.

"Why?"

Collin wished he was the kind of guy who could just assert himself, who could confidently lead her off the dance floor and outside mid-song, so they could talk tonight. Now. Immediately.

"What do you want to talk to me about?" she prodded when he didn't respond fast enough.

"I want—no, I need—to apologize for—well, for what happened between us." He started stumbling over his words, so he left it at that for the moment.

"Apology accepted," she finally said.

It suddenly occurred to him that she wasn't just staring vacantly past his shoulders. Her eyes were locked with someone else's, and when he shifted so he could see, he found Faith and her husband, Cord, dancing together, but purposefully making their way through the couples toward them. His time was running out. "Please, Prudence," he said. "I owe you more than just an apology."

"You don't owe me anything, Mr. Stewart," she replied, closing her eyes briefly.

"But I do," he insisted. "I want to talk to you about the way I left things."

"You left things," she murmured, echoing his words back at him. "You left more than just *things*, Mr. Stewart."

"I know." How else could he respond to that heartbreaking statement? "And Collin, please. My name is Collin."

"I know your name."

"Will you see me if I come out to the ranch tomorrow?" he asked, all but begging now.

She didn't answer, but he could feel her trembling against him, and it made his heart sick.

"Mind if I cut in?" The light tap on his shoulder was Faith's, and he could do nothing but hand Prudence over to her big sister. Collin moved out of the way of the other dancers as he watched the two girls spin away from him. A moment later, he felt the presence of someone else.

Cord stood there, arms crossed, his eyes on the sisters, too, and Collin understood all too well what had just happened. Big sister and big brother looking out for their own.

"How long you in town for, Stewart?" Cord asked, his tone deceptively nonchalant, even though he was speaking loud enough to be heard over the music.

"A few days," Collin told him, remaining noncommittal. He wasn't sure how he felt about Cord and Faith's intervening, but he couldn't help wondering how much they knew about what had happened between Prudence and him all those years ago.

"I see." After a few moments, Cord asked, "You know what else I see?"

Collin turned to look directly at the tall, broad-shouldered cowboy beside him, but he didn't say anything.

"I see that my wife looks worried about her little sister."

Well. How did one argue with that?

But Prudence wasn't seventeen anymore. She wasn't eighteen anymore, either. And back when she was just a teenager, he'd done nothing wrong. He had nothing but his honorable intentions to defend, and that's what he aimed to do, if only Prudence would agree to speak with him privately.

No, he'd done the right thing, and he still stood by that. He'd walked away, even though Prudence had all but thrown herself at him. He'd walked away! He'd done the right thing. He hadn't even kissed her, he'd barely touched her, except to set her away from him. And then he'd taken an emergency leave from work, not for his sake, but for hers, so that she wouldn't have to bear the humiliation of that moment every time they saw each other during the last two weeks of her senior year. He'd stayed away all summer so that she could move forward with her plans for her future without having to face him again, certain that whatever she felt for him would fade once enough time had passed. When he realized that his own feelings for her hadn't faded, that they had even grown in the months he'd spent back home in Kennedy Heights, he'd taken the permanent position he now held as a fifth-grade teacher at 7 Hills Middle School in the nearby Madisonville neighborhood. Cincinnati was far enough away that he wouldn't be tempted to give in to his own desires and run back to Plumwood Hollow to claim her for himself.

He'd done everything right. Unlike Cordell Overman, the guy standing beside him now, the guy who knocked up Faith back when she was just eighteen, then abandoned her to raise his child without a daddy while he went off to chase his dreams of being a football superstar.

Collin did *not* feel compelled to defend his actions to Cord, at least not before he'd spoken to Prudence first. He owed her that.

"I know," he said, purposely misunderstanding Cord's indirect challenge. "I was there last night when Prudence fainted. I'm the one who carried her inside the house."

Cord nodded, but the expression on his face told Collin he knew an evasion tactic when he saw one. "And I thank you for that."

"You're welcome," Collin replied. "Excuse me." And with that, he made his way toward the bar where Cass was sitting, chatting animatedly with Badger.

When Cass saw him approach, she leapt off the stool and grabbed his hand. "Come dance with me, Collin," she demanded, then dragged him back out onto the dance floor after blowing Badger a kiss.

Collin chuckled at the woman's vivacity; Cass was a lot of fun, and he didn't want his downer mood to spill over onto her. She was obviously enjoying herself. But after the oh-so-polite rebuff he'd just gotten from Prudence's family, Collin wasn't sure he wanted to stick around. What he wouldn't give to be able to just call it a night and head back to his hotel room. He should opt to come on his bike and just meet Cass here.

Over her shoulder, he caught a glimpse into the arched opening of the party room, and saw Prudence drop into a chair beside her father. She rested her head on his shoulder and closed her eyes, and everything about her posture radiated weariness. She looked like she just wanted to go home, too. A prickle of guilt crept up his spine and made his neck warm, certain he'd been a contributing factor to her discomfort.

Halfway through the second verse of the song, Cass leaned back and eyed him. "You're not here, are you?" She made a playful pouty face up at him.

"Sorry." Collin grimaced. "I'm a rotten date, aren't I?"

Cass patted his cheek in that motherly way of hers. "I'm sure you'd make the right person a wonderful date. I'm just not that person, but we both knew that already. Wanna call it a night?"

"No, no," Collin countered, shaking his head. "You're having a good time."

"Don't be silly. I'll grab my house key off my keyring, then you can take my truck back to my place and get your bike. Just shove my keys through the mail slot on my door." She started to turn out of his arms.

"Wait," he said, drawing her back. "I'm not just going to leave you here without a ride," he protested.

Cass grinned and shimmied her shoulders like she was on the verge of spilling some juicy secret. She pointed at the bar, and when Collin glanced that way, he was a bit taken aback to find the bartender watching them, his beefy arms folded over his chest. "I've got a ride whenever I need one," Cass assured Collin. "Badger's good people, don't worry." She waved at the enormous man with his streaked hair, and Badger thrust his chin out in acknowledgment before turning to make a drink for another customer.

Collin hesitated for only a moment, then nodded, reassured by the sparkle of happiness in the woman's eyes. "If you're sure," he began.

"I'm sure. He's kinda cute, don't you think?" Cass asked, tipping her head in Badger's direction.

Collin chuckled. "I guess? If you like big, hairy guys named after animals."

"And I do," Cass sing-songed. "Indeed, I do."

Collin approached the bar with Cass and leaned across it to get Badger's attention. "I'm heading out, but we came in Cass's truck." He was pretty sure Badger already knew as much, but he wanted to do this right. "I need to make sure Cass is in good hands before I leave. She says you'll take her home?"

Badger's brows lifted affirmatively, then he stuck out his hand for Collin to shake. "I'll see she gets home. Be safe, man." The bartender shot a wink in Cass's direction.

Maybe there was a good man for Cass in Plumwood Hollow after all. Badger had been around a long time, and he ran a tight ship on the bar side of The Smokehouse. Rumor had it he was a teetotaler, and with Cass's history, that was a really good thing.

Collin pushed out into the surprisingly temperate autumn night and crossed the packed parking lot to the truck. He climbed inside the cab and closed the door behind him, his shoulders relaxing in the sudden stillness. Then his stomach growled. "Dang it," he muttered. "I wanted ribs tonight." Other than fast food joints or a few other bars, there weren't many eatery options open on a Sunday night in Plumwood Hollow. It seemed pretty silly for him to leave The Smokehouse and head somewhere just for food. No, he should dash back inside and order a meal to go. In fact, he'd call an order in and wait out here in the truck until it was ready.

"Give us about ten minutes," the woman said on the other end of the line.

Ten minutes to sit and brood over how unsuccessful he'd been at connecting with Prudence over the last two days.

Ten minutes to sit and berate himself for being so inept at making amends of any kind. He couldn't even get her to agree to set up a time to talk. He didn't want to take her away from the festivities; he was happy to wait for the right time. But he couldn't get her to commit one way or the other.

Ten minutes of listening to his stomach grumble and grouch. He was suddenly starving, and every minute that passed felt longer than the last.

At eight minutes and forty-three seconds, he could wait no longer. He took a few bills from his wallet, then reached for the door handle... and paused when he saw the double doors at the front of The Smokehouse swing open. Out walked Prudence, Faith, and Cord. Grateful he hadn't yet opened his door and lit up the interior of the cab, he slouched down in his seat, hoping he hadn't been seen. "I feel like a creep," he muttered under his breath.

The three of them slowly made their way through the parking lot to a small blue car and Prudence unlocked the driver's side door. Faith and Cord lingered only a few moments, thankfully, then they both hugged Prudence and stood back watching as she settled in behind the wheel and started her car. A moment later, the couple waved, then returned inside, Cord's arm wrapped possessively around his wife's waist.

As Prudence pulled out of the parking lot onto the street, Collin could hardly believe his good fortune. He'd wanted some time alone with her, away from her attentive family, away from the busyness of the weekend's celebrating. And now, here was his chance.

TWENTY-ONE

Prudence was hiding. There was no other way to spin it. She was tucked into her daddy's side and hiding from the world.

Or rather, from Collin Stewart.

His presence at the wedding had been a shock, his attendance at the reception had all but done her in, and him showing up at The Smokehouse—with Cass Whitehouse on his arm, no less—had her wanting to fade into the woodwork. Or just go home and crawl under her covers and make the whole world go away.

But when he suddenly appeared beside Hank and asked Prudence to dance with him?

She'd wanted to step into his arms, to lay her head on his shoulder, press her face to his neck so she could breathe in the scent of him, and stay there forever.

She couldn't bear it. Because she knew he'd only break her heart again. Collin had returned to Plumwood Hollow after all these years, but not for her. And no matter how she spun it, that truth never wavered. He'd arrived on a motorcycle with only the things that would fit in his saddlebags. He wasn't here to stay, he wasn't here to woo her, he wasn't here to pick up the pieces he'd left of her shattered heart. He was better than that, after all. Wasn't that what he'd said?

Collin Stewart was here to celebrate the wedding of his friend, to hang out with some of his old crowd, to flirt with some of the eligible Plumwood Hollow ladies, and then he was heading back home to Cincinnati.

Prudence would not, could not, allow him access behind the walls she'd so carefully constructed around the empty place that had once housed her heart.

"I think I need to go home, Daddy," she said. She gestured at Jasmine and Yvette at the other end of the table. "I can take the girls home with me, and that way Hope and Faith can stay as long as they like." She looked across the table at Charlotte who seemed enthralled with the sleeping baby in her arms. The older woman's face had the dreamy look of motherhood as she stared down at Ollie's chubby cheeks and button nose. His lips parted just enough to catch a glimpse of the tiny baby teeth he'd cut last month, and his lashes were long like his big sister's.

Charlotte caught Prudence watching her and smiled. "You're not taking him with you, though. He's mine, at least while he's sleeping." She sighed and lifted the baby higher so she could sniff his little head. "I can't remember the last time I got to just sit and hold a baby like this. It's pure bliss." She shot a look at Daddy. "With this whole slew of weddings in your family over the last couple of years, I have a feeling you're going to have a lot of these little blessings running around your house in the near future, Jedediah. You're a lucky man."

"God has given me much, indeed," Jed replied, his arm tightening around Prudence's shoulders in a fatherly squeeze. "If he chooses to keep pouring on the blessings, then it's only because he sees fit to do so, not because I'm lucky. Or worthy," he added.

When Prudence looked up at him, her father's eyes were locked with Charlotte's. After a thoughtful pause, the woman said, "Beloved friend of God. Your mother named you well, Jedediah Goodacre."

Prudence pulled away when her father stiffened. She glanced back and forth between him and Charlotte, curious at the exchange.

After a long pause, her father said, "I'd like to think so."

Charlotte lifted her brows as if waiting for further explanation, but when Jed offered none, she nodded, almost like she'd expected his reticence. And why wouldn't she? Jed wasn't known for being talkative, not even among his peers.

"I'm curious by nature," she finally said. "Your daughters are obviously named for the seven gospel virtues, as is your ranch, so I figured your name must have some profound meaning, too. As you pointed out, the good Lord has given you much, so it only stands to reason that you are, indeed, as your name indicates, a friend of his."

"I'd like to think so," Jed repeated.

"Although I have to wonder about Abstinence." She lifted a brow in question, and Prudence held her breath. Where was she going with this? "Has she ever felt she got the raw end of the deal being so named just because she came seventh in line?"

Well, say what you're thinking, why don't you? Prudence frowned. No doubt many shared Charlotte's opinion about Abby's admittedly controversial name, but it was rare to have anyone do more than comment on how unusual it was. Especially to Daddy's face.

"None of my daughters bear me ill will," Jed said calmly, but there was a fine razor's edge in his tone that Prudence recognized. Could Charlotte hear it, too?

"No, no, of course not," Charlotte said. "Abby has clearly risen above any derision the name might have evoked, especially in this day and age when abstinence is seen more often as a weakness than a virtue."

Jed opened his mouth, then closed it. His jaw clenched and his nostrils flared, then he took a deep breath and tried again. Still, nothing came out.

Charlotte forged ahead unchecked. "Has she never had to deal with cruel peers? Church ladies whispering behind her back? Boys with their minds in the gutter taking her name as a challenge?" She let out a low chuckle at Jed's reddening face. "Stop looking at me like I just slapped your daughter, Jedediah Goodacre. I'm a straight-talking woman and I was led to believe that you're a like-minded man. Am I truly the first to ever be curious about Abby's name?"

Prudence studied the woman across from her, but she didn't sense malice in her. In fact, she was certain Charlotte was more than a little interested in Daddy. So why, then, was she trying to provoke him? Because that's what it felt like to Prudence, and that didn't sit well with her, regardless of the motivation. *Keep cool, Prudence, Be not wise in your own eyes.*

Daddy rested his large hand over hers and squeezed, almost as if he read her mind. *I got this,* his grip told her.

Prudence relaxed a little, but now, even more so, she wanted to get out of here. Leave them to sort things out between them.

"No, you're not the first," her father replied. "But you are possibly the most pragmatic."

Charlotte laughed outright at that. "Why Jedediah Goodacre. I think that's the nicest thing anyone has said to me in a long while."

Jed cleared his throat. "You know, Miss Rawlings, abstinence is the decision to refrain from indulgence, particularly from taking license in something that might bring pleasure in moderation or in the moment, but that could just as easily cause pain or suffering if allowed to get out of hand."

Well played, Daddy. Prudence mentally high-fived her father.

"Indulgence, hm?" Charlotte shot him an impish grin. "Is indulgence such a bad thing?" When her father remained silent, Charlotte continued. "You know, I once despised my name. When I was a child. I was taller than my teacher by the time I was in third grade, and I was sapling thin. *Charlotte's Web* was a school reading requirement, and between Spider Girl, Insect, and Twiggy, I had to learn pretty quickly how to love who I was and love my name for what it was. By the way, did you know that a Charlotte is a rather decadent dessert?"

Prudence leaned forward to rest her forearms on the table in front of her. She could no longer tell if the woman was flirting or just being obstinate. "You know, Miss Charlotte, I'm usually the one in our family to say the things that others won't, so I can appreciate your straight talking, as you put it."

Daddy squeezed her hand again, and for a moment, Prudence thought he meant to shush her. But he sent her a gentle smile, not a rebuking one, so she continued, choosing her words carefully. "However, maybe rather than pointing out the negative side of something, especially something as powerful as a person's name, perhaps consider looking for the virtues in it, no play on words intended."

Charlotte turned her full attention on Prudence, and for a moment, she wondered if the older woman was going to argue. That one brow arched high as it had earlier, but all she said was, "Is that right?"

It wasn't in Prudence's nature to challenge her elders, and she didn't get any kind of thrill from putting people in their place, but it felt like lines were being drawn in the sand on some level she couldn't quite grasp, and she felt compelled to finish what she'd started. As gently as she could, considering the music still playing loudly in the main part of the restaurant, she said, "It isn't just about refraining from things like immorality, or alcohol, or decadent desserts. It's about practicing self-discipline, about refraining from selfish indulgence in things people feel entitled to, such as speaking their minds when holding their tongues might be better for everyone around them. Or expressing their opinions when their opinions might only create strife in the company they keep."

"Pix," Daddy said, squeezing her hand again, then turning to Charlotte. "Miss Rawlings—Charlotte. There is, indeed, a story behind the names of my daughters, and I am not averse to telling you. But it isn't an easy one and this is not the time and place for its telling. I hope you can understand that."

Charlotte closed her eyes briefly, and Prudence thought she saw remorse, maybe even embarrassment cross her face. Then she said, "I can't help feeling like you want an apology from me."

"No," Jed countered, his gaze fixed on the woman's face. "It's not an apology I want."

Prudence sat back in her chair, suddenly feeling like the third wheel she was. She looked out toward the stage where Abby perched on a stool, relaxed and confident as she belted out lyrics about past loves and old flames. Great. Would this night never end? She just wanted to go home. Now. And if she didn't have to see Collin Stewart again, didn't have to dance with him, didn't have to watch him dancing with anyone else, she'd be perfectly satisfied.

"Well, then," Charlotte said, drawing Prudence's attention back to the unsettling conversation taking place before her. The woman's tone had changed once again, and now the teasing was back. "What do you want from me, Jedediah Goodacre?"

Okay. Enough. She didn't mind the idea of her father showing interest in someone; it was about time. Mama had been gone for almost twenty years. But she didn't really want a front row seat for it. "Excuse me," she said, pushing to her feet. "It was nice to see you again, Charlotte. Daddy, I'm going to head home. I have a headache starting and I think I just need to go to bed. I think I'll leave the girls here, if you're okay to keep an eye on them." Besides, they could referee or call for help if the two mature adults at the table got into fisticuffs. Prudence bit back a smirk at that notion.

At that moment, Faith and Cord swept into the room, their cheeks flushed, and smiles on full wattage.

"Walk me out, will you?" Prudence asked before anyone could say anything. "The last several days are catching up to me and I'm going to call it a night and turn in early."

Faith studied her for a moment, then nodded. After saying her goodbyes, she headed out through the crowded restaurant, her sister and brother-in-law close on her heels. She made it to her car without seeing Collin, ignoring the weight of disappointment that settled in the pit of her stomach. She promised Faith she was going straight home, got in her car, and headed for the ranch, gleefully anticipating a rich cup of hot chocolate, a piece of leftover wedding cake, and having the whole place to herself.

TWENTY-TWO

For a moment, Collin almost forgot about his order of ribs. He wanted to peel out of the parking lot and follow her, but he refrained. No, he needed to get his bike. He needed to pay for the order he put in. He probably needed to eat, too—he didn't want his stomach interrupting anything he had to say to Prudence. Besides, if he took the time to pick up his order, eat it, and exchange the truck for his bike before he headed out to the ranch, that would make him look less like a stalker, wouldn't it? Less like he'd followed her home?

Praying he wouldn't bump into any of the Goodacre party, Collin dashed inside the building. Relieved to find his order waiting for him at the front, he handed over his cash, refused the change, and was on his way back to Cass's condo. The aroma of ribs filled the cab, making him salivate, but he waited until he pulled up in front of her place before pulling the takeout container from the paper bag and popping open the foil cover. Thankfully, several napkins and a fork were included, and he dug into the side of creamy mashed potatoes first with great relish.

It was all just as delicious as he remembered it, and even though he'd scarfed down the food in record time, he was glad he hadn't foregone the meal. He checked his reflection in the visor mirror, and satisfied that he didn't have rib meat in his teeth or barbecue sauce on his face, he popped one of the mints they'd included with his meal into his mouth in lieu of a good teeth brushing, then made quick work of exchanging Cass's truck for his bike. Hunger sated, helmet on, jacket zipped against the chill of the night, Collin was on the road heading out to the ranch in record time.

His bike was loud in the quiet night, especially once he hit the outskirts of Plumwood Hollow and got on the long stretch of Carpenter Road. "Nothing subtle about this, Stewart," he muttered under his breath. She'd hear him coming miles away.

Instead of pulling up in front of the ranch house, he followed the driveway around back and parked his bike in clear view of the back door. He wanted her to know he wasn't trying anything sneaky, that he was being as transparent as possible, in spite of having essentially just followed her home from the bar. "That's not creepy at all, man."

Collin took his time removing his helmet and jacket, then squared his shoulders and headed up the porch steps. There was a light on in the kitchen, but otherwise, the house appeared unoccupied. He glanced around, second-guessing his decision to come. Had Prudence gone somewhere else? No, her car was parked in front of the barn at the end of the drive. Had she already gone to bed?

He took a fortifying breath, then knocked firmly on the wooden frame around the back door.

The house remained still. No lights flickered on. No footsteps sounded.

Collin knocked again, a little harder this time.

Still nothing.

He turned and stood at the top of the porch steps, peering out over the lawn to where the reception tent had been just yesterday. If he hadn't been there to see it himself, he wouldn't have been able to imagine the celebration had ever happened. A dog barked in the distance, a deep, throaty alert, and a responding bark came from inside the big barn, reminding Collin that the Goodacres had a pair of Great Pyrenees whose job it was to protect their cattle and horses from predators. He hoped the dog in the barn wouldn't think of him as a predator and come for him. He was suddenly glad he'd parked his bike nice and close, just in case he had to make a run for it.

Hope giving way to overwhelming disappointment, he knocked one more time. If Prudence was inside, she'd have heard him. Which meant that either she wasn't home, or she didn't want to see him.

After waiting another minute or two, he finally resigned himself to giving up. He paused again at the top of the steps and let his gaze wander, until it finally landed on the garden on the far end of the house. His eyes widened in surprise at the sight—it had grown enormous in the years since he'd last seen it. But the rustic arch and the gate, that quirky piece of artwork Prudence and her father had constructed together, still marked the entrance into the fenced in spread.

And the gate stood partially open.

Collin knew the gate was not just ornamental. He knew Prudence and her father would never leave the house with that gate standing open. Which meant that Prudence—or her father, he supposed with a grimace—was most likely out there right now.

And if she was, then she also knew he was standing on her porch banging on her back door.

The fact that she hadn't spoken up, hadn't intentionally made her presence known to him, made it pretty clear how she felt about him being there.

Collin bowed his head and stared down at the toes of his boots. He should just leave. He should get on his bike and go back to his hotel room. No, go back home to Kennedy Heights, his condo, his job, the life he now lived.

But his feet wouldn't move. He shoved his hands in his front pockets and kept his head down. "God? What do I do?" he muttered.

He *couldn't* just leave. He'd come this far. How could he walk away without giving it every shot he had?

He reached up and wrapped one hand around the back of his neck, almost as if he was going to pick himself up by the scruff and get himself moving. But to his bike? Or to the garden and Prudence and all that could come of—or end with—facing her there?

With a low grunt, Collin made up his mind and started down the steps. "Prudence?" he called out, not loudly, though. He didn't want to scare her; he just wanted her to know that he knew she was there, and to make his intentions about approaching her clear. "Can we talk?"

At the bottom of the steps, he paused and listened for a response. When none came, he walked slowly toward the garden gate. "May I come in?" The question sounded ridiculous once it was out, especially if the garden was empty. He couldn't see any movement in the dark, since he was still bathed in the motion sensor lights from the back porch and the side of the barn. But something about the way the whole night seemed to be holding its breath told him that Prudence was, indeed, out there. Not hiding, exactly, but not revealing herself, either.

He drew close to the gate, and then he saw her. She wasn't hiding after all, he saw. She stood in front of the bench under the old apple tree, a blanket draped around her shoulders, watching him. The moonlight overhead shone down on her upturned face, and even from where he stood, he could see the mix of emotions playing across her features. She still didn't speak, but nor did she send him away.

"I'm coming in," Collin said, almost reverently. But then, this did feel a bit like he was stepping onto holy ground. He had a good inkling of how precious this place was to Prudence.

He stopped several feet from where she stood. Prudence still hadn't said a word.

"It's a beautiful night," he began, then berated himself for starting with something so banal.

"It is," she finally said, her gaze still locked on his face.

Collin cleared his throat and tried again. "The party last night. It was beautiful." *Really, Stewart? Really?*

"It was," she agreed.

Third time's the charm, right? "Thank you for letting me come."

"I didn't let you. It wasn't my decision."

Aaand... why hadn't he just gotten on his bike and gone home?

"But thank you for your help with me—with my—well, thank you for your help. And with getting Abby to the church on time. It seems you have a penchant for rescuing damsels in distress."

Relief flooded through him. It wasn't much, but he'd take the mere centimeter of rope she'd just given him. He only hoped she wasn't going to dole out just enough for him to hang himself with. "I'm glad I was able to help," he said, taking another step closer.

Prudence drew the edges of the blanket tighter around her in a defensive gesture, and he grimaced, his hand going to the back of his neck again. Should he haul himself out of the garden now?

For a few terribly awkward moments, they stood in the dark, unmoving, not speaking. Even the night creatures seemed to be waiting to see how things would play out.

Eventually, Prudence turned and gestured at the bench. "Do you want to sit down?" It wasn't exactly an invitation, but she wasn't sending him away.

"May I?" he asked. He supposed he was being overly cautious, but he wanted to be sure there was no misunderstanding between them, now that he finally had a chance to set things right.

"Please," she said. He lowered himself to one end of the bench, but instead of joining him, she remained standing.

Great, he thought. Because things weren't awkward enough, now he was sitting comfortably while she stood in front of him, hardly able to look at him. "Prudence, will you sit with me?" Might as well stick out his neck. She held the blade in her delicate hands; she could slice and dice him or cut him free of the past that kept him in bondage.

For a moment, he thought she'd refuse, but then she surprised him by sinking onto the other end of the bench and tucking her feet up under her. It was then he noticed she wore no shoes. Of course not. She pulled the blanket around her so that she looked like a shapeless lump with a head, and Collin had to bite back an amused smile.

They sat in silence for a while, both of them gazing out over the expanse of pasture and woods beyond the garden fence. The jagged line of the treetops delineated earth from sky, and the stars were out in full regalia. It really was a beautiful night.

"What is it you want to talk to me about?" Her question came out harsh, an edge to it that had his spine stiffening.

It was a beautiful night that he was disturbing, apparently. *Get on with it, Stewart.* "Prudence, I—I need to apologize for how I left all those years ago. For the way I let things happen. For not sticking around to face you."

She didn't respond. She wasn't going to make this easy.

"I know how hard it must have been for you to speak so candidly to me—"

"Do you?" she asked, that edge growing sharper. She kept her face averted from him, still staring out into the darkness.

"I believe so," he said, turning to study her profile. The muscles in her jaw clenched visibly and she narrowed her eyes. "You were open and genuine and generous with your feelings, and I—"

She cut him off again. "Was I?"

Collin paused before he spoke, considering his words carefully. "Prudence, I asked you what you wanted. I asked for—no, demanded—your honesty. Then when you gave it to me—"

"I gave you more than my honesty, Mr. Stewart." Her words cut with serrated edges, and he touched his chest as if to check for blood.

"Collin," he corrected softly. Why wouldn't she say his name? "I know. And then I walked away. What I did must have seemed calloused and cruel to you, but Prudence, please believe me when I say that was the last thing on my mind."

"How about that honesty thing, Mr. Stewart? Will you at least give me the same courtesy? It didn't *seem* cruel," she went on. "It *was* cruel. I was naive and blind with hope and—and—" She swallowed hard. "And love, and you cut me to the quick. Believe me when I say there was no "seem" about it. Your cruelty was one hundred percent real."

Her words were terrible to hear, but the fact that she was speaking to him at all, that she was engaging with him in this conversation kept the tiny ember of hope in him alight. "For that, I beg your forgiveness, Prudence. If it makes any difference to you, I have regretted that moment every day since. I have dreamed of undoing it, redoing it, of going back in time and handling it all differently."

She did look at him then. "And what would you have done differently?" she demanded. "Not asked me for honesty? Not led me on so that I thought you shared my feelings? In all honesty," she said acrimoniously, "told me up front that I wasn't good enough for you instead of waiting until after I'd bared my soul to you?" She all but spat the words out, and he felt each one like a punch to his gut.

"No! No, Prudence. It wasn't like that at all." He scrubbed his fingers over his hair and pushed to his feet, finding it difficult to sit so close to her with such a vast chasm of misunderstanding between them. "I want to explain. I am sorry for the way things happened. I wish it could have gone differently, but at the time, I could see no other way."

"No other way for what?" She remained seated, stiff with tension. She glared at him now, her anger fueling her courage.

"Don't you see?" He started forward, drawing close to her, but paused when she straightened abruptly, her shoulders lifting in a defensive posture. He took one more step, then dropped to a knee in front of her. He didn't touch her, didn't reach for her. "Put yourself in my shoes, Prudence. Please." How could he explain this without sounding like a coward? "I was—I am—a teacher. I was *your* teacher. A black adult man—"

"I was an adult, too," she declared, her eyes bright with unshed tears, her short spiky hair making it seem like she was bristling the way an angry cat might.

"I was *your* teacher," he repeated, speaking slowly, desperate for her to hear what he didn't want to say out loud. "A black adult man in a position of authority. You must have some idea of how precarious a position that put me in."

"What does you being black have to do with anything? Why do you keep saying that?" Her feet shoved out from under the edge of the blanket, so she almost kicked him in the face. He flinched, then rose, moving out of the way as she shot to her feet, too. She wrapped the blanket more tightly around her like a shield and through clenched teeth, all but snarled, "You think it mattered to me what color your skin was?"

He waved a hand wildly at his side. "Don't be obtuse, Prudence. You know what I mean. It may not have mattered to you, but it mattered. It still matters. It *still* matters," he reiterated, emphasizing each word, his voice cracking with restrained frustration.

"I didn't care!" she all but shouted. "I didn't care if you were black, blue, white, or purple, Collin. I love—I *loved* you. And I was a legal adult who freely offered you my heart."

"I couldn't accept it," he shot back, his own voice rising. "Don't you see? I couldn't do that to you. I couldn't do that to me. I was not free to accept what you were offering me."

"Oh, I know that," she said, growing suddenly still. "You made that perfectly clear." In a quiet, controlled tone, she said, "And I quote, 'I'm better than this.' And then you walked away from me."

Her words, little more than a whisper, reverberated across the pastures, echoed off the treetops, and boomeranged back into him.

Not her words. His words.

"That's not—that's not what I said," he croaked.

"But it is," she countered, a smile that looked more like a grimace pulling up the corners of her mouth. "It's exactly what you said."

He reached out to her, but she leapt back like his hand was a poisonous snake. "I didn't mean it the way you took it," he began.

"Really?" That dreadful calm again. "Then please, enlighten me. What way did you mean it?"

Please, God, help her understand. Help her see past her anger and hurt to what I'm trying to say. "I meant that I knew I could be the kind of man a woman—and yes, I thought of you as a woman back then, too." She rolled her eyes, but he kept talking. "I wanted to be the kind of man a woman like you deserved. The kind of man you and your family would approve of, that my family would be proud of. I wanted to be someone worthy of someone like you. But I put us both in an impossible situation back then—the wrong time, the wrong place, even if we might have been the right people—I knew without a doubt that I was compromising because of my selfish desires, that I was allowing myself to be less than what I needed to be. Less of a man than you needed me to be." He pressed a hand to his chest. "Even worse, my weakness forced you to be less of who you were, too. I put you in a compromising position that left us both vulnerable and in trouble. I *was* better than that, don't you see? And so I ran. Not because I didn't want you, but because I did." He ran his palm over the top of his head, wishing he knew the words to say to make her understand. "Oh, how I wanted you, Prudence," he reiterated, his voice gruff with emotion. "I ran because I believed it was the honorable thing to do. It was the only thing I believed I could do."

"But what about what I wanted?" Prudence asked, her question less vehement, her words thick with misery instead. "Did you even consider how I felt, or was it only other people's opinions that concerned you?"

"We could have waited a few more weeks," he said softly, regret clogging his throat. "We *should* have waited a few more weeks. A few more months, maybe a year to be above reproof. I could have waited until you came home from Colorado. I wasn't going anywhere—"

"And yet you did," she interjected flatly. "You left."

"I left *because* I couldn't—no, because I didn't wait for the right time," he clarified. "I left, yes..." His words trailed off, realizing that all the best reasons in the world wouldn't change that fact.

"Well, I didn't." She spoke so quietly, that it took him a moment to comprehend what she said.

"You didn't what?" He spoke slowly, drawing the words out, not certain he wanted to know. But something in him already knew what she'd say.

"I didn't go anywhere. I didn't leave."

He swallowed hard. "Colorado?" he managed to ask.

"Nope."

Collin took in the scope of the garden before them. Surely it was evidence of an herbalist in residence, wasn't it? "Did you find a school closer to home?" He already knew the answer to that question, too. He could read it plain as day in her eyes. But he had to ask.

"Nope." If possible, she pulled the blanket around her more closely, the edges of it gripped tightly in her fists.

"Was it—did I—?" Would it sound too conceited of him to ask if her decision was because of him? Oh well. He was in it this deep already. "Did you not go because of me?"

"I was sick," she said simply. "For a long time."

He closed his eyes and asked again. "Because of me?"

A silence, thick with pent up emotions, settled between them. Finally, she shook her head. "No, Mr. Stewart," she replied. "I was sick because of me. Because I didn't take good care of myself. I didn't focus on the right things for a while."

In other words, because of him.

"But I'm better now," she said, suddenly spreading her arms wide and sweeping the blanket out like wings. "I'm happy with the way things turned out. My business is doing really well—I have a line of botanical body care products, and its taken off in the last couple of years. This ranch, this hollow, is my home. It's where I'm meant to be." She folded herself back into the blanket, but she was no longer wrapped so tightly. She actually smiled up at him. "If it makes any difference, I forgave you, Mr. Stewart. Collin," she corrected herself with a nod of acknowledgment, her tone gentle, but still careful and polite. "A long time ago. But thank you for explaining your side of things to me. You didn't have to, and I know I certainly haven't made things easy."

"I didn't expect this to be easy," he began, but she waved a hand dismissively at his words.

"Please know that I release you from any obligation you feel you may have toward me and my wellbeing. You may have influenced them, but my choices are my own, and I am proud of what and who I've become because of the choices I've made. It's my hope and prayer that you can say the same thing about yourself."

This sounded like a dismissal. A frisson of panic skittered up his back. "I can," he replied. "I don't regret my choice to wait, Prudence, but I do regret how I enacted that choice, and I definitely regret certain aspects of how that choice played out for us."

"But I don't, Mr. Stewart," she insisted. "I mean, Collin. From my perspective, it's all turned out for the best. I'm where I've chosen to be, you're where you've chosen to be. I'm happy for you, and I'd like to think you can be happy for me."

"I don't want you to be happy for me," he said, sounding petulant even to his own ears.

"Okay." Her brow furrowed and she studied him for a few moments before dropping her gaze to her bare toes. Her feet had to be freezing. Then, with a quick shake of her head, she said, "I'm tired. I came home from The Smokehouse early to take advantage of a quiet evening alone out here. My plan was to be in bed before everyone got home, so I'm going to head inside now." She stuck her hand out for him to shake.

"Prudence." Ignoring her proffered hand, he dredged his mind for something he could say to keep her from walking away. Desperation was making it hard to remain calm. "May I ask you a question?"

She let her hand fall to her side and shrugged one shoulder, her attention focused on the brilliant stars in the velvet dome above. "You can ask. I can't guarantee I'll answer."

He eyed her for a moment as he considered his next question. Feeling foolish and rather juvenile, he finally just spit it out. "Do you still... um... do you think you might still have feelings for me?"

TWENTY-THREE

Feelings? Was there ever a more trivial word to describe the immensity, the enormity, the scope of what went on inside her when she thought of Collin Stewart?

Did she still have feelings for him? She turned away from him so he couldn't see her face. Did he really have to ask?

"Honesty, please," Collin said softly. When she remained silent, he added, "Because I still have feelings for you. That's why I came this weekend. Not just for the wedding, Prudence. I came to see you."

The words punched holes in her heart, and she prayed her knees wouldn't give out from under her. Her throat was dry, but it didn't matter. She couldn't, for the life of her, come up with anything to say to that.

"I know this feels sudden, but it's not. My feelings for you have never changed, not in the five years we've been apart."

We've been apart? Like their separation was a mutual decision? She closed her eyes. *I'm not the one who left,* she wanted to rail. *I'm not the one who put distance between us.* But nothing could get past the lump of misery lodged in her throat.

"Prudence, please. If you can find it in you to offer me your heart again—*if* that's what you want. If *I'm* what you want." Collin waved a hand back and forth between them in a slightly frantic gesture. "If you feel even a portion of what you once did, my answer this time would be yes. I want another chance. I'm asking you to give me another chance." He was rambling, speaking so fast he was almost stumbling over his words, as if he sensed her distancing herself from him more and more. "Because I'm now free to accept what you have to offer," he said. Then he squared his shoulders and lifted his chin. "I'm now free to—to love you," he concluded, his voice cracking on the last two words.

Prudence bit back the small cry that filled her lungs and made her whole body tremble with the need to release the sound into the night. *Free to love me?* She couldn't decide whether to laugh or weep. Collin's words reminded her of that ridiculous speech of Mr. Darcy's where he insulted Elizabeth Bennet in his effort to be forthright about their different stations in life. In his own eyes, blinded by his overzealous care about society's expectations, dear, daft Mr. Darcy thought he was being somehow noble. Honorable. Doing the right thing.

Could the same be true of dear, daft Mr. Stewart?

Because Darcy's words had indeed wounded, but it didn't make his love for Elizabeth any less genuine and sincere.

Darcy had done the right thing, but maybe not the best thing. And Elizabeth had put aside her pride and forgiven him.

It's a book, the voice in her head scoffed. *It's fiction. A romance novel where happily ever after is guaranteed.*

In real life, there were no such guarantees.

In real life, love wasn't always enough, and pride and prejudices were obstacles often too big to overcome.

Collin allowed prejudices to rule his heart, and Prudence clung to her pride to keep what remained of her heart from shattering into a million pieces all over again.

She met his gaze. "It doesn't matter what my feelings are, Mr. Stewart. We live two very different lives, and I'm no longer free to…" She paused, not wanting to validate his words. "I'm no longer free to offer you anything."

The pain that marred his beautiful face made her want to rescind her words, to throw her arms around his neck and beg him to forgive her for hurting him, but she somehow managed to maintain her composure.

"I'm glad you were here to celebrate this wedding with Joe and Brandon and my sisters. I know they were happy you came. I'm glad, too, that I got to see you again, that you're doing well. I'm glad we talked, and again, thank you for making that happen. But I need to say goodnight now." She cocked her head to the side and looked up at him. "Would you walk with me back to the house?" She didn't ask because she wanted to spend more time with him, but because she was afraid if they lingered in the garden under the sweet-tart magic of the fruit-heavy branches arching over them, that her resolve would weaken, and she'd allow herself to entertain the thoughts of what-if that she'd laid to rest years ago.

Those thoughts had nearly been the end of her, and she couldn't afford to wander down into that murky maze again.

She started through the garden back toward the house, not waiting to see if he followed her. She only hoped he'd remember to close the gate behind him so the deer wouldn't wander in and feast on the bounty of her fall garden.

He brushed past to hold the gate open for her, then dutifully latched it before returning to her side. "I have a favor," he said after a few moments of silence.

Prudence said nothing, dread welling up inside her.

"May I write to you?"

The question caught her by surprise, and she halted abruptly, turning to look up at him. "Write to me?" she repeated.

He gave her a pained, but oh-so-brave smile. "Yes. As in letters. Pen and paper. May I write to you?"

She started walking again, her mind instantly at war with itself.

Yes! Letters are forever keepsakes. Proof of the existence of love, cried the simpering romantic side of her.

No! refuted the battle-scarred, circumspect side of her. *Letters will only weaken you, make you vulnerable. He offers you nothing but words, and words are empty without actions.*

"Prudence," he said, taking her elbow and bringing them both to a stop. "I understand your reluctance to trust me after the way I handled things in the past. But I can't leave here believing there is no hope of ever mending whatever we once had between us. I'd like to believe we were friends once, and that we can be again."

Prudence caught the corner of her bottom lip between her teeth, then nodded slowly. "I'd like to believe that, too." She side-stepped away from him, though, forcing him to release her elbow.

"Let me write to you," he entreated again. "And if you feel so inclined, I'd love it if you wrote to me. You don't have to, of course, but maybe its a way we can get to know the people we are now." He hesitated, then added. "And who knows? Maybe we'll discover that the people we are now aren't so different than the people we were then."

She couldn't bear to look at his pleading expression a moment longer. "I suppose that's all right." She nodded again. "Yes, I think that would be okay." Then she moved toward the house again.

Collin accompanied her to the porch steps, but when he started up behind her, she turned to stop him. "Thank you, Collin. I'm good from here." She was one step above him, putting them eye to eye. Self-consciously, she waved a hand at his motorcycle, hoping to draw his gaze away from her. "That bike suits you," she said, in all sincerity. "It's not exactly what I expected to ever see you driving, but it seems like a good fit."

"Thank you." Collin kept his eyes locked on her face. "And thank you for hearing me out, Prudence."

She nodded, the weight of his gaze making her cheeks burn. The silence between them drew out until she could bear it no longer. She thrust her hand out again, almost afraid to let him touch her, but desperate for a way to wrap this up.

Collin reached out and ever so gently enfolded her hand into his. She watched, as though in a trance, as he wrapped his long fingers around hers. Although he looked like he had a mouthful of words he still wanted to share with her, he remained silent while he studied her face like he was looking for answers she didn't have to the questions he didn't ask. When his thumb moved in a tentative caress over her knuckles, she couldn't suppress the shiver that shot through her, causing the quilt to slip from her shoulders to the step behind her.

Collin let go of her hand and bent to pick the blanket up. Without a word, he carefully draped it back around her shoulders, his fingers brushing down the slopes of her arms in what could only be construed as a caress. She held in the tremor this time, but she couldn't help the way her body leaned ever so slightly toward him.

For a moment, she thought he might take her in his arms, and she knew without a doubt, that if he did, she wouldn't resist. The air between them seemed alive, sizzling with restrained emotions, and she held her breath.

But a moment later, Collin stepped back, and Prudence straightened, drawing the edges of the soft quilt around her like a shield of protection.

"I should go in," she murmured, not looking at him. "I'm tired," she added, wishing she could come up with something that didn't sound quite so much like an empty excuse to get away from him.

"Of course," he conceded, digging in his pocket for his keys. He moved toward his bike, but he stopped just short of it and turned back to look at her. "Um, Prudence?"

He was far enough away that she found the courage to meet his eyes. "Yes?" To her surprise, her voice sounded almost normal, calm, a complete juxtaposition of how she felt.

Collin opened his mouth, then closed it, clearly struggling with the words he wanted to say. Finally, he simply said, "I'm glad I came this weekend. Really glad. Thank you for being willing to hear me out."

Prudence let out a small snort. "I don't know that you gave me much of a choice." She smiled to take the edge off her words, but it was true. It wasn't like she was going to toss him out of her garden.

He nodded slowly, but one side of his mouth curved up sheepishly. "Yeah, I guess I did kinda put you on the spot, didn't I?"

"It's all right," she assured him. "I'm glad you came this weekend, too." And she was. At least she had some closure. At least now she knew *why.* He'd chosen their reputations over what might have been, and she couldn't fault him for it. There was honor in that decision, she knew, even if it wasn't the choice that she would have made. In fact, it wasn't the choice she *had* made. Back then, Prudence had known without any reservation that her heart belonged to Collin.

It still does, that haunted voice inside her head declared.

But he'd refused it, rejected her, and run.

Collin grabbed his handlebars and straddled his bike. Right before he slid his helmet on, he said, "I'm heading home in the morning. But I'm staying at The Holiday, if for some reason, *any* reason, you want to get a hold of me before I leave."

Odd, that he hadn't asked for her phone number or offered her his. For a moment, Prudence considered suggesting the exchange, but the words stayed locked inside as she considered how lovely it would be to get a letter—would it be handwritten?—from Collin instead of a text, or even an email. It seemed such an antiquated form of communication, and yet, there was something incredibly romantic about it, too.

Romantic? She bit her lip in an attempt to quell the notion. "Okay," she said. She wouldn't call and ask for him between now and tomorrow morning, not for all the stars in the sky. Like that wouldn't start the gossip chain rattling. "Drive safely, Mr. Stewart."

His helmet slid into place right as the title crossed her lips. She thought he hadn't heard her, but he cocked his head at her and frowned slightly.

"Drive safely, Collin," she amended with a smile. "Good night."

Prudence moved to the back door, but she didn't go inside. Instead, she stood on the porch under the globe light, and watched him as he knocked back the kickstand, started the bike's engine, and turned the machine around in a tight circle before heading down the driveway away from her. Without warning, tears gathered in her eyes and spilled over, but she didn't bother dashing them away. There was no one around to see her weep, no one to witness her misery. No one to tell her everything was going to be all right, that she'd done the right thing.

She didn't need anyone to tell her anything. She knew she'd done the right thing, after all, no matter how badly it hurt.

Because Prudence couldn't bear to have anyone else abandon her. First, her mother. Then her father in his grief, and her sisters as they paired up to care for each other. And now they were leaving her all over again, for new families, new homes, new careers—except for Justice, who probably would have preferred Prudence to be the one to leave.

And of course, there'd been Collin, abandoning her in her garden, broken in heart and spirit.

Once nearly killed her. She wouldn't survive if he left her again. No, by sending him away, she would not give him the opportunity.

TWENTY-FOUR

Everything about the ride home felt wrong.

That morning, Collin had been awakened by a laser beam of sunlight slicing through the crack in the drapes at the window, practically blinding him before he even opened his eyes. The clock on his phone told him the hour was far too early for a man on vacation, but no matter how hard he tried, he couldn't seem to find his way back into the land of slumber. He finally staggered out of bed and into a cold shower, hoping the frigid water would clear the fog from his sleep-deprived brain, but to no avail. Standing at the sink, it took several minutes of whisking the warm foam around on his face before his skin softened enough to get a clean shave. Even then, he nicked the cleft in his chin, and even after he finally got it to stop bleeding, he somehow managed to drag the collar of his shirt right across it as he got dressed, leaving behind a rusty smear.

Even the weather seemed to be messing with him. By the time he was dressed and packed and no longer bleeding profusely, a thick bank of clouds had moved in to block out the early morning sun that had disrupted his sleep earlier. Checking the forecast, he saw the chance of rain increased with every hour he stayed in Plumwood Hollow, so instead of stopping for a bite to eat at Serendipity's as he'd planned, he opted to get on the road right away. Cass had texted him the night before to let him know she'd made it home safely, so he didn't feel too badly about leaving without seeing her, but he'd miss out on a second cinnamon roll.

Less than a half an hour out of town, the wind kicked up, bringing with it a cloudburst that tossed stinging raindrops at him. He pulled over at a truck stop in Muldoon to get a bite to eat while waiting out the rain, and by the time he got back on the road, his stomach was telling him the lumberjack breakfast probably wasn't the best choice that morning.

The next several hours passed in a blur of discomfort and turmoil, both physical and emotional, as Collin fought to stay alert and focused on the road rather than on the girl he'd left behind. Once again.

At his apartment complex, he pulled his motorcycle into the parking space allotted to him and expelled a groan of relief that he'd made it in one piece. All he wanted was to crawl into bed and sleep the rest of the day away. But as he approached his front stoop, the door of the next apartment over flew open and Jess practically threw herself into his arms. "You're home! Come over and tell us all about it!"

Collin was shaking his head before she even got the words out. But that didn't stop her or her roommates. A moment later the other two girls had joined her, and Beau, Tracy's boyfriend, stood framed in the doorway, wearing an expression of long-suffering. "Dude, it's all they can talk about, this wedding you went to. They've been watching chicks in spandex doing tricks on horseback all weekend. They won't let you rest until you spill."

He should have known. All three of the girls, especially Jess, had texted him incessantly all weekend long, begging for details. He'd given them none, knowing they would demand a detailed retelling upon his return anyway. But he could barely keep his eyes open, and with the heaviness in his heart over how things had ended with Prudence, he knew he wouldn't be able to do the wedding justice. "I'm beat, guys," he insisted. "I need to go lie down. Can we maybe do pizza tonight? I'll buy."

"Don't be silly," Jess said. "We're the ones making demands of you, not the other way around, so pizza will be on us."

"Besides," Tracy quipped. "You've been gone for several days. You probably have nothing in your fridge anyway, and if we don't feed you, you may not eat." She stepped close to her boyfriend, slipped her arm around him, and added, "And if you don't eat, you'll never grow up to be as big as my Beau, here!"

The brawny man grinned smugly and planted a kiss on her temple.

Collin rolled his eyes. "I have a feeling that's a hopeless cause, ladies," he said. "But I promise to give you a full recounting over pizza tonight, okay?"

For a moment, he wasn't sure they were going to let him escape, but thankfully, Beau took matters into his own hands and herded the girls back inside their place. "We have a movie to finish, ladies. I have to go to work in less than an hour, and I have to see how Lorelei wins back Chad's heart. You know," he added dryly. "Since I somehow missed it the last three times we've watched this movie."

The girls next door had an addiction to sugar-sweet Hallmark movies, and any man willing to sit through any of them—multiple times, to boot—was truly valiant. "You're a champ, Beau Templeton!" Collin called after them as they trooped back inside. The man lifted a hand in acknowledgment, but the look on his face had Collin chuckling as he pulled his door closed behind him.

He dropped his pack at his feet and leaned back against the door, not certain he had the energy to make it all the way to his bedroom. It was moments like this that Collin wished for a dog, or even a cat, something alive that would acknowledge his return at the end of the day. He was grateful for his neighbors, that they plugged into his life, but it had occurred to him on more than one occasion that they were on parallel tracks, that nothing in their world would change if he didn't exist. The women embraced those around them, and it could be anyone in this apartment, and they'd still feed and coddle that person, too.

A dog, a cat, even a fish, would make him feel important, needed. Maybe just to feed and water them, but they would be his responsibility, and their comfort, their ability to thrive or not, would be on his shoulders.

Better yet, wouldn't it be wonderful to have a person waiting to welcome him home at the end of the day?

A woman.

Prudence.

He sighed, and pushed off the door, peeling out of his jacket as he went. He draped it over the back of one of the barstools at his kitchen counter before starting a pot of coffee. Not for the caffeine, but for the warmth of a hot drink, and the sense of comfort and home the bitter brew conjured. While it percolated, he headed to the bathroom for another shower; this one would be hot. He needed to wash away the grime of the road, and to soothe the lingering anxiety that seemed to have settled between his shoulder blades.

What could he have done differently this weekend? Should he have contacted Prudence first to let her know he was coming? Was it fair that he had surprised her, that he had all but forced her to hear him out?

Then again, he'd thought for sure she'd know he was coming. She was a sister of the brides; surely, she'd helped with the guest lists, the invitations. Besides, he'd discovered at some point, that she was the wedding planner, after all. Did the wedding planner have access to all of that stuff, too? Didn't she arrange who sat and stood and walked where?

Was it possible that she really hadn't seen his name on the list, or that they hadn't received his RSVP?

Even worse, had she seen his name, and simply not cared?

This whole thing felt ridiculously juvenile, reminding him of his high school years when he'd struggled to know where he fit in. He'd grown up in a predominantly white neighborhood and had attended an elementary school where, at least as far as he'd been aware of, folks had remained fairly color blind. Being biracial had never been an issue, not until he became a teenager, and then it seemed everyone had something to say about it. Until he started high school, he'd never realized that there was so much animosity and even hate toward him simply because of the color of his skin. What surprised him even more was how freely people verbalized their opinions about his parents. And it wasn't just from his fellow students, either. The names he'd heard his mother called still made his ears burn and his skin crawl, and the macho jokes about how his black father had landed himself a white woman had him throwing punches on more than one occasion. Unfortunately, his efforts to defend his parents never turned out well for Collin, since he'd suffered the fate of being a late bloomer. He'd discovered firsthand that size really does matter when you're duking it out in the school yard.

It was the feelings of uncertainty stirred up by his trip to Plumwood Hollow that had him reliving those trying years. He'd struggled terribly over identity issues; one group of peers couldn't see past the golden eyes he got from his mother, while the other couldn't see past the Afro he got from his father. His mocha skin didn't help, either; it was too dark for one group, and not dark enough for the other.

He'd somehow managed to live through those years, and by the time Collin graduated from high school, he'd made a couple good friends from both communities. It hadn't been easy, and his parents had practically arranged play dates with some of their friends' kids, much to Collin's dismay. But in the end, he was grateful for both Reggie and Dax and the friendships that had turned into long-lasting relationships. They had each other's backs their senior year, and although they'd gone their separate ways for college, they continued to stay in touch, managing to get together at least once a year in person. Reggie still lived in Cincinnati, but on the other side of town working construction for an industrial company. Dax joined the military, but his parents and siblings still lived in Kennedy Heights, and whenever he could get back to visit, Collin made sure to set aside time to visit with him, especially after the guy's marriage failed a few years back. Military life wasn't for the weak; that was for sure. Dax and his wife hadn't survived the long separations, and his was a common tale.

University had offered Collin a reprieve—his fellow collegians seemed to care little who his parents were or what neighborhood he lived in—but even so, his preferred company to keep were the humanity found between the pages of the books he read and studied. His favorite place to meet them was at the school library where he providentially ran into Joe Lynxwilder and struck up a quick and easy friendship with the farmer.

Half an hour later, Collin lay sprawled across his bed, the pillows uncharacteristically uncomfortable and lumpy under his head, his blanket twisted around his legs like an anaconda, sleep a fanciful pipe dream.

It wasn't the caffeine keeping him awake and agitated.

Nope. It was Prudence the Pixie from Plumwood Hollow. Every time his lids lowered, he saw her face, those enormous eyes surrounded by fringes of dark lashes, her perfectly defined mouth, her petite form drifting in and our among the guests at the ranch, flitting around the dance floor at The Smokehouse.

The fear that had rushed through him like a freight train when she collapsed at the sight of him.

The feel of her limp in his arms as he carried her inside her home.

The frustration and longing and self-loathing that had followed him down her driveway as he left her standing on her back porch watching him disappear into the night.

Why was he always leaving her?

Collin dragged a pillow over his face and released a growl of frustration into it. He'd left because she'd asked him to. Because Collin was a man who understood *no* to mean *no*.

So why had he asked if he could write to her? Hadn't she made it clear that she was over him? That she'd moved on from her girlish teacher-crush on him?

But there'd been a few—no, *several* moments....

When he'd set her down on the couch and their eyes had met and held. When they danced for half a song at The Smokehouse, and she'd trembled in his arms. He hadn't imagined it; she'd trembled, and he was certain it was the good kind of tremble, too. There was last night in the garden—it had almost seemed to him like she'd been waiting for him there under the draping branches of Henrietta the apple tree. Had she known he'd come? And then on the porch steps after he'd settled her blanket around her shoulders? She'd *leaned*. Leaned toward him, her face slightly lifted. If she hadn't already told him the night was over, he would have kissed her, and he was fairly certain she would have let him.

That was why he'd asked to write to her. Because of those moments. Because of that lean.

That lean gave him hope.

He tossed the pillow away and sat up on the side of his bed, scrubbing his face with both hands. "No time like the present, I suppose." Since sleep eluded him anyway.

TWENTY-FIVE

Abby headed back to Nashville Wednesday afternoon, leaving Prudence alone with her father in the big ranch house for the remainder of the twins' honeymoon. As much as she loved having Abby around, her youngest sister had an air of transition swirling about her, which left Prudence feeling unsettled and on edge. Not because she wanted what Abby wanted—to fly free of the hollow in pursuit of far-off distant dreams—but because Prudence wanted nothing more than to immerse herself into the life she had carved out at the ranch.

Although the house felt too big for just the two of them, the place was all cleaned and put back to order after the chaos of the wedding. A sense of peace had settled over the home, in spite of the empty rooms.

As he did every morning, Jed awoke first, put on the coffee, then headed out to the porch to greet Jack, who had crossed the pasture from the ranch next door, just as the dog did every morning. The man and beast made their way to the big barn, greeted the three stabled horses inside with feedbags and nose scratches, then meandered over to the smaller barn where Courage and Justice kept Flash and Fire. Young Jasmine insisted that she wanted the full responsibility of caring for the horses in her twin aunts' absences, but it hadn't taken much arm twisting before she'd agreed to let her grandfather do the early morning feedings so she wouldn't have to rush over before school.

By the time Prudence got up and began putting together some breakfast, Jed had settled into a chair on the back porch with his second cup of coffee in hand, the dog sprawled on the planks near his feet.

"Good morning, Daddy," Prudence called through the screen door, pulling the lapels of her heavy flannel shirt together against the brisk morning air. "I've got a couple of sausage patties in the skillet already. How many eggs do you want?" She hoped she didn't sound as weary as she felt, but her father turned to eye her without answering her question. Even through the mesh of the screen door, she could see the deep groove of concern that formed between his brows. She lifted her own steaming mug and smiled brightly in an effort to put his mind at ease. "The coffee's good!"

"Two eggs. Fried, please," Jed finally said, but continued to study her. She started to turn away, but he stopped her with a quiet, "Pixie Cut."

Keeping her back to him, Prudence grimaced. "What's up, Daddy?" she asked, still trying her best to sound like everything was fine. Normal. Like she didn't have a care in the world. Hoping against hope that she'd fooled him, she proceeded to open the refrigerator and pull out the carton of eggs.

But Jed wasn't having it. "Child, where are you?" It was a question he often asked of her. In fact, she couldn't ever remember him using the same phrase on any of her other sisters. It was his way of asking her *how* she was.

Granted, of all his daughters, Prudence was the most prone to flights of fancy and imaginary adventures. She was also the most likely to disappear inside her head, her own thoughts, often without even realizing it. And Daddy had a knack for knowing when she was distancing herself from the rest of them, from him.

Like God in the Garden of Eden, Prudence thought. She'd grown up hearing the story of Adam and Eve's sin in Eden, followed by their shame and hiding. Then along came God—they could hear his footsteps and were dreading facing him—and his voice calling out to them, "Where are you?" So often, that Bible story painted a God who seemed almost patronizing, speaking down to them. *You foolish humans. You think you can hide from me?*

But Prudence always imagined God asking that question the same way Jed did. A father longing for the company of his wayward—or simply distracted—children. Not because he couldn't find Adam and Eve, but because he wanted them to long for him in the same way he longed for them.

Jed asked, "Where are you?" instead of "How are you?" to draw her out of herself and into an engagement with him.

This morning, though, she didn't think she had the energy to process everything that was on her mind and in her heart. And she had no doubt that if she cracked open the door the tiniest bit, it would all spill out, and she wasn't sure she was ready to tell her father everything.

"I'm right here, Daddy. I promise," she said, tossing a quick smile his way. "Just tired." It was true. She hadn't slept well the night before. Or the night before that. In fact, she hadn't slept well since the wedding almost a week ago. Collin Stewart had plagued her thoughts every night. He'd plagued them every day, too, but at least during the day, she could keep herself busy with chores around the ranch, the after-party cleanup, and time spent in her herb shop. At night, the moment she turned off the light and closed her eyes, he was there before her, his imploring expression, his romance novel words.... So she kept the light on and read books on natural remedies and homeopathic treatments, herbal lore and plant medicine, until she couldn't keep her eyes open, often drifting off mid-sentence, only to awaken hours later with the light on and a book still clutched in her hand. That still didn't eradicate Collin from her thoughts. He showed up in her dreams, too, so that she often awoke in the turmoil of mixed emotions.

There'd been tears trickling from the corners of her eyes when she roused that morning, but she couldn't remember the details of her dream. Only that Collin had been in it.

In a slightly louder voice to be heard over the sizzling skillet, she added, "I guess I'm feeling at loose ends without this wedding hanging over my head. I keep waking up thinking I've forgotten something." Again, all true. She did often find herself wondering what still needed to be checked off her wedding to-do list. It was strange not having the big event looming over her.

After a few long moments, she heard Jed tell Jack to "Go on home now," then her father entered the kitchen. She held her breath, expecting him to push her to talk, but he just asked, "Want me to make toast?" He pulled a loaf of Charity's homemade bread out of the pantry without waiting for Prudence's answer. "How many slices do you want?"

"Just one for me. Thanks," she said, releasing her breath in relief. The two of them did life together like a couple of old married folks, Prudence often thought, and she wondered again, as she often did these days, how Daddy would do living on his own in the new house he was building across Carpenter Road. Who would cook his hearty breakfasts for him in the morning? He managed to get himself lunch without help, but that was because his daughters kept the refrigerator and pantry well-stocked. Prudence and the twins—it'd only be Justice now, she supposed—took turns cooking supper, and they all ate the meal together. She pressed a palm to her chest at the thought of him eating his evening meal all alone across the way. Maybe she could convince him to continue eating supper here at the big house.

And what if he refused? Prudence sighed dishearteningly. Then she'd have to sit across the big table from Justice and Brandon. Ugh. Because being a third wheel wasn't bad enough. Nope. She'd be the third-wheel-spinster-sister trying to keep her gaze averted from their newly-wed touchy-feely public display of affection, and all their lovey-dovey lingering looks. She could hardly bear the thought of it, even now.

Maybe she'd join Daddy at his place for supper, instead.

She sighed again. This was *not* how she envisioned her life playing out.

She forced her lips to curve up at the corners as she flipped the sausage patties and dropped three large eggs into the drippings in the middle of the pan. As they popped and sizzled, she pulled plates from the cupboard and set them on the counter to load up straight from the stove top.

At the table, Daddy reached over and took Prudence's hand, then they bowed their heads, and he lifted his voice in prayer. He blessed the food, the hands that prepared it, and prayed for each of his daughters by name, asking for God's protection and provision in their lives. Prudence squeezed his hand when he got to her name, then stilled at his next words. "Father, I ask especially for Prudence, that you would give her wisdom, discernment, and direction, that she would keep her eyes and ears open to your leading in her life."

Could he read her thoughts so clearly? After he finished, she smiled brightly and thanked him for his prayer, but then turned immediately to her plate of food before her.

"What's the plan for the day?" Jed asked. The question might have been mundane, but the shrewd look in his eyes told her he was just offering her a reprieve.

Glad for the change of subject, Prudence finished chewing her bite, then said, "I've got to get out to my workshop this morning. I have a ton of orders to fill, and I need to replenish my stock this week. We're coming into dry skin season, and my customers love their body butters this time of year."

Jed chuckled softly. "That wood smoke and whiskey one is my favorite."

Prudence grinned back at him, his compliment warming her from the inside out. The fact that the old rancher actually knew what body butter was, no less that he had a favorite, always tickled her, but she also knew that he didn't just like the stuff because his daughter made it. He liked it because it worked. There was no reason for a hardworking man to have cracked and bleeding hands, or to have hands greased up with petroleum products, not with Prudence in residence. It also helped that she was happy to massage the stuff into his hands for him, loosening up and easing the ache of his arthritic old joints.

"It's your signature scent," she quipped. She also made both his shaving and bath soap in the same fragrance—she worked on the formula for over a year to find the unique blend of ingredients, and she called the scent "Jed." It had been her most popular line of men's products three years running.

After a few moments of silence, she added, "I need to put in some time in the garden later this week, too. From the ten-day forecast, it looks like the temperature's going to dip pretty low the end of next week. I need to lay down mulch around what's left out there, but I'll be working in town Monday, Tuesday, and Wednesday, so I'm going to get started on that this afternoon after I get a handle on my Pixie Cut stuff since I'm home the next few days." Trilby had made her take this week off work after the hundreds of hours she'd put into the wedding, and Prudence was grateful for the extra time to put the ranch in order.

"I can bring a trailer full of straw over from the barn. Abby helped me clean out the stalls yesterday morning, so it's all loaded up and ready to be put to good use."

"That would be great," she said, relaxing into the normalcy of the conversation.

An hour later, Prudence was in her shop, slouched on a stool at the workbench, gazing out the window toward the garden. She absentmindedly stripped dried lavender flowers from their stalks into an enormous bowl, trying to keep her mind from wandering in the direction of Cincinnati, but to no avail. Collin's reappearance in her life, even as brief as it had been, had stirred something in her that had lain dormant for so long, she had almost believed it was gone for good. But all it took was one look into those honey-amber eyes and she was awash once again.

Was that how it had been for Faith when Cord showed up after abandoning her ten years earlier? Had she, too, been practically knocked off her feet at the mere sight of him? Had her heart felt like it was going to rocket right out of her chest?

"But Cord came back to stay," she mumbled. "Big difference." With a sigh, she set aside the lavender spikes, stood, and stretched. Maybe she should head out to the garden and get her hands dirty for a while.

As she pushed open the workshop door, the sound of voices stilled her. She peered toward the house, and to her surprise, she saw Daddy and Charlotte Rawlings standing toe to toe in the driveway. They weren't exactly arguing, at least not that she could tell, but they definitely seemed to be in some kind of a standoff, just by their postures alone.

Should she intervene? Call out to them? Or leave them alone? Or was she misinterpreting the tension between them? Prudence could usually read people well, could get a sense of how things were with folks, but the interaction between her father and this wild woman shepherdess had her at a loss.

"Hey, guys!" she finally called out, making her presence known.

Charlotte spun toward Prudence and lifted an arm in a wave. "Why hello, Miss Prudence!" she called before turning back to Jed. Charlotte reached out and rested her fingertips on Jed's forearm, and if Prudence wasn't mistaken, her father actually flinched at the contact. He didn't pull away, but he'd reacted, nonetheless. Charlotte spoke quietly to him, let out a low chuckle, then started toward Prudence. "I was hoping I'd run into you today, young lady. I was out on this side of town looking at properties, and thought I'd stop by and see if this was a good time to see your workshop and gardens. Maybe pick up some of your products. I checked out your website, and I can already tell you, I'm going to be your most faithful customer." She slowed when she drew close, but kept talking. "I love working with my wool, but my hands get so rough, and I have a hard time finding stuff to keep them from turning into sandpaper. When I shook your daddy's hand the other night, I admit I was surprised. I know he's a hardworking man, but I think my hands are rougher than his." She shot a wink at Jed over her shoulder and called back to him, "You've got great hands, Jedediah Goodacre." Then she chortled at the look of consternation that crossed his face.

Prudence couldn't help smiling at the exchange, not just at Daddy's reaction to the woman's compliment, but also because it suddenly struck her that Miss Rawlings was acting nervous. A bit flustered. Her stream of nonstop words seemed to be an attempt to cover her agitation. Up close, Prudence could see the color high on her sharp cheekbones, the flush across her chest, the way she fluttered her hands while she spoke.

Was Daddy making her nervous? Was that a good thing?

"Come on in," Prudence said, holding open the door and stepping back to let Charlotte past. "Daddy," she called out to her father before he could head back inside the house. He stopped and narrowed his eyes like he was trying to convey something to her. She had a good idea what that was, too, and she wasn't going to torture him by having him join them in her little shop. "I'm going to start in the garden after we're through here. Do you think you could haul that trailer of straw over now?"

Jed just nodded, touched the front of his hat with his finger, then spun on his heel and made for the barn.

By the time the two women stepped back out into the morning sunshine, Charlotte carrying a muslin bag filled with an assortment of body butter, healing salves, a set of herbal shampoo and conditioner, and a few samples of other products, Jed was just finishing up unloading the straw from his trailer. He'd made four piles in strategic spots around the garden plot, and Prudence thanked him with a quick kiss on the cheek.

"Ew," she teased. "You're all sweaty." She tugged the handkerchief from his back pocket and dabbed at his forehead before he snatched it from her.

"Evidence of a hardworking man," he said, reaching out like he was going to tweak her nose. Prudence jerked back to avoid his dirty hand. "In spite of my soft hands," he added, shooting a dark look in Charlotte's direction.

"I never said they were soft," Charlotte countered, her teeth flashing in a wide grin. "I believe I said they were great."

Jed's scowl deepened, but so did the color suffusing his face, and Prudence had to bite back a grin of her own.

"A man who isn't afraid to sweat is a good thing," her father went on. "Something you need to remember whenever you decide you're ready to look for a man of your own, Pixie Cut."

Prudence mimed pulling a pad of paper and pen from a hip pocket and then pretended to write something down. "Marry a sweaty man. Check."

Jed rolled his eyes and snapped his handkerchief in her direction, then started to climb onto the tractor to which the trailer was hitched. "I'll get this out of here. Need anything else from the barn?"

There was a tiny tool shed built into one corner of the garden where they kept most of their hand tools. "I think I'm good." Charlotte was only going to stay long enough to do a quick walk through of the garden, but then she'd be on her way. She had to check in with Sarah for lunch, then go see another property in the afternoon.

"All right, then," Jed said with a nod. He dipped his head toward Charlotte. "Good seeing you, Miss Rawlings. Safe travels tomorrow."

"Actually," Charlotte said, taking a quick step in his direction. "I was going to ask you for a huge favor." There was that telltale color blooming up her neck again. Prudence was beginning to wonder if it was contagious. She'd never seen two old people turn so many shades of red before.

"What can I do for you, ma'am?"

"Well, this afternoon, that property I'm going to look at? It's being sold by a fellow named Glisson. Randall Glisson. Sarah said you'd know him."

Jed frowned. "I do," he said slowly.

Prudence knew Randal Glisson, too. The man had a small homestead north of Plumwood Hollow, and although he raised a few animals and grew an enormous garden—mostly corn, root crops, beans, and a few other things that stored well and wintered over—it was widely rumored that Glisson operated a still hidden somewhere on his property, or he had connections with someone who did since the local law enforcement had never managed to uncover one out there. And they'd tried. They'd had enough evidence on many on occasion to show up with search warrants, but to no avail. However, the rough crowd who found their way to Glisson's door at all hours gave the rumors validity, and Prudence couldn't imagine any law-abiding person choosing to live in close proximity to the man and his shady dealings.

"I didn't know he was selling," Jed continued.

"Oh, it's not his personal property," Charlotte said quickly. "He heard I was looking—word travels at lightning speed in these parts," she added with a wry chuckle. "I guess he picked up a really nice piece of property that adjoins his—some kind of debt paid, I think?"

Jed nodded slowly, but his expression remained serious. Glisson was also known to engage in other forms of shady dealings, including money lending and gambling rings. He wasn't a nice man. "Sounds about right."

"Anyway, I'm looking at everything that's available while I'm here this week and I don't want to leave any stone unturned. I'm a tough cookie accustomed to looking after myself. I have been all my life. But Sarah strongly suggested that I not go out there alone, that I might ask you to join me. She thought Glisson might behave a little more... well, *respectable* if I brought you along." To Prudence she added, "And of course, you're welcome to join us."

"No," Jed said before Prudence could respond. Both women turned to stare at him in surprise.

"No?" Charlotte repeated. "No, you won't go with me? Or no, Prudence can't join us?" she asked, her tone equally wary and challenging, as though she were trying to bite back some kind of emotion.

Jed was shaking his head, but he spoke to Prudence first. "Pixie Cut, I'd rather you steer clear of that man and his property, but you already know that." To Charlotte, he said, "Miss Rawlings—"

"Charlotte," she corrected quietly.

"Charlotte," he amended. "I'll go out to look at the property with you, yes. If it's the land I'm thinking it is, then it's a fine property, and could work well for you. However, having Glisson as a neighbor isn't for the faint of heart. I don't believe he'd be a danger to you himself, but the folks that come and go on his property are another lot altogether."

"Then you'll have to fill me in on the details on the way out there," Charlotte replied, nodding sagely. "You know this place and these people; I don't. I consider your opinion invaluable."

Jed only nodded, the look on his face telling plain as day that he didn't like the idea at all.

"I'll come back by here after lunch to pick you up. I'm supposed to be out there at two." Taking Prudence's arm, Charlotte steered them both toward the garden gate. "Show me your plant magic, Pixie Cut."

No one but Daddy called her that, but Prudence found she liked the way the nickname rolled off Miss Rawling's tongue.

TWENTY-SIX

I feel like I should start singing, but don't worry; I won't. I can't carry a tune in a bucket, as my father would say.

I have started this letter more times than I can count, and honestly, with an opening line like the one above, I should just crumple this up and try yet again. But last night, after once more tossing my latest attempt into the trash can, I made my way empty-handed to the bank of mailboxes at the end of my block. It was late—after eleven, long after I should have been in bed on a school night—and I was surprised to see someone else already standing there. It was a man I'd encountered several weeks ago on another late-night sojourn to the mailboxes; he and his little scruffy dog, Walter Matthau.

I discovered the dog's name when the stupid little thing tried to lift its leg on my shoe in greeting, and his human called him off in the nick of time. I still don't know the old man's name—the incident with the dog had us chuckling together awkwardly, and introductions somehow never got made. Walter Matthau does, indeed, bear a striking resemblance to his namesake, by the way, complete with droopy jowls, mournful brown eyes, and salt and pepper fur with a side part. Did you ever see the Barbra Streisand version of "Hello Dolly"? Think Horace Vandergelder. This dog could play the part. I'm not kidding.

Why am I telling you all of this?

Because the last time I ran into said gentleman and Walter Matthau, I was debating whether or not to mail the RSVP to your sisters' wedding. He took one look at me and must have read my indecision, because he said, "Better drop it in before you lose your nerve." How he knew my quandary, I have no idea, but his words did the trick. And I'll be forever grateful that he was there that night; in all honesty, I might have chickened out and missed the opportunity to see you, to reconnect with you.

I can't help but wonder what his story is, though. That first time I saw him, he seemed... forlorn. That's the best word I can think of to describe his vibe. It makes me sad to think of it, and even more determined to learn what I can about him. He left shortly after his dog tried to assault me, but I wish I'd had the presence of mind to at least ask him his name. It's been bothering me all day, so it's nice to be able to tell you about him. I hope you don't mind sharing the burden of Walter Matthau and his human with me.

You know, I think I'll take a late-night stroll down to the mailbox tonight with this letter. Who knows? Maybe the mystery man and his mutt will be there waiting, and I can make up for my lack of manners.

...

Collin told her briefly about his job and the school where he worked, along with a favorite story about Vice Principal Storm Trooper, hoping Prudence might get a chuckle out of the anecdote. He also confessed that as much as he enjoyed working with fifth graders, he missed teaching high school students about the joy of reading and studying literature. There was nothing quite so satisfying as having a teenager who thought he or she hated reading discover just how much the world of books had to offer.

Not wanting the letter to turn into a tome, he opted to close there. "You have time," he reminded himself. "You don't need to catch her up on the last five years in the first letter.""

TWENTY-SEVEN

MORE THAN TWO WEEKS had passed since the wedding, and still, there was no letter.

Not that she was waiting for one. Of course, she wasn't.

Life was going back to normal—or at least a new normal, now that Justice and Brandon were settling into the big house with them—and with the winter months approaching, there was a lot of work to do on the ranch to prepare the place to hunker down for the cold. Daddy and Brandon were working together to make sure the barns were in good order, the hay and feed dry and well-protected from the weather, and Faith was spending more time than usual with her Dexters, preparing the herd for what was being forecast as a colder-than-usual winter. She had an exceptionally high success rate with her spring breeding earlier that year, and she wanted to make sure her pregnant mamas were fat and happy before the first snow.

Prudence had already received nearly double the number of Christmas gift orders as last year, so she was spending much more time out in her workshop than inside the house. Which wasn't a bad thing, considering the number of times she'd inadvertently walked in on Justice and Brandon taking advantage of their married status. Clothing intact, of course, but if Prudence had to witness them making out or Justice openly fondling her husband's backside one more time, she might just scream.

Jed, on the other hand, seemed oblivious to the couple's amorous activities. Either that, or they were just more careful around him than they were around her. But then, Prudence sometimes got the impression that he was already half moved out and into his own place, and no longer concerned himself with what went on inside the ranch house walls.

Sometimes, she found herself stopping in front of a mirror just to make sure she still existed. That feeling of being forgotten, the one she'd warred with as far back as she could remember, wanted to creep back in and bury her.

Every morning, she forced herself to be grateful for another day, to look for ways to serve others, to find God's presence in the small things. After the first week had passed, and she hadn't received so much as a postcard from Collin, she'd disappeared for several hours out to the clearing in the woods, spilling her heart to her mother while she cleared her memorial cairn, the pile of stones that the girls and their father had collected from all over the ranch, of leaves and other autumnal debris that the wind and rain had knocked loose from the surrounding woods. She'd returned after dark, chilled to the bone, only to discover that nobody had even worried over her absence.

In fact, Justice had cooked and served supper early that night, even though it was Prudence's turn. "I just thought you were working tonight," she'd said without malice. *Blissfully happy*, Prudence thought, looking at her smiling sister. *Blissfully oblivious.*

Invisible. That's how Prudence felt these days. Cast off. Unwanted. Not important enough to remember.

Even her garden seemed not to need her these days. The straw mulch was doing its job to keep the soil from getting too cold too early, which would allow the remaining root crops—beets, carrots, a few turnips, and plenty of radishes—to remain in the ground for at least another month and protecting the roots of the plants that would winter over in dormancy. There was little else she could do out there other than wrapping things in burlap when the temperatures dipped especially low and clearing snowdrifts or fallen branches from the apple tree.

Which made her especially thankful that she could get away to her little shop and while away the hours making more products, working on her website, and spending more time than usual on social media, connecting with customers and followers.

At that moment, she was sitting on a stool, watching droplets of steam-processed lavender hydrosol and essential oils spurting from the tiny outlet tube of her copper alembic distiller. The air in her workshop was thick with the heady scent that made Prudence feel sluggish and sleepy. She'd love a cup of coffee or tea, perhaps even hot chocolate, but she wasn't about to head into the house at the noon hour. Not if the love birds were in there have lunch together.

"I need to grow up and be happy for them," she berated herself, straightening on her seat and running her fingers through her spiky hair. "I mean, I am happy for them." She picked up a framed photo of her and Daddy on the bench under the apple tree and poked him in the nose. "I just don't want you to leave me alone with them," she grumbled. "I already feel useless enough around here."

A knock sounded at the door, startling her so that she almost dropped the photo. She quickly returned it to the sill and called out, "Come in!"

Jed pulled open the door and entered, clutching the handles of two mugs of hot coffee in one hand. "Phew! Smells like the quilting club in here," he said with a teasing smile. He knew her opinion of the smell of lavender.

"Is one of those for me?" she asked, reaching with both hands toward the mugs he carried.

"Been waiting for a chance to catch you all morning," Jed said after handing her the smaller of the two, then taking a sip of his own.

"Yeah?" she asked, eying over the lip of her cup. "I've been out here; sorry. Did you need my help with something?"

"No, no. Nothing like that." He set his mug down on the counter and drew a second stool a little closer so he could sit facing her. "I just haven't seen much of you around the house these days. I know you're busy with all of this," he continued, waving a hand to indicate the goings-on in the small shop. "But you've been noticeably more absent than usual."

Prudence shot him a sardonic look. "Yeah, well, the newlyweds have been noticeably *less* absent than usual, and sometimes it's more than I can stomach. I mean," she qualified quickly. "I'm so glad they worked things out, I really am. And I'm glad I'm not going to be the only Goodacre left in this big old ranch house after you move out..." She trailed off, then grimace up at him. "Are you sure you have to move out? Couldn't you stay here with me? I bet you could sell that place for a pretty penny and live high on the hog for the rest of your days. Like a king, Daddy!" She leaned forward and rested her fingers on his knee, a though suddenly occurring to her. "Hey! Why don't you sell your place to Miss Rawlings and stay here with me? It would be perfect for what she's looking for!"

Charlotte Rawlings had returned to Colorado after spending a week in the hollow looking at various properties. She had found two she thought might work—thank goodness, *not* the place next door to Randall Glisson's—but hadn't yet found a place that would make packing up her flock and moving them halfway across the country worth her while. She intended to return in the early summer after shearing season, hoping there might be more options available by then.

Jed chuckled and shook his head. "I am not selling my place to anyone, least of all that woman."

"That woman?" Prudence straightened, her brows lifting. "The way you say that sounds so... I don't know. Disgusted? Disgruntled? Disquieted?" She put a finger to her chin. "Hm. What other 'dis' words can I come up with?"

"I'm not dis-anything over Miss Rawlings, Pixie Cut. I just have no inclination to sell that place to anyone. I bought and built it to my own specifications so that I can live out my mature years in a place constructed to my liking."

"You built this house, too," Prudence began.

"I did, and I know you know this; I built it for your mother and you girls. Now, I've done my part in providing for you all, and it's time to pass this home on to the next generation." He narrowed his eyes at her briefly, then glanced past her, his gaze landing on the photo she'd just been looking at. "Prudence," he began, causing her to stiffen in alarm. He never called her by her given name.

"What?" A wash of trepidation flooded through her. What had come out here to tell her? Was he sick? Was something wrong with one of her sisters?

"Child, I feel like I've left this too long, but with the wedding and all that you've been carrying on your shoulders, I thought it might be best to wait. Now, I'm not so sure."

"What is it, Daddy? You're scaring me." She set her coffee down and crossed her arms defensively.

"Everything is fine. Every*one* is fine," he assured her, all but reading her mind. "It's you I'm concerned about."

"Me?" Prudence pressed a palm to her chest.

Her father took his time in responding. "I worry that I haven't paid enough attention to what's going on in your heart and mind, especially in the last few years. I think I've gotten comfortable with how comfortable you are here at Seven Virtues, and I believe I have been remiss in making plans for my own future without making sure you're on track for what you want out of life."

"Oh, Daddy," Prudence replied. Maybe he wasn't so oblivious after all. "That's not your responsibility. I'm an adult."

"You will always be my child," he interjected before she could say more. "And now with Justice and Brandon living in the big house, I fear you're going to start feeling misplaced. Perhaps you already do."

Prudence shot him a wry half-smile. "Third wheelish. Yeah. But that's to be expected; I know that," she assured him. "We'll all adjust in good time."

Jed nodded slowly, but his expression didn't change. "That's my worry. You always manage to adjust to whatever gets thrown your way. But what about you? Don't you have anything you feel like throwing back?"

"I—I don't know what you mean," she stammered. Except she kind of did. Wasn't his question right along the lines of her own ponderings of the last several weeks?

"I'm only asking if maybe you have some notions or ideas—dreams, if you will—that you'd like us to adjust to." His gaze traveled around the small room. "This business of yours? Miss Rawlings tells me you're doing quite well by it."

"Miss Rawlings? Charlotte told you that?" Her father and Charlotte Rawlings had talked about her? When? Hadn't he, just a moment ago, spoken Charlotte's name like he wanted nothing to do with her?

"She tells me that your online store is doing well, that you have—what did she call it? A really active customer base, I believe. And a strong social media following; does that sound right?"

Prudence's eyes widened at her father's casual use of the terms. These were words she'd never heard him use before, and the fact that he'd learned them from Charlotte Rawlings indicated that he'd spent more time with her than Prudence had been aware of. "Um, yes," she said, nodding quickly. "My business is doing well." A smile tugged at the corners of her lips, and she shrugged self-consciously. "I started selling my products a few years ago because I always made too much to use before it went bad. I was also burning through my meager paycheck from Trilby paying for supplies that I didn't have on hand, so I originally hoped to just to break even." She gestured to the shelves of products that lined two walls of the shop. "I never planned for this, but my Pixie Cut line has taken off, Daddy. For whatever reason, people seem to like what I do."

"Of course, they do. You have always given more than a hundred percent to every endeavor you set your mind to." He studied her, his brow still furrowed. "Let me ask this: Do *you* like what you do? Is this something you see as your future?"

Prudence hesitated, not quite sure how to answer him. She did, indeed, see Pixie Cut Botanicals continuing to thrive and grow, but with so many changes happening around the ranch, she couldn't help wondering if those changes might affect her business—and her general way of life here—as well.

"What about that herb school you were so keen on after high school?" Jed asked when Prudence didn't speak right away. "I know you said the timing wasn't right back then, and I'll admit that I was a relieved papa, knowing you wouldn't be leaving your old man so soon," he said with a sheepish grin. "But have you considered pursuing that again? With all the changes around here—the riding school, your sisters moving in and out of the place—have you given any further thought to it?"

Caught off guard by the question that seemed to come from out of left field, Prudence's mind raced around his words, searching for any underlying motivation or meaning behind them. Was he suggesting she go away for a while? Leave the ranch to Justice and Courage to get their program off the ground? Or was he simply encouraging her to take a firm hold of her future? "I haven't really thought of going back to school," she began, choosing her words carefully. "I mean, with my business taking off the way it has, it seems counterproductive for me to put things on hold and go get an education I may not need." She lifted a hand to wave away her words. "That sounds elitist, and I don't mean it that way. I will keep studying and learning about plants and plant medicines and products for the rest of my life, I'm certain, and if I were to go through an official educational program, it would be wonderful." She paused, imagining what it would be like to study alongside other like-minded students. It brought a soft smile to her lips. "It really would be like a dream, I admit. But honestly, I think I'd rather try to find someone local who might mentor me, who would teach me more about what grows in our area. That way I could keep the business going, the garden, help around here. Help you get settled in your new place. Help take care of the ranch." Okay. That last bit might have been overkill. She had no gifting when it came to chickens and cows, riding tractors, or electrical fencing. She knew it, Daddy knew it, everyone knew it. Which was why she had been able to spend so much time building her business; no one expected her to do much more than the gardening and her share of the chores around the place.

"I see," her father began, but she wondered if he really did. They both sipped their cooling drinks, lost in their own thoughts, before Jed spoke again. "Pixie Cut, it's more than just your future on my mind." He held his hand out between them, palm up, and she rested hers in his large one. "I can't help but notice you're fading a bit. Somethings eating away at you, and I—I worry. The last time—"

"Stop. It's not like that. I'm just a little adrift, I think. Like you said, a lot has changed over the last few years. I'm adjusting, that's all."

Jed took a deep breath, then let it out slowly. "I'm not so sure I believe you," he finally said. "I'd like you to give your future—what *you* want, not what you think everyone else thinks you want—some thought. If you want to pursue that herbal college again, this might be a good time."

"I don't want to leave here, Daddy," she said, pushing up from her stool and circling around to the other side of it to straighten the packing supplies scattered untidily on one end of her workbench. She hated how her voice pitched up significantly, making her sound less like the adult she'd declared herself to be. "Please don't send me away."

"I'm not sending you anywhere, child. I'm giving you the freedom to go, if that's what you want to do."

"But it's not," she insisted, and yet, she had a sudden image of herself behind Collin on his motorcycle, riding off into the sunset together. "I feel like you're trying to push me out of the nest, or something, but I helped make this nest, too, you know. This is my home."

"It is," Jed agreed. "And it's not going anywhere. But that doesn't mean *you* can't, even for a short time. Just think about it, okay?"

"I have thought about it," she said firmly. "I've thought a lot about what I want to do around here. Here, being the key word. I just haven't talked about my thoughts—my plans or dreams—because we've been busy with other things."

"Want to talk about them now?"

"No," she retorted petulantly. "I would just feel like I was trying to defend my position here." She sounded more and more like a child with every word. "Besides, I'm still researching and trying to work out details, and I'm not ready to talk about it all yet."

Jed nodded, then he, too, rose and came to stand beside her at the workbench. He wrapped an arm around her shoulders and drew her gently up against his side. She resisted for only a moment, then leaned her head on his shoulder. Out the window, a bright red cardinal and his tawny mate perched on the bird feeder hanging from one of the eaves of the shop, eating heartily together. A moment later, as if on cue, they both took flight. "I'm not trying to push you out of the nest," he murmured against the top of her head. "I just want you to know that if you want to spread your wings a little, you have my blessing."

"Okay," Prudence whispered in acknowledgment. "Thank you." She gave her father a quick side hug, then straightened and stepped away. "I'd better get back to work. I need to get these orders packaged up and off to the post office before they close today."

"Speaking of the post office," Jed said, reaching into his back pocket. "This came in the mail for you. I thought maybe it might be what you've been looking for the last couple of weeks." In his hand was an envelope, her address written in a script she recognized immediately, even after all these years. She'd seen that fine print on many a graded paper her senior year, seen her name written in his writing dozens of times.

It was all Prudence could do not to snatch it from her father's grip. She did her best to maintain a neutral expression, but when Jed's eyebrow lifted, she knew she'd failed miserably. "From Mr. Stewart?" she asked, then wanted to kick herself. Talk about sounding guilty. "I mean, Collin." She held her hand out for the letter.

"It appears so," he said, turning the missive toward himself and reading the return address as if for the first time, holding it just out of her reach. "Did something happen between you and that young man that I'm not aware of?"

Prudence swallowed hard, lowered her hand, but didn't look away. She wouldn't concede that easily. "Um," she began, not sure exactly how to answer that question. "You mean, during the few days he was here for the wedding?" Then she closed her eyes briefly, realizing that in her effort to be evasive, she'd just given away far too much. She went back to busying herself with items on her workbench, hoping he wouldn't read anything into her question.

Not a chance.

"Well, now," Jed began, his tone contemplative as he waved the letter between them. "I suppose a weekend isn't too little time to have things happen." He paused, cocking his head as if waiting for a response. "But then, I remember you had a thing for him back in high school, and I can't help wondering if maybe you two revisited that notion while he was here."

Prudence gulped and felt her eyes go wide. "Daddy," she admonished, but she sounded a little breathless, and she could feel her cheeks flush. "The only thing that happened is that I fainted, and he carried me into the house. I wish everyone would stop making such a big deal about it."

There went Daddy's eyebrow again. "I see." But he just kept staring at her like he was waiting for her to expound. She decided that silence was her best defense at this point.

Except that her mouth didn't seem to get the message. "I mean, I *did* have a crush on him my senior year," she said. "But then, I think every Plumwood High girl did. The twins couldn't stop talking about him when they were in his class, too. Remember?" If she kept going, she was only going to make things worse.

"I remember," Jed said, his posture deceptively relaxed. Prudence knew better; she felt like she was being played like a fine-tuned instrument.

She thrust her hand out again. "Let me have it, please."

Jed handed her the letter. "I just don't ever remember any of my other daughters exchanging long distance correspondence with him."

As nonchalantly as possible, she glanced quickly at the envelope, then tucked it into the pocket of her craft apron and picked up a roll of brown packing paper. "He probably just wrote to make sure I was okay. I mean, I did faint in front of him. And he was always very courteous that way."

"I remember," Jed said again.

"Besides, we haven't been long-distance corresponding, as you put it. It's one letter, that's all. And now, I really do need to get back to work." She slid her tape dispenser closer, then picked up a pair of scissors, holding them up as proof. "Thanks for bringing it," she said, as she tore a strip of paper from the roll and began wrapping a brown glass jar. *Please leave, please, please, please.* The letter was practically burning a hole in her pocket, and she thought she might explode with anticipation if he didn't go soon.

"Let's have that conversation about your plans in the next couple of days," her father said after a moment. "All right?"

Prudence met his eyes briefly, glad for the change of subject. "Okay. Sounds good."

The moment Jed closed the workshop door behind him, Prudence plucked the envelope from her pocket, pressed it to her chest, covering it in both hands.

For whatever reason, she'd had her doubts that Collin would actually write to her. When a week passed, then two, her doubts had seemed valid. But now, here it was. She could hardly believe it... and part of her was almost too afraid to open it, lest it all be a ruse. A trick. Or worse, him apologizing, rescinding the things he'd said.

Almost too afraid. But not quite.

Prudence crossed the room to the opposite corner of the room to the diminutive slipper chair open sitting near another window. It was her brainstorming chair, and on a shelf close by were her collection of idea journals and photo albums she'd collected over the years. She lowered herself into the seat and held the letter toward the soft autumn daylight. Before opening the envelope, she lifted it to her nose and breathed in. For a moment, she could almost imagine that it smelled like him.

"Don't be so silly," she admonished herself, then slid her finger under the flap and carefully pried it open.

Two days later, another letter arrived, but this time, Prudence was the one who plucked it from among the pile stuffed into the mailbox at the end of the driveway. Jack had wandered over from next door and had followed her down the long gravel lane and back, his smiley face and energetic trot making it extra hard for her to hold back a smile that might expose her secretly giddy mood to anyone watching.

Three more days passed, and yet another envelope with her name on it was tucked into their mailbox. Like the previous letter, this one was short and conversational, a slice-of-life kind of missive. Collin told her about the family who lived in the next condo over, a young husband and wife and their two young boys.

...

The kids call me Mr. Collink. Yes, with a 'k' on the end. I think one of them said it that way when they first met me, and they decided it was more fun to say than plain old 'Collin'. If they weren't so cute, I might challenge them to a duel or something manly and heroic, but let's just say I'm glad it never has to come to that. I'm what some might call a magnet for sharp objects. I can cut myself just by watching a knife commercial. Don't get me started on the numerous altercations between my razor and this mutant chin of mine.

...

"Your chin isn't mutant," Prudence murmured defensively as she climbed the porch steps, the letter pressed to her chest. "I love your cleft chin. Talk about manly."

"What was that?" Jed asked as he stepped out of the kitchen and pulled the door closed behind him.

"Oh, hey, Daddy. Just talking to myself," she said, but she knew her cheeks blazed with telltale color.

"Is that another letter from your young man?"

Prudence rolled her eyes dramatically. "He's not my young man."

"But it is a letter from your Mr. Stewart," he persisted.

"Again, he's not my anything," she began, then shook her head at the teasing glint in his eyes. "Never mind. Yes, I have here a letter from Collin Stewart. Would you like to read it?" She fluttered it at him with a display of false bravado. The last thing she wanted was for her father to read Collin's letter. Not because they had anything in them that she didn't want him to see, but because everything he'd written, he'd written to and for her. Not "Dear Prudence and Jed." Not "Dear Prudence and family."

Simply "Dear Prudence."

Jed chuckled and reached over to gently pinch her chin. "I'm just giving you a hard time, Pixie Cut. It's nice to see some of your color back. If it's because of that fellow and his pen, then he has my blessing." And with that, he strode past her and out toward the barn, calling Jack to follow him.

"You're a funny guy, Daddy!" Prudence called after them, then headed inside and to her room where she could read the letter again, pouring over each sentence, each word, each stroke of the pen in private.

She couldn't decide if three letters in six days was romantic or borderline creepy, but if the way she felt when she saw her name in his distinctive handwriting was any indication, she was going with romantic.

It scared her how badly she wanted it to be romantic.

TWENTY-EIGHT

Dear Prudence,

His name is Abraham Stone.

Mr. Abraham Stone and Walter Matthau, it seems, go out for one last stroll to the mailbox before bed every single night. Mr. Stone goes hoping that there will be a letter from Mrs. Stone. Walter Matthau, I'm beginning to believe, goes because he hopes I (along with my left slipper) will be there. Yes, once again, that little dog tried to lift his leg on my foot. Why does he have it in for me? What did I ever do to him?

Mr. Stone didn't exactly apologize for Walter Matthau's rude manners, but he did keep the dog on a much shorter leash while we spoke.

He's lonely, Prudence. What word did I use when I told you about him? Forlorn, right? I think that was it. Forlorn, and lonely. It's clear that he misses his wife fiercely. He says it's hard going to bed without her.

It's all rather tragically romantic, don't you think? Mr. Stone tells me Mrs. Stone — Evelyn is her name — went into the hospital with a mild, but lingering case of bronchitis at the beginning of the year. Within a few days of being there, it had turned into pneumonia, and she has yet to recover. In April, they moved her to a short-term facility, then when she didn't get better fast enough there, they moved her again in August to a long-term facility, which is where she remains for now. Mr. Stone visits her every day, he tells me, and she writes letters to him on her good days. He says getting those letters right before bed helps him sleep, but that her good days are getting fewer and farther between.

I need to ask him how long they've been married. I get the sense that theirs is one of those lifetime deals. He does seem to be a little lost without her.

I have these neighbors next door, Tracy, Jessica, and Belinda. They remind me of that show, Friends. I never watched it, to be honest, but the way they live and interact with each other feels a lot like a television show. But they bring over their leftovers, which means I eat well on a regular basis. Why am I telling you this?

Shortly after I moved in here, when introductions were being made, I discovered that Tracy and Jess are actually from Southern Indiana, only about fifty miles north of the Ohio River. Neither of them had heard of Plumwood Hollow, but they'd both been down in Kentucky numerous times and we all thought it a small world, etc., and that was kind of the end of the list of what we all had in common. Then in September, Tracy and her boyfriend stopped by to bring me leftover enchiladas, and she happened to see your sisters' wedding invitation on my counter and just about lost her mind. She knew exactly who the Twisted Sisters were—apparently she and Jess had been fans for years. Tracy later told me that she'd even taken some trick riding lessons when she was younger, but after a scary fall that ended with a broken ankle, made the decision to enjoy the sport from the sidelines. (No regrets, she says.)

Anyway, Tracy told me in no uncertain terms that my only option was to attend, if for no other reason than because she wanted me to come back with the up close and personal scoop on the wedding. If she hadn't had a boyfriend, I'm pretty sure she would have latched onto me like a barnacle, and come along as my plus one, whether I asked her to or not.

Which I didn't, just to set the record straight.

All three of them are lovely girls, but I'm pretty sure there might be the equivalent of half a book in their condo. Which means there is never, and I mean NEVER, a moment of silence over there. I'm not sure they even sleep.

They might even be vampires. Don't worry. I always keep my doors and windows locked at night.

Wow. That got weird.

So as you might have guessed, since this is actual pen on paper, not email or text, and therefore, I'm not able to simply "delete" the unwanted stuff, I've decided I'm going to send whatever I write. Like we're having a conversation.

A one-sided conversation, I know. But still, if you were sitting in front of me and I went off about vampires, I wouldn't be able to take it back, right? I figure this way, you're getting to know the real me, not just the carefully edited, scripted version of me.

By the way, if you ever get the notion to write me back, I'd like that.

...

Collin stared at the last line he'd written. Well. He couldn't say it any plainer than that, could he?

TWENTY-NINE

...

Prudence's mind went completely and utterly blank, devoid of anything even remotely interesting to share with the man her heart insisted she still loved. It had taken her almost a week—and two more short, conversational letters from Collin—since his request before she worked up the courage to write back to him. She should have plenty of fodder to respond to. Five letters in less than two weeks. "Count them," she said out loud. "Five, Pru!"

...

I like the idea of not being able to erase words already out there, the transparency of it. You did say this might be a way we could get to know each other, right? No delete button. I'm not sure I'm that brave, but I'm willing to give it a shot.

...

For the next hour, Prudence carefully chose her words, her sentences, paying attention to structure and prose, her tone, in an attempt to make certain Collin wouldn't read anything more into the letter than what she wrote. It was nice to have someone interested in her and her alone, someone who really wanted to know how and who she was. It felt good to know she was being thought of—often, in fact—that someone thought her worth pursuing.

Because that's what he was doing. She knew it, even though she was reticent to admit it. His letters might sound lighthearted and conversational, but she knew better. No one wrote letters anymore, especially not two and three or more a week, not unless they were lovers separated by bodies of water, land masses, or war.

She also knew that if she actually worked up the courage to mail this reply, for all intents and purposes, she'd be accepting his courting of her, no matter how casual and unassuming she made her letter to him sound.

...

I'm glad you made it to the hollow for the wedding. It really was good to see you again, Collin. I hope you'll find your way back to these parts before another five years passes by.

...

Prudence stared at the last line she'd written. Well. She couldn't say it any plainer than that, could she?

THIRTY

Dear Prudence,

Your letter arrived yesterday, and it's taken me a full twenty-four hours to recover from my shock. Not the "shock and horror" kind of shock, mind you. The "happy surprise" kind of shock. I honestly held little hope that you would ever respond, no less so soon. Not after the way things were left between us.

Maybe I'm being too transparent now, but I want you to know that you have put a smile on my face that I haven't been able to wipe off. My cheeks are aching, I'm telling you, and I think I might have been drooling just a little during the study hall class I monitored today. One of the students, a kid name Jerome, shot a paper wad at me. It hit me in the side of the neck, and I hardly felt it. I should have given him detention, but I didn't. I just made him stay after class and straighten the bookshelves at the back of the room. Big mistake. It meant I had to stay after class, too. I made it about fifteen minutes, then cut him loose after eliciting a promise from him never to shoot anything at me again. I'll be tougher on him next time, of course.

Something unusual and kind of cool happened today. Jessica—one of the girls next door—stopped by with two containers of beef stew right before supper. At first, I thought she was planning on joining me for supper, and I almost panicked. I didn't want company. I wanted to reread your letter for the hundredth time, to plan out what I would write back to you. She surprised me when she told me the second container was for my new friend, "the old guy I've been hanging out with." Those were her words.

Apparently, my neighbors have seen us standing at the bank of mailboxes together on several evenings. Nights, I should say. It's usually a lot closer to midnight than what I think of as the evening hours. That tells you the hours the trio next door keep... Anyway, she said they all thought it was "just adorable" that the two of us were standing out there in our matching old man slippers and pajamas, and of course, that his dog was "soooooooooooooo cute" (Again, her words). They tell me it's like looking at me and me in fifty years, and then they laugh hysterically and threaten to get me a little dog of my own for Christmas. They have no idea how much I dislike that dog. Or how much he dislikes me.

So tonight, when I take this letter to the mailbox, I'll be carting along with me a container of homemade beef stew. I hope he won't be offended—some people don't like others thinking they're in need in any way. I'll have to pay attention to his response. I suppose if he seems put off by the gesture, I'll tell him it's for Walter Matthau.

Hey, maybe that will help win WM over to me. And yes, the little mutt still tries to put me in my place every time we meet. Go figure.

So what are your plans for Thanksgiving? I'm off for the whole week, so I've been commandeered into helping a buddy move on Monday and Tuesday, then I'm taking my parents to London to visit my aunt and uncle (Mom's older sister) for Thanksgiving. Yes, London.

Sounds exciting, right?

London, Ohio, that is. Nothing so grand as dashing off to London, England, for this American holiday.

It's not something we usually do, but Aunt Janet has finally retired this year—at 74 years old, mind you—and she wants to cook an enormous turkey. Mom says it's probably a good think I'm not a big turkey fan; says my aunt has never been a skilled hand in the kitchen. Which is one of the reasons we're going up a day early... so Mom can help with the cooking. I'll be hanging with the old guys in the den. I offered to help cook—I make a mean sweet potato pie—but since it's Mom's recipe anyway, she told me I'd just be in the way.

It seems that hanging out with old guys is something I do a lot of these days. Then again, I do spend a lot of time hanging out with fifth graders, too. Maybe I'm just trying to maintain some balance in my life. Yeah. We'll go with that.

Speaking of fifth grade boys, even though I know I once was one, they still have the capacity to surprise me, sometimes even in a good way.

The other day, all the kids were supposed to take their tests home and get a parent's signature. I do this fairly regularly - rather than isolating a kid who gets a bad grade, I randomly make everyone in class get signatures. It's also a way to let parents know when their kids are doing great, too. Anyway, there's this kid, Jerome. Yes, Jerome of the spit wad. He's kind of a big deal in the fifth grade—class clown, has something to say about everything, you know the type. So he positions himself at the end of the line to turn his paper in, then when he is the only kid standing at my desk, he starts patting his pants pockets frantically. After some futile digging and dramatic exclamations of concern, he slaps his forehead and says, "Oh! It's in my other pants." Then he proceeds to pull down his pants to reveal another pair underneath, in which the signed test is, indeed, tucked into a back pocket. I thanked him, he picked up his discarded jeans and returned to his desk, and class went on as usual. I have learned to take things in stride—there is always a Jerome in every class, Prudence. The ironic thing is that Jerome always manages to get exceptionally good grades. He's probably the smartest kid in my class this year. Sadly, he will likely be one of those who get so bored with standardized education that he drops out early - I see it happen time and time again when there isn't someone at home teaching these kids how to harness their minds and develop their potential. They either end up as social derelicts or the next Steve Jobs.

With Jerome, I'm betting on the next Steve Jobs.

...

Collin paused to read over what he'd written. He marveled a little over how much he wanted to keep writing, how much he liked the idea of Prudence sitting off by herself somewhere, reading the words he wrote for her. Throughout his day, he found himself thinking, I need to remember to tell Prudence about this, or, I wish Prudence were here to share this moment with me.

"Careful there, Stewart," he muttered to himself after wrapping up the last few lines of the letter and tucking it inside its envelope. "Move too fast and you might mess things up all over again."

He wrote to her again a few days later, not at all bothered that she didn't send him a reply right away. Then he penned one more the Tuesday before heading to London with his parents.

...

Dear Prudence,

I looked up your website and I'm blown away. I'm so proud of you! I don't mean that in a patronizing way, either. I'm proud FOR you, thrilled about your success. You have hundreds, no, thousands of reviews on all your products, and every one of the reviews is fantastic. Your customers don't just love your products, either. They love you, don't they? But then, of course they do.

I ordered something from you last week. Did you notice? Or do you have one of those automated systems that does all the paperwork for you, and all you have to do is print out a label? I bought one of your honeysuckle and lemon balm gift sets, the one with lotion and lip stuff and a bath bomb. I think that's what you called it. Sounds a little intimidating, but the set has rave reviews on your site, so I took the plunge. It got here yesterday, and I admit that I immediately smelled it. Not because I worried it wouldn't smell good, but because I wondered if the fragrance would remind me of you.

It didn't, not really, and in hindsight, I'm glad. There's something not quite right about my aunt smelling like you.

Aaaaaand... I think it's time to change the subject.

I've started stalking you online, but not in a bad way, I promise. It's nice to see what you've been up to in the last five years, through your posts, your pictures, your videos, etc. You've got a great eye for photography—again, I'm kinda blown away! You seem to capture some kind of magic in all your images, whether of your plants, your products, the scenery shots, the animals you photograph. I especially love the pictures you've taken of Jack. I've never seen a dog smile like that before. And of course, the pictures of you. Something in your eyes makes me think you know things no one else in the whole world does. You're quite captivating, Prudence.

It's Thanksgiving in two days, but I wanted to write to you before I get swept up in the fun fest that is me and the golden oldies in London to tell you that I have a lot to be thankful for this year. My job, my family, my friends, my neighbors, Abraham Stone and even Walter Matthau. I think we're growing on each other. It might have been the beef stew—Mr. Stone admitted to sharing some with the dog.

But most of all, I'm thankful for you, Prudence, that you didn't refuse me completely, that you haven't torn up my letters, or worse, sent them back unopened.

I hope you'll write to me again. I want to read your voice.

...

Was it too much? Was he pushing too hard?

Perhaps he was, but the words had already spilled from his pen, and he now had no choice but to let them go.

THIRTY-ONE

Dear Collin,

I did see your order! Thank you - I hope your aunt enjoyed the set. That one is a customer favorite, especially the fizzy bath bomb. I think it's one of those decadence things. Like we're bathing in champagne or something. Except that sounds kinda gross. Sticky. And wasteful. I'd probably be sneaking sips of my bathwater. Which is more than kinda gross.

And I'm not sure why I'd need to be sneaky about it?

Aaaaaand... I think it's time to change the subject.

But just so you know, I personally packaged up your order, hand-wrote the label, and took it to the post office myself. But then, that's what I do with every order. That doesn't make your order any less special. It means that every single order I get is special. Next year, though, if things keep going the way they are, I'm going to have to hire some help, at least around the holidays. I'm having a hard time keeping up with the orders. But I'm not complaining! I mean, that's a great problem to have, right?

In fact, things have been going so well with Pixie Cut Botanicals (PCB from now on, okay?), that last year, I actually started issuing myself a paycheck instead of putting everything back into the business. I even have a savings account, one that's growing! Sometimes I'm afraid to look at my monthly statements for fear I've just been dreaming, but for whatever reason, God has seen fit to turn my little hobby into a success.

Thanks for letting me brag a little. I think Daddy is actually starting to realize how well PCB is going, but that's because I'm always recruiting him to help me harvest and dry my plants. But the rest of my family has no clue, so it's our little secret, okay? Not that I don't want them to know, but it feels like something that's just mine right now, and I like that feeling.

So I guess you were right. I do know something no one else knows. Well, now YOU know.

And I don't mind.

Thanksgiving here at Seven Virtues was just as chaotic as usual, but in the best of ways, all things considered. For the first time ever, we were not all gathered around our ridiculously large table for the meal. Abby couldn't make it because she was doing a show with several other musicians for some big sports event on Thanksgiving Day. Faith, Cord, Jasmine, and Ollie were also missing. They went to Louisville to spend the holiday with Cord's parents. But inevitably, we always end up with extra people joining us, folks who don't have somewhere to be or anyone to be with on Thanksgiving, and yesterday was no exception. Which means we always have way more food than we know what to do with, since in these parts, everyone brings something, even when they're told not to. A few of Daddy's old codger farm and ranch friends join us every year, and rather than feeling like a third wheel with the disgusting married couples (thanks, Abby, for abandoning me), I, too, hung out with old guys all day. It was actually kinda fun for me. Was it fun for you? The stories they can tell, Collin. My goodness, but we have things easy in this day and age, don't we?

In light of that, it makes me feel a bit petty when I get overwhelmed by all the changes that have taken place around here in the last few years. Five of my sisters—five, Collin!—have married (or remarried in Hope's case) and three of them already have families (or families in the works in Charity's case). I am so happy for each of them, I really am. It's good to see my big sisters so well loved by good men. Courage and Justice don't have plans for kids just yet, but they are "birthing" their trick riding school next year, did you know about that? I wonder if your friend, Tracy, has heard about it. Anyway, they plan to open in April, and they already have a waiting list of students. They deserve for this to succeed. They've worked so hard their whole career, and now to be able to hand down their knowledge and experience to the next generation? What a gift for everyone involved. And Abby, dear, daring, darling Abby, is off following her dreams in Nashville, and I couldn't be prouder of her.

Even Daddy is different these days. He's preparing to move to his own place early next year - not sure if you knew that or not, either. He bought several acres across from Seven Virtues on Carpenter Road and has spent the last year building a log house for himself. He'd hoped to move in by this Christmas, but with all the events of the last year, he's a little behind schedule. I think if he had his way, he'd move in anyway, but one of the things he's still waiting on is a custom wood-burning stove that has been delayed. Our winters here, as you know, are usually pretty mild compared to some parts of the Midwest, but not nearly mild enough to convince us to let him move in without heat. He acts like he's so tough, but the moment he drops into his lounger in front of the fire, groaning all the way down, mind you, he is out like a baby. Or a weary old man. He doesn't fool any of us.

And honestly, I can't help wondering if he's feeling a little nostalgic this holiday season. He's had to hand over so many of us girls into the care of other men. Even Abby, although the only guy in her life is her manager. At least as far as we know.

That said, I did pick up on something about her that isn't sitting well with me. It's like a hint of disillusionment, or something like it. I hate putting it into words, especially a word as discouraging as disillusionment, but something was definitely off, Collin. I made a point to ask her how she was really doing, if everything was going the way she'd hoped—she has a good head on her shoulders, my little sister does, so I know she hasn't gone into things with pipe dreams and unrealistic expectations—but she insisted that she couldn't be more pleased with the journey she's on. I think it's true. I think she's really happy about the road her music has taken her on, but it's the condition of her tender heart that has me feeling in a bit of a quandary. And knowing Abby, she'll just push that aside if she can. Any sacrifice is worth it for her music, you know? But I'm going to try to get her alone at Christmas and see if I can't figure out what it is.

What are your plans for Christmas? How much time do you have off for the holidays? Do you have any special or unique Christmas traditions in your family?

THIRTY-TWO

Dear Prudence,

Your secret is safe with me. Thank you for entrusting it to me.

And now that I know your secret, I'm that much happier for you. What are your plans for the future? Do you think you'll keep the business at Seven Virtues Ranch and expand on site? Are you able to use more of the ranch for your business, or is it allotted for other things? Or do you think you'll start looking for a place of your own? A place you can name after your company?

A lot of questions - sorry. I must admit that I am not entrepreneurial at all, so I don't even know if I'm asking the right ones, but it all sounds pretty exciting to me.

I read what you wrote on your website, about closed doors and open windows, but maybe one day you'll tell me more about your decision not to go to Colorado, about how Pixie Cut Botanicals was birthed out of that decision. I can't help but be impressed by what you've accomplished, in spite of how your plans got rerouted.

You are brave, Prudence Goodacre.

Both brave and beautiful.

I hope you know that.

I'm sorry to hear that about Abby. She seemed her same effervescent self to me, but then I didn't get to have her in any of my classes, so I didn't know her as well as I did you and the twins. I'll definitely keep her - and you and your talk with her at Christmas - in my prayers.

Speaking of Christmas plans, I will be joining my parents at their place, as usual. This year, though, Mom is "letting me" make the sweet potato pie! Will miracles never cease?

My folks host a neighborhood Christmas Eve party at their place every year and people come and go all evening. People bring their family favorite treats so there's this giant smorgasbord spread out in the dining room. It's madness, I'm telling you, but I think they're afraid if they take a year off, or God forbid, hand off the hosting baton to another family on the block, the whole neighborhood might stage a mutiny.

My parents were the first mixed race couple on the street when we moved here. I was just a kid and had no clue that we were odd. Well, at least not because of our skin color - ha-ha. But my folks didn't let their pride or their neighbors' prejudices sway their intent to become a part of their community. That first Christmas Eve, they opened our home and invited everyone on our block and the one behind us. Only two other families showed up. Undaunted, they did it again the following year, and at least half a dozen families made an appearance. By the third year - the first one I really remember - we had the makings of a new neighborhood tradition. The Annual Stewart Family Christmas Eve Party. Next year will be their twenty-fifth one, so I'm pretty sure they've got at least one more in them after this one!

Oh! I almost forgot to tell you! I'm also bringing Abraham and Walter to the party. Yes, Mr. Stone AND Walter Matthau. I didn't have the heart to invite one without the other. Mr. Stone says it's been weeks since he received a letter from his wife, yet he's faithfully checking the mailbox before bed every night. The old guy just about breaks my heart, Prudence. He spent Thanksgiving with his wife, but he says that more often than not these days, she doesn't even know who he is. Sometimes she even gets agitated when he visits; her developing dementia has her becoming paranoid, and she seems afraid of him, which is just brutal. He'll visit with her Christmas morning, but he seemed pleased at the idea of spending Christmas Eve at a traditional neighborhood party. I just hope Walter Matthau will be on his best behavior!

Christmas day, since it's just the three of us, we all sleep in, especially now that I'm older and have no desire to try to catch Santa kissing Mama or leaving gifts under the tree. When we do finally roll out of bed, we open gifts, eat leftover party food so Mom doesn't have to cook, and reminisce about the success of the party and all of the previous ones that came before it. Which inevitably includes recounting the new heights of inappropriate behavior achieved by Lisa and Fred Harding, thanks to the "adultified" eggnog they insist on bringing every year, even though they are the only ones who drink it. I'm pretty sure everyone else is too afraid to try it after witnessing its effect on the Hardings. The craziest part about it all is how normal the couple - who are in their sixties now - behave every other day of the year.

I usually end up walking them home, just to make sure they end up in the right house. Which is next door. No joke.

Every time I spend Christmas there, it's like a nostalgia explosion. The sounds, the sights, the tastes, the smells. All the familiar faces are a little older, and inevitably, there are new faces, too, folks who have moved in, or family members grown and starting families of their own. But the spirit of Christmas feels untainted by time when I'm there, and I'm proud of my parents for somehow preserving that and then sharing it with everyone they know.

Now it's my turn to thank you for letting me brag. I feel like I've led a charmed life in so many ways, Prudence, and I don't take it for granted. My parents have spent their lives fighting - and graciously, I must say - to defend their right to be who they are, no matter what anyone else thinks of them. I'd like to think I've come away with even half their courage and determination.

THIRTY-THREE

Dear Collin,

You asked about my plans for the future of PCB. I'm not sure, to be honest. I'd love to stay here at Seven Virtues. I've never really imagined myself anywhere else, but only because I've never really thought that far ahead. Whenever I think of the future, I have this hazy picture of Daddy and me sitting on the back porch with our coffee cups, shooting the breeze about all the young whippersnappers taking over the countryside. Even though I know full well that Daddy is making plans to move out of here - and off the back porch - in just a few short months.

I have to tell you, though, I worry about what will become of this place. I want to preserve this home's dignity, you know? I want to make her young and pretty again, not let her become some old dowager no one wants around anymore. I want her to be alive, and not just alive with memories, but with people, with friends and neighbors, the way your parents have done with your childhood home.

I don't know what Justice and Brandon's plans for the future are, but I almost feel like they live in the ranch house by default. Out of convenience, since it's here where the trick riding school is going to be, not because it's home to them. I'm sure my own selfish desires play a big part in my perspective, but for whatever reason, I simply can't conjure up an image of them raising a family here, or growing old here.

Sigh. I know I'm being melodramatic about this wonderful old place, but I swear I can almost hear her walls, her floors, that big old fireplace, begging not to be abandoned, not to become a relic.

I want to fill this place, Collin. I don't know how, not without help, but I hate seeing her standing here empty except for a few times a year, her rooms cavernous and her halls echoing.

I love what I do. I love growing things. I love making things with what I've grown. Not cooking things - that's more Charity's forte. No, I love making things that make people feel good about themselves. I love creating fragrances that stir deep-seated emotions like love, passion, bittersweetness, even grief. Of course, nostalgia, too.

I'd love to try to capture the aroma of your Annual Stewart Family Christmas Eve Party. I wonder what it would smell like....

I love hearing that my products help soften work-roughened hands, help lift the spirits of heart-weary bodies. I smile when my customers tell me they have to resist the urge to pour their shampoo over ice cream!

But do you know what I'd love even more? I'd love to help people learn to make these things for themselves, to discover God's design for our bodies and minds to heal themselves by nurturing and tending to the right things and with the right ingredients. There is a place for hospitals and pharmaceuticals, absolutely. But I believe health and healing start in the home, in the food we eat, in the way we treat and are treated by others. And of course, in the kitchen garden where plant medicine abounds.

I think if I could do anything with Seven Virtues, I'd keep Pixie Cut Botanicals small and manageable for me and maybe a few employees, but I'd turn the ranch house into a school of my own. Start small, you know? Hire a real herbalist to teach me and a few other boarding students....

Anyway, I'm dreaming, I know, but you asked. None of this is possible without the consent and support of the rest of the family, and the twins have already got their trick riding school all but locked and loaded. Justice and Brandon aren't going anywhere any time soon, so turning the house into an herb school is pretty much out of the question, at least for now.

So I guess I'll just keep running my business the way I have been, and see what happens.

Sigh. That last sentence makes me feel pretty discouraged. But I don't know what else to do.

THIRTY-FOUR

Be brave. Tell your family what your dreams are. They love you, that's as plain as day. I can't imagine any of your sisters being blind or cruel enough not to see what you've accomplished once you show them. In fact, I imagine they'll be blown away, just like I was, and so proud of you. Your family will want to encourage you, not stand in your way; that's the kind of people they are.

I've been thinking about your ideas, and although it's been a while since I was inside the ranch house, I can absolutely picture it being a learning center. The house kind of had a dormitory feel, didn't it?

Have you talked to Justice and Brandon about their plans? Have they said they intend to stay in the house indefinitely? Or are they just living there until they find a place of their own? In fact, maybe Justice opted to stay there so that you wouldn't be alone in that big old house. Have you ever thought about that?

I suppose it makes sense that at least one of the twins lives on the property with the school going in, but who knows? It's possible Justice and Brandon want something that's theirs, not a house that's co-owned by all of you.

Talk to them. And once they all hear your ideas, you might be surprised by what changes come about.

You won't know until you ask, right?

Be brave, Prudence. Like you were in the garden with me when you looked me in the eye and told me what you wanted.

...

Collin paused, wondering if he should have added that last line. But she had been brave all those years ago. Far more so than he'd been.

He sighed, his stomach twisting at the memory of his actions. Honorable intentions or not, he'd handled things badly with her. No wonder she'd been reticent to give him the time of day.

...

You know, I've been sitting here telling you to be brave, but somethings been eating at me, something I've been too afraid to bring up.

Until now. If I am going to expect you to be brave, then I should expect nothing less of myself, right?

In hindsight - always twenty-twenty, isn't it? - I think things might have gone differently with us if I'd been more like my parents, resisting barriers and standing my ground. If I'd been bold enough to do the right thing at the right time in the right way. I honestly don't know what that would have looked like, and I don't want to waste time playing 'what if' with our past, but if I had it to do all over again, I would do things differently. I wouldn't run, for starters. Okay, maybe I still would have run away out of the garden that particular night. I was scared out of my mind of what might happen if you let me kiss you. It didn't help that I knew your daddy was sitting in his arm chair just inside the front door waiting for us. So, yes, I probably would have still left you standing under that apple tree with my sweater. But if I'd stayed in the hollow, waited until you graduated, until you returned from your school in Colorado? Who knows?

Let me ask you something, Prudence.

Did I do the right thing this time, leaving you standing there on your Daddy's back porch? Or should I have kissed you in your garden, out there under that old apple tree?

I admit that I have spent a significant amount of time playing 'what if' on this subject, and I can assure you, none of it has been wasted time.

THIRTY-FIVE

Dear Collin,

Change. It's a deceptively simple word, yet it wields a heck of a punch, you know?

I am beginning to believe that the only thing that hasn't done much changing around here is me, Collin. I know I said that we'd both changed so much in these last five years, but the more I think about it, the more I wonder how true that is. I mean, I HAVE changed. No one goes from childhood to adulthood without some kind of metamorphosis. I have a business that I've developed almost by accident, one that I love and can see myself doing for years to come, maybe even for my whole life. I'm four times more awesome of an aunt than I was back in high school because I've got four times the number of nieces and nephews now. That IS how it works, isn't it? And I've kinda taken over as the daughter who watches out for Daddy. I'm not nearly as attentive (translate: as bossy) as Faith was, but Daddy and I get along out here like an old married couple. Or like an old man and his spinster daughter. Ha.

Wow. That makes me sound like I feel sorry for myself. I don't. Really, I don't.

But if I'm being honest, and I'd like to think I can be with you, Collin, underneath all those things I just listed, I'm still the same old me, the same girl, still standing under the same apple tree in the same garden. And I'm starting to think that may not be such a good thing. I'm kind of stuck. You say I'm brave, but I'm not. I'm afraid of everything. I think I've always been afraid. I may dress weird and do odd things with my hair and makeup, but that's just for show. A facade of false bravado, one I've gotten comfortable hiding behind. I have always played it safe, always gone the way the wind blows, taking the easy way so I didn't have to fight against the current.

You want to know why I didn't go to Colorado?

Sure, part of it had to do with my oh-so-tragic broken heart. There was a time I wasn't sure I'd ever heal from it. But to be fair, my bleeding heart was really just the straw that broke the camel's back, so to speak. The excuse I needed not to go.

In fact, had you responded positively to my offer, I might have used you as my excuse anyway.

The real reason? I was afraid. I was afraid I'd fail. That I wouldn't be good enough, wouldn't be tough enough. That I wouldn't BE enough to make anything of myself.

I haven't ever said all of this to anyone before, so forgive me if I'm rambling, but I want you to understand where I'm coming from.

I am a watcher. A listener. A discerner. I have this "ability" to read people, to understand what makes them tick, to recognize things that are out of balance in other people's lives, sometimes even before they do. My Daddy tells me it's a God-given gift. I'm not sure I agree, at least about the God-given part, and I'm not sure others think of it as a gift, either, God-given or otherwise. I have put people off with the things I say, that's the truth of it.

Why don't I see it as a gift? Because I came by this "ability" to watch and listen and discern out of necessity. Desperation, even.

I have a problem with change, Collin. It scares me, because change in my life usually equates to someone leaving me behind, forgetting about me. I have struggled all my life with feeling transparent. Maybe not invisible, but not truly accounted for. Does that make sense?

My mother died—she "left me"—when I was four. And in his overwhelming grief, my father left me for a time, too. Thank goodness that was temporary. But it wasn't just my parents. Faith took over caring for Abby, who was just a baby, then. She had lots of help from Mrs. Flanner next door, but Faith stepped into the matriarchal shoes in the family like a warrior. I don't know that any other thirteen-year-old girl could have filled those shoes as well as she did. We are a whole family because of Faith, I'll have you know. Anyway, Charity and Hope had each other, Courage and Justice had each *other. Because I was introverted by nature and didn't really know how to express my needs—then again, what four-year-old does?—I was left alone to process all of it. I know both Daddy and Faith, at least, feel some guilt over how all of that played out, but hindsight is twenty-twenty, and it was never anyone's intent to forget about me. Sometimes things like that just happen.*

But they treat me like I'm fragile, like they used to treat my mother, who actually was fragile.

Faith says that out of all us girls, I look the most like her. Most of the time, that makes me feel good. But when I see my father watching me as if afraid that I might break, it makes me want to scream.

I may be afraid, Collin, but I am NOT fragile. I am not my mother.

I admit that I've given them reason to worry in the past. I didn't thrive as a child, but because of the above circumstances, that should be no surprise. When I started school, I was easily overwhelmed. It was too loud, too crowded, and too... well, too many hours spent inside. I often ended up in the nurse's office complaining of a stomachache - there was a window by the sick station that looked out toward the woods. But by the time I made it to high school, I was finding my way. I had friends of my own, a boyfriend or two, but it all felt—I don't know. Transient, I suppose. Temporary. Like I was just there passing time.

Then I fell for you.

...

Prudence set down her pen and took a deep breath. Could she keep going? Should she keep going?

Collin said she was brave. Did she believe him?

...

I did kind of fall apart after high school, Collin. You leaving like that only validated my fears about myself. Please know that I don't hold it against you. I never have. In fact, I always thought it was my fault, that I'd behaved badly and cost you your job. So I'm glad you told me your reasons for doing what you did, because its allowed me to look back and see things a little more clearly.

Unfortunately, what I'm seeing now isn't a whole lot better. I think I understand what better now those verses in the Bible that talk about a bruised reed and a smoldering wick. That's what I feel like. Bent and bruised, a flame that could easily burn out.

But if those verses are to be believed, God can still use me, right? He doesn't want me bent and bruised, hiding my light under a cloak of fear so that it's in danger of burning out.

You're right, Collin. It's time for me to make some changes. To stop waiting—in fear and trembling—of what's coming around the corner toward me.

It's time for me to be brave, to believe in myself and my own dreams as much as I believe in everyone else's.

I'm going to talk to my family about my dreams this Christmas.

...

Prudence studied the words she'd just written, doing her best to ignore the voice of her four-year-old self, the one that pleaded with her to hide, to be afraid of the great big world out there. She didn't know how this decision would play out, what changes she would implement first, but something shifted inside her, a flutter of hope, of anticipation.

Maybe Daddy was right. Maybe it was time to spread her wings a little, see what kind of air she could get.

...

Do you remember how much fun Plumwood Hollow's downtown annual New Year's Eve party was? Well, it still is. I'm sure your December is busy with school and then Christmas with the family, but if you don't have anywhere else that you'd rather be, I'd love to have you come celebrate with our family this year.

Hindsight. Mistakes. Second chances. Brand New Years. Don't they all kind of work together?

You know, I believe there's a tradition on New Year's Eve, something about a clock striking midnight, champagne, and kisses. Maybe this New Year's Eve can mark the start of a second chance for us, a way to right past mistakes, now that we're both seeing more clearly.

What do you think? Shall we be brave together?

THIRTY-SIX

DEAR PRUDENCE,

Yes, I remember Plumwood Hollow's annual New Year's Eve parties.

No, there is nowhere I'd rather be.

Yes, I'd love to celebrate with you, Wild horses couldn't keep me away.

Yes, let's be brave together, my dear Prudence.

DEAR PRUDENCE,

This letter will be another short one, not because I don't want to write more, but because I want to get straight to the point.

I have been asked, last minute, to chaperone a group of kids from our church who are going on a skiing retreat between Christmas and New Year's Day. The chaperone—Roy—whose place I'm taking has developed acute bronchitis and has essentially been put on bed rest for the week, which means he's down for the count until the 29th at the earliest. Needless to say, because it's such late notice, they've had trouble finding a replacement chaperone for the group.

When they approached me, I agreed to fill in, but made it clear that someone would need to take over for me on New Year's Eve. Roy assures me that his antibiotic treatment is already working, that his doctor says he should be up and running again by then, but the youth pastor also promised me he would arrange a backup for that night, just in case.

I'm writing to let you know about this for two reasons. One, please pray for these kids. They're going to enjoy the skiing, of course, but it's a small group *who are quite serious about their faith, and the skiing is happening around some intense sessions of prayer and worship and searching for God's purpose in their lives. This time could be life-changing for them.*

The second reason is that I know how church volunteering works, the whole "twenty percent of the people do eighty percent of the work" thing. Which means there's a definite possibility that Roy might not be well enough to come up to the retreat after all, and that the backup plan the youth pastor is still trying to get in place won't work out either.

Which also means that there is a slight chance I'll be stuck up at the retreat center through to New Year's Day and end up missing the New Year's Eve party with you.

If that happens, I will do everything in my power to be there before the day is out so we can at least celebrate the first day of the New Year together.

I don't foresee any of this happening, Prudence. I am sure Roy will show—he's really bummed about missing out on the skiing. Ha ha. But even if he doesn't, I am counting on Seth and Sierra (the youth pastor and his wife) to find someone to cover for me. I told Sierra a little about you, about us, and about how important it is that I'm in Plumwood Hollow on New Year's Eve—I hope you don't mind—and she said she'd make it happen.

But famous last words and all, right?

So just in case, I'm telling you now what's going on next week. Please know that I would not have agreed to do this had it not been for the fact that they haven't been able to find anyone else.

I am and will continue praying for you as you prepare to share your heart with your family.

I can't wait to hear all about it. In person!

I can't wait to see you again, my dear Prudence.

...

He added his phone number to the letter under his name, and asked her to please call to let him know she'd gotten his letter before he left in the early hours of the day after Christmas, since he wasn't sure what the retreat schedule would be like or how much down time he'd have to himself.

THIRTY-SEVEN

COLLIN'S LETTER ARRIVED TWO days before Christmas. Prudence skimmed it quickly, holding her breath as she did, certain, up until the very last word, that he was backing out of coming to Plumwood Hollow for New Years.

But he wasn't... or was he?

She read it again, her fingertips drifting over the grooves his pen had made in the paper. She could practically hear him reading the words to her, the regret in his voice.

Regret, but not remorse. There was no apology in his letter.

No, he'd written to tell her that even though he still *hoped* to join her for New Year's Eve, there was a good possibility he wouldn't make it.

And he expected her to be okay with it.

To be okay with being pushed to the back burner, yet again.

Tears prickled behind Prudence's eyes. She lay the letter face down on her workbench so she wouldn't search the words for a different message. "He's doing something so much more important than partying with you, Pru," she whispered into the quiet of her shop. "He's helping teenagers discover who God wants them to be."

And Collin had such a heart for teenagers; she knew that. She wasn't surprised he'd agreed to step in, and she shouldn't be hurt by his decision, either. In fact, she should be proud of him for giving up his time to fill in where there was a need. That was who Collin was: selfless, kind, generous, and available...

To everyone, but her, it seemed.

"Stop it, Pru," she admonished herself. "He went out of his way to let you know what's going on, to give you plenty of warning, should the worst-case scenario turn out to be the real one."

But in the back of her mind, another voice, this one no longer four and afraid, stomped her foot. *He said he'd be here. He said wild horses couldn't keep him away. He promised.*

She lifted her hands to her face and let the tears fall, her shoulders sagging in defeat and disillusionment. Once again, he'd abandoned her to do the right thing, the good thing, because he believed it was the best thing.

"But what about me, God?" she cried out, the words muffled behind her hands. "I want to be the 'best' thing in his life. Is that too much to ask? The thing—the *person*—he'll drop everything for to be with?"

Prudence thought she heard the tiniest snick of a latch coming from somewhere inside her ribcage. She couldn't be certain, but she thought maybe it was the sound of her heart locking down the wings she'd just started using again.

She wouldn't call him today, not with her emotions in such turmoil. She wouldn't call him tomorrow, either. Not with the Annual Stewart Family Christmas Eve Party going on. Nor would she call him on Christmas Day, no matter how badly she might be tempted. And there'd be no need to call him after that—he'd probably be out of cell phone range for the week.

She'd see him when she saw him.

Whenever that might be.

CHRISTMAS MORNING DAWNED QUIET and cold, and outside, the gray sky hinted at the storm the weathermen had been eluding to the last few days. When Prudence, wrapped in her thick fuzzy robe, shuffled down the hall to the kitchen a few minutes later, she was surprised to find the lights still off, no coffee brewing, and the thermostat still set low for sleeping.

Gone were the days of little girls practically dragging their parents—then, just their father—out of bed at the crack of dawn. Gone were the days of noisy giggles and excited exclamations at the sight of stuffed stockings and too many packages to count under the Christmas tree. Gone were the days when the heady scent of cinnamon rolls mingled with the first hint of roasting turkey that filled every crook and corner of their home.

Prudence didn't turn any lights on, but busied herself setting up the coffee pot and preheating the oven. She peeled the plastic wrap off the pan of cinnamon rolls Charity had prepped and brought over the night before, and when the oven beeped that it was ready, she slid the special treat in, holding the stove door open a little longer than necessary as the heat warmed her hands and face.

She didn't raise the thermostat in the hall, but instead, headed into the living room and laid new wood in the fireplace. It didn't take her long to get a good blaze going, and by the time the coffee had finished brewing, and the sweet, cinnamon scent of the rolls filtered into the room from the kitchen, Prudence had the tree lit up, soft Christmas music playing on the television, and she was beginning to feel a little warmer, a little cheerier, if not exactly any more festive.

She filled a mug and added a generous splash of heavy whipping cream to it, along with a dollop or two of real maple syrup, then headed back into the living room and curled up in Daddy's recliner to wait for the rest of the gang to wake up.

It wouldn't be the whole family gathered around the tree this morning; only Justice and Brandon, Abby—if they could pry her out of bed—Daddy, and Prudence. Faith and Cord and their two children would spend the first hours of Christmas morning in the home Cord had built for them just beyond the strip of trees that marked the property line between Whispering Hills and Seven Virtues Ranch. Now, with all the leaves gone, Prudence could see the pretty little home from her back porch. Charity and Frank would start their morning at the grand old house next door—opening in spring as the new Whispering Hills Bed and Breakfast. Hope, Levi, Yvette, and Levi's mother who still lived with them, would also do their own family stuff, and for the first time in their lives, Courage and Justice would awaken to Christmas Day apart from each other, with

Courage at the Lynxwilder home, celebrating her first holiday with Joe and his mother, Sarah.

But then, starting around noon, the different families would descend upon the Seven Virtues Ranch house, bearing gifts and food, joy and laughter, ready to create new memories to tide them over for another year.

It was Daddy who made his way from the hall first. "Merry Christmas, Pixie Cut," he said, his voice gravelly and deep. "Smells good in here."

Prudence smiled over at him. "Merry Christmas, Daddy. Need any help with the horses?" She was feeling quite cozy all curled up in a ball under a heavy fleece throw. The fire was burning hot and the room had thawed considerably. But she hated seeing him head out there alone, especially under such a moody sky.

"I got em. You keep my chair warm for me." Jed shot her a grin as he slipped into his heavily lined barn coat. "Be back shortly." He would be, too, Prudence was certain. He hadn't even stopped for coffee first.

Brandon made an appearance shortly, but after taking one look into the living room and finding only Prudence there, he said poured two mugs of java, then headed straight back down the hall toward the bedroom he shared with Justice. The door closed loudly behind him, then Justice's laughter rang out. Prudence hunkered down a little lower in the chair, pulling the blanket up around her ears. She quietly hummed along with Taylor Swift singing George Michael's "Last Christmas" in an attempt to block out any other sounds of holiday cheer coming from down the hall.

Daddy swept back inside, bringing with him a gust of frigid air, just as the timer went off for the cinnamon rolls to come out. While Prudence put the finishing touches on breakfast, Jed went pounding on doors, booming out "Ho ho ho! Merry Christmas!" at each room.

Faith and Cord and their kids arrived just after the noon hour only moments ahead of Hope and her little family. Yvette and Jasmine latched onto each other the moment they entered the room, and after helping settle Nona into a low armchair near the fire, Hope and Levi headed back out to grab their contributions to the family meal they'd be sharing later that afternoon, a gorgeous standing rib roast he had dressed and ready to put in the oven, a crock pot of Nona's Spanish rice, and a platter of assorted homemade cookies and other treats. Faith handed Ollie over to Cord and headed straight to the kitchen where she would, for the rest of the day, commandeer the show.

Courage, Joe and Sarah came an hour later, having decided that morning to stop by the cemetery to take Christmas flowers to Joe's father's grave. In spite of the cold, they'd spent a little time cleaning the stone and trimming up the grass that was trying to creep across the flat base of the marker. They brought with them a beautiful fresh salad made from the tender greens Joe had growing in his greenhouses year-round. Sarah and Courage had made an apple crumb pie and a pumpkin pie, too.

Charity and Frank made their appearance just as the kids were getting antsy, and for the next hour or so, they drank coffee, ate goodies, talked about Christmases past, and filled the room with love and laughter. Nona seemed to be enjoying the melee from her post by the fire, and Jed, in his recliner, watched his burgeoning family, a gentle, self-satisfied smile on his face.

Prudence observed it all from her corner of the sofa, marveling at how large the family had grown in the last few years, and at how easy it had been to embrace every new member as one of their own. To adjust, as Daddy had said, to changes that were manifested in love. Her sisters seemed so happy, so content these days, and Prudence knew much of that had to do with the men who loved them. Abby, too, seemed to be settling comfortably into this new season in her life, and although she reverted to being the goofy kid sister inside the walls of their home, to the world around her, she presented a composed, confident, self-assured young lady ready to take on whatever life had to offer. Prudence still worried about her—she'd overheard snippets of a heated phone conversation late last night, but this morning, there was no indication of a rough night's sleep in her little sister's behavior.

Maybe you're just trying to project your own disquiet onto poor Abby. She's happy, can't you see? Why do you always have to look for trouble? This time, the voice sounded suspiciously like Justice's. Prudence lifted her cup to her mouth to hide her smile. Trust Justice to say it like it was, even in Prudence's head.

Her hands were trembling as she lowered her cup. She needed to stop drinking coffee. And eating sugar. If she didn't get some protein in her system soon, she was going to crash and burn. She lifted her gaze to find her father's eyes on her, studying her. She saw love there, deep and abiding, and she smiled back at him. It didn't matter that Prudence didn't have a man of her own, a man who considered her the best thing in his life, the most important thing. She had this ranch, her gardens, a remarkable family, this town she could call her own. She had Daddy on her side, a king of men, and that was far more than most people could say.

A couple hours later, the kitchen counters were full to overflowing with all the fixings of a Christmas meal. Levi pulled the rib roast out of the oven to rest while Charity and Frank headed back over to Whispering Hills for the turkey, and to pick up Binks, the old foreman, who'd made a habit of joining the Goodacres for Christmas dinner for the last couple of years.

"You should see the two of us in the kitchen these days," Charity said as she stood near Frank, who had pulled out one of the dining chairs and had sat to put on his boots. She bumped his shoulder with her hip, then smoothed her hands over her suddenly protruding belly. "Between his fake leg and my baby bump, we are about as coordinated as penguins."

Frank shot her a leer as he straightened from tying up his boots. "You think I bump into you by accident?" He reached out and laid his hand over hers where they rested on the half-moon curve of her stomach.

Prudence turned away from the tender tableau, filled with a deep and sudden longing that made the spaces between her ribs ache.

The rib roast was just about ready to serve by the time Charity, Frank and Binks returned, bringing with them the turkey and a tureen of aromatic gravy. The foreman's contribution was a Mason jar of his spicy, candied pecans, a family favorite among the Goodacre clan. Abby snatched the jar out of his gnarled hands, threw her arms around him, kissed him loudly on the cheek, then thanked him effusively before disappearing down the hall with the jar.

"Bring those back here, young lady," Faith called after her.

To which Abby responded, "You're not my mother!" But she did return shortly, and with the jar, no less. Although enough of the nuts were missing to make it obvious that she'd stashed a good handful or more somewhere in her room.

It took a bit of finagling, but eventually, everyone found seats around the table. When Daddy stood at his place and offered a prayer of blessing over the meal, over his family, and over the day they were celebrating, it all felt rather momentous, and there were more than a few surreptitiously dabbed eyes when it was over.

By the time they all went their separate ways, the storm that had been threatening for two days drifted off course, leaving the sky cold and clear. The stars above were so bright, it was as if the angels had decorated for Christmas. With the house set to right, Justice and Brandon off to spend the evening with Courage and Jo, and Abby out with friends, it was just Daddy and Prudence in the big old place. They sat in companionable silence together, the living room lit only by the fire crackling and dancing at the hearth and the white lights of the Christmas tree.

It hurt to think that this might be the last Christmas night spent like this, but Prudence refused to focus on that. "It was such a great day, wasn't it?" she said, taking a small, almost obligatory bite of the pumpkin pie she'd served them both to have with her hot chocolate and Daddy's coffee. The man could drink the black brew right up until bedtime and never have it affect his sleep. *Caffeine is no match for manual labor,* he always insisted.

"It was, indeed, a great day," Jed agreed solemnly.

The silence fell around them again, but when Prudence glanced over at her father, she found him watching her. He didn't speak, but she could tell by the look in his eyes that he was waiting, biding his time, giving her the floor.

"I've been thinking about what you said out in the workshop a few weeks ago, Daddy," she began, surprising herself just a little. She hadn't intended to open this conversation up today, to rock the boat in any way, but suddenly, the opportunity to talk about her ideas was presenting itself. *Be brave.* If she was going to be brave, with or without Collin, then the time was now.

THIRTY-EIGHT

Jed nodded encouragingly at Prudence, but he remained silent.

"I do have ideas for my future, things I'd like to explore. I've been hesitant to talk about them for many reasons, one of them being, as you said, that I adjust. I accommodate. I want people to be happy, Daddy, and if my sacrifice brings others happiness, then I'm happy to do so."

Frown lines formed along her father's brow.

"Another reason I've been hesitant to share them is because I often feel like I'm not taken very seriously. I feel like you and my sisters, most people in this town, in fact; you all metaphorically pat me on the head, like I'm some fragile child who needs special treatment. But I'm not, Daddy." She straightened in her seat, squaring her shoulders, and shifting a little so that she faced him more fully. "I am a good businesswoman. Did you know that? I have taken my hobby and turned it into a successful online business. Do you know that I have more than enough money in my savings account right now to purchase my own home, complete with a couple acres for my own gardens? That's solely from profits, Daddy, from what I'm paying myself. The meager wages I make from Trilby is almost pocket change these days. I heard Miss Rawlings talking about some of the places she was looking at, and although I wouldn't want or need nearly as much as she does, for the first time, I realized that I was in a position to spread my wings, like you told me to."

Her father nodded slowly, contemplatively. "I must admit, I had no idea. But I am not surprised; not one bit. I see the way you pour yourself into every aspect of your work, from the jobs you do for Trilby, to your own products, your gardens. You have what it takes, and I am not at all surprised by your success. Well done, Pixie Cut. Well done."

"Thank you." Prudence felt tears welling, but she blinked them back. Hadn't she just finished telling him that she was a good businesswoman? Crying wasn't professional, and it certainly wouldn't help her in making her case.

"I'm proud of you," her father added, as if sensing that she needed to hear the words. "I hope you're proud of yourself."

"Thank you," she said again. "That means a lot to me. And I'm starting to take pride in who I am, in what I've accomplished. I'm learning what it means to do so, anyway, although, I have to admit this level of success scares me. It doesn't seem real to me, and a big part of me feels like I don't deserve it. But that's the other reason I've been reticent to even make plans."

When she paused to collect her thoughts—she wanted to say this the right way so as not to garner pity or sympathy, but to simply state facts—Jed said, "Don't be afraid to tell me what's on your heart."

Be brave. Prudence nodded quickly, swallowed hard, and continued. "I have spent my whole life waiting to be let down, to be left by the wayside, to be passed over. And the thing is, it's happened time and time again, like a self-fulfilling prophecy. When Mama died, I felt so abandoned, but also guilty because I knew she hadn't done it on purpose." She reached up to touch the spiky hair on top of her head. "Why do you think I've never changed my hairstyle? It's the last one she gave me, remember?"

"I remember." Jed said softly, smiling tenderly at her.

"Then you... well, you kinda checked out for a while," she said, not wanting to hurt him, but needing him to know all of it. "Then all my sisters went off to school, leaving me at home alone with what seemed like the shell of you. And Faith took my baby from me," she added in an attempt to lighten the weight of her words. "I'd asked Mama for a twin of my own, just like Justice and Courage had, and when she told me about Abby coming, I just assumed she'd gotten pregnant for me."

"She said as much to me," he said. "I remember how much you hovered after Abby was born. Like you weren't quite sure we'd gotten what we ordered."

"Exactly," Prudence said with a giggle. "But I wasn't about to complain. I loved her before I even laid eyes on her because I believed her to be mine. Then when Mrs. Flanner stepped in to help?" Prudence shook her head in mock dismay. "I thought that woman was going to steal our baby from us. Faith assured me we got to keep Abby, but that she would be responsible for taking care of her, not me, and that Mrs. Flanner was only helping us figure out how to go about doing that. At that point, handing her over to Faith felt like an acceptable compromise."

"I'm so sorry, Pixie Cut," Jed began. "I wish I had been a stronger man, a better husband and father. I'm not prone to dwell on the way things would or could or should have been, however, I do take responsibility for the wrongs I have done. Forgive me, child, for leaving you alone when you needed me." He swallowed audibly, and looked like he wanted to say more, but Prudence didn't let him continue.

"Oh please don't, Daddy. There was never anything to forgive. It was all so messed up back then, for all of us, and I never held any of this against anyone. We have all done the best we can in this family, and I think we've done pretty well, don't you?" She didn't wait for his answer but went on. "I only told you because I'm just now realizing how much it all has played into the person I've become. I guess I kind of thought I just hovered over all of it, that I stayed unaffected and safe. But in the end, those experiences are the reason I hover, the reason I distance myself from the things I want. Does that even make sense?"

"Makes perfect sense," her father confirmed, but he waited, clearly sensing that she wasn't finished.

"Out of self-preservation, I have learned to be content with pouring myself into other people's lives and futures." She snorted sardonically, then voiced the epiphany that had just occurred to her. "It's kind of ironic, isn't it? I'm a wedding planner, Daddy. I'm paid to launch other people's dreams." She shrugged. "But I've been content with that. At least, I suppose, content enough."

"Why, then, do I feel so dissatisfied for you?"

Prudence shrugged again. "Maybe because I'm no longer satisfied with that, myself."

"So what do you want?" Jed asked, sitting forward a little. "Do you want to look for a place of your own? A little cottage with a custom workshop, a greenhouse, a massive garden—"

She interrupted him with a shake of her head. "No, that's not it." She started to bring her knees up, wrapping her arms around them like a hedgehog curling into a defensive ball of prickly quills. Realizing what she was doing, she immediately shifted to sit taller, her legs folded ladylike—and rather professionally, Prudence thought—at her side, the way proper ladies did in paintings of picnics in the garden or on the beach. She took a deep breath and said, "I'm not interested in spreading my wings, Daddy, not if they take me away from here." She shook her head emphatically. "I just can't see myself anywhere else."

Jed's frown deepened, but she kept going.

"Don't worry. I'm not clipping my wings, so to speak. I already have those things you asked about, or the possibility of those things, I should say. I mean, I have big ideas—no, big plans." *Be brave*, she reminded herself, not in Collin's voice this time, but in her own. "Big plans for *this* place," she repeated, speaking the words emphatically, her voice growing firmer as she spoke. "Right here at Seven Virtues Ranch."

"Well, what about your young man?" Jed asked. The question seemed to come from out of the blue.

"My—you mean, Mr. Stewart? Collin?" She fought the urge to curl up again.

"Yes. Collin."

Prudence dropped her gaze to her lap. With one finger, she traced the pattern of snowflakes on her flannel pajama pants. Finally, she met her father's eyes again. "I don't know. He's not really mine, at least not that I'm aware of. Maybe he never will be, and that would break my heart all over again."

"Again? So it's been him this whole time? Since high school?"

"Was it so obvious back then?" Prudence asked, cringing.

"To everyone."

Prudence's eyes widened, then she closed them in surrender. "You mean, the whole family knows?"

"I think everyone suspected as much. Even Abby had an inkling back then. She asked me yesterday when his letter came for you if you two had ever sorted things out after that night he came to supper."

Prudence sighed. "She teased us mercifully when he was out for the wedding. I just thought she was being an irritating little sister. I had no clue she thought we were picking up where we left off."

"Which was where?" Jed asked, a steely edge cutting through his words.

"Nothing happened, Daddy," Prudence assured him, locking eyes with him. "Not like that. Collin was the perfect gentleman in every way, I promise you. I'm the one who stepped across the line." She tried to swallow the lump of misery that was forming at the back of her throat. "I put him on the spot. I confessed my feelings to him, knowing he could do nothing about them, even if he did reciprocate. He did the right thing. He left."

"Ah." Jed nodded slowly and lifted a hand to rub at the scruff along one side of his jaw. His expression was one of revelation and regret. "Passed over. Left by the wayside," he said in reference to the fears she'd admitted earlier. "Just like everyone else in your life."

"Right or wrong," Prudence agreed, her voice cracking around the words. "He left me."

Jed shifted in his big old recliner, making room for her the way he used to when she was younger. "If you're not too grown up," he said, holding out his arm to invite her in.

Without a moment's hesitation, Prudence rose and crossed the room to squeeze into the narrow space at her father's side. He wrapped his arm around her and she laid her head on his shoulder, feeling small and childlike, at the same time, more aware than ever at how age had inexorably altered the feel of her father's embrace.

"And you stayed in Plumwood Hollow instead of going away to school," he said, his voice rumbling in his chest under her ear. It wasn't a question; he was just putting two and two together. "Here at home where you felt safe."

"Yes." She wiped away a rogue tear that had breached her guard. "But it's turned out all right, in spite of myself, hasn't it?"

Jed wasn't finished, though. "And now I'm bailing out on you again, aren't I?" he asked softly. "Abandoning you to figure out your future alone."

Prudence shook her head. "No. You're not. You're stepping into a new season of your life, just like everyone else in this house is doing. Something I should be doing, too." She waved a hand in the general direction of his new place. "I'm proud of you for venturing out on your own. I had no idea—none of us did—that you didn't plan to die here."

"Oh, I still plan to die here, don't you worry. I figure I'll wander back over one morning and set my weary old bones under that apple tree in the garden when it's my time to go. If Jack's still around, he'll keep me company until one of you girls stumbles across my carcass."

"Daddy, that's awful!" She elbowed him in the ribs.

Jed let out a delighted chuckle. "Give you girls one last scare. Make up for all the times you have raised my blood pressure through the roof or stopped my heart for one reason or another."

"Stop it. You're not allowed to die, you hear?" Prudence admonished. "You're a legend, you know, and legends never die."

"Well, we'll see about that," he said, without really conceding. "But let's not get off track. Tell me what's happened between you and Collin. I thought, by the letters, by your rosy cheeks and ready smiles," he added playfully, "that you were finding your way back to each other."

Prudence sighed, more confident now that she was tucked into her father's side. "I kinda thought so, too, but I am having reservations. They seem selfish, I suppose, but they're there, nonetheless. In invited him to the New Year's Eve party next week, and he said he'd come."

"That's good news, right?"

She made a derisive sound. "It was until he accepted a better offer."

Jed flinched and drew back a little so he could see her face. "A better offer than one from my daughter?"

"It was from God." She wrinkled her nose. "I can't compete with the Almighty, Daddy."

"Explain," Jed replied, not smiling at her wry response.

"He had to fill in last minute for someone who got sick. To be a chaperone for his church's youth group *ski retreat.*" She made air quotes around the last two words. "Even I wouldn't say no to an all-expenses paid ski retreat," she added.

"Not true," Jed countered, that hard edge back in his voice. "If you'd promised to be somewhere else, you would definitely turn down the offer."

"It wasn't an offer, though. They needed him. He was the only one who could do it at such late notice."

Jed pulled back again. "You're trying to tell me that out of all the people in Cincinnati, Ohio, Collin Stewart was the only man available to chaperone at this youth group's ski retreat? Somehow, I find that hard to believe."

"They asked everyone at church," Prudence said, not sure why she was defending Collin now. "I mean, that's the way it sounded from his letter. And they're doing everything they can—" Again, she made air quotes, indicating that she knew exactly what happened to best laid plans. "—to arrange a backup for him so Collin can still come to the hollow for the New Year's Eve party."

"What about the parents of these youngsters? One of them couldn't step up? Too excited about getting a break from their rotten teenagers?"

"Daddy!" Now it was Prudence's turn to rear back. She frowned at him. "It's not just a ski retreat. It's also supposed to be like some mountain top experience with God."

"Quite literally, by the sound of it." Jed was not impressed. "Seems to me your Mr. Stewart has trouble with priorities. You know, young lady, I believe there is no such thing as 'the only one' in God's kingdom. Especially in a church. The Almighty is perfectly capable of finding the help he needs when he has a job that needs doing. It's our own pride that tells us we're the *only one.*" He didn't use air quotes the way Prudence did, but he said those last two words as if they tasted like bitter herbs. "I dare say more people would step up to do God's work if it weren't for folks like your Mr. Stewart jumping in headfirst, prior commitments be damned, who believe they're the only ones who can do the job."

Her father was getting all riled up, and Prudence wasn't sure whether to chastise him for cursing—something completely out of character for him—or shout, "Preach it, Daddy!"

"A man is only as good as his word, and a good man honors his commitments. Someone else would have stepped up, had young Stewart said he wasn't available." Jed shook his head in disgust. "A man willing to set aside the woman God gives him because he believes he is the *only one* who can perform a certain church activity?" He left the statement unfinished, but his sentiment was more than evident.

"Wait, Daddy. You're reading into things. I'm not so sure—"

"Am I?" he asked, but it wasn't really a question. "Tell me what you read into this. 'Husbands, love your wives, just as Christ also loved the church and gave Himself up for her.' That's straight out of the Holy Bible, child. Ephesians 5:25." He didn't wait for Prudence to tell him anything, but she was so flabbergasted by the turn the conversation had taken, she was pretty much mute anyway. "I'll tell you what I read into it. It doesn't say, 'Husbands love the church the way Jesus does.' No. It says, 'Husbands love your wives—"

"Wives!" Prudence finally got out, her voice rising in alarm. "He isn't my—I'm not his wife, Daddy. It's not like that." She leaned forward and twisted in the chair so she could look at him without cranking her neck so hard. "Collin and I are just friends right now. We're not even really dating. At least, I don't think we are. Not officially, anyway. We just reconnected about two months ago." It was two months, two weeks, five days, about nineteen hours, and fifteen letters ago, but who was counting?

"I see," Jed said, clearly *not* seeing. "How long have you loved that boy?"

She hesitated only a moment, then opted for honesty. "Since the winter dance my senior year." It hardly seemed much of a secret anymore.

"And how long has he loved you?"

"I don't know," she shot back, but she could feel heat flushing her cheeks with color.

Jed narrowed his eyes at her.

"I guess since sometime between the winter dance and that terrible, awful, humiliating night in the garden," she mumbled. Hadn't Collin said as much? Or had she only heard what she wanted to hear? He'd said he was now free to love her… but that didn't mean he actually did. She blew out a huff of discouragement. "I don't know, Daddy. I really don't."

"From my perspective, there's no 'just friends' about it." This time, he did use air quotes. "I met your mama on a Sunday night and asked her to marry me one week later. We tied the knot barely two months after that. Have a familiar ring to it? Barely two months?"

"I'm not you and Mama, Daddy. Things are different these days."

Jed shook his head. "When you know, you know. And correct me if I'm wrong, but you've known all along, haven't you?" He tugged her close again and kissed the top of her head. "You may not be us, but you're cut from the same cloth."

"Well, it doesn't matter anyway. Because it doesn't change the fact that he's still, you know…" She trailed off, not wanting to say the words.

"Passing you over. Leaving you standing in the garden all alone again." Jed shook his head long and slowly.

"Please don't let your next words be 'Why, I oughta…'" Prudence said under her breath, biting back the giggle that wanted to escape.

Jed burst out laughing, then squeezed her hard one more time before nudging her out of the chair. "Stop elbowing me in the ribs and go sit in your own chair, child. Drink your chocolate and eat your Christmas pie, and tell me about your plans for Seven Virtues Ranch. I'll figure out what I oughta do to that boy tomorrow."

"Oh, please leave him alone. He's doing the Lord's work, remember?"

Jed only shook his head in response.

Prudence settled into her own chair again, but left the treats where they were. Instead, she shared with him her vision of investing her money back into Seven Virtues, of possibly buying out her sisters' share of just the ranch house and turning it into an education center, filling the rooms with a handful of dedicated students each year who would learn hands on, from the ground up, about herbs and flowers, foraging and conservation, natural remedies and personal care products like she made for Pixie Cut Botanicals. She laid out her plans to expand the garden, to build a few greenhouses so she could grow her plants year-round. She shared with him her desire to build another pole barn on the property, but to use it as a combination classroom and workshop. "Faith can keep running her Dexters here, my plans won't interfere with the trick riding school in any way that I can see, and my students won't be here for the holidays, so we can still do our big family gatherings here: Christmas and New Years, Thanksgiving, Easter, any of them. And of course, I'll take your big room after you move out," she added cheekily. "Although, I suppose I should offer it to Justice and Brandon. I don't want them to feel like I'm kicking them out."

The whole time she talked, Daddy listened. Awake and attentive, pride oozing from every pore.

When she finally stopped, completely emptied out, it was as if the weight of the world had been lifted from her shoulders.

"Well?" she finally prompted. "What do you think?"

THIRTY-NINE

Before Jed could respond, from behind Prudence, a voice called out, "Prudence Goodacre, you rock!" followed by a round of applause, as Abby, Justice and Courage, trailed by Brandon and Joe, made their way into the living room from the kitchen. Abby reached her first and launched herself into Prudence's lap, wrapping her arms around her with abandon.

"Oof!" Prudence grunted. "Get off me, you big lug."

"But I'm your baby," Abby whined, throwing her legs over the arm of the chair so that Prudence was practically cradling her against her will.

"How much of all that did you hear?" Prudence gasped. "Were you guys eavesdropping this whole time?"

"Get off her, Abbers. You're going to crush her before she ever finds a way to be useful to us." That was Justice, of course. But when Abby stood and pulled Prudence up with her, the twins joined in for a group hug. "You might just have saved our marriage," Justice added.

Prudence pulled back and darted a look of alarm between her sister and new brother-in-law. "What does that mean?"

"We want a place of our own," Justice explained. "One that doesn't come with sisters in the rooms on either side of ours, or Daddy in the master suite at the end of the hall."

Brandon chuckled self-consciously and grimaced at Jed, but their father just smiled and shook his head at their antics.

"But we felt like we were being selfish, wanting so much when we already had everything we needed here. We have been trying to come up with a good reason to ask everyone how you all felt about us building our own house on the ranch." Justice gave Prudence another forceful hug before returning to Brandon's side and slipping an arm around his waist. To him, she said, "Problem solved, sweet cheeks. We can blame her for wanting to kick us out."

"I love the whole thing," Courage said, grabbing Prudence's hands and squeezing them. "I can't imagine a better way to use this property, this home that we all love so much. I know Mama would be so proud of what you've come up with. She'd be all over this with you." She cocked her head at her husband, who was shaking Jed's hand in a silent greeting. "And you know Joe and I will help in any way we can. He's got all the right contacts for your gardening and greenhouse supplies. Right, honey?" she asked over her shoulder.

"I'm your man," Joe agreed. He sat on the edge of the sofa and Courage joined him.

"Actually," Abby contradicted. "Professor McHottie Pants Stewart is her man."

"He's not my anything," Prudence declared, throwing her hands up in mock frustration. But they'd apparently heard everything, so there was no trying to deny it. "I mean, I'm his if he'd ever take me up on the offer, but that continues to be the problem, doesn't it?"

Joe exchanged a curious look with Courage, who just shrugged.

Prudence eyed them suspiciously. "What are you two doing here, anyway? In fact, why are all of you here? You were supposed to go out tonight and give me and Daddy a quiet night in."

"Oh please," Abby groaned. "You sound soooo old when you say stuff like that."

"I'm an old soul," Prudence declared. "And proud of it."

"Well, nothings open tonight, not even Schooners." Abby shot narrowed glances at both twins. "Apparently, the waitresses who usually work Christmas night both bailed because they had other things to do. You know... like their husbands."

"Abby!" Prudence, Courage, and Jed said collectively. Justice high-fived the youngest Goodacre, then Brandon did, too. Joe turned all shades of embarrassment and pointedly did *not* look at his wife's father.

"Anyway," Courage said, taking over. "We came back here to play some games so you could join us." She turned to Jed. "You, too, Daddy."

Jed chuckled and shook his head. "I'm not fit for much more than resting my eyes in this recliner tonight. But you kids go on. Play your games."

"Get dressed, Pru," Justice ordered, pointing at her over-sized snowflake flannel pajamas. "You're embarrassing our husbands with your lingerie."

Prudence just rolled her eyes.

"Seriously," Abby joined in. "It's too early for pajamas. Pictionary or Exploding Kittens, since Daddy's not playing. We'll get the game set up. You get dressed."

"I am not changing out of my cozies for any of you. You're in my house, remember?" She pulled a Jed gesture and waved two fingers between her eyes and Justice's.

"Suit yourself," Justice shot back with a shrug. But her tone said she thought Prudence just might regret it.

"Suited," Prudence replied, elbowing past them to head for the bathroom. Maybe she had a chocolate milk mustache or something.

Her upper lip was clean, but she brushed her teeth to get rid of the aftertaste of rich desserts. She'd eaten so much all day long, and the thought of anything but cold, refreshing water made her stomach clench. She'd washed all her makeup off an hour ago, but her hair was still spiking in all the right places. "Nothing wrong with this," she said with a sassy nod to her reflection, then she headed out to the living room to join her family.

She was just settling cross-legged on the floor in front of the large coffee table when the doorbell rang. Abby jumped up. "I'll get it. Hope you all don't mind. I invited a friend."

"Seriously, Abbers?" Justice complained. "I thought it was just going to be family. Otherwise, I would have asked Terrell Jackson if he wanted to join us."

"Seriously, Abbers?" Brandon echoed. "I would have asked Ellie Baker if she wanted to join us."

"You're a funny guy," his wife said, rolling her eyes and laying her head on his shoulder. Ellie Baker, a girl they'd all known since elementary school, had never before been on anyone's radar, at least not as a home wrecker. But for whatever reason, more than once over the last few months, she'd made it abundantly clear that if Brandon ever had any doubts about his marital status, she'd be happy to show him what he was missing out on.

Brandon planted a kiss on top of Justice's head, then patted her knee affectionately. "Not as funny as you are, wife of mine."

Prudence groaned inwardly. She didn't mind Abby's friends, not the ones she knew anyway. It didn't matter that they saw her without her makeup or in her pajamas. But she, too, was looking forward to spending what was left of Christmas playing games with her loved ones and talking about all of their futures together. For the first time in as far back as she could remember, she wouldn't be an outsider, a wallflower, watching and listening. Because this time, she actually had something to contribute to the conversation.

"Prudence."

The room fell silent, and all eyes turned first to the man—the oh, so beautiful man—standing just inside the front door, then to her. Prudence stared, open-mouthed, eyes wide, at Collin, words having escaped her. Thoughts having escaped her. Her brain short-circuited; his presence simply didn't register.

"Sir," Collin said, turning to Jed with an outstretched hand.

Jed pushed to his feet and shook the proffered hand. "Merry Christmas, Mr. Stewart."

"Merry Christmas," Collin replied before his eyes swept back to Prudence. "I'm sorry to show up unannounced like this."

"You announced it to us," Abby said cheekily from behind him. "Well, to Courage and Joe, who then announced it to Justice, Brandon, and me."

Words came rushing back and Prudence pointed at Courage who sat on the floor across the table from her. "You knew he was coming? You *all* knew?"

"We all knew," Justice admitted casually. "Well, Daddy didn't."

"But—but why? Why didn't you say anything? After—after you heard—" Prudence's pulse throbbed so loudly inside her skull, she thought her head might explode. "I don't—I don't understand," she stammered, pushing abruptly to her feet. The room swayed around her, and she grabbed for the armrest of the chair beside her, feeling all the blood rush from her face.

"Whoa!" Both the twins leapt to their feet in an effort to get to Prudence's side before she went down. But Collin managed to get there first, catching her around the waist, and pulling her up against him.

"I'm okay," she said breathlessly. "I just stood up too quickly. I'm okay," she repeated when he didn't let her go.

"I don't think she is," Abby said from where she still stood next to Jed's chair. "She looks like she could go down any minute, Mr. Stewart. I'd keep a tight hold on her if I were you."

Jed chuckled, then, shaking his head at his daughters' antics, he lowered himself back into his recliner. "It doesn't happen often, Mr. Stewart, but I'm actually in agreement with my youngest daughter." He casually popped up the leg rest and sat back, lacing his fingers together over his stomach. "In fact, I suggest you take Pixie Cut outside for some fresh air. Maybe a stroll out under the starlight."

"Daddy," Justice cooed melodramatically. "You're such a romantic old man!"

"Hush, child," Jed said with a wink. "I'm a grumpy old man. Now I'm going to sit here and rest my eyes for a bit. You kids do whatever it is you kids are going to do. Don't mind me."

FORTY

COLLIN DIDN'T NEED JED or Abby's instructions to keep a hold of Prudence. If he had things his way, he'd never let go of her again.

But Prudence wasn't having it. She pressed her hands flat against his chest and pushed away from him. She didn't move far, but he felt the physical distance between them like a chasm.

"Will you step outside with me, Prudence?" he asked in a low voice, his eyes never leaving her face. She still looked pale, but that could very well be because she wore no makeup. He could see the flush rising in her cheeks, and although she still seemed shaken, she definitely seemed steadier on her feet. "It's clear—you can certainly see the stars—but it's cold. Do you have a jacket? Or a blanket?" Behind her, thrown haphazardly over the back of the sofa, was the quilt she'd draped around her shoulders back in October when he'd followed her home from The Smokehouse.

"Don't let her go out there barefoot," Jed said from his chair, his lids lowered. He wasn't fooling anyone, though. He was very much aware of everything that was going on in what was still his house.

"I'll get your shoes," Courage said to Prudence, squeezing her hand encouragingly before disappearing out of the room to the kitchen.

"Grab my jacket, too," Prudence called after her. "The old green barn coat."

Courage returned a moment later and handed the coat to Collin.

Justice pointed at the sofa. "Sit, Pru. Put your shoes on or Daddy won't let you go out and play."

Collin bit back a smile as an obviously flustered Prudence settled on the edge of the couch cushion and shoved her feet into the thick-soled military-style boots Courage set in front of her. By the time she stood, he had her jacket held out for her to slip her arms into.

"We'll play the first round without you," Abby quipped, dropping back to her seat on the floor beside Justice. "But if you two stay out there too long, we'll start thinking dirty—"

"Child," Jed admonished. "Hush. Let the lovebirds find their wings."

"See?" Justice interjected. "Romantic as a red, red rose, Daddy."

"Shall we?" Collin asked, grinning at the unrelenting teasing among Prudence's family members. To his relief, she nodded and slipped her hand in his proffered one before following him to the door. "I'll bring her back safe and sound, sir," he said to Jed as they passed the lounging man.

"Take your time, young Stewart." He waited until Collin had pulled open the door before opening one eye and adding, "Just remember that I won't go to bed until my daughter does."

Collin nodded with a grin. "Got it."

As they stood side by side on the front stoop, gazing out into the beautiful night, Collin had to force himself to breathe normally. Prudence's hand in his felt small and fragile, and he wasn't sure which of them was trembling more. *Be brave,* he told himself. *You've come this far. Don't hold back now.* "Shall we walk to the garden?" he asked, hoping he sounded more confident than he felt.

Prudence nodded. "Sure." The word came out just above a whisper. "The ground. It's wet. Your shoes." She pointed at the dress shoes he wore.

"I'm not worried about my shoes," he assured her as he led them down the steps to the horseshoe drive in front of the house where his car, the same blue Toyota Corolla he'd had since graduating from college—a gift from his parents who both knew how meager a new teacher's salary could be—was parked. Collin hadn't been bold enough to assume he could park behind the house with the family vehicles, and although he wouldn't admit it out loud, parking alone out front made making a quick escape easier if the need arose.

Thank goodness, it didn't seem like that would be a major concern.

They followed the walkway that led around the end of the house toward the sprawling garden shrouded in a thin veil of mist that settled low on the ground. The bare branches of the old apple tree spread like tattered lacework against the starlit sky, her arms outstretched in welcome. Collin held open the whimsical gate for Prudence to walk through, then he followed behind her as she led the way to the bench beneath the tree.

"It's damp," she said, reaching down to run her fingertips along the rough surface.

"Here." Collin whipped off the wool scarf his mother had draped around his neck earlier that day, telling him it made him look smart and debonair.

"What woman can refuse a man who has the guts to wear a white wool scarf?" she asked, brimming with excitement as she sent him on his way to "woo and win the fair maiden."

"It'll stain," Prudence said, holding up both hands to stop him.

He grinned down at her and folded it in half lengthwise, then laid it on the bench. "I'm not worried about my scarf, either." He sincerely hoped she'd start speaking to him in more than two-word sentences at some point. "Come," he said, settling on the bench and patting the seat beside him. "It's wool, so by the time any moisture soaks through to our backsides, we probably won't even notice." He grimaced as soon as the words were out. He sounded like an idiot.

Prudence hesitated, only for a moment, but it didn't escape his notice. Then she acquiesced and perched on the edge of the bench beside him. Before he could say anything else, she asked, "Why are you here, Collin?" Each word was weighed down with caution, but at least there were more than two strung together.

"I never heard back from you." It seemed the simplest place to start.

"But don't you have to leave for the retreat first thing tomorrow morning?" She crossed her arms tightly, her shoulders hunching forward in a defensive posture. In what sounded like a carefully modulated voice, she added, "Please don't tell me you bailed on those kids because of me. I was fine with you missing the party, especially for such a good cause."

"Oh, Prudence." In that moment, he knew he'd made the right decision. "Those kids? The church? That's not who I bailed on," he began, hoping he could make her understand the gravity of his actions tonight. "I don't know what I was thinking when I said yes." He shook his head and started again. "Actually, I do know what I was thinking. I didn't want to let Seth and Sierra and those kids down. I didn't want to let anyone down." He cleared his throat. He wanted to reach for her hand, but he couldn't, not with hers tucked so tightly against her ribcage. "I didn't want them to think less of me for saying no, you know? I got caught up in this pompous desire to sweep in and save the day."

His eyes were adjusting to the dark and he could now make out her furrowed brow, the pressed line of her delicate mouth. Was she upset at his admission? Disappointed in him?

"This is something I've struggled with my whole life," he confessed. "I'm a people pleaser, Prudence. I have bent over backwards more times than I can count to make people like me. And the crazy thing? People seem to like me better when I stop trying so hard." He tapped his temple. "I know that up here. I've seen it play out time and time again. But still, somewhere inside of me there's this confused little mixed-race kid in me who's afraid of being judged. So I play it safe, try to please everyone, and end up leaving messes behind me everywhere I go." He stopped talking, not wanting her to think he felt sorry for himself.

"I get it," Prudence said, but the caution was still there. "I really do. I'm kind of the same way."

Collin nodded. Of course, she got it. Hadn't she been the victim of one of the worst of the messes he'd made?

She shot him a quick, commiserating glance, then looked away again.

"I shouldn't have sent that letter asking you to accommodate my poor judgment," he said, changing tact. "I should have called and told you about the situation in person. I should have called and *asked* you about it, if nothing else."

"You didn't have my phone number," she interjected, her gaze drifting over the garden and past the fence toward the open pasture.

Collin chuckled. "I know people," he said wryly. "I could have had my people call your people to get your number. But the real issue is that I shouldn't have agreed to fill in for Roy in the first place."

"I understood your reasons for going," Prudence countered. "And I wasn't upset. Not really. And now I feel bad that you made a special trip all the way out to the hollow just for—" She broke off as though unsure of how to finish that sentence. "You didn't need to come all this way just for this," she finished lamely, but something in her voice—the slightest softening around the edges—gave him hope.

"I disagree, Prudence. I believe this is exactly where I need to be right now."

She sighed deeply, her exhale turning to a puff of mist before dissipating.

"I owe you," he began, but paused when she stiffened, almost like she might be preparing for what was coming next. Putting up her defenses. He hurried on, hoping his next words would alleviate her tension. "I owe you an apology, first and foremost, for not making my commitment to you my number one priority. Do you know who pointed that out to me?"

Prudence frowned and shook her head. "Who?"

"Mr. Abraham Stone. Last night, when I picked him and Walter Matthau up, he asked me if he was going to get to meet my girl at the party. When I told him you weren't going to be there, he asked, 'Then what on earth did I get all gussied up for?'" The memory of Mr. Stone's umbrage made Collin smile, but he continued. "When he got over being perturbed, he asked if he'd be meeting her—*her* is you, by the way. He was asking about you. He calls you my pen pal gal." Prudence's lips curved up into a brief smile at that, making Collin's heart race with joy. "Anyway, he asked if I'd be seeing the New Year in with you, if I'd be kissing you at the stroke of midnight."

Her tiny intake of breath told Collin she was hanging on every word, and once more, his heart soared. "Needless to say, when I told him what I'd done to you, he refused to talk to me the rest of the car ride over to my folks' place."

"Oh, dear." Prudence's nose still crinkled when she smiled, Collin noticed.

"Yeah. Well, I thought he was done berating me, but when I pulled into the garage, he started in on me again. Do you want to know what he said to me? Or am I starting to bore you?"

Prudence rolled her eyes and nudged him with her shoulder, although her arms remained tightly crossed. "Don't leave me in suspense, Mr. Stewart."

"I don't plan on leaving you at all, Miss Goodacre. In suspense or otherwise." He held his hand out to her, palm up, fingers spread, emboldened now that he'd said those words. She couldn't possibly misinterpret his intentions, but he asked anyway. "Will you let me hold your hand again?"

It seemed an age passed before she looked over at him, her luminous gaze finding his for just a moment. Then she uncrossed her arms and settled her hand into his, threading her fingers through his. He let his breath out in relief.

"Mr. Stone wanted to know how I was going to convince you that I loved you if I wasn't going to make your heart the most important thing in my life? If I wasn't going to put you first, before all others. That includes extracurricular and volunteer activities, even church functions, work, sports," he added with a snort. "You don't have to worry there, by the way. Oh, and books," he said with exaggerated seriousness. "You are more important to me than all the books in the world."

Prudence's fingers tightened in his with every word that left his mouth. She turned and lifted her face, her eyes wide with... disbelief? Hope? "You—you—I mean, do you—"

"Yes," he said, nodding slowly, his gaze locked with hers. "I do. I have waited far too long to tell you this, and I'm here now, tonight, because I don't want to wait another moment to tell you what I came to say. I love you, Prudence Goodacre. I have loved you, and only you, for the last five and a half years."

Her eyes filled with tears as he spoke, her hand once again trembling in his. She lifted her other one to her mouth and held it there while he finished. "And I want to spend the rest of my life telling you, showing you, just how much."

She reached up and touched his cheek with her fingertips. "I love you, too, Collin," she whispered.

Collin stood and pulled her up with him, then crushed her to him, wrapping her in his arms like a prisoner just released from a life sentence. He was desperate to finally, *finally*, kiss those rosebud lips he'd thought far too much about over the last half a decade, but he didn't want to let her go, either.

"You're crushing me," she whispered shakily, her breath warm on his neck. "And I really want you to kiss me," she added, still in a whisper, but a rather seductive one.

Collin obliged her immediately.

When he finally lifted his head so he could look at her beautiful face, he saw in her eyes everything he'd hoped for. Loosening his hold, but not releasing her, he reached inside his jacket pocket and pulled out a small blue satin drawstring bag. Her gaze darted from the bag to his face and back to the bag, but he drew her close again. "I was going to give this to you on New Year's Eve," he murmured, their faces only inches apart, foreheads almost touching.

"What is it?" she asked breathlessly.

Collin kissed the tip of her nose, then her mouth, reveling in the feel of her soft lips against his before he lifted his head. He needed to finish what he'd come here to do so he could kiss her again and again. "It wasn't meant to be an engagement ring," he began, leaning away just enough to pull the small pouch open. "But I had it custom made just for you, so until I can get you the real thing, I'm hoping you'll accept this as a place holder." From the bag, he pulled out a ring that looked like something one of J.R.R. Tolkein's elven queens might wear. She gasped as he slid it on the third finger of the hand that she readily held out to him. A perfect fit: silver and gold strands were intricately woven together so that the piece looked alive; tendrils of precious metals wrapping around her ring finger, binding her to him forever and ever. "Will you marry me?" he asked in a voice thick with emotion. "Will you be my wife?"

"I will," she replied, almost before he got the last word out. "Yes, Collin, yes. I want to be your wife more than anything in the world." She threw her arms around her neck and buried her face against his neck and lifted her lips to his.

A soft buzzing filled his ears, and for a moment, Collin thought it was just another sensation caused by the long-awaited kisses he couldn't get enough of. But when it didn't stop, he suddenly realized that it was his phone going off in his jacket pocket. "Sorry," he muttered, hoping it wasn't his mother calling for an update. "I should have left this thing in the car."

"Who is it?" Prudence asked, but her eyes were fixed on her hand where it rested over his heart, on the ring that suited her so perfectly, just as he'd known it would. "Please don't get me any other ring, Collin," she whispered, resting her head back on his shoulder. "This is better than anything I could ever hope for."

Collin couldn't help the surge of satisfaction when he heard the breathless quality of her voice. He glanced at the screen in his hand. "It's Joe's number, but I think the text is from Abby." He held it up for her to see.

You two done making out? Come inside before your lips fuse. We need one more player for Exploding Kittens, and we are all dying to know when you two are going to make it official and get this knot tied.

"Do you want to respond or shall I?" Collin asked.

Prudence took the phone from him, but instead of answering the text, she dropped it back into his coat pocket. "Let them wait. We have five years' worth of kissing to catch up on."

Collin pulled her to him, perhaps a little rougher than necessary, but she threw back her head and laughed at his enthusiasm. He captured her smiling mouth beneath his, relishing in the knowledge that he was exactly who he was meant to be, where he was meant to be, and with whom he was meant to be.

FORTY-ONE

Six months later...

"I't's beautiful, isn't it?" Prudence whispered, leaning her head on her father's shoulder, her hand resting in the crook of his elbow. They stood together beneath the arching branches of Redbuds in full bloom, peeking into the small clearing through a narrow gap in the muslin panels that had been strung up between the two trees.

Family members and a few close friends were seated on the beautiful hand-hewn Black Cherry benches Jed had made as a wedding gift—benches that would later be used in the new education program gardens. The trees around them were in full leaf, and the dappled sunlight that fluttered down from the cerulean May sky felt like showers of blessing on all who gathered there to share in this momentous occasion. Pastor Treadwell had not yet taken his place under the white and pink flowering Dogwoods that had burst into riotous color only two weeks earlier, nor could they see Collin from their limited view.

But Prudence didn't need to see him to know he was there. Every cell in her body pulsed with the awareness of him, and she reveled in the undeniable, irrefutable, incontestable knowledge of his love for her, and hers for him.

"It makes my chest ache to look at it," Daddy murmured, just like he did every time he stood in this place, preparing himself to hand one of his beloved daughters over to another man. Then he patted the back of her hand and turned to smile down at her. "But the ache eases when I look at you, my dear Prudence. You are so lovely, child."

"Daddy, I can't cry yet," she whispered, blinking ferociously.

Jed planted a gentle kiss on her temple. "Your mother—" His voice hitched, and Prudence heard him swallow hard before he continued. "I know she's here in spirit—I see her every day in each of you girls. But today..." He nodded slowly. "Today, she would be in her element."

"I'd like to think so, too," she whispered, squeezing his arm. It was why Prudence had chosen this place, this small clearing in the woods beyond the pasture, the secret place Caroline Goodacre had carved out of the woods so many years ago. The family still gathered there to celebrate Mother's Day, and Prudence had taken it upon herself to tend to the little glade, keeping it as natural and and organic as possible, gently reclaiming the space whenever the creeping wild roses and blackberry brambles breeched its borders.

Caroline's memorial stone pile beneath the largest white Dogwood didn't seem out of place at all for a wedding, not with the rambling Carolina Jessamine vine spilling its sunshine yellow flowers everywhere. Another vine Prudence had to keep cut back, but one she and her sisters had planted there themselves because of its lovely name.

Out of their line of sight, Abby played soft prelude music on her Hummingbird acoustic, the sounds sweet and mellow over the accompaniment of quiet chatter and late May breezes. At any moment now, Pastor Treadwell and Collin would take their places, Abby would transition into "Starlight in the Garden," a dreamy, lyrical composition she'd written for this moment, and Jasmine and Yvette would pull back the curtains to reveal the bride waiting for her groom. Daddy would walk Prudence through the middle of the small gathering and present her to the man with whom she would spend the rest of her life.

The man she would spend the rest of her life with right here at Seven Virtues Ranch.

It had taken nearly four months of negotiating—there were no open positions and a new one had to be created and approved by the board—but Collin was returning to teach Language Arts and Literature classes at Plumwood High, come the fall. He'd had to take a significant wage decrease, but the sacrifice was well worth it to both he and Prudence. Not only would he be back in the hollow teaching young adults the riches of the written word, but he'd be doing so with Prudence as his wife.

While Collin finished up the school year in Cincinnati, Prudence focused her energies on setting in motion her plans for Seven Gardens at Seven Virtues Ranch Education Center. She took advantage of having a law school student living in the same house, and after spending long hours consulting with Justice over the business and legal aspects of operation, Prudence had made the decision to keep her Pixie Cut Botanicals product line its own entity, thus allowing her to launch the education program as a non-profit organization.

In doing so, she hoped to make her program more accessible to those who might benefit most from it, particularly to students who might have financial impediments. There were many small communities in the surrounding hollows where traditional medical care was considered more of a luxury, and Prudence hoped her program would give rise to a new generation of home herbalists who had a good knowledge of what they could do for themselves, as well as knowing when it was time to seek outside help. She had just hired a brilliant young man to write grant proposals for her, and she was currently in negotiations of her own with two local herbalists, as well as a naturopathic doctor who worked out of Bowling Green, all of whom seemed as excited as Prudence was about Seven Gardens.

There were, indeed, to be seven different teaching gardens spread out over four of the five acres allotted to the program, plus two enormous high tunnel greenhouses, with plans for more in the years to come. But the name of the business had an even greater significance to Prudence. In the Bible, the number seven represented completion and perfection, and she couldn't imagine a more perfect place to complete her journey and put down roots. She'd found it in her own back yard.

Both she and Collin had come full circle, ending up right back where they'd started. From the bench under the apple tree, the view encompassed all of Seven Gardens, and every time Collin drove out to see her, he found her there, waiting for him with welcoming kisses and the latest updates of the comings and goings of Seven Virtues Ranch.

Jed had *finally* officially moved into his new house, and although he did, indeed, have supper at the ranch house most evenings, he usually went back to home to rest his eyes in his recliner in front of his own fireplace.

Justice and Brandon had broken ground on a log home of their own tucked back into the woods, a place that all but disappeared for most of the year until the trees lost their leaves. They hoped to be settled under its roof before the year was out, but for now, the young marrieds and Prudence had managed to cohabitate peacefully. It would definitely make things easier on Prudence once she and Collin were married and living together in the ranch house, too. She wouldn't feel like such a third wheel all the time, nor would she care how much her sister manhandled her husband in public. Prudence would be far too preoccupied with a husband—and a future—of her own.

A hush fell over the clearing as Abby's guitar faded away, then returned with a new melody that rippled out from her fingertips like rays of sunshine. A happy bark went up in response, making Prudence and Jed—and everyone else, it sounded like—chuckle appreciatively. Apparently, Walter Matthau was ready to get the show on the road. At Collin and Prudence's insistence, he and Mr. Abraham Stone had come from Cincinnati with Collin's parents. Jessica, Belinda, Tracy, and even Beau, were also in attendance. "To balance out my side of the seats," Collin had explained.

And then, Jasmine and Yvette, their young faces lit up with beaming smiles, swept aside the muslin panels, and the small group of guests stood and turned to face the bride and her father.

Prudence wore a stunning 1920's-era beaded gown in the palest of pink, the underskirt falling in asymmetrical layers of chiffon to just above her ankles. She'd found the dress two years earlier, hanging on a rack with a multitude of other wedding and party dresses at a secondhand store in Muldoon. It looked authentic, and Prudence could hardly believe her good fortune when she stepped into it and the piece slipped down over her body like it had been made for her.

"I always knew that dress would find the perfect home," the saleswoman had said when Prudence stepped out of the dressing room to show her.

At the time, Prudence had no idea where she might wear such a gown, but that had mattered little. It belonged to her, and that was all there was to it. On this special day, she couldn't imagine stepping into her new life in anything else.

On her head was perched a delicately woven crown of Honey Bracelet stems, sprigs of white Baby's Breath, and wild Carolina Roses with their freckled yellow centers and pale pink petals that almost perfectly matched the hue of her dress. Her bouquet of wildflowers had been gathered during the walk to the little glade not more than an hour ago, and it was made up of wild red and blue Columbines, Northern Blue Flag Irises, crowns of yellow Golden Alexander and white Yarrow, bundled together with trailing vines of the Carolina Jessamine from Mama's cairn.

The couple had chosen to have a quiet, intimate wedding, not because they worried what people might say, but because they were quiet, intimate people. Those who knew and loved them best weren't at all surprised.

The bride wore no shoes. Those who knew and loved her best weren't at all surprised.

The groom wore glasses and a tweed coat with elbow patches. Those who knew and loved him best weren't at all surprised.

There was a Honda Shadow 750 with tightly packed saddlebags parked near the back porch of the ranch house. Two helmets hung from the brand new cushioned sissy bar that had been mounted behind the passenger seat a few weeks earlier. Someone had tied several tin cans and colorful streamers to it, too, taking extra care that they didn't dangle too long so they wouldn't tangle in the back tire. The newlyweds were leaving for their honeymoon first thing in the morning on a cross country motorcycle ride. Those who knew and loved them best were concerned... but not at all surprised.

Granted, they weren't riding all the way to Alaska—at least not this time—but all the way across the state of Kentucky and up to Cedar Falls, Ohio, where they had reserved a colorful canvas yurt at a bed and breakfast tucked into the woods near Hocking Hills State Park. The diminutive abode was decorated in bold, eclectic fabrics, complete with a canopied queen size bed, a spa bathtub for two, a tiny kitchenette with a wood burning stove, and a balcony from which they could watch the sun set each evening.

The groom couldn't wait to carry his bohemian bride over the threshold; he was quite certain he'd be kissed into oblivion the moment he kicked the door closed behind them.

Aren't you glad that Prudence and Collin waited for love and found their way back to each other and their happily ever after?

Are you ready for Book 7 in the Seven Virtues Ranch Romance Series?

Abby thinks she might be broken.
Everything she does seems to wind up in one big mess.
Can she figure out a way to set things right before anyone finds out?
And what about the indomitable Goodacre patriarch, Jedediah?
With all his daughters grown and starting families of their own, what's to become of him and his great big heart?

Something About ABBY
A Seven Virtues Ranch Romance Book 7

FOLLOW YOUR DREAMS, THEY said. *We believe in you*, they said. *You're going to be a superstar*, they said.

Two years ago, Abby Goodacre, the hollow's hometown hopeful headed off to Music City to seek her fame and fortune. But the road to super-stardom has proved to be a whole lot bumpier than she'd expected.

Now she's hiding out in a friend's spare room, too ashamed to show her face around town. She's let them all down - her band, her fans, her father, her sisters, her friends, yes, all of Plumwood Hollow.

They just don't know it yet.

At least, that's what she thought. Until the hollow's hometown heartthrob shows up at her back door... and he's not willing to be shut out of her life again.

Jedediah Goodacre has watched all seven of his daughters discover their own paths, and he couldn't be prouder of each of them. He's looking forward to living the gray and grizzly bachelor life now that he's no longer sharing a roof with all his womenfolk.

But the Almighty seems to have other plans for him—in the guise of a long-limbed shepherdess hellbent on getting under his skin. It seems Jed can't get away from her... either that, or he can't get enough of her. One thing he's sure of, though, is that she's nothing like his late wife, his beloved sweet Caroline.

Well, there is that one little similarity. He can't seem to say 'no' to Charlotte Rawlings any more than he could to Caroline.

And that woman knows it.

~ ~ ~

Keep reading for a sneak peek from
Something About ABBY: A Seven Virtues Ranch Romance Book 7

A Note from Becky

Dear Reader,

How did you feel about Prudence and Collin's story? I know the teacher/student relationship can often be considered taboo and can stir up all kinds of different emotions, right? Do you think Collin and Prudence handled things the right way?

I have been happily married for well over thirty years to a man almost ten years older than I am, a man with whom I fell in love when I was seventeen. He was twenty-six at the time. Fortunately, we didn't have the legal/ethical issues of a student/teacher relationship between us, but we did endure our share of side-eyed, judgemental looks. We were married six months after my eighteenth birthday, and in spite of all the naysayers, we continue to live out happily ever after.

I am pleased to tell you, Dear Reader, that Prudence and Collin will also spend the rest of their long, *long* lives together in wedded bliss!

I like to say that I write hopefully-ever-after contemporary romance and women's fiction. Books you'll want to hug. Because romance and relationships can be predictably unpredictable, and that's what makes a great story, right?

Where hope lives and love triumphs,
Becky Doughty

Come visit me at BeckyDoughty.com. I'd love to send you my newsletter about new releases, sales, and giveaways. ***Subscribe today and introduce yourself!***

An Excerpt: Something About Abby

Chapter 1

~ ~ ~

...And home is still out of reach to me,
But if I close my eyes and sing
With the cicada serenade
In the maples on my street
For a moment, that's home to me.

THE WORDS POURED OUT of Abby like a lament, the homesick child inside her aching with every note, every syllable. It wasn't how the tender song was meant to be performed, but she couldn't help it. The longing for that old familiar sky, the rich and ruddy earth beneath her feet, the tangy scent of fresh hay bales stacked rafter-high in the barn. The background music of the feminine voices of her sisters—tears and laughter, too—filling every corner of the ranch house.

But I don't think that I'm sad now,
I'm not anything more than I was when I left
But maybe that's my problem.
I'd sooner crack in two than let myself forget.
All I can do right now is take a breath...

The rumble of a tractor, the lowing of cattle, the pounding of horses' hooves marking the pulse of life at Seven Virtues Ranch. And Jedediah Goodacre. *Oh, Daddy. I miss you.*

> *How does one hold onto this?*
> *How do you keep from losing*
> *What you never had?*
> *Standing in the whirlwind,*
> *Trying not to let all of the change make me sad.*

It was all she could do to keep the quaver from her voice as she sang. She swallowed the lump of emotions that kept trying to close her throat and pushed the poignant words out—words meant to make people smile and remember, not weep.

> *The moon has fallen from that old familiar sky*
> *In both of my hometowns....*

She bowed her head over her guitar as she gently plucked the last notes of the song and let them hang there.

A smattering of applause jarred her out of her reverie, and Abby lifted her head, her wide stage smile in place, and nodded in acknowledgment.

It was time for a break, wasn't it? A bead of sweat trickled down her spine between her shoulder blades before getting absorbed into the fabric of her shirt. Her hair clung like spiderwebs to the back of her neck, the fans in front of the stage doing little to counteract the sticky summer heat that pushed in through the open windows at their backs.

Glamorous was not a word she'd use to describe gigging on Honky Tonk Row in Nashville. In fact, if the Seattle music scene hadn't already laid claim to it, Abby was certain someone would have coined it Nashville Grunge. Not for the music style, but because of how a person felt performing on the tiny front window stages in the packed bars and restaurants all along the busy downtown street. The owners and managers knew how to draw folks in and sell them lots of drinks—as long as the weather cooperated, the plate glass windows were opened wide to the elements, and the better the band sounded, the more attention they got from passersby. The more attention the band got, the more likely it was that those passersby would duck inside to listen. And then eat and drink. Spend their money.

Abby didn't judge people for eating and drinking. She didn't judge people for spending their money. In fact, lately, she was doing a little too much of both herself.

She leaned closer to her microphone. "Folks, y'all are fabulous," Her speaking voice was naturally husky, so she was pretty sure no one would notice the catch in it. She poured on the twang, just in case. "You remind me of my people back home, and that's sayin' a lot."

Someone at the back of the room called out, "We love you, Abstinence!" A dark-haired woman waved from where she sat leaning casually against the shoulder of a barrel-chested man. Regulars the last couple of weeks—Starla and Robert? Bob? No, Bill, maybe. She couldn't quite recall. She was usually great with names, but his wasn't coming to her. Tonight, she was finding it difficult to focus on anything except getting through this gig.

"Hey, you two lovebirds." Abby pointed in their direction. It was still weird to hear strangers calling her by her full name. She'd gone by Abby her whole life, but Remington Sounder had suggested she use the unique and memorable Abstinence to give her a leg up in the industry. "Do I need to call for a hand check?"

That got a reaction out of the crowded room, lightening the mood that had settled after her song. She raised her voice to be heard over the cat calls and wolf whistles. "Listen, we're going to take a short break. Ten minutes, then we'll be back for more. Y'all behave while we're gone now, ya hear?" She waggled a finger at Starla and her man again. "I'm talking about you two, especially."

Amidst another round of hooting and applause, Abby unplugged her guitar and set it on the stand behind her, skirted the conglomeration of microphone stands, cables, and monitors, and headed off the side of the raised platform.

She intentionally did *not* look at Bucky. She could feel his eyes on her as she made her way to the tiny room at the back of the bar used by the different bands. She hoped the guys would mingle and let her have the space to herself for a few minutes. She needed to get her act together, and ten minutes was hardly enough time to use the bathroom and touch up her heat-warped makeup.

"What the hell, Abby?" Bucky's voice caught up to her before he did, but his hand on her upper arm made it clear that he had no intention of leaving her in peace.

She didn't even flinch at his abrasive language, even though he knew she didn't like it. It could get a lot worse when he was really ticked off. She stopped mid stride and waited for him to continue, partly because she wasn't sure how to answer his question, and partly because she knew it wouldn't matter anyway. He wasn't really looking for answers. At least not ones she could give him.

"Lay off, Buck." Tad wasn't far behind, shoving his drumsticks into his back pocket as he approached. "Everyone has a rough night now and then."

"Yeah, maybe," Bucky shot back, still gripping Abby's arm too tightly. "But the princess here doesn't seem to get the whole 'now and then' part of that equation."

Had it been so obvious that she was in a funk? Could her audience tell, too? Abby grimaced and let her hair fall forward to hide her face from Bucky's glare. A bubble of anxiety behind her ribs threatened to burst into a full-blown panic. She tried to pull away from his bruising fingers to no avail. "Give me a minute, okay?" she ground out, doing her best to keep the tremor from her voice as she met her guitar player's eyes. Hard, unyielding, and definitely condescending.

She hated when he called her princess. He was the only one in the band who did, and it had been a long time since he'd said it nicely.

"You've got ten. No, make that eight minutes." Bucky pointed at the digital clock mounted crookedly on the wall just outside the small band room. "You better find your happy place and make it snappy. We have an audience to get fired up, and you're acting like a wet rag."

From behind him, Tad gave Abby a bolstering smile, but said nothing.

"I'll make it snappy," she retorted, snapping her fingers emphatically. But her voice cracked on the last word, and Bucky didn't miss a beat.

He bent forward, his face too close to hers. "Don't—"

"Hey." Tad moved around Bucky to step between them. "Let's not do this here, okay?" He eyed the clock pointedly.

Abby jerked her arm from Bucky's grasp and pushed open the door of the little storage room. It should have been locked, but she didn't bother acknowledging it. She knew well who'd been the last one out of there, but she wasn't about to point fingers at her guitar player right now. Fortunately, her most important possession, her Hummingbird guitar, Blossom, was up on stage under the watchful eye of the band manager. She snatched up the backpack she used instead of a purse and shoved past both guys. "I'll be in the little girl's room. Don't come looking for me."

"Don't make me!" Bucky snarled after her.

Abby was relieved to find the bathroom empty. It didn't happen often, and she lifted a quick "Thank you for small mercies," heavenward. Ripping several paper towels from the dispenser, she let the water run as cold as it would get and held them under it. Then she peeled her shirt off over her head and pressed the cool towels to her neck and chest, then tucked one under each arm. She smelled just fine, thank goodness—the Pixie Cut deodorant Prudence made for her worked like nothing store-bought ever could. But she knew a thing or two about how to keep from overheating; she'd spent far too many long hours rounding up cattle in the dog days of summer not to. Closing her eyes, she leaned against the vanity and counted backwards from twenty-five.

She could get through this. She had to get through this. They still had an hour-long set to go.

Two minutes later—which left her fewer than five remaining before Bucky came looking for her—Abby tossed the paper towels and slipped her arms back into her shirt. She eyed her makeup and hair. Actually, her hair seemed to be holding up all right despite the humidity, but her eyeliner was smudged and her lipstick sung clean off. "I look like one of those crying clowns," she muttered to her reflection, just as the bathroom door swung open. It was the woman from the audience.

"Hey, girl," Starla said when her eyes met Abby's in the mirror. The woman didn't exactly smile at her, which made Abby wary. "You okay in here? That hot guitar player of yours is out in the corridor waiting for you." She came to stand at the counter, too, but kept studying Abby. "And when I say hot, I don't mean his appearance. Although I do have eyes in my head, and he is easy to look at." She waved a hand dismissively, as if to flick away her own comment, then continued. "He just seemed a little riled up to me, that's all. Hot under the collar, you know?" She leaned forward and made a kissy face at her own reflection. "I'm trying to be a girlfriend, but if I'm just being nosy, you can tell me to hush and mind my own. Do you like this lipstick on me?"

For a moment, Abby didn't respond. She swallowed hard, resisting the urge to ask the woman for a hug. Something about her reminded her of someone from Plumwood Hollow, someone good, someone genuine. "You remind me of..." Who? Abby shook her head in frustration. Not any of her sisters. None of them were quite so—quite so *vivid*.

Starla let out a good-natured, albeit slightly self-deprecating, chuckle. "I hope it's someone good and kind. And pretty," she added with a wink.

Cass Whitehouse.

Starla reminded Abby of Cass and her baked goods. The cinnamon rolls at Serendipity's. Her mouth began to water. "Good and kind and pretty. That's exactly right. You remind me of someone from home." She thought her voice was steady, but Starla was more than just good and kind and pretty. She was also astute.

"Need me to run interference with Mr. Hot and Bothered out there?" Starla pulled a tube of lipstick from the depths of her suede leather shoulder bag. "And you never said if you like this color on me." She uncapped it and held it out for Abby to see. "It's called Girl Talk."

"How apropos," Abby said, giving her a warm smile. "I do like your lipstick. That color is perfect for you. And don't worry about Bucky. He's always in a fit when we're in the middle of a gig. It takes him forever to unwind, so breaks aren't really his thing."

"Huh," Starla replied noncommittally, her mouth forming an open 'O' while she applied a thick coat of Girl Talk to her lips. She straightened and dropped the makeup back in her bag. "Well, you just say the word and I'm there, okay?" Then she ducked inside one of the stalls.

"Thank you," Abby said, choking back the unexpected well of emotion at the woman's kindness. "I'll see you out there, okay?"

"I'm rooting for you, girlie!" Starla said from behind the stall door. "Bert and I are your biggest fans!"

Bert. That was the guy's name. She was inexorably grateful for Bert and Starla being out in the crowded room tonight. She'd buy them another round of whatever they were drinking as a thank you.

Abby smiled at her reflection and decided the smudged eyeliner wasn't so bad after all. "Nashville Grunge," she whispered so the other woman wouldn't hear. "I like it." Then she headed out of the sanctuary of the restroom.

Sure enough, not more than ten feet from the door stood Bucky. Tad was nowhere in sight.

"I still have two minutes," she stated, not even slowing her pace as she tried to veer around him. Bucky side-stepped to block her path, forcing her to pull up short just inches from plowing into him. "Get out of my way."

Bucky didn't step back. He crossed his arms, one of his elbows grazing her breast. She stood her ground; she didn't even flinch at the inappropriate contact. She would not let him see how close she was to a breakdown. She had to keep it together.

"I said, get out of my way." Abby swung her backpack up onto her shoulder, and Bucky took a quick half step back. She scowled up at him. "I'm not going to hit you."

He narrowed his eyes at her menacingly.

"Move," Abby demanded.

Bucky didn't move.

"Move!" she said, this time much louder. Behind her, the bathroom door swung open.

"Hey there, Guitar Man!"

Starla. *Thank you, God.*

"Sounding great up there," the older woman cooed as she sidled up to Abby. "Our Abstinence has the voice of an angel, doesn't she? You are one lucky guy to be a part of her band." Starla nudged Abby's shoulder with her own. "You know how to pick 'em, woman."

Bucky's face transformed from dark and foreboding to charming, beguiling, engaging. To Abby, it didn't make him seem any less threatening, though. And definitely just as repellent. How had she not noticed the act back when they'd first started working together? How had she missed it? She was usually such a good judge of character. But somehow, she'd been blind to the real Benton "Bucky" Jarlsburg. Until now.

Well, until a couple of months ago when his true colors started showing through that pretty outer layer.

"Why thank you, ma'am. And yes, I am indeed a lucky man." Bucky reached for Abby's hand, but Starla intercepted the gesture as if she'd thought he was reaching for hers. His expression registered momentary displeasure, but then he lifted the older woman's hand to his lips and planted a quick kiss on her knuckles.

"I was just telling Abstinence here how much we love her music," Starla gushed. "I bet you love getting to work with someone so gifted."

Okay, now she was laying it on a little too thick; surely, Bucky would start to get suspicious. Abby had to stop her before she said something that might make him blow. It already sounded like the woman thought he was some half-rate musician for hire.

Technically, Abby supposed he was. Maybe not half-rate: Bucky was a strong, solid guitar player who filled in nicely around her own playing. She'd chosen him for that reason—because he *wasn't* a virtuoso. When Remington Sounder had brought her to Nashville almost two years ago, the man had advised her to hone her own guitar skills so that she wouldn't be dependent on the skill and ability of another musician to keep her afloat. She'd come a long way since then, especially in the last year since being out in the big world all on her own, and it hadn't escaped her that perhaps that was one of the reasons Bucky was always so moody. Over the ten months they'd been working together, he'd slowly come to realize that Abby could play anything he could, maybe even better than he could.

But just because she could play all his parts didn't mean she no longer needed him. The band wouldn't be complete without him, or Tad, or even Gregor. Gregor, who'd be sitting at the bar until the rest of them returned to the stage, she knew. Not for the drinks, although he always seemed to have one in front of him, but for the women who really, really liked her bass player. Who probably bought his drinks for him, too.

"I need to stash this," Abby said abruptly, shaking the backpack that was still slung over her shoulder. "Did you lock the gig room this time?" She wanted to bite the words back the moment they were out.

"You were the last one in there," Bucky retorted. He tried to pull his hand from Starla's, but the woman played dumb and didn't let go.

Abby shot her a grateful glance. "I'll see you on stage then." Abby pushed past him. Oh, she'd hear about all of this later, but she could handle it then. *After* the show was over and she didn't have to put on a brave face for her adoring fans.

Chapter 2

~ ~ ~

Tuesday night's performance hadn't gone much better than the night before. Bucky had all but refused to acknowledge her, even on stage. By the end of the night, she was wrung out and ready for a day off. She didn't work Wednesdays, thank goodness, at either of her jobs, and she wanted nothing more than to head back to her tiny studio apartment, wash off the clinging vestiges of night life at The Whiskey Vault, and fall into the blissful abyss of sleep.

Tad and Bucky were loading up their gear into the back of Tad's van, but Abby was stuck inside with Stan waiting for a check. She'd put her foot down early on when they'd first started gigging, refusing to let the guys run a bar tab against the night's payout—Gregor, in particular, since he had a propensity to use their tab to purchase drinks for the pretty faces around him, too. It was shocking how how quickly those drinks could whittle away at the total owed them at the end of the night.

Gregor had helped haul Tad's drum kit out the back door, but then he'd disappeared with a girl who'd plastered herself to his side as soon as he left the stage. Abby knew they likely wouldn't see him until Thursday morning when they got together to run through their set for The Stage where they played the rooftop.

Stan, stout and stoic as a tree stump, but wickedly good at keeping the band working, waved at the hustling barman to get his attention. "Can you let Jack know we're still waiting on him?" Stan called out. "My band is done for the night and ready to go."

In other words, pay up. Now.

A minute later, Jack Hindlay came around the end of the bar toward them and gave Stan a sealed envelope—presumably, their week's pay—completely disregarding Abby's outstretched hand. "Thanks for waiting," he said, his gaze shifting to Abby, then back to Stan.

Shifting. Shifty. That word stuck in Abby's craw. There was a look in Jack's eyes that didn't bode well. His next words made her heart race. "We need to talk about next month's contract."

"Call me tomorrow," Stan told him, his tone casual, but brooking no argument. "This kid needs her beauty sleep."

"Nah," Jack insisted, just as coolly. "Let's talk now. You and me, Stan. The little princess can go get her beauty sleep without you."

Abby frowned at the exchange. How many ways had these guys just insulted her? Kids? Beauty sleep? And little princess? Really?

"Excuse me." She reached over and snatched the envelope out of Stan's hand, then slipped it into her backpack without even bothering to look at it. "If you're talking about my band playing here next month, then you're talking with me, too."

Jack crossed his hairy, tattooed arms, a gesture that said far more than any words might.

Abby appreciated Stan. He was great at his job, and she was grateful for all that he did for them. When Abby first came to Nashville, she'd thrived under the mentoring of Remington Sounder, an icon in the country music industry. Remington was famous for plucking no-name musicians off tiny no-name stages and giving them a jump start into the big arena. He'd heard her perform at Plumwood Hollow's Smokehouse Grill near the end of her senior year, and he'd offered her a half-hour opener spot on his tour and to produce her first album... in exchange for the rights—and ninety percent of the royalties—to said album.

As painful as that concession had been for her, the majority of the up-and-coming musicians he'd taken under his wing had gone on to super stardom, and it had been an offer Abby couldn't refuse. She'd gotten a taste of that super stardom on the road with him and his extensive production caravan, and she'd been hooked. So when the tour was over, she'd opted to stay in Nashville so she could get on the Broadway circuit. Rem had introduced her to Stan who made her promises that he'd kept for a whole year now. The Abstinence Goodacre Band had indeed been busy.

But there were things about Stan she didn't care for. His curmudgeonly silence. The toothpick he always had sticking out of the side of his mouth, that he somehow kept lodged in place, even when he talked. How he studied her while she performed, like she was a product, not a person. The way he shifted his tone of voice, his language, his behavior, ever so subtly to match those of the people he did business with. Sure, that chameleon ability probably had a lot to do with his exceptional managerial skills, but it always left Abby feeling a little unsettled, unsure of which Stan was the real one.

"Let's talk, then," Stan said after a moment. "The three of us. Shall we step into my office?" He nodded toward the back door that led out into the alley behind the bar. He didn't wait for a response from Jack, but turned and headed that direction after gesturing for Abby to go ahead of him.

Tad was just closing the doors of his van when they stepped out into the night. The heat and humidity of the summer day hadn't let up more than a few degrees in the last several hours, even this close to midnight, but the air was fresher than it was inside the crowded bar, and Abby took a deep breath. She ignored the slight stench that emanated from the dumpster nearby. She turned toward Stan and Jack just as Bucky came around the back of the van to join them.

"What's going on?" he asked, his voice ringing with surliness.

Abby glanced over at Tad who shrugged noncommittally. Tad was a good ol' boy, a great counterbalance to Bucky's volatile nature. He opened the driver's side door and got in behind the wheel, then rolled his window down so he could still listen in on the conversation.

Without preamble, Jack said, "I've only got one spot a week for your band next month, Stan."

"My band," Abby said, her hackles rising.

"Our band," Bucky interjected, his scowl deepening as he edged in closer to her.

"Nope. We need two nights." Stan ignored them both. "Mondays and Tuesdays."

"You get one or none."

"Why the change? You got someone else better than these kids?" The question came out sounding like the very idea was ludicrous.

"Your band is on the rocks," Jack stated, crossing his arms again. "I can't take a risk on a no-show. Especially the last gig of the night twice a week."

"Excuse me?" Abby stepped forward, standing shoulder-to-shoulder with Stan. "I don't do no-shows, Jack. Neither does my band."

"Our band," Bucky growled from just over her shoulder. She side-stepped slightly to try to edge him out, but he just moved with her, crowding her obnoxiously.

"That's what I'm talking about." Jack spoke to Stan, but he thrust his chin in Bucky's direction. "You got trouble brewing, Stan, and I don't want any part of it. So Mondays and Tuesdays are going to someone else. I can give you Sundays at 2:45 PM, and that's it. Take it or leave it."

"There's nothing wrong with my band," Stan said, his voice bland as ever. "You don't want to put an end to a good thing, Jack. You got people in there who come just to hear Abstinence sing." Stan never called her Abby. Nope, to him she was a commodity, not a small-town girl with a sweet nickname.

Jack lifted his hands at his sides. "I know they do. But I'm not paying for the drama, and my customers aren't, either. There's been talk, and I don't like it."

"You won't get another Abstinence," Stan started to say, but Jack cut him off.

"No, I won't. But I'll get a Sarah, and a Brittney, and a Jessica. Who knows? I might even get myself a Taylor. There's always another pretty young starlet waiting for an opening on my stage, Stan. Don't kid yourself."

The words cut deeply, just as they were intended to. Pretty young starlet. That's all she was to these people. A product. A commodity. And an expendable one at that.

Keep her in her place. Remind her she's nothing special.

"We don't need this kind of crap, Stan," Bucky spoke up, widening his stance and nudging Abby aside. "We walk away."

"Shut up, Benton." Stan's tone didn't change, but the use of Bucky's real name was remarkably effective in putting the musician in his place. To the bar manager, he said, "We'll take it, Jack. But you and I aren't finished discussing this."

"No discussion. Take it or leave it. There's nothing more to my offer, and I'm not budging. I'm already giving you handouts as it is."

Bucky said a foul word and turned on his heel. Behind her, Abby heard the van door open and slam shut again.

Jack cocked his head at Stan with an expression that said, "Didn't I tell you?"

Without another word exchanged, Stan and Jack shook hands, then Jack nodded curtly and headed back inside, leaving Abby and Stan alone at the back door stoop.

After a brief uncomfortable silence, Bucky exited the van again and stomped toward them, his face a mask of rage. He opened his mouth to speak, but Stan lifted a hand to silence him.

"Here's the way I see it," he began, his voice raised a little so they all could hear him. "You two—" he waved a finger back and forth between Abby and Bucky. "You two better figure out who's in charge here. When you do, let me know and then we'll get back to work."

"I'm in charge," Abby said, her voice shaking with anger and fatigue. "I've always been in charge."

"Well, that's what I thought when I signed you on, but it seems to me that your guitar player is starting to think differently."

"I'm in charge," Abby said again.

"Not if you're letting him walk all over you," Stan argued. "Not if you're letting him dictate the quality of your performance." Bucky made a garbled sound that might have been another bad word, but Stan talked right over him. "Jack's right, Ms. Goodacre. I've seen it a thousand times, and so has he. Your band is on the rocks. You're going down if you don't get this sinking ship repaired. And quickly."

"But—but I—"

"If you're in charge, you don't get to make excuses." Stan pulled the toothpick from between his teeth and pointed it at Abby. She couldn't help it; she took a step backward, repulsed by the disgusting object. The man kept talking like he hadn't noticed. "Like I said. Let me know when you figure out which one of you gets to be on top." And with that crude indictment, Stan headed back inside the bar after Jack.

Abby had no false hope that he was going in to try to get a different response from the guy. Stan often stayed after the band left, listening to the feedback of the unwitting customers, assessing the quality of the band that took the stage next when there was one. It didn't hurt that he got to write off his food and drink that way, either. More often than not, someone recognized him, and his meal would end up costing him nothing but a shared table.

She turned to Tad before getting in the van. "Would you mind dropping me off at my place first?" Usually, they all went back to Tad's to unload the gear. Most of it was his drum set, but because he also happened to be the only one of them who had a garage, he kept some of the other stuff at his place, too. It was a good time to hash over the night's performance and make any necessary tweaks to the next gig. But tonight had her utterly deflated and she didn't think she'd be any good to any of them. She tensed, certain Bucky would have something to say about that.

He did. He gestured dramatically in the direction Stan and Jack had gone. "This is on you, Princess Abby."

"Buck. Enough." Tad raised his voice, something he rarely did. "Let's call it a night."

"Fine. We'll call it a night. You can drop me off at her royal highness' place, too."

"Bucky, please," Abby breathed out, tired of his ugliness. To Tad, she said, "Never mind. I'll come help with the gear." That meant getting a ride back to her place from Bucky, which was what she'd been hoping to avoid in the first place, but she certainly preferred that to him getting dropped off with her and then not having a car in which to leave. At this point, she just wanted the night to end without any more drama than was absolutely necessary.

Because with Bucky, drama was always necessary. Which meant it fell on her shoulders to determine how much of it there'd be.

"Nah, I don't think that's going to work," her guitar player said, his tone suddenly smooth. "I just remembered that I've got someplace to be, so I'm leaving straight from Tad's. You'll have to find another way home."

Yep, drama.

Abby wanted to throw something at him. Something hard. She wanted to punch him in that beautiful face. She wanted to wring his neck, the same neck she'd pressed her face into far too many times. She wanted to turn back the clock and undo the things they'd done together. No dancing, no long afternoons in the park co-writing songs, no squeezing together into the one and only armchair in her tiny studio apartment so they could watch movies on her laptop. No holding hands, no holding each other. No kissing. No promises. No roller coaster romance.

"I'll take you home," Tad said, circling the van to open the sliding passenger door for her. She climbed in beside her guitar, glad to be alone in the back with the equipment. Bucky got into the front opposite Tad and pulled his door closed with far more force than was necessary. He shot an ugly glare at Abby over his shoulder while he fastened his seatbelt.

She ignored him the best she could, but she was immeasurably relieved when she saw that Tad was, indeed, taking her home first.

She and Bucky didn't exchange another word until she stepped out onto the sidewalk in front of her apartment. Bucky had his head down scrolling through his phone, making an exaggerated point to ignore her, but Tad nudged the controls on the driver's side so the passenger window rolled down.

"Thanks, Tad," she said, looking past Bucky, who still didn't acknowledge her.

Tad gave her an apologetic smile. "Sure thing."

"Goodnight, Bucky," she finally said. How she wished things were different between them. "You sounded good tonight."

"Thanks," he muttered, but he didn't look up.

Abby patted the side of the van, and then turned to go inside her building, knowing Tad would wait until she was safe behind the security door before he pulled away.

The tiny foyer had a bank of mailboxes along one wall, and Abby set her guitar case down so she could check hers. There wasn't a single piece of mail in it, not even an advertisement flier, but that was no surprise. For some reason, the sight of the empty box brought on another wave of homesickness, one that left her weak at the knees. But she had three flights of stairs to climb before she could fall apart, so she took a deep, shaky breath, picked up Blossom, and started up.

A few minutes later, Abby stood at the one window in her apartment and gazed down into the narrow back street—an alley, really—below. She had no view, unless you counted what went on inside the apartments across from her, but most of those residents kept their curtains drawn for that very reason. She braced herself with a hand on the window frame while she toed off first one boot, then the other, kicking the pair aside before peeling off her socks, too. She needed a shower. She needed something to eat, something that wasn't battered, fried, or eaten with dip. Why was it that the band always got to eat stuff for free, but only from the unhealthiest items on the menu?

She needed some sleep. She needed to shirk off the shroud of Bucky's anger and the stench of another late night at the bar. She needed some peace. A little bit of oblivion.

"I need a drink."

~ ~ ~

Read the rest of Abby – and Jed's—story today!

Something About ABBY: Seven Virtues Ranch Romance Book 7

~ ~ ~

Love series about sisters?
Then check out The Gustafson Girls Series!

Juliette & the Monday ManDates

Juliette is perfectly content with her quiet nights at home alone, especially when they include Chinese takeout and sappy rom coms.

But her sisters think she's teetering on the brink of spinsterhood. So, they've come up with an intervention plan: weekly blind dates until their Jules finds her knight in shining armor... or until they run out of single guy friends.

They're calling it The Monday ManDates.

Survival skills kicking in, Juliette secretly names each new Monday man. There's TheraPaul, Frisky Frank, and TAZ the Rock Star, for starters. Then there's the Officer Manly Man, the policeman with a penchant for pulling Juliette over when she's at her very worst.

With a lineup like that, positively identifying her happily-ever-after seems like a long shot.

Pick up Juliette & the Monday ManDates today and fall in love with this family of wild and wonderful women!